Praise for *The O*

"With the historical authent... ...
perfectly observed family rel...
and the gut-wrenching twist of Jojo Moyes... It is historical
fiction at its heart-breaking best. Epic, enthralling and deeply
emotional, to say I loved it is an understatement. Jenny
Ashcroft is a superb writer."
Iona Grey, *Letters to the Lost*

"An unforgettable story of great love torn apart by war, of
heroism and betrayal, passion and pure evil, all set against
an idyllic Greek island backdrop. It's a genuine masterpiece,
a book to lose yourself in."
Gill Paul, *The Secret Wife*

"What a beautiful novel. So romantic, so epic, so tear-
jearking. I absolutely adored it and can't wait to read the next
Jenny Ashcroft novel. Five stars all round."
Lorna Cook, *The Forgotten Village*

"I was completely spellbound. A beautiful, poignant love
story with a clever twist, all set against the backdrop of war-
torn Crete. It's the best book I've read this year."
Kathleen McGurl, *The Forgotten Secret*

"*The Officer and The Spy* has simply blown me away! Such
a powerful and poignant love story set against the beauty and
danger of wartime Crete. At times I could hardly bear to read
on, and yet couldn't put it down."
Liz Trenow, *Searching for my Daughter*

"*The Officer and The Spy* is beautifully written, powerful
and poignant. Time and place are brilliantly evoked, with
a moving love story at its core. It is excellent."
Tracy Rees, *The House at Silvermoor*

Jenny Ashcroft is the author of several historical novels, including *Beneath a Burning Sky* and *Island in the East*. She previously spent much of her life living in, working in and exploring Australia and Asia, and now splits her time between Australia and the UK.

The Officer and The Spy is in part inspired by her Greek grandmother's stories and is Jenny's most personal novel to date.

Also by Jenny Ashcroft

Beneath a Burning Sky
Island in the East
Meet Me in Bombay
Under the Golden Sun

Jenny Ashcroft

The
OFFICER
and
THE SPY

ONE PLACE. MANY STORIES

HQ
An imprint of HarperCollins*Publishers* Ltd
1 London Bridge Street
London SE1 9GF

www.harpercollins.co.uk

Harper Ireland
Macken House, 39/40 Mayor Street Upper,
Dublin 1 D01 C9W8, Ireland

This edition 2023

1
First published in Great Britain by
HQ, an imprint of HarperCollins*Publishers* Ltd 2022, as *The Echoes of Love*

Copyright © Jenny Ashcroft 2022

Jenny Ashcroft asserts the moral right to be
identified as the author of this work.
A catalogue record for this book is
available from the British Library.

ISBN: 978-0-00-860312-0

MIX
Paper | Supporting
responsible forestry
FSC™ C007454

This book is produced from independently certified FSC™ paper
to ensure responsible forest management.

For more information visit: www.harpercollins.co.uk/green

This book is set in Sabon by Type-it AS, Norway

Printed and Bound in the UK using 100% Renewable Electricity at
CPI Group (UK) Ltd, Croydon, CR0 4YY

For my grandmother, Maria Rosis

'Remembering wartime Greece.' Transcript of research interview undertaken by M. Middleton (M.M.) *with subject seventeen (#17), at British Broadcasting House, 4 June 1974*

M.M: You knew Crete well then, before the occupation?
#17:   I did.
M.M: Chania . . . ?
#17:   Chania especially.
M.M: I gather the town was much changed by the invasion.
#17:   The entire island was.
M.M: I realize it was heavily bombed . . .
#17:   It went well beyond that.
M.M: How so?
#17:   [Pours glass of water] Freedom, vanished. Safety, vanished. Crete was cut off, from almost everything. [Drinks water] You must understand what that was like.
M.M: Perhaps you could help me.
#17:   It became a world in itself. We were all of us there, and that was it. Tremendously isolated. Life outside felt [searches for word] *theoretical*.
M.M: Theoretical?

#17: Not real. Suspended. For the duration. None of the normal rules applied. Or at least . . . one could forget they should.

M.M: And have you been back since?

#17: No.

M.M: Some will consider it odd, that you've decided to speak out about it all now, after so many years.

#17: I am sure some will.

M.M: And what would you say to them?

#17: That they're quite correct.

M.M: Can you offer an explanation for why you're doing it?

#17: [Long silence]

M.M: An encounter?

#17: [Sighs. Shakes head]

M.M: A new recollection, perhaps . . . ?

#17: No. No. I've always remembered everything.

M.M: Then . . . ?

#17: I've recently become . . . unwell.

M.M: I am sorry.

#17: Yes. [Deeper sigh] It rather . . . *illuminates* . . . one's life, knowing it's drawing to a close. [Pauses] If there really is to be some grand reckoning, then mine is now dauntingly imminent.

M.M: And how do you feel you will fare?

#17: Poorly.

M.M: You feel guilty?

#17: Yes. Yes, I feel guilty.

M.M: For what though, exactly?

#17: For so much. [Coughs] Every single day.

BEFORE THE WAR

Chapter One

Crete, June 1936

It felt like the beginning of so many summers that had gone before. Eleni, sitting beside her grandfather in his beloved Cadillac, roaring along the dusty coast road from Chania – sticky with sweat beneath her travelling clothes: the skirt suit that had been so appropriate in Portsmouth, but in Greece was too thick, too dull; grey with lingering English chill – gave not a moment's pause to the possibility that the one ahead might be different. Why should she? She'd been summering in Crete since she was a baby. This was to be her nineteenth stay. She trusted in what the island held waiting for her, entirely.

The road grew quieter, the further her *papou*, Yorgos, drove them out of Chania's bustling centre. There were no other motorcars on the winding hillside pass, just the odd farmer and laden donkey, goats that grazed in the dry, golden heat. Yorgos overtook them all, at a speed Eleni's British father would have called reckless, had he been there, but which she hardly noticed. She rested her head back, feeling the balmy wind in her tired eyes, the ebbing sun a warm cloth on her face, and, heedless of the Cadillac's wheels skimming the cliff edge, luxuriated in the relief of her three-day odyssey across Europe finally being over.

She'd travelled by herself that year. Her father, Timothy – a naval captain, and off to sea himself for the summer – hadn't been happy about it. He'd wanted her to take her usual chaperone: a retired teacher by the name of Miss Finch. But Miss Finch had, only the week before, broken her leg – playing croquet, of all things – leaving Timothy no time to recruit a replacement, and little choice but to give in to Eleni's assurances that she could manage the trip alone. Which she had. Happily. Sorry as she'd felt for Miss Finch (and really, *poor* Miss Finch), it had been such a relief, not having to spend endless hours nodding along to her tales of various nieces and nephews, so many pet rabbits, and pure liberation, deciding for herself when to have a drink, or read, or simply stare from the carriage window in silence.

And now she was here.

Here.

She tilted her head, looking down and out at the sea below; a glittering cloth tinged rose by the dusk, sliced in two by the furrows of the ferry that had brought her from Athens. Idly, she watched it steam away to the horizon, wondering who was now on it, what kind of lives they led, and all the while Yorgos talked, his gruff voice raised above the engine, grilling her on her solitary passage through France, Mussolini's Italy, speaking in rapid Greek, no concession to the months that had passed since she'd last used the language, his tolerance for it not being her mother tongue extremely low.

'Did the trains run on time?'

'They were fine,' she said; *ola kala*.

'Not crowded?'

'No.'

'You had no trouble in Italy? The blackshirts . . . '

'I hardly saw any,' she said. 'Only at the border.' Having her documents scrutinised by the abrasive soldiers was never comfortable, but she'd survived the ordeal many times before. The fascists had, after all, been running Italy since she was a child. She'd known to keep her expression blank as the men had studied

6

her, then her papers, then her again. She'd distracted herself by looking at the posters on the railway sidings. 'Mussolini never gets older in his pictures,' she mused. 'Apparently he shaves his head so no one will guess he's going grey.'

'I don't want to waste oxygen talking about him,' said Yorgos.

'You started it . . .'

'And now I'm finishing it.' He shifted gear. 'You had enough to eat?'

'Plenty.'

'Really?'

'Yes.' She smiled. 'Really.'

He grunted, disbelieving.

Still smiling, she didn't attempt to convince him.

He'd never be convinced she ate enough anywhere but on Crete. Her diet was an obsession for him. He'd feed her now until September, not happy unless she left having gained at least a stone to see her through the British winter. She'd manage it, with remarkable ease, but couldn't be nearly so pleased about it.

'Why?' Yorgos would demand. 'What, you want to be one of these *magazine models*?'

She wouldn't entirely mind.

He'd arm her with fruits and vegetables to return to England with as well, refusing to accept that any food could be got there that wasn't brown. She'd take the heavy box, even though it was a pain to carry, the fruit would inevitably bruise, and she *really* didn't need it, because she hated denying him anything. And because she knew how his certainty that the British diet had killed her mother plagued him – as though more tomatoes and olives and spinach could have saved her from the Spanish flu.

Perhaps they might have.

'Here we are,' he said, unnecessarily, rounding the bend Eleni had been waiting for, veering on to the steep track of rocks and wildflowers that led down to the villa.

She braced her feet against the motor's floor, stopping herself from lurching forward as they sped on, feeling a wave of joy as the bougainvillea-shrouded house came into view.

It hadn't changed.

It never changed.

She stared, drinking in its perfect *sameness*.

She had no place she'd grown up in, back in England. She'd moved with her father countless times around their Portsmouth suburb of Gosport, their naval quarters upgraded with each new promotion he'd secured through the ranks (an indoor latrine, running hot water, that kind of thing). When she'd turned eleven, Timothy had spent long periods in Africa, and boarding school dormitories had joined her rotation of bedrooms. At fifteen, he'd taken a desk job back in Portsmouth and summoned her home to complete her school certificate there. She'd only just finished. She wasn't sure what should come next, only that her father expected her to be waiting in their newest house – a modern detached with both garden and garage – when he returned from his summer patrol of the Libyan Sea. (*I feel a . . . hole . . . of sorts, without you,* had been his farewell at the docks, delivered without him once touching her, or meeting her eye. *Take care now. I miss you. Dear. In my way.*)

This villa had been her constant. Perched in the elbow of land between Chania and Souda, overlooking the sea, it was, like so much of Crete, built in the style of the Venetians who'd occupied the island before the Turks had invaded, back in the 1600s. It wasn't grand, and needed repair in parts, but to Eleni, flattened by the functional monotony of Gosport, its imperfections only added to its beauty. The terracotta walls, fissured by age, battered by centuries of heat and wind, were as pale as peach flesh; the shutters, no bluer than a hazed sky. At night, they'd creak in the breeze coming up from the shore, and she'd lie listening to them, soothed by the thought that her mama must have once done the same.

'And she watches,' said Yorgos, as he always did, pulling to a halt at the front door. He turned off the ignition, flooding them in a silence broken only by the song of the cicadas, the lapping waves below. 'Happy, because you are here.'

Eleni smiled.

Slowly, she climbed from the motor, drawing deep on the villa's layered scents: citrus from the lemon trees; the bougainvillaea's pollen; the thyme that grew, everywhere. She closed her eyes, losing herself in them all, these smells she'd missed too, too much.

She didn't think about Yorgos watching her, his satisfied nod at her contentment.

She didn't think about much at all.

She simply breathed.

It was her favourite breath of the year.

The breath that truly started summer for her.

The breath when her monochrome world shifted fully into colour, and her loneliness gave way to belonging.

The breath when – however impossible she'd find it to ever admit to her father – she came home.

It was dark by the time she set off to swim that night, picking her way down the stairs a long-gone Venetian had cut into the hillside. She could hear Yorgos clattering around on the terrace above, readying the grill for their dinner. The light of his oil lamp oozed into the blackness, joining the glow of the moon, helping to illuminate her rocky path downward. She wore her bathing costume beneath her robe, held a towel under her arm. The costume's new elastic was stiff, clinging in a way that made her very conscious of how little of her it covered. She'd bought it for the summer at Landport Drapery on Portsmouth's

Commercial Road, using the money she'd saved working as a weekend receptionist at Queen's Hotel.

'Don't fritter it away, now,' her boss, Mr Hodgson, had instructed, handing over her final payslip.

Did he give similar instructions to the male staff, she'd wondered.

Regardless, the costume was navy blue, cut with a sweetheart neck, down to a daring high thigh, and she loved it. It was the most glamorous thing she'd ever owned. She had no idea what her *papou* was going to say when he saw it, or the shorts she'd impulsively bought at Landport's as well.

Don't wear them anyone can see, probably.

She'd taken her time unpacking it all upstairs, unfolding her older, less controversial, sundresses, hanging them in the ancient wardrobe, then pausing – out of habit, old longing – at the bureau, staring into the photograph that stood there: the only one that existed of herself and her mama. It had been taken at a studio in Portsmouth when she'd been just a few months old, and her mama not much older than she was now; just twenty. Her mama was wearing a winter coat, and held Eleni bundled up in a blanket, clasping her hand. Eleni had her fist wrapped around her forefinger; tight, trusting. She'd known her mama, then. Once, she'd known her.

They looked alike; even Eleni could see that. Aside from the fair hair she'd inherited from her father, her mama had given her everything: olive skin, oval face; *curves.* Yorgos said they shared mannerisms, as well. *She used to sink her face in her hands when she laughed, and fiddle at her earlobe when she was trying to ignore me telling her off.* Did Eleni's father notice their similarities? He never spoke of it if he did. And he kept no photographs up. He wasn't one for ornaments or memories. Eleni wished he was, but not even a wedding portrait graced his well-ordered desk.

She shivered. The June air had cooled since sunset, and her

bare skin prickled in anticipation of the sea's liquid touch. She could hear the waves licking lazily over the cove's pebbles below. The Greeks had a word, just for that fizzing sound they made. *Flisvos*. It was a beautiful sound. It deserved a word of its own, Eleni thought.

It grew darker as the steps gave way to the small private bay, and she disappeared from the reach of her *papou*'s lamp. The sea, beyond the shallow shore break, was calm; a mirror to the stars, the beam of the white moon. She continued towards it, not hesitating as she shrugged off her robe, letting it fall to the ground. It was the only way to make herself get in, at this time of year, this time of night. No pause for thought.

Except then she did stop, startled by the crack of a branch behind her. She turned, glancing up at the shadowy hillside. An animal, she thought. A goat, or stray dog. She waited to see if it would show itself . . .

But no, nothing.

'Fine, be like that,' she said, in Greek, so it understood.

And, without further ado, she ran at the sea, diving, her breath leaving her as the biting water quenched her face, her sluggish, weary limbs. She swam deeper, on and on, diving again, reaching for the sandy bottom, lungs bursting until she could bear it no more and had to resurface, gasping for air. Sinking backwards, she floated, pulse pounding in her ears, eyes fixed on the stars – so much brighter, away from Portsmouth's city lights, so much closer – thinking of the freedom of the months ahead. The wonderful reality that she was lying in the Aegean Sea, staring at Venus, and not revising for her exams, or doing the washing up, back in Gosport.

She wasn't sure how long she might have gone on drifting like that.

Not so very long, probably. Soon enough, the sea's chill would have propelled her from her reverie.

But the call came first.

'Otto,' it rang out, high and clear from the shore, '*Otto Linder.*'

Intrigued by the unfamiliar voice, the unfamiliar name, Eleni kicked herself upright, peering through the night for the person who'd spoken, finding her easily on the dark water's edge, marked out by her white evening gown; a ghostly kind of silhouette. The gown was full-length, elegant, making its wearer appear more adult than she'd sounded. She'd *sounded* like a girl. Eleni studied her, wondering who she was, and what she could be doing on the rocks beneath Nikos Kalantis's villa. A villa which, now Eleni looked, had several lamps of its own burning. Her brow creased. She'd only ever known Nikos's home to stand empty in the past. He'd always been absent on business when she'd visited. ('This is no loss,' Yorgos had once said.)

Was he here this year?

Or had he leased his villa to tourists?

Certainly, this girl wasn't Greek. German, maybe. They were hearing it spoken more these days in England; those newsreels that played at the pictures of Hitler shouting, the ecstatic crowds cheering . . .

'Otto.' That name again. Something else followed. '*Wo bist du?*' Definitely German. And whiney. '*Essen ist fertig.*'

Then, another voice: male, deep, and so very close to Eleni, she all but lost her heart through her mouth.

'*Ich komme.*'

I'm coming?

Eleni hardly considered it.

She was much more concerned with absorbing the revelation that she hadn't been nearly so alone in the water as she'd believed.

That, and the jolt of the stranger, *Otto's*, eyes meeting hers when she spun reflexively towards him, no more than twenty strokes away.

Hand to her exploding chest, she stared.

For a moment, so did he.

As shocked as she was?

He didn't appear particularly shocked.

The night was too deep for Eleni to see him clearly – she drew an impression rather than a picture: the symmetry of his face, accentuated by the shadows; those eyes, holding hers – but it was enough for her to feel sure that he'd been a deal more aware of her presence than she had his.

Indignantly, she arched a brow.

Did he smile?

She was pretty sure his lips moved in a rueful smile.

She had no time to decide. The girl in white called for him again – '*Otto, wo* bist *du?*' – and, with a flicked glance in her direction, he bade Eleni, '*Guten Nacht,*' (she understood that) then was gone, slicing through the water for the shore.

Too stunned to move, Eleni watched him go.

He swam fast. His strokes, clean and assured, hardly made a noise. Vaguely, she made sense of why she hadn't noticed him before.

How long had he been aware of her own presence though?

Turning the unanswerable question over, she kept her attention on him as he reached the rocks, pulling himself from the sea. His back was broad, muscular, his movement easy and athletic. The woman threw a towel for him, and he caught it. He obviously joked, too, because the woman laughed, her peals slicing through the night. At the sound, their familiarity, Eleni felt the strangest tug; that hollowness of being on the outside. In the ensuing silence, she, replaying Otto's smile – certain now that's what it had been – found herself wishing she knew what he'd just said.

Much more than that though, she really was becoming freezing.

With a breath of resolution, she forced her cold body back into motion. She swam as swiftly as Otto had, not looking at him again, so not knowing whether he did, or did not, glance back at her. By the time she'd realized how much she wanted to check, it was already too late; she'd reached the shore and was wading through the shallows, Nikos's own rocky inlet hidden from view.

She stared in its direction, curiosity over Otto, and the girl, growing.

Then, teeth chattering, thinking she could quiz her *papou* on them, she reached for her towel and robe, and, wrapping herself in both, set off at a jog for the villa.

She heard no more noises on the way up; no cracks, nor rustles. It was only when she came across a kitten, curled right at the top of the stairs, that she recalled the snapping branch that had stopped her in her tracks before.

'Was it you?' she asked the tiny animal, scooping it up. It mewed plaintively, its back leg sticky with blood. 'Now who did this?'

Another mew.

Cradling it close, she carried it on with her, back into the light of her *papou*'s lamp.

'Don't bring that animal in here,' he called from up on the now-smoky terrace.

'It's hurt.'

'That's life.'

'*Papou*, you're a doctor . . . '

'For humans.'

'Just take a look at it.'

'And all the other cats on the island?'

'Please. Whilst I get changed. I won't be long.'

She wasn't.

And, as she and her *papou* ate beneath the stars – the kitten, clean of blood, purring at their feet ('What shall we call him?' she asked. 'Nothing,' Yorgos said. 'That's not a very good name,' she observed) – she mentioned the Germans she'd seen at Nikos Kalantis's villa. She learnt that Yorgos knew disappointingly little of them, only that they must be part of the family that had flown in that morning from Berlin to stay for the summer. *The Linders.*

'Friends of Mr Kalantis?' she asked.

'Let's hope better of them than that,' he said, and frowned, scolding her against throwing fishbones for the kitten to eat.

She ignored him on the fishbones, but let the matter of the Linders, and Nikos Kalantis, go, knowing he was only being short-tempered because she'd raised the subject of his neighbour in the first place. They'd been at odds her entire life: a dispute over land that went back generations. The island was littered with such family feuds. The story went that Eleni's grandmama had, for herself, been good friends with Nikos, before she, like Eleni's mama, had died too young, leaving Eleni's mama just a baby (a troubling family trait), but not even she'd been able to heal the rift between the pair. If anything, Eleni suspected her friendship with Nikos had made it worse. There'd been some incident involving her mama too, back during the Great War, when Nikos had lost his temper at her – Eleni didn't know why ('You think a man like him needs a reason,' Yorgos had said, when she'd pressed him on it), only that it was another thing Yorgos could never forgive, and hated remembering.

Hating that for him, Eleni had long ceased asking him to.

Dropping more fish for the kitten, she moved the conversation on, coaxing him back into a better mood by mentioning the whispered rumours of King Edward's affair with the American divorcée, Wallis Simpson, giving him – no royalist, but every inch a moralist – all the opening he needed to vent about values and duty and the importance of modesty. (*He's really going to hate my shorts,* she thought.) As he talked on – jumping from Edward, to the newly reinstated Greek monarchy, his fury at their support for yet another would-be European dictator, General Ioannis Metaxas in Athens, and from there to the welcome news that Dimitri, the owner of the harbourside café Eleni had waitressed at the summer before, had called by, offering her employment again – she did her best to keep up, fighting a smile at his gesticulations, forgetting all about her watery encounter.

But later, as she fell onto her mattress, an oil lamp flickering on the bedside table, the kitten snug on a cushion by the door, her mind moved once more to the memory of Otto's face in the darkness. The warmth in his voice. *Guten Nacht.* She stared sightlessly at her chipped ceiling, listening to the shutters creak, and thought not of her mother, but of him in his villa down the way, and about what relation the girl in white could be to him.

A sister?

Girlfriend?

Or a fiancée?

Somehow, sister felt better.

She expelled a short laugh at herself, for caring.

Then she rolled on to her side, extinguished her lamp, and wondered how long it would be before she saw him again.

Chapter Two

She woke early the next morning, a Saturday, wrenched from sleep by Yorgos rapping at her door, telling her to hurry, *grigora,* stop wasting the day, it was almost seven.

'Almost seven?' she croaked, slipping into English in her groggy disorientation. 'That's not even five in England.'

'This is Greece—' he wedged the door open '—and we have things to do.'

'You didn't say last night.'

'Because I knew you'd moan about getting up. What—' he pointed '—is that cat doing on your pillow?'

'I don't know.'

'You'd better hope it doesn't have fleas.'

She did hope it.

In that moment though, with him clapping his hands at her impatiently, it was the least of her concerns.

She shouldn't have arrived on a Friday, she realized belatedly. Normally, the boat and train schedules delivered her earlier in the week, when Yorgos – refusing to retire, for all he was in his sixties – was occupied at his nearby general practitioners, leaving her all the time she needed to adjust to the Greek clock's head-start on England, and take her fill of swimming and reading down at the cove before Saturday rolled around, and the reunions commenced.

It wasn't that she didn't look forward to seeing the rest of the family. She did. She loved them, missed them, would choose time with them over her father's parents any day of the week. (Every couple of months or so, her father would, in response to a wounded letter from his mother, make his own excuses, and despatch Eleni like a sacrificial lamb for Sunday lunch at his childhood home in Sutton: anaemic greens, floury mash, Bisto gravy, all washed down with suet pudding, a silent game of chess with Eleni's grandfather, and a gentle but firm lecture from her grandmother on how, if she'd only agree to secretarial college, she might find herself a nice, steady husband. 'Like Grandpa here,' Grandma would say, with a pained smile at him in his braces, agonising over what to do with his knight.) There'd be no Bisto in Crete, no career advice, nor suet either; nothing to dread whatsoever, other than that Eleni had been travelling for three days straight, and truly would have loved a couple more off before spending hours in the motor with Yorgos getting to everyone.

They didn't have many stops to make, at least. Their family wasn't large, not by Crete's standards. Eleni's mama (Petra; she'd been called Petra) had, like Eleni's father, been an only child. Yorgos had no brothers or sisters either, and his parents, along with Eleni's grandmother's parents, had sadly gone before she was born. But her grandmother's sister, great-aunt Sofia, was still very much alive, way up in the white mountains, where she'd moved with her husband, Vassili, at the turn of the century, to make wine. They'd made a son too, (another Vassili), who himself was married with a Vassili of his own. *Little Vassili.*

Other than them, there was just Spiros and Maria, who weren't really family at all, but felt like family, because Eleni had known them forever. Spiros had been at school with Yorgos, studying medicine in Athens with him, and was his partner at the general practitioners. He and his wife Maria lived much closer to home, alongside the island's politicians and diplomats in the Chania suburb of Halepa. Eleni was as familiar with their shoreside townhouse as she was the villa. When she was little, she'd spent every day there with Maria, just as her mama had used to: playing, baking, learning to swim, whilst her *papou* worked.

It wasn't them, though, that Yorgos had arranged to see that Saturday, as Eleni discovered over breakfast. No, they were expecting them the following morning. Saturday was to be all about the long journey into the mountains; lunch with Sofia and the Vassilis.

'And I don't want to be late,' said Yorgos. 'So upstairs, quickly. Get ready.'

'All right,' said Eleni, going, before he could start clapping again.

She didn't forget about the kitten in the rush. Once she was dressed, and had checked him for fleas ('None,' she declared triumphantly), she made him up saucers of milk and fish scraps and settled him to snooze on an old blanket beneath the terrace awning.

'What *shall* we call him?' she pondered, running her finger over his bony head.

'I told you,' said Yorgos, 'nothing.' *Tipota.*

Eleni sighed. 'I don't know why you're so set on that name . . . '

She didn't forget about Otto either.

The thought of their brief meeting returned to her, vividly, when, at length, she and Yorgos were in the motor, roaring past the gateway to Nikos's villa, on their way to the road inland. The gate was nothing to look at. Simple, lined by shrubs; Eleni had passed it thousands of times before without notice.

Yet this time, she looked.

There was no one there. Just a pair of butterflies that flitted weightlessly above the splintered wooden posts. It was so early, the sun barely risen past the sea's misty horizon. Eleni expected everyone was in bed.

Still, she couldn't help but glance back as they accelerated away, holding the gate in her sights . . .

But no, nothing.

Yorgos sped on, wheels throwing up dust, and even the butterflies disappeared.

'Who was that?'

Henri's question cut through the silence in Otto's room, startling him, although he didn't give away how much. Still in just the trousers he'd slept in, he remained exactly as he was, hands resting on the windowsill, gaze fixed on the now-empty road above.

'Could you knock?' he said.

'You haven't answered me,' said Henri.

Otto still didn't. He set his jaw on the things he might say to his father, and leant harder on the windowsill, the heels of his hands numbing. A baby lizard darted up the side of the pane, then stopped, stringy legs splayed, seeming to realize it was being observed. Otto imagined its miniscule heart pounding. That instinct for survival . . .

'Otto, who was it?'

The lizard didn't blink. It was as though it believed it could make itself invisible through stillness.

If only.

'Otto?'

'I don't know,' Otto lied.

He'd seen her blonde head, caught a glimpse of her face as she'd turned in his direction.

Smiled, because she'd looked for him.

Eleni Adams, Nikos Kalantis had said she was called, when Otto had asked him about her, after the welcome dinner they'd both been late to the night before. *An English father*, Nikos had gone on, in perfect, dismissive, German. *I have nothing to do with her.*

'You were distracted last night,' said Henri now. 'I noticed . . . '

'I'm sure you did.'

'So did your mother. I'm worried—' Henri paused, looking to the wall, reminding Otto – not that he could forget – who was on the other side of it '—that Lotte might have been upset.'

Otto continued to study the road. The motor's dust had settled.

Where had she gone to?

'You need to be careful,' said Henri. 'You and your sister need to be *careful.*'

'So you keep telling us.'

'Krista —'

'Makes her own choices.'

'Yes,' Henri snapped, voice rising, 'so you need to make smarter ones. I . . . ' He broke off at a sound from Lotte's room. The creak of her bed, and a slow sigh.

Did she sigh like that, Otto wondered, when her father talked about his day at work?

'Look at me,' said Henri, quieter now. 'Turn around.'

Otto didn't move. Nor did the lizard.

'Be nice to Lotte today,' Henri said, at length.

'I always am.'

'Do it better.'

'Is that an order?'

'If it must be,' said Henri, 'then, yes.'

They weren't late to Sofia's, for all Yorgos's certainty that they would be, and the protracted drive – which was somehow always longer, and more beautiful, than Eleni could ever recall. Beauty and pain were alike in that respect, she decided, as they left the coast behind and climbed into the mountains: never sharper than in the moment of experience. With every turn of Yorgos's wheel, the cliffs, lush with pine and cypress trees, enveloped them, reminding her, effortlessly, of their splendour: streams that glinted at the bottom of plummeting ravines; peaks that soared up and up, bruising the beating sky. Churches sugared the rock faces, white paintwork reflecting the hot sun – so bright it made Eleni's eyes water, even with her shades on (another Landport's purchase). Occasionally, they passed through a village, and the locals – herding goats, drinking coffee in the sleepy shade of *kafeterias* – raised their hands in stiff greeting, stern but hospitable, always, to strangers. They dressed timelessly: the men in black breeches, cummerbunds of deep red, and embroidered waistcoats; the women in high-necked dresses and headscarves. Eleni for herself wore no headscarf, but had chosen a long-sleeved dress for the day, in spite of the heat. Chania was one thing – they'd just about moved into the twentieth century there – but here, up in the mountains . . . no; they weren't ready for her shorts here.

She wasn't sure they were ready for her sunshades either.

'What's wrong with your eyes?' asked Sofia, when they finally reached her pretty, stone house, and she greeted them at the door.

'Nothing,' said Eleni, removing her glasses. 'See?'

Sofia took her by the shoulders, examining her. Tiny, with white hair rolled in a chignon, gravity-defying cheekbones, and worry lines that, she said, had been etched by a lifetime of Vassilis, she had a broad face that was kind and strong, brooking no nonsense.

'Good,' she said, squashing Eleni in a talc-scented embrace, 'you have such beautiful eyes. Better something happened to your ears.'

'Better neither,' said Yorgos.

'Better what?' said Katerina, wife of middle Vassili, joining them, pulling Eleni from Sofia's arms and into her own tight hold. 'Better here, with us, yes, Eleni-mou?'

'Yes,' said Eleni, muffled by her bosom.

They spent that afternoon like they'd spent countless others, out in the vine-latticed garden, squashed in at the table with its wine barrels for legs. The three Vassilis – all moustaches, and cheek pinches, and jokes about how they hoped Eleni hadn't turned too quiet, too *English,* over the winter – had roasted a goat, Sofia and Katerina had prepared platters of salads, and cheeses, and there was much, much wine.

There was arguing too, that was par for the course; a bit about politics, but mainly Little Vassili – who was two years older than Eleni, well over six feet, and had, it transpired, just that week enlisted in the Cretan division of the Greek army.

'You want to fight?' Yorgos asked him.

'I want to stand on my own feet,' he said.

'Well,' said Yorgos, with a grudging turn of his lips.

'No,' said Katerina, 'don't encourage him. It's too danger-ous . . . '

'It's safe, Mama,' said Little Vassili, reaching for a hunk of bread.

'It *is* the army,' Eleni felt compelled to chime in. 'I've heard they use these things called . . . now, what's the word?' She pulled a musing face. 'Guns, is it . . . ?'

'Eleni-mou, go back to being quiet.'

'No.'

'Anyway—' he bit into his bread '—there's no one to shoot, in Crete.'

'Then stay here,' his father said. 'Crush grapes. We have plenty of those.'

'I don't want to make wine.'

'What's wrong with making wine?'

'What's *wrong* with the army?'

And so they continued, voices rising, shouting over one another, until Sofia smacked the table, ordering them all to be quiet, *behave,* she would not have the day ruined. 'We'll talk about this another time, yes?'

Silently, like chastised schoolchildren, they all nodded.

Obediently, no one did say another word on the matter. Uncle Vassili relayed a tale about a donkey who'd recently broken into the wine cellar, making itself drunk ('Walked like this,' he said, demonstrating, black eyes twinkling in his swarthy face), and, within no time at all, it was as though the row had never occurred. It was one of the things Eleni loved most about everyone; how swiftly they could switch from anger to happiness, no brooding in-between.

For herself, she was sure Little Vassili *would* be safe, for all her tease about guns. The island had been peaceful for years – neither of them had even been born when Crete had last had to fight, for independence from the Ottomans. And he'd been dreaming with her forever of the adventures he might have, if he could only escape the mountains. More than anything, she was excited for him. As the sun rose higher, bouncing off the tomato plants, perfuming the charcoaled air with sweetness, she forgot all about his parents' worry; she thought only of the beating heat, the sight of her *papou* with his head thrown back in laughter, and each piece of news that was shared: of friends' marriages, engagements, new babies.

Everyone wanted to hear about her winter too, of course, and Timothy; his summer tour of the nearby Libyan Sea.

'Will we see him, here?' Sofia asked.

'I doubt it,' said Eleni. 'You know he never comes.'

'Well, there was that once,' said Katerina, and off they went, reminiscing about Timothy's only trip to the island with

Eleni, back when she'd been about to turn twelve, more than a decade after he'd first sent her from England, couriered to her *papou* with a nanny, like a babe with a stork. He'd remained at the villa for a fortnight, where he'd uttered not a word of his memories from the war, when his ship had been docked in Souda for repair, and he'd met Eleni's mama; most of the time, he'd read journals on a deckchair whilst Eleni had swum. One morning though, he'd taken her fishing, she was fairly sure at Yorgos's suggestion, but the hours they'd spent on their rented boat, silently casting out, had nonetheless stuck in her mind. He'd shown her how to bait her hook, putting his arms around her to help her reel it in. They'd caught nothing but seaweed. 'We've left the fish happy, I think, Eleni,' he'd said, and she'd laughed, loving it when he had too. He'd let her steer the boat back, showing her how to guide the prow into the waves, both of them dodging the spray.

She'd loved that as well.

And the next day, they'd come up here, to the mountains.

'Do you remember when Sofia got him dancing?' said Katerina, eyes streaming.

'Oh, don't,' said Eleni, covering her face with her hands, seeing him again, stiffly copying Sofia's movements, in one of the short-sleeved shirts he'd bought especially for the trip. 'Poor Dad . . . '

'Maybe that's why he never came again,' said Katerina, wiping her tears. 'We blame you, Sofia.'

'Blame Little Vassili,' said Sofia. 'He was the one who spilt wine all over him.'

'Ah, he didn't mind,' said Yorgos. 'It was Petra not being here he couldn't bear.' He moved his glass, rotating it between his thumb and forefinger. 'Until he came, I'm sure he'd managed to believe she somehow still was.'

It wasn't the first time he'd said such a thing.

It always felt horribly sad though, when he did.

Eleni reached across the table, squeezing his hand.

He smiled, squeezing hers back.

'Well, I'm still blaming Little Vassili,' said Sofia at length, dispelling the grief. 'Now come—' she surveyed the table '—Petra's probably looking down on us thinking there's too much food left. Everyone, eat.'

Everyone did.

None of them moved for hours, other than to top up the wine. As dusk fell, the sun dipping behind the peaks, Katerina fetched orange pie for dessert, Eleni and Little Vassili lit the garden's lanterns – stumbling, after all the wine – and Katerina's parents and the neighbours arrived, bringing more cheek-pinching, and carafes of their own *krassi*. Inevitably, Katerina's father got out his bouzouki too, and Sofia kicked off the dancing Timothy had fallen prey to, dragging everyone up until they were all on their feet, arms slung over each other, crouching low, springing high, so many *opa-a*'s rolling into the valley, the mountains soaring around them, silent and watchful, like indulgent gods.

'I'm broken,' Eleni said to Yorgos when, at last, they were back in the motor, speeding through the blackness to the coast. The temperature had dipped again. The mountain air was crisp on her hot face, her skin shivery beneath the dress she'd spent most of the day melting in. Wrapping herself in the blanket Yorgos had brought, she rested her head on his shoulder. 'How old *is* Sofia again?'

'Always twenty.'

His deep voice reverberated beneath her. She felt her heavy eyes close.

'I hope the kitten's all right.'

'I hope he's gone.'

'No,' she said, unconsciousness stealing over her, 'you don't.'

She slept the entire way home. A deep, swallowing sleep, in

which her father was once again dancing, out on the mountain-side, and she was stepping backwards, then falling uncontrollably down, reaching in vain for Timothy, still dancing, until she wasn't, because Yorgos was shaking her awake outside the villa, a lit oil lamp in hand.

'We're here, Eleni-mou. Come. Your cat is still on his throne.' He offered her the lamp.

Shakily, dozily, heart pummelling from her dreamt terror, she took it, and, bidding him goodnight, eased herself from the motor, then padded out to the terrace, where the kitten was indeed purring on his blanket, lost in happier slumber, deaf to the cicadas' chorus.

The saucers of food she'd left him were empty. She smiled, picturing him hungrily tucking in.

'*Papou* wants to call you *Tipota*,' she said, crouching to stroke him. 'What do you think?'

He moved in his sleep, pushing his head against her palm.

'Really?' she said. 'You like that name, too?'

With another stroke, she yawned and, feeling her calves protest from the dancing, so long in the motor, stood to return inside and fall at last into her own bed.

Faintly, she became aware of the cello's music.

The melody carried on the cool night, across from Nikos's villa.

Holding the lamp, she moved to the terrace edge, listening.

Below her, the moon's beam carved through the sea. Far out, a lone fishing boat bobbed at anchor.

The music went on, serene, smooth; so different to the bouzouki that, until that moment, had been ringing in her ears, her muscles.

Whoever was playing did it expertly.

Patriotically, too.

Eleni wasn't usually one for being able to name composers.

Unlike the parents of her school friends, Timothy hadn't spent his evenings drilling her on recordings so that she might one day hold her own at a dinner party; he'd taught her Morse. But she recognized Bach, and that this was the first of his Cello Suites. Mr Hodgson at the hotel had used to play a recording on the lobby gramophone all the time. It had sounded crackly there, repetitive and impersonal.

Here, in the still night, it was beautiful.

She closed her tired eyes. Behind her lids, she pictured the bow moving over the strings. She felt each of its strokes, deep within her.

Was it Otto playing?

Or her? That woman with the child's voice, who'd called to him from the rocks.

A sister?

Hearing again the flirtatious tinkling of her laugh, she reluctantly decided, *probably not.*

She'd thought no more of either of them, in the noisy distraction of the day. Now, though . . .

Now, they filled her mind.

Whether they were out together, alone so late at night.

Or if it was somebody else playing. Another member of this Linder family from Berlin.

The cello stopped, giving her no answers.

She waited for it to start again.

The waves rippled, the cat purred, but no more music came.

When it became clear that none was going to, she turned again, and, still hearing the echo of the cello in the night's dark silence, went inside.

'Remembering wartime Greece.' Transcript of research interview undertaken by M. Middleton (M.M.) with subject seventeen (#17), at British Broadcasting House, 4 June 1974

M.M: What was she like, Eleni Adams?

#17: I can't think how to begin answering that.

M.M: She wasn't straightforward?

#17: Who is?

M.M: Not Eleni Adams?

#17: [Coughs] No, no, not her. She was a . . . [frowns] What are those animals called, that change?

M.M: Butterflies?

#17: No, God no. Too fragile. No, the ones that shift colour, to confuse predators. You know, camouflage . . .

M.M: Chameleons?

#17: Yes, that's it. Chameleons. That was her. She was able to . . . morph, instantly. One would see her, hear her, and not question that she was Greek. Not even with her [gestures at head] curls. Obviously, there are Cretans with fair hair. And she had the right expressions, the gesticulations. Entirely . . . authentic. And then, just like that, she'd break into English, and the Greekness it . . . well, it fell away from her. It was incredible. [Reaches for water] I remember the first time I saw it happen, back in thirty-six. At that café she worked at, with . . . with . . .

M.M: [Consults notes] Dimitri?

#17: Yes, of course. Dimitri. [Sighs] She was with him, wearing these white shorts. You should have seen her. She could have been on a poster. That hair, such dark skin, blue eyes that took up her whole face, and legs, legs that, well . . . [Stares at glass] I don't think she'd yet realized the effect she had on men. She came to. It was what made her so dangerous. An assassin dressed up as a goddess. But then [frowns] I believe she was still as innocent as she looked. Then.

M.M: She was nineteen, yes?

#17: Not even. God [drinks more] nineteen thirty-six. It was a different world. There was . . . hope in it. Trust, in the future. Not for everyone. But for a lot of people.

M.M: For you?

#17: I don't know. Maybe. Jesse Owens won four gold medals at the Berlin Olympics that August, and people cheered. That was still possible. Then the Spanish Civil War came.

The next year, Hitler took over the German
army . . .

M.M: And Eleni?

#17: Eleni?

M.M: You were talking about the first time you
saw her morph.

#17: Morph?

M.M: Into an English girl.

#17: Ah, yes. Remind me what I was saying?

M.M: She was with Dimitri . . .

#17: So she was. Yes, yes. [Stares at glass]
They were dancing together, actually. Right
by the harbour's edge. She was talking
away, every inch the Cretan, and then, she
stopped, spoke in English. [Long silence]
Oh, hello. That was all she said. But just
like that, she was pure . . . Pure . . .
Vivian Leigh. It was as though an artist
had taken a paintbrush to her portrait and
reworked it. Her father was an officer
in the Royal Navy. You know that. She
was . . . *cut glass*. Apart from . . .
[stops]

M.M: Apart from?

#17: Apart from her laugh. There was nothing
stiff, or precise about her laugh. It
was . . . unconstrained. [Takes several
breaths] She laughed with her heart. Her
whole being.

M.M: A good laugh?

#17: [Nods]

M.M: You liked it?

#17: [Silence]

M.M: Yes?

#17: Yes. [Brushes eyes] I should have stayed away from her.

M.M: But you didn't.

#17: By the time I realized I should have, she already meant too much.

Chapter Three

It wasn't Otto that Eleni had heard on the cello.

It wasn't Lotte either.

Lotte, whose pale skin had burnt that afternoon, in the restless hours they'd all spent baking on the rocks, was upstairs, in her room beside Otto's – sleeping, just as Otto's parents, Henri and Brigit, were sleeping – when those first chords rent the night.

No, it was eighteen-year-old Marianne who played.

Otto heard her himself, on his way back from another swim, out to where he'd seen a fishing boat anchored. He knew it was Marianne, from the moment her bow touched the strings. He'd listened to her play too often to doubt it. His mother, Brigit, had taught her. He and his younger sister, Krista, had used to get into trouble as children, for disrupting their lessons.

'I finally have a student worthy of my attention,' Brigit had used to say, shooing them out of the drawing room, 'unlike you philistines.' They'd laugh, not knowing of what the word meant. 'Go, into the garden.' She'd tickle them. 'Marianne will come soon.'

Otto felt her touch again, as he ran up Nikos's dark steps. For a moment – dripping wet, breathless with cold and exertion – he stopped, smiled. But then he let his smile fall, because those lessons, his mother's tickles, were trapped in a vanished world.

Fixing his sights on the glow of lamplight above, he climbed the final steps, through the olive trees, towards where Krista and Marianne sat alone on the terrace: Marianne in her nightgown, the cello wedged between her legs, her plait slung over her shoulder; Krista, on the paved floor beside her, elbows resting on her knees, one of the cigarettes Hitler hated smoking in her hand.

When Marianne finished playing, she held her bow against the strings, not moving. Krista offered her the cigarette, and Marianne stared at it, then bowed her head.

Her shoulders shuddered. She made a quiet, choking sound.

It took Otto a moment to realize that she was crying.

It shook him, deeply. Marianne was one of the sweetest people he knew, perpetually smiling, game for anything, always the first up and out on her bicycle, plaits flying, since the day she'd learnt to ride one. *Krista, Krista, come on.* It was hideous, seeing her upset. She never cried.

I can't let myself, she'd said, the year before, when the Nuremberg Laws had stripped her, and anyone with three or more Jewish grandparents, of their citizenship. *They want me to give up, to feel worthless. The only power I have is not allowing them.*

Something must have happened whilst Otto had been swimming. He wanted to ask Marianne what, but held back, instinctively leaving her the privacy she believed she had.

She continued to cry, vicious tears that she seemingly couldn't contain now she'd set them free. She clung to her cello and bow like they were all she had to cling to, but then Krista stood, wrapping her arms around her, giving her something else. Letting her bow go, Marianne reached up, placed her hand over Krista's, and Krista rested her cheek on her head, holding her closer.

Quietly, heavily, Otto slipped through the terrace doors, into the villa, leaving them both alone.

Lotte was waiting for him upstairs, hovering with a candle at her bedroom door. Not asleep, after all. He sighed inwardly. She was always appearing when he was least expecting it. Here, now. Last night, down at the rocks. *Otto. Otto Linder.* It had taken every ounce of his self-control not to betray his irritation that she'd come.

'Who was that?' she'd asked, after he'd swum to her, looking out at where he'd left her, *Eleni Adams*, in the water.

'A mermaid,' he'd said.

It wasn't funny, but she'd laughed like it was.

She was in white again tonight: a silk nightrobe. Her hair was loose, reaching in a sheet to her waist. The candle's flame rippled gold on her scalded skin, bare where her robe had slipped from her shoulder.

Had she dropped it like that on purpose?

She'd used to be so scruffy. Her family had once rented rooms on the outskirts of the same leafy suburb of Grunewald that Otto's own, and Marianne's, lived. Brigit, and Marianne's mother, had used to invite Lotte around for dinners, to stay on weekends, saying it was safer for her out of the way of her parents. Otto, three years older, with his own friends, had had little do to with Lotte himself. She'd been too timid to interest him; always so afraid of muddying her pinafore, the possible pain of falling.

Sometimes, though, he'd seen her staring up from the bottom of one of the trees they'd all scampered into, or standing alone on the edge of the frozen lake, and felt a tug of pity.

Is the ice strong enough? she'd ask, whenever he went back to help her find her footing, clinging to his arm through threadbare mittens. Her father had been a poor man, before he hadn't. *I don't want to fall in.*

You won't fall in, he'd say.

If I did, would you help me?

'Otto?' she whispered now, porcelain voice bringing him back to the moment. 'Is Marianne all right?'

He met her gaze. Her doll's eyes reflected the candle. Probably, if he looked further into them, he'd still find a trace of that childish vulnerability. Some reason to pity her again.

He probably wouldn't even need to search that hard.

But he was tired. He didn't have the energy to search.

And he didn't want to pity Lotte.

'How do you know there's something wrong with Marianne?' he asked.

'I went down. You . . . I wondered where you'd gone.'

'A swim,' he said.

Stop following me.

'I overheard Marianne tell Krista her parents have to give up the house.' She didn't blink. 'Did you know?'

'No,' he said, flatly – saddened, but unsurprised. Marianne's parents had been struggling for money for years. Her father, Ernst, once a music professor with Otto's mother at the University of Berlin, had been dismissed with the rest of the Jewish staff back when the Nazis seized power in 1933. He now scraped by teaching piano to the children of parents who'd still send them to him. Marianne's mother, Nicola, cleaned, but didn't have much work either. *Friends feel uncomfortable,* she said. *Strangers don't want me. Thank God for your mama.* 'Why didn't they say anything?' Otto asked, more of himself than Lotte, realizing as he spoke that they probably had, and that that was why Henri had invited Marianne along on this trip: to save her the pain of moving. Henri wasn't a bad man, just desperate.

'Marianne only found out herself yesterday,' said Lotte, 'before we flew. When we go back, they'll be living in her aunt's flat. I told Marianne they shouldn't . . . '

'Why?'

'Because they need to leave Germany.' She took a breath. 'It can't be their home anymore.'

Otto stared. 'You actually said that to her?'

'Yes. She needs to face facts.'

'She's beside herself, Lotte.'

'She was upset already. She's been bottling it up.'

'So you decided to make it worse?'

'No . . .'

'She's your friend.'

'I know . . .'

'Her mother used to look after you. She made your birthday cakes . . .'

'That's the past. This is now. No one *wants* them in Germany.'

'No Nazi wants them.'

'That's all that counts anymore.'

'Is it?'

'Otto, you know it is.'

Don't tell me what I know, he almost snapped, but clenched his fist, stopping himself.

Be nice to Lotte.

'I'm tired,' he said, and carried on to his room. 'I need to sleep.'

'I was trying to help her, Otto. Help all of them . . .'

'All right,' he said, and didn't add how much he despised the cowardice of such help. That she, who, out of any person he knew, might actually attempt to do *something* more for Marianne – something that counted too – did nothing but sit, night after night at her father's dinner parties, taking the place of her mother, who'd long since run off, smiling prettily, at Nazis. She'd been afraid of her father her entire life. Nothing he said was going to change that.

Would she really help his own family, as Henri was counting on her doing, if – *when* – it came to it?

Otto held little hope of it.

But, whilst there was even a shred of a chance that she might, he accepted that he couldn't alienate her.

So, with as much civility as he could muster, he bid her good-night, and closed his door.

Crete hadn't been in Otto's plan for the summer. He was heading into the final year of his architecture degree, up in Munich, and keen to make the most of his freedom before he graduated and went into uniform. Conscription was a new development in Germany, introduced the March before, breaking the Treaty of Versailles, and – less significantly for international law, but certainly significant for Otto – forcing him to give up the post he'd been offered in a Berlin design studio and resign himself instead to military service. There was no way out of it. He and several of his classmates had looked for one.

'Are you mad?' one of their tutors had demanded, when he'd found out about their investigations. 'Want someone to open a file on you? Get flagged as non-patriots?'

Obviously not.

But neither had they been inclined to stick around through the vacation and wave swastikas at the Olympic Games. They'd decided to escape, on their bikes, cycling through Austria, down into Italy, back to Switzerland.

Henri, however, had been plotting an escape too.

'I have to get your sister out of Berlin, before she gets herself killed,' he'd said, arriving without warning at Otto's digs in Munich, just three weeks before. 'And your mother . . . Ah, Otto. Your mother is getting worse. She needs rest and peace. And you. We need you.'

He'd arranged everything, no expense spared: air tickets, so Brigit wouldn't have a long journey by sea, then a two-month lease on the villa. Brigit's doctor knew Nikos from way back;

it had been he who'd suggested renting his house to Henri. 'Mr Kalantis prefers to work the summer in Thessaloniki,' Henri had told Otto, without so much as a pause to ask whether Otto *minded* giving up his plans for the break. 'He'll leave once we're settled, and there'll be plenty of room for all of us, Marianne as well. Lotte, too.'

'Lotte?' Otto had said, interrupting. 'Seriously, Papa. *Lotte?*'

'Yes, Otto. Lotte.'

'Does her father know Marianne is coming?'

'No . . . '

'You don't think Lotte will tell him?'

'No, because you're going to ask her not to.'

That had done it. Otto had exploded, refusing to go along with any of it, flaming at Henri's high-handedness, the stranglehold of obligation he could feel closing around him. Henri, in turn, had accused him of being selfish, unfeeling, and slammed from the room, instructing him to come by his hotel when he'd seen sense.

'Has it ever occurred to you?' Otto had yelled after him, from the top of the stone stairwell, 'that our versions of sense don't align?'

'Never once,' Henri had yelled back.

'Beer?' one of Otto's housemates had enquired, sloping from his room.

They'd cracked several, climbing on to Otto's window ledge to drink them, convincing each other, in Munich's early summer sunshine, that Otto wouldn't be going to Crete to babysit or cajole anyone – least of all the daughter of a man who might fairly expect to spend his eternity in hell. No, he'd be cycling with the rest of them.

Otto had believed it.

Until his mother had telephoned.

'I want you to go on your adventure, my darling,' she'd said.

'I've told Papa that there *will* be other summers.' He'd pictured her gentle smile. Imagined her, alone in their hallway, fingers touched to the wall to still their tremor. 'I'll think of you having fun with your friends, and it will make me so happy. It's all the medicine I need.'

How could he have enjoyed a second of anything, after that?

'Good man,' his father had said, at the door of his hotel room. 'Are you drunk?'

'Yes.'

'It never helps . . . '

'It's helped a bit.'

The others had gone off to Austria, and Otto had returned to Grunewald, hugging Krista when she'd charged down the driveway to greet him, hugging his mother too, at the front door, hiding his grief that she hadn't been able to run anywhere. *Your mother is getting worse.* It had only been then, seeing the oil-spills of exhaustion beneath her eyes, feeling her bony fragility, that he'd accepted the truth of Henri's words. Realized that, whatever his disappointment, it was right that he'd come home to her.

He'd still dreaded the weeks ahead, though.

He'd dreaded them all through that evening, as Henri, taut with forced jollity, had talked over dinner about the many excursions he was excited to make: to Knossos, various beaches; a plan to rent a boat.

'Perhaps you can teach Lotte to sail, Otto. I'm sure she'd enjoy that.'

He'd dreaded them as he'd failed to fall asleep in his childhood bedroom, listening to the pipes' familiar creaks, the rustle of the garden's trees.

He'd dreaded them more when, the next morning, through the kitchen window, he'd caught sight of Lotte's father, SS-Oberst-Gruppenführer Becker, turning into the driveway in his motor with its swastika flags, delivering Lotte to the porch.

'Stay here with me, darling,' Brigit had said to Marianne, who Henri had been careful to collect much earlier. 'His ignorance is our bliss, yes? We'll enjoy our breakfast, not give him the satisfaction of ruining it. Otto will see him off.'

'Thank you,' Marianne had said to Otto, as, leadenly, he'd gone to do just that.

At the porch, Becker had clamped his hand in his own, watery eyes willing him to flinch. 'Look after my little girl,' he'd said, and then he'd smiled. 'I know you will.'

Otto hadn't returned the smile. Not even for Marianne.

The vice of Becker's fist had tightened, and he hadn't flinched either.

But he had sat with Lotte for the taxicab to the airstrip, then again in the aeroplane. She'd fumbled over her belt, asked for his help, and he'd clicked the metal into place for her.

'I don't know what Papa is going to do when he finds out about Marianne,' she'd whispered.

'Does he need to know?' he'd asked, true to the lines of his father's script.

'You want me to lie to him?'

'Just not tell him about it.' He'd held her eye, despising himself when she'd blushed. 'Please, Lotte.'

'All right.'

For the rest of the flight, with the propellors' noise mercifully blocking conversation, Otto had stared through the window, thinking of he wasn't sure what, until, at last, they'd descended towards Crete. The island from the sky had been beautiful, undeniably so, its great bulk shimmering beneath the blazing sky, yet Otto hadn't been moved. He'd looked coldly at the beaches scalloping the perimeter – the iridescent sea so transparent he'd been able to see the shadow of the plane's wings in its fathoms – too buried in his own bleak mood to want to surface. As they'd bumped into land, Lotte had gasped, and he'd pretended not to hear. When, minutes later, they'd all disembarked into the airstrip's peace, he'd felt no urge to exclaim on the blissful warmth, like everyone else had. He'd simply filled his lungs with the hit of pure, earthy air – that scent he would, eventually, with a clearer mind, come to crave – and told himself, *it's not for long*. Lotte would, at least, be gone before the rest of them, too, flying back to Germany to be her father's ornament for the closing days of the Olympics.

They'd have a week free of her at the end.

'It's something,' Krista had consoled, when they'd reached the villa, and he'd carried her and Marianne's trunks to their room.

It was.

Just not very much.

At nightfall, Lotte had hummed as she'd dressed for dinner, and Otto, hearing the noise through their thin, shared wall, had gone for that first swim to escape. He'd wanted only to move, raise his heart rate, exorcise the tension trapped in his limbs.

He'd hoped for no more than that.

But he'd caught sight of Eleni Adams on the moonlit shingles. He'd watched her run at the sea like she belonged in it.

Dreaded the summer ahead, for the short time he was near her, a fraction less.

It had been her abandon that had appealed to him. *A mermaid*, he'd called her, and she could have been one, diving, swimming, not giving a *damn*. All of them, in Germany, had become so conditioned to picturing themselves through the eyes of others, second-guessing the impression they were making: a self-obsession borne of terror. But Eleni; she'd been . . . *free*. He'd felt her freedom in himself, vicariously.

Until Lotte had come, calling him to dinner.

Otto. Otto Linder.

Aside from that one dawn glimpse of Eleni, in her grandfather's

Cadillac, he'd seen nothing of her since. Not out on the road, nor down by the water, nor in it.

Hour by hour, she'd dropped from his mind. His thoughts had filled once again with his mother, how washed out she looked in her basket chair, reading; how pensive his father was, watching her; Lotte, so watchful too.

Lotte, at least, remained in bed the following morning, a Sunday.

'Bathed in cold cream,' said Marianne, returning to the kitchen, where Otto and Krista were having breakfast. (Marianne, with a magnanimity Otto struggled to understand, had taken Lotte up a tray.) 'She's staying hidden until tomorrow.'

'How red does she look?' Krista asked, dolloping yoghurt into a bowl.

'Quite,' said Marianne. 'But, you know, still pretty.'

'I don't think she is,' said Krista. 'She's always reminded me of a lily, which—' she sat at the table '—stains everything it touches.'

Marianne said nothing. Krista had told Otto, whilst she'd been gone upstairs, that she was determined to forget the night before had happened. *She says she doesn't know when she'll get another holiday. She's promised her parents she'll enjoy this one.*

In part to help her do that, in part because he couldn't face idling away another day in the villa, Otto suggested the three of them head out, explore the island.

'A good idea,' said Nikos, making them all turn as he too came into the kitchen. 'You can use my motor.'

'Are you sure?' Krista asked.

'Yes.' He crossed to the sideboard, poured coffee. 'I rarely use it. I have a man who taxis me, so I can work. He'll take me to the port tomorrow. The motor's yours for the summer.' He sipped his coffee. 'Please don't crash it.'

Was he joking?

His hooded expression gave nothing away.

They thanked him. He told them it was nothing, that he'd fetch them a map.

'Who was that playing the cello last night?' he asked, at the door.

'Me,' said Marianne. 'I hope I didn't disturb you.'

He turned his heavy eyes on her.

'You disturbed me a great deal,' he said.

Then went.

Marianne grimaced. 'Oh . . . '

'Don't worry about it,' said Otto.

'He'll be gone to Thessaloniki tomorrow,' said Krista. 'Now come on, let's get going too, before Papa comes and insists that we stay with Lotte.'

Otto drove. He was the only one who knew how. He saw Lotte through the motor's rear mirror as he shifted into gear. She was at her window, staring down at them. She could have been six again, watching longingly from the edge of the icy lake.

Frowning, flooring the gas, Otto accelerated away.

It was evening by the time they reached Chania.

The day had turned into a surprisingly good one, the three of them speeding along the rutted island roads, pulling up at various beaches, swimming in the cerulean sea. But they'd long since run out of water and were now intent on finding somewhere, anywhere, that was open on a Sunday, to have a drink.

Leaving the motor in a tree-lined square, they set off through the town's shuttered alleyways, eventually coming to the harbour, where, to their relief, they discovered one *kafeteria* open for business, at the very end of the long, sleepy quayside – past the fishing boats bobbing at anchor, the pelicans that stood on bollards, observing the bruising horizon – its tables bustling, a gramophone blaring out Fred Astaire.

Krista and Marianne made a beeline for it, selecting one of the few vacant tables. It was next to a noisy group who, with their Anglo-Saxon features, could only be tourists too. There were lots of Greek customers besides, mostly men, all drinking coffee.

Then, a girl in white shorts and a lemon blouse, dancing with a dark man in shirt sleeves by the water's edge. Otto noticed them, and Nikos watching them both from the back of the café, in sequence. He was taken aback to see Nikos. He drew breath to call hello, but then the girl reclaimed his attention, exclaiming as her dance partner spun her around. She clutched her ankle, spoke in rapid Greek, and laughingly pushed her partner towards the café door.

The man grinned, unchastised, and retreated inside.

Otto didn't watch him go. He was too busy looking at the girl. Realizing who she was.

I have nothing to do with her, Nikos had said.

Why then had he been watching her so closely?

And where had he gone? Otto glanced back at his table, but it was empty.

Bemused, but actually not caring about Nikos, and ignoring Krista calling for him to sit, he turned again to Eleni. She filled her cheeks with air, seeming to catch her breath. Her hair – gold to Lotte's white – escaped from its ponytail in waves, sticking, damp, to her skin. She ran her fingers around the back of her neck, looking down as, gingerly, she pressed on her ankle.

She had red nail polish on her toes.

Slowly, as though sensing the weight of his attention, she looked up, towards him.

He watched her do it.

Saw her eyes – such a deep blue that they appeared almost black – widen in surprise, just as they had in the water.

Only this time, she didn't remain silent.

'Oh, hello,' she said, in the most perfect, cut-glass English; it was impossible not to laugh.

'Hello,' he said.

'You speak English?'

'Yes,' he said. His mother had spoken it to him from the crib. 'I can manage.'

She smiled.

What a smile.

'I think you must be Otto Linder,' she said.

Chapter Four

I think you must be Otto Linder.

She cursed inwardly, hearing her own words back, realizing how readily she'd given away that she knew his name. *Play hard-to-get,* the dog eared magazines back in the hotel staff room had always advised. *There are few things so alluring as disinterest.*

Had she put him off?

He didn't seem put off.

He laughed again, pushing his hand through hair that was salt-matted, and messy, and would have had Timothy sending him straight for a crew cut, and somehow she – who absolutely shouldn't be letting him off so easily for the fright he'd given her in the sea – was laughing with him, unable to help herself.

He really was the last person she'd been expecting to see.

She'd looked for him again earlier, driving past his gate on the way to Halepa, but that had been hours before. In the time since, she'd swam at Maria and Spiros's bay, eaten slow-baked lamb in their courtyard, talked of a hundred different things, but never once of a stranger from Berlin. She'd come to the quayside that evening thinking only of assuring Dimitri that she wanted his job for the summer, at which news he'd been unsurprised ('Eleni, who you could work with, but me?') and much less interested in discussing her hours ('We'll do the same as last year, *no problem*') than in showing off his new gramophone, then dancing with her to 'Cheek to Cheek'.

'Come, Eleni. Let's be in heaven . . . '

'This is heaven?' she'd said, as he'd turned her painfully on her ankle. 'I had higher hopes . . . '

The recording was still playing. Fred's voice carried above the café's buzzy chatter . . .

. . . *My heart beats so that I can barely speak* . . .

Eleni had some sympathy.

Otto made to join her, passing two girls at a table. One pulled at his arm, and he said something to her. *Hang on,* maybe. Hazily, Eleni registered their exchange. Much more vividly, she was conscious of Otto leaving the girls, closing the short distance between himself and her, until there was none left.

'I think *you*,' he said, 'must be Eleni Adams.'

'You know my name too,' she said.

(She probably shouldn't have said that.)

'I do,' he agreed.

She smiled again. She didn't try to contain the urge. It was already too late.

Besides, did it *really* matter?

He, after all, was smiling with her.

She liked his smile. Liked his accent, so much subtler than she'd heard on any newsreel. Liked his face, no longer hidden by the night. His features had a Slavic slant to them; all firm lines, save for a dent to the bridge of his nose, which looked as though it had once been broken. She lingered on it, wondering how it had happened. Unquestioningly, she decided she'd have guessed just by seeing him that he was German. Or, at least, that he wasn't British. He had none of the soft edges of the sailors around Gosport; her classmates' brothers. There wasn't a trace of schoolboy ruddiness in his sun-drenched skin.

He didn't look like a boy at all.

Her eyes snagged on his – no Aryan blue, but green, near grey, in the mellowing dusk, and alight with amusement. He'd noticed she'd been taking the measure of him.

There are few things so alluring as disinterest.

Smile spreading, cheeks flushing, she said, 'Tell me, do you make a habit of startling lone women in the sea?'

'Only on Fridays,' he replied, without missing a beat, making her laugh again.

He was fun.

She liked that, too.

'How's your ankle?' he asked.

'Fine,' she replied, which it almost was.

'You don't need to sit?'

'No.'

'All right,' he said, and made no move to sit, or go, either.

He wants to stay, she thought, *he wants to stay with me.*

And wanting – very much, suddenly – for him to go on doing that, she combed her mind for something else to ask him, settling, with another glance at his hair, on whether he'd come from a beach.

'I've come from a few,' he said. Then, as she drew breath to ask which, 'I have no idea.'

'No?' she said, smiling more, because he'd read her mind. 'How is that possible?'

'Our map was in Greek.'

'How inconvenient.'

'I know.'

'But you still managed to find some good ones?'

'We found some beautiful ones.'

'Well, there's no shortage of those.'

'So I'm discovering.'

'And you can't have got too lost,' she went on, the words

coming to her as she spoke. 'You made it here—' she kept her expression level '—to Rethymno.'

He stared.

Valiantly, she fought another smile.

'Damn,' he said, all seriousness, 'we were aiming for Heraklion.'

And she let her smile go, loving that he'd played along.

Beside them, a table of customers got up. They moved, letting them pass, then immediately stepped back together again.

Inside the café, the recording crackled to an end, then, after a moment's pause, restarted.

'I am sorry about Friday night,' Otto said, apropos of nothing, letting Eleni know he was still thinking about it too. 'I didn't mean to shock you . . . '

'Good.'

'I would have talked to you sooner, if I'd known you spoke English.'

'Really?' It was a nice thought. 'And what would you have said?'

'Hello, probably.'

She considered it. 'Is that so different in German?'

'Not to English. But to Greek—' he broke off. 'You tell me.'

'I suppose it is a little different.'

'Just a little?'

'Yes, a little.'

He gave her a long look.

She widened her eyes. 'What?'

'I don't think I believe you.'

'I don't think I believe you came all the way to Greece not knowing how to say hello,' she riposted.

It was his turn to fight a smile. 'Fine, so tell me how.'

'You really don't know?'

'I really don't know.'

'It's *yassas*,' she said, relenting. '*Yiassou*, with someone you know.'

'Ha,' he said, vindicated, 'so pretty different.'

'Pretty different,' she conceded.

'So, I'm forgiven?'

'I suppose you are.'

'Well, thank God,' he said, teasing, she knew, but . . . maybe he meant it too.

They fell silent.

She looked at him.

He looked at her.

Heaven. I'm in heaven . . .

'Would you . . . ?' he began.

'Eleni,' came the call, making them both turn.

'Oh no,' Eleni breathed, her heart (that had once again been beating so that she could barely speak) sinking as she caught sight of Yorgos, who she'd left waiting round the corner in the motor, striding along the waterfront in his Sunday three-piece, swinging his worry beads, face stern, impervious to the charms of Fred's voice, and the gradually sinking sun.

'I see you see me,' he shouted to her, in Greek. 'You said five minutes.'

'I'm coming,' she called back, also in Greek.

'Walk, then.'

'Your grandfather?' Otto asked.

'Yes.'

'He looks nice.'

She laughed.

'*Eleni Juliet Adams* . . . '

She stopped laughing.

'I'm coming,' she called to Yorgos again. Then, in English, to Otto, conscious, so conscious, of how much she wanted to stay, 'I'd better go. He's not in the best mood.'

'Why?'

'My shorts.' He hated them, predictably enough. He'd almost refused to leave the house with her that morning, adamant that Maria and Spiros would be as appalled by them as he. But Spiros had been impartial (*what do I know?*), and Maria, who Eleni had known would be on her side, had told Yorgos to not be so stuffy. *If I was as young as I feel, I'd wear them too.* He was still sulking. 'He wants me to burn them.'

'That's drastic.'

'Isn't it though?'

'Eleni.' Yorgos again. He was getting close. 'Who is that boy you're talking to . . . ?'

'God, I have to go,' Eleni repeated, only this time – propelled by Yorgos's rapid advance, her desperation to avoid the awkwardness of introductions – she went.

'Wait,' Otto called after her.

'Yes?' she said, looking back over her shoulder.

The sun's last rays reached out, bathing him, everyone at the tables, in its last drops of heat.

'Promise me something.'

'What?'

He grinned. 'Please don't burn those shorts.'

She kept smiling, hearing those words over, all through the evening that followed: on the drive home, scooping Tipota up at the porch (Tips, she decided, for short), feeding him Maria's leftover lamb, helping Yorgos prepare their own supper, playing backgammon with him on the terrace (winning, as though he wasn't sulking enough). She kept smiling about all of it, half of her back at the harbour, reliving each moment, recalling fresh details every time. How Otto had pronounced her name, *I-leni*, with his accent that she'd liked. The way he'd dropped his head when he'd laughed, then raised his gaze to hers again. That question he'd begun, yet failed to finish.

Would you . . . ?

Have a drink with him?

Is that what he'd been going to ask?

She had to bite her lip, just at the possibility, lest Yorgos see and ask what it was she kept smiling about.

Perhaps that would have stopped, eventually.

Perhaps, given time, the elation of those heady minutes at the harbour would have faded in her mind.

Perhaps Otto might have.

But there was no chance for that to happen. She saw him again so soon.

She saw him that very night.

It was past eleven. She was in the kitchen, ironing, Tips winding around her feet. Otto was swimming, away from his villa; those clean, precise strokes. She caught his movement through the open window, felt the stillness of recognition; smiled again without knowing it.

Setting the iron down, she stepped to the window.

It really was late for him to be out swimming.

Did the others in his villa know he was gone?

Would that girl who'd called for him before come again?

Eleni had been thinking of her too, these past hours. She hadn't done that at all at the café, swept up, entirely, in the moment. But, ever since, she'd found herself picturing her again, in her willowy white gown, picturing those girls at the harbour too, becoming increasingly certain, the more she had, that neither of the pair had been her; they'd looked too casual, too relaxed. She'd become curious about them as well: who they were, why the girl in white hadn't been with them; frustrated with her own guessing games . . .

She pushed the window wider. He was swimming so far. He'd almost reached that boat at anchor.

'The iron's going to scald,' said Yorgos, appearing from the terrace with an empty brandy glass. 'Are those things beneath it?'

'They're called shorts.'

'Is that a yes?'

'A no. It's a dress.'

'I'd rather it was those things.'

She laughed, but didn't move to attend to the iron. She kept her eyes on Otto. Waiting, although she wasn't entirely sure why.

He reached the boat, stopped.

For a few seconds, he didn't move.

Then he turned in the water, looked directly up at her at the lit window, waved.

And she realized what she'd been waiting for.

Everything felt changed somehow, when she woke the next morning. In the space of a night, the summer ahead, so predictable, had . . . pixelated, into unknowns: the endless possibilities of when or where she might run into him next.

It wasn't comfortable.

Yet, she, pulling off her nightdress, reaching for her bathing costume, couldn't for a second wish it another way.

Was that normal?

She had no idea.

She had no experience to tell her. Really, none. The only interactions she'd had with the opposite sex – beyond her family, customers at the café and hotel – had been fleeting civilities with her father's subordinates, all of whom were too scared of a disciplinary charge to do more than tip their caps at her in greeting. There were her classmates' brothers too, she supposed; she'd danced with some of them at the year's spate of eighteenth birthday parties. She wasn't sure such clumsy fumblings counted as experience, though. Certainly not the kind she wished to repeat. Those clammy fingers creeping south of her waist, the damp puddles of hot breath on her forehead, had all left her feeling . . . queasy. Desperate to be home in her bedroom. And a bit worried that there was something wrong with her, because wasn't one meant to feel palpitations and happiness in such circumstances?

She'd felt happy with Otto.

She was pretty sure she'd felt palpitations. (It was all a bit of a blur.)

She definitely felt them now, grabbing her towel and heading to the cove, where there was at least a working chance he'd be swimming again.

The Monday dawn – the last of June – was already warm; her warmest yet since returning. It would happen like this now, the heat building until September, the long days and short nights cooled only by the whim of the Meltemi winds that whipped from island to island through July and August. The breaking rays made the chill sea much easier to wade into than it had been on her first night. The light was pure, sharp, beating with a lucidity she'd experienced nowhere outside of Greece. She stood, waist-deep in the translucent water, momentarily mesmerised by the snakes of sunlight on the pebbles at her feet. Then, closing her eyes, she dived, kicking, swimming on, determinedly not glancing back over her shoulder, superstitious enough to believe he'd be more likely to come if she didn't check.

She kept going, to as far out as he'd been the night before, maybe further; the boat had disappeared, doubtless taken by its owner in search of squid and snapper. It was only when her arms began to tremble, her legs to shake, that she finally swivelled, searching the glassy expanse she'd crossed, and exhaled a sigh.

It was all emptiness.

Nikos Kalantis's villa remained shuttered and silent.

The only sign of life came from Yorgos, stepping out onto his and Eleni's own terrace, suited and ready for the surgery, raising his arm, beckoning her home.

She waved back, but hesitated before setting off.

She took her time too, returning to the cove, just in case . . .

'Please don't go so deep,' Yorgos cautioned, when, wrapped in her robe, she finally joined him in the kitchen. He was brewing coffee on the range. 'I wouldn't be able to get to you if you needed me. It's my worst nightmare.'

'I was fine,' she said, kissing him, 'I promise.'

'I fed your animal.'

'Tips.'

'A ridiculous name.'

'It's better than nothing.'

As soon as she was dressed, she called to Yorgos that she'd cycle to the bakery for breakfast. There was a small one not far inland, past Nikos's villa as it happened, but that absolutely wasn't the reason she went. If you got there early enough, they still had *bougatsa* left: the cinnamon-dusted, custard-filled pastries Eleni fantasised about through winter and never, not ever, considered trying to resist (hang the extra stone). It was the thought of enjoying one of them, warm from the oven, that motivated her. Only that.

She still looked out for Otto though, when she passed his gate (that forever-deserted gate) on her way to the bakery.

She looked out for him again as she made her way home, her basket wafting tantalising vanilla sweetness.

She was poised for the sight of him with every push of her pedal.

But, other than Irena, who ran the bakery, and her husband, Philip, out in the sunshine, loading the morning deliveries onto a cart, she saw no one.

The morning wasn't a complete bust. There was the *bougatsa* at least. She devoured hers leaning against the kitchen counter, chatting to Yorgos about his day's appointments, offering to see to their dinner since he wouldn't be home until late. She was working herself – her first shift at Dimitri's – but that didn't start until noon. She had plenty of time, she assured Yorgos, to put something in the oven before she'd need to catch the bus to Chania.

'Thank you,' he said, kissing her goodbye. 'In return, I'll try and say no more about those things.'

'Shorts,' she corrected, swallowing another mouthful. 'And you probably will say more.'

'Yes,' he agreed, heading off. 'I probably will. Don't miss your bus.'

'I won't,' she said.

She very nearly did.

Tips got into the pantry whilst she was out in the garden picking aubergines for an imam, and wrought havoc with a bag of rice and jar of honey, covering the villa in sticky, grainy paw prints. She had to mop the floors before they ended up with an ant infestation, then prepare the imam, then extract Tips again from the pantry (locking the door this time. *Fool me once . . .*), all of which left her mere minutes to make some rolls for her lunch, pack her bag, and race for the bus stop.

It was several hundred yards away, uphill along the dusty, unshaded road, past Nikos's villa, that gate. The sun, directly above, blazed, so fiercely the static afternoon seemed to quiver with its force. Sweating in her sundress, sandals slapping the crackling shrubs underfoot, Eleni cursed, hearing the tell tale protest of the bus's engine behind her, and picked up her pace, only just beating it to the stop.

Clutching her smarting waist, handing her drachma to the driver, she collapsed in a sprung seat beside the window, turned to yank the murky pane down, and felt her breath catch in her mouth because, oh god, there he was.

He was there, right there, coming over the verge of the roadside, climbing from the shore below. He'd been swimming. His hair was wet; he wore shorts, an open shirt, a towel slung around his neck.

Heart racing (palpitations!), still holding the window, she wondered if she should say something, then, before she could decide not to, called, 'Hello again.'

Play hard to get.

Too late.

In that moment, she couldn't have given less of a damn. Because he looked up, their eyes connected, and, just as the bus jerked into motion, he smiled.

A smile that lifted his contemplative face.

A smile that made her pumping heart expand.

A smile that felt entirely for her.

'Where are you going?' he shouted, above the engine.

'Work,' she said.

'Work where?'

'That café,' she said, leaning out of the window so that she could keep looking at him, heady with the turn of events.

He said something else.

She put her hand to her ear, unable to make it out. The bus, moving faster, was too noisy.

He shouted again.

'I still can't hear you,' she shouted back.

Now he was laughing. He yelled a third time.

She heard an 'I,' a 'see', a 'you.'

I'll come and see you?

Had it been that?

It might have been.

She really thought it might have.

The bus rounded the bend, she flopped back in her seat, laughed too, and, ignoring the odd look her neighbour gave her, hoped so much that it had.

She floated on the possibility, all the way into town.

Even when the journey took longer than it should have, thanks to an unscheduled stop for a herd of goats, she floated.

They were, inevitably, late in, compelling her to run, yet again, for the café, dodging the throngs at the harbour, which, unlike the evening before, was packed, the colourful, Venetian terraces in business, baskets of produce on display, fishermen haggling to sell their morning's catch.

'I'm sorry,' she gasped, sprinting the final stretch to Dimitri, visibly run off his feet, laden tray aloft, tables heaving with customers around him. 'I'm so sorry.'

'It's fine,' he said, with an airy wave. 'The world has not ended, I don't think. *No problem.*' He said the latter in English, an American accent. He'd done the same the night before, talking about her hours. The turn of phrase was, like the gramophone, a new development. 'Come,' he continued, in Greek, beckoning her on into the café's serving room: a hole-in-the-wall at the bottom of his narrow, lemon-painted home. There was hardly any furniture inside, just a mahogany bar, on which the gramophone and a coffee stove stood, then shelves full of cups, sacks of oranges on the floor. 'I need you to juice.'

It was Eleni's least favourite job. The oranges made her hands go yellow, and quickly stung invisible nicks in her skin, but not even a half-hour spent doing that dampened her mood. Nothing could. Not the smell of the rubbish bin behind the café, when she carried the orange shells out to throw them away. Not the flies who gusted up when she opened the bin's lids. Not the soaring temperature when she set to waiting tables, wiping spills, emptying ashtrays. Not even the tourists who spoke to her in too-loud, too-slow English. (She found them funny.) Whatever she was doing, she had one eye out for Otto (*I. See. You.*), her heart hovering between her chest and her mouth in case he appeared.

But three o'clock rolled around, the quayside emptied for the siesta, and still he hadn't come. Resolutely telling herself, *there's still time,* Eleni left Dimitri to head for his rest upstairs and set off for the quiet stretch of beach at Paralia Koum Kapi, where she'd spent so many of her siestas the summer before. Just as she had then, she ate her sandwiches alone on the sand, wriggled into her swimsuit beneath a towel, and indulged in a long soak in the sea. After, she lay down to dry, watched the sun through the web of her raised fingers, but didn't pick up the book she'd brought, too preoccupied with wondering where Otto was.

Impatient to be where he might appear, she returned to Dimitri's well before it opened again at five. She didn't have long left in her shift; whilst the customers would keep coming until gone ten, she always left at seven. It had been Yorgos's one stipulation when, seeing Dimitri's '*help really needed*' sign the previous summer, Eleni had offered up her services: she must be home before dark. Dimitri, who'd been a patient of Yorgos's since the day Yorgos had brought him into the world – quite a regular one, thanks to the asthma Dimitri refused to admit being bothered by to anyone *besides* Yorgos – had readily agreed. *Anything Doctor Florakis says.* Sometimes, Yorgos collected Eleni himself, if his appointments allowed. Mostly she caught the bus home, as she would be doing that evening.

It was always quieter, after the siesta, trade not really picking up again until the sun started to go down. Pleasanter too, in the softening heat. There was time for Eleni to sit and chat with Dimitri, hear his news. He told her about a friend of his, Socrates, who'd moved to Athens as a child, but had recently returned to Crete to take up a post at the local school come September. He was, like, Dimitri, in his late twenties, and had leased an apartment close by. It was a bit of a state. Dimitri was helping him redecorate it each night after the café shut.

'He sings when he strips the wallpaper,' he said, tapping his cigarette into the ashtray. 'He makes up his own songs. He used to do that when we were boys too. He loves music. Actually, he helped me buy the gramophone.'

'Ah,' said Eleni, smiling. 'And does he by any chance say, *no problem*, all the time?'

Dimitri's brow furrowed. 'How did you know that?'

'Never mind. When will I meet him?'

'Soon. He's going to help me when you go.'

'You're expanding, Dimitri. Two staff . . . '

'No, Socrates doesn't want wages. He says it's repayment for the decorating.'

'That's very nice of him.'

'Ye-es,' said Dimitri. '*Very* nice. If only . . . '

'Don't even think it,' she said. 'Look at my yellow fingers.' She wiggled them. '*I* need payment.'

Socrates arrived, as promised, just as Eleni was getting ready to leave for the bus. She saw him from the café's doorway, laughingly clasping Dimitri's hand in greeting at the waterside, slapping his shoulder. The first thing that struck her was how pleased both he and Dimitri were to see each other. They must really have been good friends when they were children. The second was that Socrates was very nice looking. *Comfortable.* Different to Dimitri's other acquaintance, indeed to Dimitri himself; he had none of their lean height, Grecian features, or dark moustaches. He had no moustache at all. But he was broad, with a square frame, even squarer jaw, light-brown hair, and tan skin that creased around his eyes when he smiled.

She saw that up close, when, moments later, bag on her shoulder, she crossed over to the pair, apologising to Socrates that she had to run off so soon.

'I promise not to take it personally,' he said. 'But are you sure you don't want me to walk you to the bus?'

It was a sweet offer.

She liked him for it. Liked him for having come to help Dimitri. She'd felt bad, the summer before, leaving him in the lurch, knowing, whatever his insistence to the contrary, that he'd have been better off hiring someone full-time. Given that, she really wasn't about to steal Socrates away, just as he'd arrived.

'I'll be fine,' she assured him, 'but thank you.' Determinedly, she found a smile to repay his, concealing how low she'd by now started to feel.

It was hardly his fault, after all, that he wasn't Otto.

Otto, who she'd foolishly waited for all day, and who hadn't come.

Otto, who she still, ridiculously, looked around for as she bade Dimitri and Socrates goodbye, and retraced her steps through Chania's dimming streets to the bus stop.

She didn't see him.

She realized, of course, that there could be any number of reasons for that – not least that there was every chance she'd misheard him earlier. He might not have said *I'll come and see you*, at all. It could have been, *I'll see you soon*. Or, *I'll see you again*. Possibly, he'd already had plans for the day. Plans he couldn't change.

That was actually entirely likely.

All of this she repeated to herself, waiting for the bus beneath the bird-filled trees in the square, then on the rickety ride home. Yet, no matter how hard she tried to reason her disappointment away, it wouldn't budge. It sat, heavy and stubborn, in her chest.

She'd really believed he was going to come.

Foolish it may be, but now that he hadn't, she felt shunned.

It confused her.

He'd looked so happy to see her, earlier. As happy as she'd been to see him.

Hadn't he?

She rested her head against the bus's cool frame and sighed, increasingly unsure.

The sun was almost down by the time she got off the bus. Above, the first stars glinted through the sky's pale, purpling sheen. The sea, beyond the cliff-edge, had begun to darken. The water was no longer still, but choppy, teased into ruffles by a sudden, thyme-scented breeze. The road, once the bus had lumbered off, rustled; all shadows and cicadas, a couple of grazing goats.

Go straight home, Yorgos had reminded Eleni, only that morning. *I'll be counting on you doing that.*

She hadn't argued, knowing he already gave her a deal more freedom than most Cretan girls her age had. She loved him for it. Loved that, for all his despair over her shorts, King Edward's morals, he – who'd taught her to read Greek with the aid of newspaper articles campaigning for women to vote (something they still weren't allowed to do here) – didn't treat her as though she were a china figurine.

She certainly couldn't have resembled one less now, grubby and tired, her salty hair sticking to her skin as she reached up to release it from its ponytail. She felt instant relief, pulling the band free. It had been hurting. She ached, everywhere. In her shoulders, her back, the soles of her feet.

The stroll home, downhill in the wind, was at least much easier going than her morning race up to the stop had been. She let her mind wander, to the imam, her hope that it hadn't turned too dry in the oven; Tips, and if he was hungry; the bath she was about to have. Nikos's damned gate, when she passed it.

Still no one there.

From somewhere, she found a laugh, that she'd bothered to check, and carried on, down the last stretch, around to the entrance to the villa.

Then stopped short.

Was she imagining it?

She didn't think she was imagining it.

Her heart, well and truly back palpitating, didn't think she was either.

It was him.

It was.

He was sitting on the ground, at the head of her driveway, in shorts, a jumper rolled up at the sleeves, his back against the tree there. He had a sketchpad on his lap. His attention was on the paper, the line he was measuring. His hair fell over his face. Absently, he moved it behind his ear.

'Hello again,' she said, just as she had that morning.

And, just as he had that morning, he looked up.

Grinned.

At her.

Her disappointment evaporated. What disappointment? She wasn't disappointed.

'Finally,' he said. 'I've been waiting for you.'

'You have?' she said, delighted, audibly. (*Play hard to get.* Who cared? Not her.)

'Yes. For quite a long time.'

'Oh,' she said, enjoying that, *quite a long time.* Enjoying it very much.

He set his pad aside, and stood, moving towards her.

She moved towards him, off the road.

'I thought . . . ' she began.

'I wanted to come into town,' he said, speaking at the same time.

They both laughed.

'I'm sorry I didn't,' he said. 'I got caught up in . . . something. By the time I was free, I thought it might be too late. So I came here.'

'To wait.'

'To wait. And now you're here too.'

'I am.'

'Are you in a rush?'

'No rush,' she said, forgetting the imam, forgetting poor Tips. Was this happening?

'Would you like to sit with me, then?' He held out his arm to the tree, as though to a chair. 'It's very comfortable.'

'Really?'

'Not at all.'

She smiled.

Not taking her eyes from his, she sat.

He joined her.

His hand rested on the grass, almost touching hers. She knew it was close, even without looking, from the tingling in her skin.

'So,' he said, 'I have many questions.'

'Yes,' she said, 'I have a fair few myself.'

His smile grew.

She felt hers do the same.

Without thinking, she stretched out her hand.

Or, he did his.

Either way, their fingertips touched.

In the Greek twilight, on the hard, baked ground, they kept touching.

And off she went, again.

Floating.

#17: Do you believe first love can be real love?

M.M: I thought I was meant to be the person interviewing you.

#17: Do you, though? Or do you think it is simply the force of attraction, novelty? Overwhelming, shocking. Selfish, often. But ultimately doomed to burn out?

M.M: Doomed? No, I don't think it's always doomed.

#17: Really?

M.M: No. If that was the case, there wouldn't be so many people who choose to spend the rest of their lives with their first love.

#17: But that choice is so often made in the initial flush, without clear thought.

M.M: I don't think that necessarily makes it less genuine. I think a choice to spend a lifetime with someone is one that's taken again and again, year after year.

#17: Out of obligation. Societal
expectation . . .

M.M: No. Not always.

#17: [Frowns]

M.M: You don't agree?

#17: I'm not sure.

[Silence]

M.M: Are you feeling unwell? Would you like to
rest?

#17: No, no. I was simply thinking. You see,
perhaps I'm a cynic, but I find it just
a shade too . . . tidy, too [searches
for word] coincidental, that one should
discover one's real love, a love that can
truly last a lifetime, in one's first
infatuation.

M.M: You really believe that?

#17: Yes.

M.M: Truly?

#17: Have I not just said so?

M.M: You have. I apologise.

#17: You don't sound at all sorry.

M.M: No?

#17: No. And you look as though there's
something else you want to say.

M.M: Do I?

#17: Yes, so please do say it.

M.M: Can I be blunt?

#17: I would much rather you were. As I've
mentioned, I have little time, and even
less energy, for interpreting subtext.

M.M: I am sorry about that.

#17: Yes, yes. And; so?

M.M: Well, you can be very compelling. Very convincing.

#17: I suppose so.

M.M: You've told me yourself that you've fooled many people.

#17: Yes . . .

M.M: I can't help wondering if this time, with regard to the validity of first love, if . . . Well . . .

#17: Well?

M.M: Well, to be blunt, if it's yourself that you're trying to fool. To assuage your guilt.

[Prolonged silence]

#17: That really was very blunt.

LONDON, 1940

Chapter Five

St James's Park, November 1940

'I say, do you by chance have change for a shilling?'

The question broke into Eleni's reverie as she sat on her usual bench beside the lake, the remnants of her lunchtime sandwiches on her lap. She glanced up to see the man who'd spoken, eyes streaming in the instant at the glare of the low winter sun spraying across the water behind him. She had a stinking cold. Too many nights trying to sleep in the damp Anderson shelter with Helen and Esther. She couldn't remember the last time the siren hadn't had them scrambling from their beds, on a blind dash through the blackout for the shelter. What it felt like to wake from a full night of sleep. A warm one . . .

And oh, she was going to sneeze again. Hastily, she yanked her kerchief from her sleeve, containing first one eruption, then another, the third, a charm. And, the fourth . . . ? No.

No fourth.

Shuddering, she put her kerchief away.

'Bless you,' came the man's voice.

'Thank you,' she said, and thought of Esther, with her funny beliefs. *You'll kill a fairy.* 'Here . . . ' She reached for her purse. 'I'm sure I have something. Oh, hang on.' She dropped her purse, reclaimed her kerchief. The fourth sneeze, after all. 'Sorry.' She wiped her nose, pressed the backs of her wrists to her eyes. 'I think that was the last.'

'You poor thing.'

'I'm fine.'

'You look like you should be sitting beside a fire, with a bowl of soup, not on a cold park bench.' The man gestured at the ducks on the bankside, hungrily eyeing her crusts. 'Even they're shivering.'

She laughed.

He did too, expelling a puff of ice.

He wasn't shivering. He was dressed snugly for the frozen November day, in a smart raglan overcoat, trilby hat, leather gloves and scarf. He was in his thirties, she guessed, now her vision had cleared and she could see him properly; clean shaven, and refined. If she hadn't been so bunged up, she was sure she'd have been able to smell an expensive cologne – the kind that came in a crystal decanter and lingered in the stuffy, stale air of the Cabinet War Rooms on King Charles Street. She'd been working down there since the start of the war. A typist, after all. (Her grandma in Sutton would have been so proud, had the pair of them still been on speaking terms.) Really, this man struck her as being cut from *just* the same cloth as the politicians and generals who paced the subterranean corridors there. He had the same assured smile, the perfectly polished shoes. He was even wearing a signet ring. She spotted the tell tale impression beneath his leather glove, and, habitually playing the game she amused Esther with, sitting at her first-floor window, sketched in his background: school at Harrow or Eton, university at Oxford or Cambridge. And a year travelling around Europe after graduation. (A lot of them in the War Rooms had travelled; they loved to chat to her in their schoolboy Greek.) He'd have a house in the country, a family flat here in town that his politician father used too, and would be called Rupert, or Edward, or Hector, or some such. Frankly, it disappointed her that he didn't have the correct change.

He was the sort that should.

'A shilling, yes?' she said, reclaiming her purse, opening the clasp.

'If it's no trouble.'

'Not at all. You're in luck.' She fished out sixpence and some loose pennies, proffered them in the flat of her own gloved hand. 'Will this do?'

'Perfect.' He dropped his shilling into her palm, extracted the coins from hers. 'You know—' he closed his leathered fist around the pennies '—your face is most awfully familiar.'

'Is it?'

'It is.' His smile grew. 'We've met.'

'I don't think so.'

'Yes.'

'I'm sure not.'

'I'm sure *of* it. Have you been to any parties recently? The Callaghans'?'

'No.'

'Tony Hicks's, then?'

She shook her head. 'Sorry.'

'Leighton's?'

'Leighton?' She blinked her sore eyes, feigning recognition. '*Angus* Leighton?'

'*Yes* . . .'

'No.' She laughed, wiped her nose again. 'I don't know an Angus Leighton.'

'How very odd that I do.'

He certainly was smooth. 'Isn't it just?'

'Ha—' he raised his fist '—I've got it now.' She was sure he didn't. 'You were at the Café Royal on Friday.'

'Was I?'

'Yes.'

'No.'

'*No?*'

'No,' she repeated. 'But aren't you social?'

'Hmmm,' he said, appearing to consider it. 'What were you doing on Friday?'

'I was at the pictures,' she lied, since what did it matter to him?

'Seeing what?'

'*Gone with the Wind.*' Her nose tingled. Her eyes gushed again. She drew breath, braced for another sneeze . . .

None came.

She hated it when that happened.

'Did you like it?'

'What?'

'*Gone with the Wind*?'

'Doesn't everyone?'

'I didn't.'

'You must be the exception.'

'Nothing wrong with that.'

She smiled, politely, and reached for her handbag, deciding it was time to make a move. Talking to strange men who professed to know you was hardly encouraged at King Charles Street (*careless talk may give away vital secrets*), and whilst she honestly doubted this man *was* a fifth columnist trying to charm her into betraying state information – truly, he was Eton to a *T* – she was starting to suspect he could well be interested in charming her into something else, and she was hardly in the mood for that either.

'I'd better run,' she said, scattering her crusts to the ducks, rendering them hysterical. 'I only have a few minutes left of my lunch break.'

'Well, now, that's a fib.'

She stopped short. 'Excuse me?'

He met her stare, calm and steady. 'I said you fibbed, Miss Adams. Miss Carter isn't expecting you back at King Charles Street for another—' he consulted his watch '—*twenty-eight* minutes. And you weren't at the pictures on Friday. You were at home, with Esther and your landlady.'

She said nothing, stilled by shock.

He didn't speak either. Just appraised her.

For a few disorientated moments, it was as though everything around her retreated – the frenzied ducks, the steely barrage balloons in the sky, the traffic in the distance – and there was just her and this man, with his polished shoes, polished voice, and strange knowledge.

Then she breathed, coming back to herself.

'Who are you?' she said.

'Hector Herbert.'

Hector. It gave her no satisfaction that she'd been right about his name. Or at least, very little satisfaction. She was far too uneasy to be smug.

She couldn't think what was happening.

'You're a very believable liar,' he went on, unsettling her more.

'I might say the same to you,' she somehow managed to riposte.

He narrowed his eyes, then laughed, shortly.

'I was sceptical,' he said. 'I really was. I'm old-fashioned, I admit. But I can see it.'

'See what, exactly?'

He didn't reply. He stepped back, letting a woman with a perambulator go by.

A wind gusted across the water, lifting his scarf, stinging Eleni's stuffy nose, her flushed cheeks.

'I think it's worth us talking more,' Hector said, once the woman had passed, still not answering Eleni's question. 'Shall we walk?' He gestured at the wet, glinting footpath, in the opposite direction to where the woman had headed.

Eleni didn't move.

'Miss Adams?'

'I'm not going anywhere with you. Not until you tell me what it is you see, how you know when my lunch hour ends, or what I was doing on Friday. Or, for that matter, why you've just been pretending you don't know who I am.'

'I was simply drawing an impression. Weighing up whether there was any point in us proceeding.'

'You were testing me?'

'I still am.'

'Oh, wonderful.' She was growing angrier the more confused she became. She very nearly told him as much, and that she had no interest in being tested by him, or anyone, any further. Then she realized that if she did that, she might well never discover what any of this was about. It would simply become a strange thing that had once happened. She was far too curious to allow that.

Besides, he spoke first. 'Are you afraid, Miss Adams?'

'Do you want me to be?'

'No, I assure you. And you're quite safe. I'm not your enemy. I . . . ' He broke off, glanced briefly around them, hazel eyes alert beneath his trilby, then brought his attention back to her. 'I must remind you, now, that you've signed the Official Secrets Act.'

That made her look at him twice. 'I'm aware.'

'Everything I say from this point on is bound by that.'

She frowned. 'Who are you?' she asked again.

'Have you heard, Miss Adams, down in your hallowed chambers, of an organisation called the Special Operations Executive?'

She stared.

'Good,' he said. 'I see you have. So, please—' he gestured at the footpath again '—let's walk.'

She didn't return to her typewriter that afternoon.

They did call by King Charles Street. Eleni insisted, despite Hector's assurances that her superior, Miss Carter, had been told not to be alarmed if she didn't reappear, wanting to be certain all was above board. 'Forgive me, Mr Herbert, if I'm not completely inclined to take you at your word.'

'Are you inclined now?' he enquired drily, when after a brief, to-the-point conversation with Miss Carter, she reappeared at ground level.

'I'm becoming that way.'

'I'm so pleased.' He set off, along the busy Westminster pavements, compelling her to follow. 'We've started off as liars, Miss Adams. Let's see if we can learn to trust. Might I call you Eleni?'

'You might, Hector. Just as soon as you tell me what's going on.'

'Yes, yes.' He turned for the road, looked left at the buses, right at the taxicabs, preparing to cross. 'We need to go somewhere quieter first. Walls have ears, especially around here.'

'Where are we going?'

He darted off. 'You'll see.'

'Baker Street?' she persisted, running to catch up. It seemed as good a guess as any. The offices of the Special Operations Executive had recently moved there. She'd typed up several dossiers now on the covert organisation's growing number, their activity in occupied France.

'A pub actually.' He raised his voice above the clang of an approaching fire engine's bell. There was always somewhere burning in London at the moment. 'We'll get you a hot toddy.'

She didn't *not* like the sound of that.

*

The pub was in Vauxhall. It took them a half-hour to reach it, along the chill London streets. Whilst they walked, Hector remained tight-lipped about why he'd approached Eleni, enlightening her instead on the myriad disconcerting things he knew about her, presenting her with each fact of her life much as though he were a magician, revealing his hand of cards.

In the shadows of Westminster Abbey, he listed her school certificate scores, which had been respectable, then the names of all her old headmistresses, her house mistresses, a select few of her classmates. As they passed Victoria Tower Gardens (stopping briefly for Eleni to succumb to another sneezing fit), he moved from her school days, to her secretarial diploma, then her first agency post, with the Greek shipping company, Lemos & Pateras Ltd, in 1937, and her second, at Lloyds Bank, in 1938. He informed her that both employers had supplied him with character references, as had several staff at the War Rooms, all of which he professed himself satisfied with, as indeed he was with her final qualification, in conversational German, which she'd studied for at the same time as her diploma, learning to speak it quite passably.

'*Sehr gut*,' he said, speaking it too.

Strangely, he didn't ask her what had motivated her to take such a course.

For the time being, he asked her nothing at all.

They reached the river, where the bank's mud had frozen solid, and he kept talking, detailing how she'd turned twenty-three on 24 September, and had celebrated over lunch with her fellow typists, eating cake in St James's Park, but not with her father, because he, now a Vice Admiral with the navy, had been off sailing somewhere in the Atlantic, ever since she'd turned twenty-two.

'And do you know how I celebrated *that* birthday?' she asked, with a raised brow.

'No. No one mentioned that detail in their references.'

'A hole, Hector.' She tsked, blew her nose. 'How lax of you.'

She teased, not because she found it funny that he'd investigated her so thoroughly, but because she felt quite violated, shaken by how oblivious she'd been to it going on, and didn't want him to guess as much. He might perceive it as weakness, possibly use it as a mark against her in his test. She didn't want that either.

She *wanted* to pass his test.

She'd started to suspect what it might be for.

She'd been silently picking it over while they'd been walking, racking her stuffy mind for any plausible reason that he, an agent of the SOE, whose entire raison d'être was running covert operations behind enemy lines, might be interested in her, a secretary. Whichever way she looked at it, she could only find one reason. A reason that felt at once ridiculous, yet heart-quickeningly possible. A reason she was almost afraid to acknowledge, in case she was wrong.

Except, maybe she wasn't wrong.

He'd been so pleased she knew German.

Sehr gut.

And when they reached the pub in Vauxhall – a small, shabby affair with criss-crossed tape on its windows, and jars of pickled eggs on the bar – he ordered their drinks, led her to a small, private backroom, and commented on what a world away it must all feel from the tavernas of Crete.

'Yes,' she said. *Oh my God.* 'Quite a world.'

'You must miss it,' he said, gesturing for her to sit at the room's only table, beside a stuttering, coal-rationed fire. 'It's been such a long time since you were there.'

'You know that too, do you?'

'I do.'

Fighting to stay calm, her pulse not really cooperating, she sat, as directed, sipped her hot toddy, shivered at the tingling warmth of rum, lemon and spices coating her sore throat, then set her glass down.

'I don't think I need you to tell me what's going on,' she said, deciding as she spoke that if she was right about it, he should know she'd worked it out. Surely it would count as a tick in her favour. 'I think I might have guessed.'

'Really?' He leant back in his chair, peeling off his gloves, studying her.

She waited for him to say something else.

He didn't.

'I know what the SOE does,' she said, filling the silence. She didn't go into more detail. She hardly needed to familiarise him with the work of his own people, fluent in French, who were dropped into occupied France to aid the resistance. 'What I also know is that, at this very moment, whilst you're weighing up whether you're wasting your time with me, Italy is attacking the Greek mainland, and it probably won't be long before Germany arrives to support them.' That much had been all over the papers since the end of October, when Metaxas had rejected Mussolini's ultimatum to be allowed free passage for his troops through Greece, and Mussolini had invaded. Eleni had been combing the broadsheets morning and night, hungry for details of Greek counter-offensives, torturing herself with images of bombs dropping in Athens, jackboots marching into Crete. But, for now, she buried her panic, kept her fear from her face. *No weakness.* 'What I also feel sure of,' she continued, 'is that you're aware my mother was Greek.'

The corner of Hector's lips moved. A smile?

'You feel sure of that?'

'I do. Given you could tell me how I spent my birthday this year, it would be rather ridiculous if you'd missed that detail. In fact—' she didn't lift her eyes from his '—I think it's the reason

you've approached me.' There were certainly any number of
staff at the War Rooms who might have suggested he should;
all those conversations in Greek over her typewriter. 'It simply
feels too coincidental that, just as it's becoming possible Greece
may be occupied, you've vetted me so . . . forensically. We have
troops on their way to Crete, RAF squadrons at the Albanian
front, and here you suddenly are, with my loose change in your
pocket.'

For a few moments, he didn't speak.

He ran one finger around the rim of his glass. His signet ring
caught the glow of the fire.

'And what is it you believe we're interested in you doing?'
he asked.

'Going to Greece,' she said, and, despite her growing conviction, the words, spoken out loud, felt preposterous. Perhaps
because she wanted them to be true, too much.

But Hector didn't laugh, or shake his head, or act in any way
like she was talking in fantasies.

So she carried on.

'I believe you're considering whether I could be part of
a resistance there, if it comes to it.'

The muscles around his eyes tightened. She could see him
thinking, evaluating.

She wasn't sure she breathed.

'Would you do that?' he asked. 'Go?'

'In a heartbeat,' she said, her own racing all the more.

'You wouldn't be afraid?'

OhGodOhGod. 'Not as much as I would be sitting here,
wondering what was happening, knowing I should be there helping.' Was this real? It was all too much. Her sinuses re-exploded.
She reached for her bag, a fresh kerchief, catching yet another
sneeze. 'You said that you were old-fashioned in the park.'

'You remember?'

'Yes. I think you meant because I'm a woman. But you shouldn't underestimate us. You mustn't underestimate me.'

'Don't worry.' He removed his hat, placed it beside their steaming glasses. 'I won't be making that mistake. But, Eleni, you're sprinting ahead. First . . . ' he broke off, shifted to Greek. '*Echo kapies erotisis na sou kano.*'

I have questions.

'Then please,' she replied, also in Greek, 'ask them.'

So he did.

For the rest of the afternoon, they didn't speak English again. He grilled her, relentlessly, about everything from her earliest memories of the island, to the food she ate there, the names and ages of everyone she knew, their religion (Greek Orthodox), church habits (infrequent), politics (democratic), and person-alities ('How long have you got?' she said. 'All the time we need,' he replied). No detail seemed insignificant to him: not Yorgos's quick temper, nor his warm heart, nor even the variety of Sofia and the Vassilis' wines. He combed over every detail she gave him, making her repeat herself again and again, with such scrutiny, such suspicion, that she very nearly started to wonder whether she was in fact making everything up.

But no matter how drained she became, how dizzy with her cold, the rum, she maintained her focus, considering every word she said before she said it, allowing herself not a single slip. It felt like one of the games of chess she'd used to play with her grandpa in Sutton, only exponentially more important, because the stakes were so much higher than they ever had been then. Yorgos was turning seventy that year. She hadn't seen him, or anyone in Crete, since 1936, because of her own short-sightedness, and now they were all in danger, and she might not have another opportunity to get to them for years to come.

She really needed to pass this test.

'How did your family react when Metaxas took power?'

Hector asked, the light through the room's one, grimy window beginning to fade. 'You were there, yes, that August of thirty-six?'

'I was,' said Eleni, and didn't add how little attention she'd paid to the power struggles in Athens at the time, or why she'd been so distracted. She wasn't a fool. She'd realized by now that Hector might already know about Otto (a Nazi army officer, the last she'd heard, and, oh, she hated picturing it); he'd mentioned Esther earlier, after all. But whilst there remained a chance he'd somehow missed the connection – that Otto, like her twenty-second birthday, had escaped his net – she wasn't about to bring any of it up.

Not doing that, she talked on, of the general unhappiness in Crete when Metaxas had staged his August 1936 coup with the support of the Greek king. She said that the island in general wasn't in favour of the monarchy, and her family no different. 'Except Uncle Vassili. He loves Metaxas. And the king. I'm sure he's feeling quite proud that Metaxas has refused to let Mussolini bully him. Actually—' she considered it '—I suspect a lot of Cretans are, whatever the past. They'll be pleased he's standing against fascists.'

'And were any of your family involved in the uprising against Metaxas in thirty-eight?'

'No, no.' She drained the dregs of her drink. '*Papou* wrote to me about it though.' He'd been furious at the chaotic insurrection, planned by Crete's politicians, and kicked off with a broadcast from Chania's radio station, calling Greece's rebels to arms. *It was all over in a few hours,* Yorgos had written, *and now we have martial law, arrests everywhere, and all our weapons confiscated. Your cousin took my father's gun.* 'Little Vassili is in the army,' Eleni said. 'He helped quash it all.'

'But you weren't in Crete yourself.'

'No, I was here.'

'You haven't been back since thirty-six, have you?'

'No.'

'Yet, before that, you visited every summer since before you were a year old.'

'Yes.'

He cocked his head to one side, a dent forming between his sharp eyes.

Determinedly, she didn't let her own gaze waver.

'Did something happen,' he asked, 'the last time you were there? Something that kept you from going back?'

'No,' she said, smiling, shaking her head, her mouth running dry on the lie, the suddenly very stark possibility that he absolutely did know about it all. 'What could have happened?' She left no pause for him to answer. 'I couldn't go. I was working, you know that. I had a contract with the agency.' She shrugged, nonchalantly (she hoped). 'How could I have asked for so much time away?'

His head remained on one side. He didn't blink.

She didn't either.

Then, he nodded, apparently satisfied, and, silently, she exhaled.

'It's getting dark, isn't it?' he said, and got up, pulling the blackout down before switching on the room's lamps, bathing them, the peeling floral wallpaper and stained rug, in light. Whilst his back was turned, she drew several breaths, gathering herself before he returned to his seat, and the interrogation resumed.

The questions kept flowing. He had so many things still to ask her. What parts of the island she'd visited; when, and how often. Where she was known. By whom. How she'd come to work for Dimitri. Whether she'd enjoyed waitressing. If she enjoyed typing as much. Whether she'd be able to do it on a Greek typewriter. Yes, she thought so? He made a note. They might have to look into that.

It felt like there was nothing he didn't want to look into.

Except, Otto, and Esther.

Eleni waited, and waited, never anything less than on the edge of her seat, after that close call, for him to bring either of them up. Her throat grew raw from talking, her nose sore from rubbing, and there wasn't a single, draining moment that she didn't remain braced to hear their names.

But she never did.

The pub's clock chimed seven, ringing through their closed wooden door, and, to her sagging relief, Hector declared that they should call it a day.

'Have I passed your test?' she couldn't resist enquiring, once they were out in the night, breathing ice once more, and walking over Vauxhall Bridge to hail her a taxi home. A frost was setting in, glittering the bridge's steel railings; the full bomber's moon reflected off the murky river. Smoke spiralled from Vauxhall's chimneys, snaking up to the starry sky. 'In case you doubt it, I really want to have passed.'

He laughed.

He hadn't done that since the park.

She hoped she could take it as a positive sign.

A taxicab approached from the other side of the bank. He stopped walking, and raised his hand to flag it, then whistled for good measure. It was a surprisingly uncouth gesture. Taken aback, she looked at him sideways, noticing that his own eyes, beneath his trilby, were glassy with tiredness. For the first time since they'd met, she felt herself almost warm to him. He suddenly seemed halfway human.

'So?' she said, prompting him.

'So,' he said. 'There's something I keep worrying over.'

Oh God, she thought, cursing herself for having pushed, *here we go after all.*

But she had no need to panic.

He still didn't mention Otto.

He asked her to estimate how many people in Crete, besides her family, knew that she was half-English.

'No one, really, outside of Chania,' she said.

'And there?'

'I'm not sure. There's Dimitri obviously, a few of his friends, some of the customers at the café. I don't think there are that many who'd remember me though. Most of the trade's passing. And Chania's a big town . . . '

The taxicab pulled to a halt, interrupting her. The driver got out, rubbed his hands, asking them where they were headed.

'Clapham Common,' Hector told him, pulling the change Eleni had given him earlier from his pocket, handing it back to her. 'It will just be this young lady here. Could you give us another minute though, please? Feel free to start the meter.'

Eleni didn't watch the driver return to his cab. And she didn't bat an eyelid that Hector knew where she lived. She'd have been an idiot by that point to have been surprised by that. She thought only of making this final minute they had together count.

'You don't need to worry about people knowing me,' she began, once the cabby had slammed his door shut.

'Eleni,' Hector said, turning to face her, his back to the motor, 'we'd have to seriously consider whether it would be safe for you to remain in Crete, were it to be occupied. You'd almost certainly have to move. No, no—' he held up his gloved hand, stopping her from talking '—there's no point arguing now. I'm still very much of the hope that we can prevent an occupation from happening, in any case. Certainly, your immediate interest to us, to me, is how you can help us prepare to stop one. An attack *is* coming. Italy are undoubtedly eyeing the island as a potential naval base, and it's too strategic, too close to our forces in Africa, the Nazis' oil fields in Romania, for them to ignore for much longer either. No one wants to see it fall, and we have several operatives in place already, recruiting across the island for men we can rely on to arm, train to fight. Establishing trust is crucial.' He gave her a level look. 'I do believe you could be useful in that.'

'I could. I'm sure I could.' She clenched her hands into fists, holding down her excitement. 'Does this mean I'm going?'

'No.'

'Oh.'

'There are several hoops you'll need to jump through first. More interviews, with native speakers, some others I'd want you to meet . . . But before any of that, like I said, I'm worried. Things can and do go wrong, all the time, and if Crete does fall, I don't want to know that I've sent you there only for you to somehow get trapped, out of our reach, surrounded by Nazis, on an island chock-full of people who might betray you.'

'That would never happen.'

'You can't be sure of that?'

'I can. I am. Everyone I know there, I trust.'

He sighed a gust of white. Tipping his head back, he examined the icy, starlit sky.

It was the most uncertain she'd seen him.

She didn't like it.

'How deeply do you trust them?' he asked.

'Deeply.'

'All of them?'

'Yes.' She didn't even think about it. 'Every single one.'

'How deeply?'

'Extremely.'

'Would you trust them with your life?'

'Yes,' she said, again, without hesitation. 'I would trust them with my life.'

Chapter Six

It was almost eight by the time she finally slipped through the front door of the Victorian terrace she called home. The hallway was silent, and quite dark. Blindly, she drew the door's thick curtains, reached for the switch on the tasselled floor lamp, and, able to see once more, closed her gritty eyes, sinking back against the wall. Hollow with exhaustion, she felt the muscles in her face loosen, and realized just how tensely she'd been controlling them under Hector's watch, then in the taxi. The cabby had kept looking at her in the rear mirror. The more he had, the more she'd started to wonder if he was from the SOE as well; another part of her test. Or perhaps it was just tiredness making her paranoid.

She filled her lungs through her blocked nose, drawing a deep, deep sniff. A real sniff, snotty and antisocial. The kind she'd been longing to indulge in ever since she'd thrown those crusts to the ducks.

Could she smell something? Actually smell?

Stewing apples?

Her stomach rumbled. She'd put nothing in it but that hot toddy, all afternoon.

The living room door opened. Helen, *Miss Finch*, came out. She was ready for bed in her plush pink velveteen dressing gown, her white hair full of rollers. She still carried a slight limp from the croquet incident that had sent Eleni travelling to Greece alone, back at the start of that fateful summer of 1936. She'd given up chaperoning after that, decided to go into the business of sub-leasing her house instead. Eleni had been her first, and longest-serving, tenant. The fact of Helen being her landlady had helped Timothy make peace with her taking the leap, leaving home. They'd had several arguments about it, but in the end he'd gone so far as to borrow one of the navy's motors to drive her up to Clapham from Portsmouth, bought her a pot plant for her windowsill. *I miss you. Dear. In my way.* Eleni had kept it alive, diligently, ever since, carrying it with her to the Anderson each night. She couldn't leave it in there all the time, Helen's pet rabbits might eat it. The sun-starved little things never left the shelter. Poor Helen was haunted by a terror of them being bombed, or pilfered for a neighbour's pie. She was finalising arrangements to take them, along with herself, to her brother's in Cheshire for the duration. Eleni would be staying on in the house, but Esther was to go with her. It would be so much safer . . .

'You're very late, dear,' she said to Eleni now. 'I was worried. How's the head cold?'

'The same.'

'You should put some cream on your nose.'

Eleni nodded. She should. 'Is Esther . . . ?'

'Oh, you know her. Fast asleep.'

'I was hoping to catch her.'

'You'll see her when the siren goes.'

'I suppose I will. Is that apple crumble I can smell?'

'No, dear. It's chutney.'

Disappointing.

'There's stew left on the stove for you though. And post on the dresser.'

'Thank you.'

Achingly, Eleni pushed herself upright, and, removing her gloves, coat and hat, hanging them on her designated hook, carried on down to the cosy basement kitchen.

She didn't go to the stove right away. She stopped to look at the letter Helen had left on the dresser's wooden shelf, smiling, through her tiredness, seeing the American postmark. Eager as she was to open it, she decided to wait until she was bathed and in bed, and could relax. She wanted to take her time, reading it.

With another sniff, she crossed to the sink to pour herself a glass of water. Whilst the water ran, she stared sightlessly into the deep, worn basin, and saw not chipped enamel, but Hector Herbert's cold face across from her on the bridge; the penetrating focus of his stare.

'Please,' she'd entreated, just before they'd parted, reaching out to take his gloved hands in hers. '*Please*, Hector. You have to let me do this.'

She'd startled him, touching his hands. She'd felt the tell-tale jolt in his muscles and been happy. For the first time, it had felt like the power had shifted, however marginally, in her favour.

Still, it hadn't taken Hector long to collect himself.

'I'll let you keep jumping through our hoops,' was all he'd promised. Then, perhaps to regain the front foot, or maybe because he'd been saving the best for last all along, he'd startled her. 'And next time we meet, I suggest you be ready with the truth about why you haven't returned to Crete for the past four years. You're a good liar, Eleni. You could be an excellent one. But, please, no more lying to me.'

The glass in her hand overflowed, bringing her back to the kitchen.

She turned off the faucet, raised the glass to her lips and drained it, the frigid liquid rushing to her chest.

Please, no more lying to me.

How much was he going to want to know?

There was so much that she still didn't know herself.

Like, what had become of Otto. Where he was fighting. Whether he was happy in the life he'd chosen.

If he was still alive.

She thought he must still be alive. She was sure she'd know if the world no longer had him in it.

Or was it that she simply needed to believe she would?

Upset at her own question, she refilled her glass, picked up a bowl from the draining rack, and crossed to the stove, ladling herself a portion of tepid stew. Vainly, she tried to push Otto from her mind. She didn't want to be thinking about him. She wanted to be thinking only of Crete; Yorgos's face, when she saw him again, as she was by now absolutely determined that she would; the scent of thyme . . .

Please, no more lying to me.

With a chink, she dropped the lid back on the casserole, took her bowl to the table, sat, and sank her heavy head into her hands.

What could she possibly say to Hector? How to begin to explain what that summer had done to her, without crashing into one of his hoops?

Releasing her head, she reached into the table's drawer for a spoon, and took a mouthful of stew. She'd never been someone who lost their appetite when they were upset. It simply wasn't in her make-up. And she really was starving.

But God, it hurt, to be sitting in this silent kitchen, with Esther dreaming upstairs, thinking of him.

Seven weeks, they'd had together, that summer. Seven, uninterrupted weeks.

He'd been working on a college assignment, through all of them; a design for a house. It was what he'd been drawing in his sketchpad, that first June night she'd found him, waiting for her under that tree. She'd asked him to show it to her, and he'd reached for the pad, setting it on his lap, guiding her around the beginnings of a porch, the front steps.

By the end of those seven weeks, that small handful of lines had metamorphosed into a five-bedroomed home, and he'd talked to her about it like it would one day be their own.

'I'll build you a swimming pool,' he'd said. 'That way you can be a mermaid even if we're not near the sea.'

She could hear his voice now; that subtle accent. He'd spoken such excellent English. His mother, Brigit, had lived in London for years along with her diplomat parents, before the last war, and had raised him and Krista to be bilingual. So fluent had they both been that, sometimes, Eleni had forgotten they were German at all.

'We'd have to be near the sea,' she'd told Otto. 'I won't have it any other way.'

'That's fine,' he'd said. 'I won't have it any way, but with you.'

He'd been a good liar too.

She couldn't precisely recall where they'd been when they'd had that conversation. They'd spent so much time together, talked of so many countless things, that it was impossible now, more than four years on, to be certain of what detail, or secret, or dream, or regret, they'd shared, when.

Yet, there were certain things she remembered very clearly.

Such as, their first night, under that tree. The one that they'd started as near-strangers, ended as something rather different, rather better, and which – like a domino tipping, pushing them into their next encounter, then their next, until they were both of them falling, on and on – had turned the rest of their summer into an inevitability.

After it, they simply hadn't wanted to be apart.

In fairness, he had warned her about Lotte, admitting, right there, under that tree, that she'd been the reason he'd failed to get to the café that afternoon.

'She's important,' he'd said, with a sigh that had made her ache for him, even more when he'd explained about his mother's multiple sclerosis, and how much more dangerous the illness had become in Germany, where the Nazis were becoming increasingly insistent on eradicating such conditions from their Aryan race. 'It's not considered hereditary,' he'd said, 'but sometimes it does . . . recur . . . and lately my sister's eyes have been blurring, she keeps getting these pins and needles. She's tried to act like it's nothing, but Mama took her to her doctor, he did some tests. It's not nothing. It's terrifying, actually.' His head, against the trunk, had been so close hers. 'Lotte's father's a powerful man. He could protect them both. So . . . '

'She's important,' Eleni had echoed.

'Only in that,' he'd said. 'Nothing more.'

She'd believed him. Realizing how little he must want to dwell on it, already only wanting to make him happy, she hadn't asked him more.

They'd moved on, talking of easier things: his childhood in Grunewald, life in Munich, her own in Portsmouth; Mr Hodgson at her hotel in Portsmouth.

She stirred her stew, replaying how she'd told him about how cross her old manager used to become when sailors had tried to check in with girls who hadn't really been their wives.

'They always call themselves Mr and Mrs Brown, or Smith, or Jones. I wish they'd think of something more original. Like, I don't know . . . *Winterbottom.*'

'Or *Nachtnebel*,' he'd said.

'*Nachtnebel*,' she'd repeated, laughing. And, as they'd carried on, thinking up other ridiculous surnames – *Fitzhattily*, *Macloughty*, *Trinkenshuh* – they'd laughed more, until she, looking into his bright eyes, had had tears running down her cheeks.

She set her spoon down, dropping her head back into her hands.

Just before they'd bid one another goodnight, she'd tried to teach him some more Greek, beyond the word hello. The breezy night had been black by then; her bottom, entirely numb on the unforgiving floor.

He'd been awful at Greek. Truly awful. She'd told him as much, and he'd challenged her to see if she could do any better at German.

They'd started with, *good evening*.

'*Guten abend*,' she'd parroted.

'Very good,' he'd said, the tree's leaves painting shadows on his face. 'Next, we'll do, *schön, dich kennenzulernen*. It's nice to get to know you.'

'It's nice to get to know you, too.'

He'd laughed, softly.

She'd loved his laugh.

'So?'

She'd tried. '*Schön, dich kennen . . . kennen . . .* '

'*Schön, dich kennenzulernen*.'

'*Schön, dich kennenzulernen*.'

'Excellent,' he'd said. Then, '*Ich mag dich sehr*.'

'What does that mean?' she'd asked.

He hadn't answered. Tips had chosen that moment to interrupt them, pouncing on to Eleni's lap, reminding her that he needed his dinner, of the imam cooking in the oven.

Ich mag dich sehr.

Eleni had since found out what the words meant.

I really like you.

He'd known already.

I think I knew from the moment I saw you in those shorts, he'd written, in one of the many letters he'd sent after they'd parted, and which she only wished she could be strong enough to throw away.

They hadn't kissed, that first evening.

Back then, she'd still never kissed anyone, and had had to wait several more days before that had changed.

She remembered that happening as well.

She remembered it perfectly.

It had been on the Friday following. Not an evening had gone by in-between that he hadn't been waiting for her at the bus stop to walk her home, sit with her again beneath that tree.

But that Friday, he'd managed to get away from the others long enough to surprise her at the café, just as they'd been closing for the siesta. Socrates, also there, had offered to fill in for the rest of Eleni's shift so that she and Otto could spend the afternoon together.

'Are you sure?' she'd asked him, at once thrilled, and full of sudden nerves.

'Cheek to Cheek' had been playing, the sun blazing.

'I'm sure,' Socrates had said, smiling not at her, but at Dimitri.

'Go,' Dimitri had said, shoo-ing her off, 'before he changes his mind.'

'Yes, come,' Otto had said, grabbing her hand, pulling her to him, making her laugh.

She'd taken off her apron, thrown it for Dimitri to catch, and it had landed on one of the remaining customer's heads. She'd laughed about that too.

She'd laughed a lot, that afternoon.

She still counted it as one of the happiest of her life.

BEFORE THE WAR

Chapter Seven

Crete, July 1936

There wasn't a cloud in the beating sky. It was 3 July, and the temperature well into the nineties, even at close to four. The cliffs above the beach Eleni had brought Otto to were steep, netted with weeds and wild herbs, pockets of cactus, unshaded from the fierce rays. Neither of them talked as they climbed down, too focused on the effort of not tumbling, their skin sheened with sweat.

He wore shorts and a loose shirt; she wore a blue dress.

'Where *are* the shorts?' he'd asked, just the evening before.

'Waiting for the weekend,' she'd said. Their fingers had been touching again. 'When I'm not working.'

And now the weekend had started early.

They'd driven to the beach in Nikos Kalantis's motor. Nikos himself had left for Thessaloniki at the start of the week, but not before he'd first annoyed Otto, claiming to have had no idea what he was talking about, when he'd mentioned seeing him watching Eleni and Dimitri dance.

'He said he hadn't noticed you,' Otto had told Eleni, under the tree. 'He was looking right at you. I'm sure he knew who you were.'

'What does it matter if he did?' Eleni had replied, unfazed.

'It matters that he pretended he didn't.'

'I probably just brought back bad memories he didn't want to talk about. He was awful to my mama, you know . . . '

Given he had been, given Yorgos's prevailing hatred of him, it might have felt odd to her, riding in his motor from the café, had she not been so distracted by who she was riding with; the illicitness of their afternoon escape.

She'd kept stealing looks at Otto as they'd driven, eyes on his tanned hand guiding the steering wheel, the way he'd rested his other arm on the door frame, so enviably at ease; how his sun-bleached brown hair, that needed a crew cut, except she hoped would never get one, because she liked it too much the way it was, had blown in the hot wind.

He'd snuck glances at her too, smiling quizzically beneath his aviator shades. '*Where* are we going?'

'A bit further,' she'd said, reaching up to push her own hair from her face. 'Not much longer.'

It had been Dimitri who'd suggested the spot to her, several miles outside of town, past their villas, past a small, sleepy village called Chorafakia. ('Where do we go?' she'd asked him, in hurried Greek, reclaiming her apron from that tourist. 'Easy,' he'd said. '*No problem*.') She'd known the beach the instant he'd mentioned it. Maria had used to bring her as a child, when Yorgos and Spiros had been working, and the Meltemi winds blowing. The tiny, white bay, with its deep, crystal water, was one of the most sheltered on the coast. Reliably deserted too, especially on days as still as this one, thanks to its situation off the beaten track, the difficult climb down. Rarely had Eleni run into another soul there.

Which, for her and Otto's purposes, made it just about perfect.

It wasn't the risk of being spotted by Lotte that she worried about. She still hadn't met her, or any of the others with Otto at the villa, but knew by now that it had been she who'd called for him from the rocks. And Marianne who'd played the cello.

And Krista who, back in Germany, played with fire, darting around Berlin, ignoring her father, ignoring her pins and needles, distributing anti-Nazi pamphlets.

She liked the sound of Krista, liked the sound of Marianne. She certainly didn't want to cause any unnecessary trouble for them, or Lotte.

But what really concerned her that afternoon was not causing anyone on the island an unnecessary heart attack, least of all her *papou*. Because, however progressive he might be when it came to her working at the café, female suffrage, Crete in 1936 was simply not a place that she, or any young woman, might reasonably expect to get away with being seen, for any length of time, with a young man she wasn't related to. Sitting each night with Otto at the end of her driveway, under the cover of dusk, was one thing. But heading out and about on a sun-drenched Friday?

They needed to be a lot more careful about keeping hidden for that.

'It's certainly hidden,' Otto said, jumping the last drop to the sand, then turning to help her, except she'd already jumped down too.

He threw his bag on the sand and crouched to extract a bottle of water, offering it to her.

'Thank you,' she said, gladly taking it, gulping the liquid down before handing the bottle back to him.

She watched him drink, his lips touching the rim hers had just left. There was a raw intimacy to the moment, the beach's silence, the lapping of the barely there shore break. Now they were no longer on the move, her nerves about what this unexpected afternoon might hold, returned, disorientating her.

'See that rock,' she said, talking through the giddying sensation, pointing at where it jutted from the water. 'It was covered in sea urchins the last time I was here. Do you want to see if it still is?'

'Do I want to go swimming with you?' He grinned.

Her nerves evaporated.

'Yes, Eleni,' he started to unbutton his shirt (her nerves returned), 'I would like to go swimming with you.'

They hadn't done it together since the first night she'd returned to the island. Whilst she'd been out every morning that week before work, he hadn't joined her, just as she hadn't joined him when she'd seen him late each night from her kitchen window. Tempted as she always was to run down to him – alert as she remained for him to surprise her – she'd come to realize how foolish it would be; the bay, like the stage of a theatre; the villas, its seats.

Here though . . . Here, there was no audience.

He walked to the shore, wading in to waist-deep, the sun bouncing from his broad shoulders, leaving her alone whilst she wriggled from her undergarments beneath her dress, and slipped her costume on. She kept her eyes fixed on him, moving as quickly as she could, not knowing whether he might look back at her.

But, *a gentleman,* he didn't, not until she too was wading in, at which point he turned, tucking his hair behind his ear, and whistled, low and long; a gentleman no more.

'That's quite a suit. I think I like it even more than your shorts.'

She laughed, the heat in her skin growing, yet not so much that she wanted any of it to stop. 'Are we going to swim?'

'Lead the way.'

'All right—' she raised her arms in a 'V' '—I hope you can keep up.'

It was a fair distance, further than she'd recalled; it took a while before the rock started to feel any closer. But with him matching her pace, stroke for stroke, right by her side in the sea she felt so at home in, she only wanted it to go on and on. And, to her relief, the longer it did, the more caught up she became in the steady rhythm of their movement, she felt herself start to relax, her muscles loosen, her mind clear, until, by the time they reached the rock and she was clambering up onto it, footprints evaporating on the hot, porous surface, she was no longer so jittery, or trying to second-guess what might or might not be going to happen; no, she was getting onto her knees, peering over the rock's edge at the spiky garden of urchins beneath, marvelling that, in all that had happened in her own life since she'd last visited the beach – school moves, house moves, exams – here these urchins had been, clinging on. Here they still were.

'You are a *fast* swimmer,' Otto, still in the sea, said.

She turned, smiling. His high cheekbones were beaded with water, his hair darkened by it. Beneath the clear surface, she saw his chest rising and falling . . .

'Do you need to catch your breath?' she teased.

Ignoring her, he pulled himself up onto the rock, soaking it all over again, looking down at the urchins. 'Have you ever trodden on one?'

'Unfortunately, yes. Not here. Near Maria and Spiros's.' She'd been little. Maria had carried her back to the house, removed the urchin's spikes, wiped her tears, kissed the sole of her foot, and taken her to the surgery so that Yorgos could check her over, just to be safe. ('Well,' Yorgos had said, kissing her foot too, 'you won't do this twice.') 'It really hurts,' she told Otto. 'It does for days.'

'I know.' He moved, laying back on the rock, resting his head on his arms so that his tanned stomach formed a concave. 'I've done it too, in Italy.'

'Italy?' she said, lying beside him. She felt the cool drip of her salty hair down her neck, the heat of the stone beneath her drying skin. 'When did you go to Italy?'

'Years ago.' He turned his head, looking at her, his green eyes so close, they blurred. 'Puglia.'

'Was it nice?'

He smiled. 'Not as nice as here.'

She smiled too. 'Where else have you been?'

'Only London.'

'Really?'

'Hmm,' he said, 'my mother wanted us to see it.' He went on, describing the seedy hotel his father had mistakenly booked for them all, right in the heart of Soho. 'I think he'd misheard the name of a place a colleague had recommended. Something like that anyway.' He broke off, remembering. She watched him do it, in the sunshine. How he left her for a moment. 'I was fourteen, I loved it. I wanted to go to a jazz club. But he made us move the next day, to a guest house in Chelsea.'

'Oh—' she pouted in mock sympathy '—you poor thing.'

'I know. It was very hard.' He shifted his weight. 'Like this rock.'

'You want to move?'

'No.' Another smile. 'Not particularly.'

'Shall I tell you what I want?'

'Please do.'

'To know how—' she raised her hand, and, with her fingertip, touched the slight dent in his nose; the only imperfection in his face '—you did this.'

'You want to know that?' His brow creased. 'Really?'

'Really.'

'It's not a very impressive story, honestly . . . '

'Well, now I really want to hear it.'

He rolled his head back, and closed his eyes. 'Krista did it.'

'Your *sister*?' She burst out laughing. 'Your sister broke your nose?'

'My sister broke my nose.'

'How?'

'Sledging.'

'Seriously?'

'Seriously. We were children. I was facing forward, and she was sitting on my back. She thought we were going too fast, so used my head as a brake. Are you laughing again?' He opened one eye. 'Look at you, you're beside yourself. Eleni, that's not very nice.'

'I'm sorry . . . '

'No, you're not.'

'You're right, I'm not.' She placed her hand beneath her ribs. 'I am a bit hungry though.'

'You're always hungry.'

It was another thing they'd established, over the course of the week. He'd brought German chocolate to the bus stop for her the night before; she'd taken the foil wrapped squares, tasted their creamy, melting deliciousness, and felt herself fall, just a little deeper.

'What did you have for lunch?' he asked her.

'I haven't eaten it.'

'What?' He opened both eyes. 'That's insane.'

'It's your fault. I was going to have it on my break from work.'

'Did you bring it with you?'

'Yes, it's in my bag.'

'Good.' He pushed himself to sitting. 'Let's go.'

It was the nicest squashed spinach pie and bruised peach she'd ever tasted.

She ate both, once they'd made it back to the beach, with him beside her, their backs against the cliffs, legs bent up, knees touching, feet buried in the piping white sand. The sea stretched before them, beautiful and glittering, but she didn't really look at it.

She looked at him.

And they talked, they talked and talked, her nerves fading to an irrelevant memory as the words flowed between them, as easily as they had each evening, the two of them speaking more of their homes, their families, grandparents in Sutton, friends in Munich – the impossibility of eating a spinach pie anything other than messily ('I'm too hungry to be a lady,' Eleni said) – packing their questions and answers and more questions in, chasing the sun's descent to the horizon; the inevitable point at which they'd need to leave.

'I *must* be home by eight,' she reminded them both, gathering the final flaky bits of her pie, popping them in her mouth. '*Papou*'s last appointment is at seven, and I've left a moussaka baking. I can't burn that too. We *can't* lose track of time.'

'All right.'

'Seriously, though.'

'Absolutely seriously.'

'Good.' She swallowed. 'What did you tell your family you were doing?'

'Working again.'

'On your house?'

'My house, which—' he reached sideways, tugging his pad from his bag '—now has—' he flicked the pages '—a hallway and half a kitchen. See, and—' another flick '—a back elevation.'

'Is that wall all glass?'

'It is. I want lots of light.'

'Will you have a living room?'

'Of course.'

'How many bathrooms?'

'Three, at least.'

'I love it. And a reading nook?'

'A nook?'

'Yes, with a window seat that catches the afternoon sun.'

'All right.' He smiled. 'I can do that.'

'Good.' She let her head rest against the cliff, closing her eyes at the heat bathing her face. 'This is going to be an excellent house.'

The sun kept moving, she ate her peach, they had an impossible-to-settle debate about whether a planted stone would ever grow into a tree ('I'll bury it myself,' she said, tossing it into her bag, 'then we'll see'), talked more of her earliest trips to Greece, the little pieces she remembered from those summers – holding her *papou*'s hand on the stairs to the cove; him sleeping at the foot of her bed, so she wouldn't be afraid – and, as the white beach turned to shadows of blush and grey, whether she minded that her father had sent her away for the first time, so very young.

'A bit,' she admitted. 'It's quite an odd thing, isn't it, to send a baby who's just lost her mother across Europe with a nanny, to stay with a grandfather she doesn't know?'

'Your grandfather must have wanted to meet you though.'

'But he offered to come to England.' Maria had told her that; how Yorgos, broken-hearted over her mama, had been ready to leave the surgery in Spiros's hands, travel over. *He needed to hold you, be convinced you existed.* 'Dad wired him straight back, everything arranged for me to come here instead. He must have been desperate to get rid of me.'

'What about his parents?'

She pulled a face. 'I'm glad he didn't send me to them.'

'But surely if he was so eager to get rid of you, that would have been easier?'

'I don't know.' She thought about it. All those Sunday lunches he'd sent her off to them alone. 'I'm not sure he likes them.'

'So he knew you'd be happier with your grandfather.'

'I could have been though,' she reminded him. '*Papou* was going to come.'

'Maybe your father didn't want him to have to. Maybe he thought you'd be happier here, in your mama's home.'

She considered that as well.

'It's a nice idea,' she said. Certainly, she preferred it to the narrative of Timothy simply having needed her gone. 'It actually must have cost a lot to pay all those nannies to bring me here. Pick me up again . . .'

'There you go.'

She smiled, nudged him with her bare arm. 'Aren't you clever?'

'Sometimes,' he said, laughing. 'Sometimes . . .'

She didn't move her arm. She didn't want to. She leant into him; felt him do the same to her.

'I'm curious about your trip to London,' she said. 'Tell me more . . .'

So he did, relaying his family's walks along the river, around the parks, the shows they'd seen; his mother's excitement when they'd gone one evening to the Royal Opera House, then another day, to her old neighbourhood in Kensington, where she'd shown them all her house, her school, a tea room she'd used to visit with *her* mother, and the palace. 'Oh, I've been there,' said Eleni, and then they were playing snap with the landmarks they'd visited – Hampton Court, St Paul's, The Tower – laughing at Krista's disappointment in London Bridge. ('It is fairly disappointing,' Eleni said.) They moved on, to Puglia, the long journey his family had made cross-country to visit Pompeii, and her own train journeys through Italy; Mussolini's bald-headed photographs at the border.

It was as the sun really started its descent, flooding the sky with colour – the layers of gold and pink and purple so rich, they became an almost solid thing; a place where heaven might really exist – that they came to the subject of his National Service, waiting for him at the end of his degree, and the lengths he and his friends had gone to, trying to avoid it.

'Do you ever think about leaving Germany?' she asked. 'Your family, I mean. For your mother and Krista too . . .'

'We've talked about it.' He raised his face to the ethereal sky,

the light catching his profile. 'But it's really . . . complicated.
For lots of reasons. My father's law firm is in Berlin, he'd have
to start all over again somewhere else, so how would he keep
paying for Mama's care, her medicine? And my grandparents are
getting old, neither of my parents want to leave them. Or their
friends. Germany's home, you know . . . Besides—' he brought
his attention back to her '—Mama and Krista are still safe, for
now. Only Mama's doctor knows about them.'

'Nikos's friend?'

'Yes.'

'You trust him?'

'We have to.'

'And no one else knows?'

'No.'

'Not even your mother's parents?'

'Not even them. It's too dangerous. Mama only became so
bad this winter. Her lungs, they're starting to . . . give in. She got
pneumonia. Everyone thinks she's still recovering.' He paused,
visibly struggling to find sense in it all. 'We can't tell anyone.'

'I'm so sorry,' she said, only wishing there was something
else, something better, she could say.

'It's really . . . wrong.' He took a breath. 'She's dying. My
mother's dying.' His deep voice faltered. 'One day, Krista's going
to get worse too, and we have to pretend it's not happening,
because we have no idea what might happen to them if it got
out.'

She touched her hand to his wrist, felt sand, the warmth of
his skin.

He moved, threading his fingers through hers, and tried to
smile, only it was full of hurt; the same, jarring vulnerability
that had brought her up so short when he'd first spoken to her
of Brigit and Krista. She'd realized then, just how much she
could grow to care for him.

She realized now, how much she already did.

'Could it get better in Germany?' she asked.

'My parents hope it will. But—' his thumb brushed hers '—I don't know. I don't even know how we got here. There were so many protests at first. *So* many. Then the Nazis came down hard, and everyone got scared. I think . . . ' He frowned at their hands. 'I think that we all gave in. Started to find ways to live with it. Not *heil*-ing, unless we have to. Not looking at the "Jews unwelcome" signs . . . '

'You have signs?'

'Everywhere. A lot of them have been taken down for the Olympics, but they'll go back up, and everyone will look away again, so—' he raised his shoulder '—how can it get better?'

'Your sister's trying.'

'I'm not sure how much good pamphlets can do.'

'It's something.'

'Enough to be worth the risk?'

She said nothing. How could she possibly comment?

'There's an old art museum in Berlin,' he went on, 'on Prinz-Albrecht-Strasse. The Gestapo have their headquarters there. It's where Lotte's father works. Our father says Krista won't be happy until she's inside it, being interrogated by him.'

'God, don't.' Eleni felt a chill in the hot day, just at the idea; the word, *Gestapo*. 'You know, I'm coming to think you really should all leave.'

He looked at her sideways. 'You're thinking that, are you?'

'I am. Come to England. Bring Marianne. And her parents. And her aunt.'

'Her aunt's about to have a baby.'

'All the more reason, then. We have lots of good hospitals. And our art museums are still art museums. Seriously, all of you, come.'

'It's really not that easy.'

'It could be . . . '

'No. Honestly. Apart from anything, I'd never get released from national service. Not now. And we'd need visas. You should see the queues, every day, outside the British consulate.'

'Long?'

'All the way round the block, full of Jewish families who don't believe it will get better.'

'Like Marianne's?'

'They don't have the money. Not close. You need thousands to qualify for a British visa. And sponsors, an address in England . . . '

'How can anyone have an address before they get there?'

'They have to, if they want a visa.'

'I didn't know.' She struggled to absorb it. 'I can't imagine being so . . . trapped.'

'I can't imagine you ever being trapped.' He turned, facing her fully in the deepening dusk. 'You'd swim away. A mermaid . . . '

'A mermaid?'

'Yes.' He smiled, truly this time. 'One that eats really messily, and lures unsuspecting Germans to abandoned beaches.'

'A siren too?'

'A siren?'

'From the *Odyssey*. You know, the ones who sing and coax poor sailors to their deaths.'

'Jesus, Eleni . . . '

'No, you're fine. I promise I'd never try to kill you.'

'That's very good to know.'

'Not unless you did something really bad.'

'I'd better behave then.'

'You better had.'

They fell silent.

The sea lapped at the shore; above, cicadas nested.

'I'm sorry,' he said, with a rueful look, 'I feel like I've made you sad.'

'No, no . . . '

'You're too easy to talk to. In Germany, you never know who might be listening. I don't say anything anymore without stopping to think if it's safe. But with you—' he shook his head '—I don't stop at all, with you.'

She felt her heart balloon. 'That must be quite a relief.'

'It is. I'd forgotten what it was like.'

'I'm very glad I've reminded you.'

'I'm very glad you have too. You make me feel . . . ' He broke off. 'How do I put it . . . ?'

'Happy?' she suggested.

'Yes, happy . . . '

'Euphoric?' she went on, laughing, because he was. 'Over the moon?'

'All of that. But also . . . ' his fingers moved around hers, 'not alone. Not alone at all.'

'Oh.' She thought it might just be the nicest thing anyone had ever said to her. 'You make me feel that way as well.'

'Good.'

'Very good.'

The silence between them went on longer this time.

'All right,' he exhaled, 'now that we've established that—' he pulled her hand, pointing in the direction of the sea '—shall we have one more swim?'

'Really?' she said dubiously. 'What time is it?'

'Only—' he reached for his watch '—a bit after seven.'

It was the flippant way he said it.

She narrowed her eyes. 'How much of a bit?'

'A bit, you know.' Letting her hand go, he pushed himself to his feet.

'I don't know, actually,' she said, raising her arm to shield her eyes. The low sun was directly behind him, oozing over his shoulders, around his body. 'Is it a ten-minute bit? Or a fifteen bit?'

'A little over fifteen.'

'How much over fifteen?'

'About the same again.'

It took her a second. '*It's half past seven?*'

'No.'

'Good.' *Thank God.*

'It's thirty-three minutes past.'

'What?' *What?* 'We've got to go.' She reached for her dress, scrambling to standing. 'God, the moussaka . . . '

'We have time. I'm a fast driver.'

'No one's that fast.'

'You don't want to come swimming with me?'

'Of course I want to go swimming with you.'

'Excellent.'

And, before she could object further, he scooped her up, threw her dress on the ground, her over his shoulder, and sprinted to the shore, making her squeal, a little in protest, but mostly delight.

'If my grandfather is home when we get there,' she said, coming up for air, once he'd thrown them both in, 'I'm blaming you. I warn you—' she pushed her bedraggled hair from her face '—I will be flinging you under that bus.'

'He won't be there,' he said, his own hair dripping, running his arms around her waist, pulling her to him. 'And your dinner will be fine.'

'It had better be,' she said, pushing him lightly on the chest.

It was then that it happened.

She knew it was going to.

She'd never before kissed anyone, but she knew, she knew. From the way he held her, closer; each one of her quickening breaths . . .

She'd been imagining the moment all week long, on the bus, waiting tables, going to bed each night, agonising over what she should do, how she should be, dreading that she'd fumble it.

Yet, in that moment, none of that could have been further from her mind.

She thought of nothing but his face, so near to hers she could see the reflection of the setting sun in his eyes. And that she was in his arms, in the water, which felt good, so very, very good. Only, she wanted more.

She really, really wanted him.

She moved her hand up over his shoulder, behind his neck.

He dipped, towards her.

Their lips brushed, and everything went still – the sea, the beach, her heart in her chest. Then, he held her tighter, strong and sure, lifting her up, to him, kissing her again, hungrily, dizzyingly, and, with an instinct she'd never known she possessed, she kissed him back, just as hungrily, wrapping herself around him, forgetting the beach, forgetting the sea, forgetting the time; losing herself, utterly.

'So,' he said, when, finally, they pulled apart. 'Should we go home?' His fingers traced her spine beneath the water, sending shivers darting through her. 'If you're worried . . . '

'I'm not worried,' she said, pressing against him, feeling his stomach tense, smiling, guessing she was giving him shivers too. 'You're a fast driver.'

'I don't know.' His lips moved against hers. 'I think maybe we should go.'

'You do, do you?'

'I do,' he said.

They didn't move, of course.

They stayed right where they were, kissing again, tumbling into the sea, laughing, diving, swimming back into each other's arms, unable to stop what they'd at last started.

It was completely wonderful.

She realized that, even as it was happening.

They drifted deeper, him joking about her moussaka, making her laugh harder, even more as he tickled her, pulling her under, and she felt drunk with how wonderful it was: the most perfect end, to the most perfect afternoon.

And just the start, the very start, of the rest of their summer to come.

A whole summer.

She reached for him beneath the water, pressing her lips to his once more, tasting salt, sunshine.

A whole summer.

It all felt so utterly, blissfully endless.

Chapter Eight

Otto did get her home before they were found out; it was a fine-run thing, and they made more than one grazing donkey stare as they careered along the dusty, winding roads, but he got her back. When he left her, running to her front door in the silver half-light, her tangled hair dripping rivulets down the back of her blue dress, there was no one besides that kitten of hers waiting for her at the porch. Tips, she called the striped scrap of a thing. He leant on the steering wheel, replaying her indignation, a couple of nights before, when he'd suggested her grandfather had possibly had a point, saying it was a ridiculous name.

'What name isn't ridiculous,' she'd demanded, 'when you *really* think about it?'

'Fitzhattily,' he'd said.

And her laugh, her laugh . . .

He watched her scoop Tips up, knowing he should head home before Yorgos could return, yet lacking the will to go. In just a few short days, it was the way it had become: he only wanted to be where she was.

It was strange to him, how much he wanted that.

There'd been others, back in Germany: girls he'd met at parties, at dances, around the university. He'd liked them, had fun, moved on, and never thought twice about doing that. Not one of them had occupied his mind when he wasn't with them, or compelled him to spend time with them over his studies, his friends.

None could have made him forget, with a single glance – an absent catch of peach juice with their finger – that those friends existed.

She tucked Tips against her, opened the door, peered in, then turned back to him.

'I think we're safe.' Her clear voice rang through the balmy air. 'I can't smell burning.'

'So the moussaka's fine.'

'I'm going to go and check . . . '

'You do that.'

'Goodnight, then.'

'Goodnight, Eleni.'

She lingered, staring up at him with those dark-blue eyes; impossible to look away from.

'*Kalinichta*,' she said.

'*Kalinichta*,' he repeated.

Which, for some reason, made her smile and shake her head.

Then, with a wave of her free hand, she slipped inside.

He watched the space she'd left a moment longer, drew a steadying breath, shifted into gear, and, resignedly, went too.

The villa's hallway was empty when he let himself in, filled with the scent of lemon, roasting meat. The Greek lady, Christina, who'd cooked for them all on their first night, kept returning to cook again. Nikos had arranged for her to keep house until the end of the summer.

'*Should* we offer her money?' Henri had asked, again, at breakfast that morning.

Krista had sighed. 'I'm sure Nikos has it in hand, Papa.'

'Are you?' Otto had said, irritated, still, that Nikos had lied to him about watching Eleni and Dimitri dance at the café, the night before he left. ('I can't think what you're talking about,' he'd said, when Otto had mentioned seeing him. 'I didn't notice anyone, certainly not you.')

'I don't want to insult her,' Henri had gone on, 'but we can't leave her short . . . '

It was really bothering him. Otto could hear him now, through the ajar kitchen door, fumbling to talk to Christina with the aid of his Greek dictionary. He briefly considered going in, rescuing them both by drawing Henri away, but then he heard his mother and Krista too, out on the veranda, and decided to go to them instead.

'Poor Papa,' Brigit said, as he pulled up a deckchair. 'Everything keeps running out of his control. It doesn't suit his lawyer's mind . . . '

'And what about you?' Otto said. 'How are you feeling?'

'Better,' she said, and, to his relief, was starting to look it. There was colour in her skin again; some energy in her eyes.

She'd had a difficult week, shaken from a fall on Monday. The fall itself hadn't been too bad, just a twisted wrist, but bad enough that Otto hadn't been able to follow Eleni to the café, as he'd promised he would. When he'd reached the villa, high from seeing her on the bus (*hello again*), he'd collided with Henri and Brigit in the driveway, off to have Brigit's wrist looked at.

'I want you to keep Lotte company,' Henri had said to Otto. 'She's upset enough, after the way you all went off and left her yesterday, and I can't have her fretting about this whilst we're gone.'

Otto hadn't protested. Brigit had reached for him, telling him not to worry, and he'd held her, feeling his throat constrict at the familiarity of her scent, her warmth; a child again, for those few moments, terrified of losing his mother. He'd helped her into the car, seen them off, and, burying his sadness, and anger – at all of it – had dutifully spent the rest of the afternoon with Lotte, playing cards in the shade, watching Krista and Marianne swim, trying not to look at Lotte's sunburn, or too much at the time, waiting for his parents to reappear.

As soon as they had, and he'd been assured Brigit's wrist wasn't broken, he'd left Lotte to change for dinner (a lengthy procedure), and headed out at last, down the road, where he'd waited again, more happily this time, for Eleni; that first, incredible evening, under their tree.

'Where's Marianne?' he asked Krista now. 'Still swimming?'

'Having a bath,' said Krista. 'Mama's been giving me a lecture, with—' she raised her glass '—wine to sweeten the deal.'

'Be grateful for that,' said Brigit. 'Papa wouldn't have given you anything.'

'What lecture?' Otto asked, stretching his legs before him. His feet were still covered in sand. White sand . . .

'A Lotte lecture,' said Krista. 'I need to be nicer.'

Otto raised a brow. 'Join my party.'

'You're being fine, Otto,' said Brigit.

'Thank you, Mama.'

Krista stuck her tongue out at him.

'How old are you?' he said. 'Twelve?'

'She's certainly behaving like it,' said Brigit, not unfairly. Even Otto, hardly inclined to take Lotte's side, could see Krista had been pushing things too far with her that week – ignoring her, ever since she'd made Marianne cry, speaking to her only when forced to, and then in curt monosyllables. *Can you pass the salt?* Increasingly, Otto had noticed Lotte turn quieter whenever Krista was near, appearing, sometimes, on the edge of tears, as Krista pointedly asked Marianne to go for a walk, a swim.

'You're being very unfair,' Brigit scolded Krista. 'Lotte is not her father, but she is our guest.'

'Only because Papa wants Otto to marry her.'

'Papa does not want Otto to marry her.'

'Good,' said Otto, 'because that won't be happening.'

'No?'

'No.'

'I suspect he wouldn't object if it did . . . '

'Mama . . . '

'Fine, fine.' She smiled, then quickly became serious again. 'All he wants is that you both be kind to her, make her feel part of the family, as she was, for a long time, before all this Nazi nonsense. I want you to do that, too. Not—' she lifted her hand '—for any agenda, but because she's already had *too much* unkindness in her life. Why do you think she spends all this time getting ready every night? She's grown up believing she must always work to make people like her. She deserves better.'

'I—'

'No, Krista.' Brigit shot her a quelling look. 'Enough. You are making everyone uncomfortable, including Marianne, including yourself, I suspect, being such a bully.'

'I'm not being a *bully*.'

'Yes, you are.'

'It's her.'

'She's not doing anything.'

'She told Marianne that she wants them all to leave Germany.'

'Well, not exactly,' said Otto, interjecting, against his better inclination, not wanting to argue – certainly not to ruin his *excellent* mood in a row with his sister, especially defending Lotte – yet unable to help himself, because this wasn't being quite fair. 'She said that she *thought* they should leave. It's not what she wants.' Lotte had been at great pains, convincing him of that, over their countless games of cards that week. *If I didn't care about them all so much, I wouldn't have said it.* 'She's given up, because she's Lotte, and that's what she does, so thinks they all should too.'

'How does she even suppose Nicola and Ernst could afford to go?'

'I don't think she's considered that.'

'I expect she hasn't,' said Brigit. 'She's frightened, probably not thinking straight at all. We'll never know what it's like for her, in that house, and these are frightening times for everyone. You're frightened, Krista.'

'No, I'm not.'

'Yes, my darling, you are. And it's nothing to be ashamed of. But never forget, you could go on for decades without becoming poorly like me . . . '

'Mama . . . '

'You could. You will, Krista, if you're careful. If we're all careful.'

'I don't *want* to be careful.'

'I don't want you to have to be.' Brigit took her hand, face softening in the lowering light. 'This is life though. It will pass, I believe it, but until it does, making Lotte miserable won't solve anything.' She smiled. 'The two of you used to be such friends . . . '

'Did we?'

'You know you did. You'd keep me up all night, chatting. Remember the plays you used to put on? Yes, you see, you do. Try being friends again tonight, yes? Please. For me.'

Maybe it was her tumbler of wine, which Krista drained before going to change, or that she, like Otto, couldn't bear to let their mother down, whilst she was still here – or, perhaps, a combination of the two – but whilst Otto was in his room, changing himself, he heard Krista knock on Lotte's door, asking if she'd like to go down to the rocks with her and Marianne before dinner, sneak a quick cigarette. 'I know you don't smoke, but—'

'I'm coming,' said Lotte, with an eagerness difficult to hear. 'I'll get my shawl. Shall we ask Otto?'

'I think he wants to keep working,' said Krista. 'Let's leave him.'

Sending her a silent thank you, Otto listened to them disappear down the stairs, shrugged on a clean shirt, and, genuinely wanting to work, pulled up a chair at his wooden desk, getting started on the designs he'd been sketching mentally since the beach. He'd been stealing moments like this all week, catching up on the progress he'd claimed to be making on his assignment when he was out with Eleni. The better he'd grown to know her, the more he'd found himself picturing her as he'd drawn; with each new doorway he'd added, he'd seen her shadow falling through it; with every window, he'd wondered what she'd make of it. That evening, she was very present in his mind. *Will you have a living room?* He would soon.

He became immediately immersed in the task, leaving his room, leaving the villa, existing wholly in the page. In Munich, he'd go on for hours in such a way, uninterrupted.

But this wasn't Munich. And it wasn't long before Henri's voice fractured his focus, calling him downstairs. Cursing, he shouted that he'd be there in a minute, remained where he was for several more, finishing the measurements he'd been calculating, then – surveying the little he'd managed to get done, already impatient to be back at his desk, carrying on – reluctantly went to join everyone.

They ate on the terrace. Lotte smiled across the table at Otto as they took their seats, visibly lighter after her trip to the rocks with Krista and Marianne, which he deduced hadn't been a disaster. Unlike Krista, who'd dressed for the meal in her dungarees, and Marianne, who wore the same simple dress she wore most nights, Lotte had once again come much as she might to an opera, in a black silk gown. Her sunburn had faded, leaving the very lightest of tans on her pale skin. *A lily.* She wore long gloves, and had pinned her white-blonde hair.

Eleni's had been loose, all day; curled and salty.

Turning from Lotte, Otto looked across the water, in the direction of her villa, imagining her there. Occasionally, as the meal wore on, and Henri steered them around the same safe subjects they talked about every night (the weather, everyone's plans for the next day, how delicious the food was, the weather), Otto swore he heard her laughter, carrying on the still night air. It distracted him, made him even more restless to escape the table's polite pretence.

As, at length, he did. They all dispersed, as soon as the dishes were cleared, as relieved as each other, he suspected, to be free again. Brigit went to bed, like always, Henri with her. Normally, Lotte would follow them up, and Otto would go swimming. But that night, Lotte remained in the kitchen, hovering around Krista and Marianne, nodding quickly when Marianne asked her if she'd like some tea, and Otto, who'd swam enough, headed back to his room, taking the stairs two at a time, going straight to his desk.

He remained there into the small hours, working by the light of a candle, the cicadas clacking outside. The living room wasn't the main thing he wanted to complete, simply the part he needed to design first. He didn't pause until he had, covering his desk in rubber shavings, erasing whatever wasn't perfect, getting it right, for her. The candle burnt down to a wax puddle, and he lit another; at some point, the girls all came upstairs, whispering, and he ignored them; through the window, the night deepened into the darkness before dawn, and still, he kept going.

When, at last, he leant back in his chair, running his hands through his hair, his back ached. His wrist ached. His brain ached.

But . . .

He looked at the papers before him. The living room was wide and deep, with doors onto a garden, and a high, vaulted roof. Off it was another room, smaller, but still airy. On one side was a fireplace. On the other, a window seat.

He smiled.

She had her reading nook.

It would catch the afternoon sun.

The date all of them, apart from Lotte, were to return to Berlin was 15 August. Lotte was to leave the Saturday before, on the eighth, flying home for the Olympics with an escort sent by her father. Keenly as Otto had been anticipating her departure, he no longer wished away the days between now and then.

Waking late the next morning, he wished away nothing of the summer.

Infinite, Eleni had called the six weeks they had left together, as they'd raced for the motor the night before.

They'd felt like it, whilst he was still with her.

But, now, lying alone in his bed, turning to face the fierce Greek light seeping through his shutters – reflecting on how it had, unbelievably, already been a week since she'd passed by that same window in her grandfather's Cadillac, no more than an intriguing stranger – they seemed anything but.

He didn't want to think about them ending. Didn't want to dwell on everything waiting, back in Germany, once they did.

He heard everyone in the kitchen below, making breakfast, and didn't want to join them either.

He wanted only to go in search of her, so she could make time feel infinite for him again.

It wasn't possible that weekend. She was gone for all of it, working until the siesta on Saturday, then out with her grandfather the rest of the time, driving around the island, wearing her shorts ('Not always,' she said, with a roll of her blue-black eyes, when they were finally together again), calling on Maria and Spiros, spending another day in the mountains, leaving Otto to get on with life at the villa, where the quiet hours passed in a sultry rhythm, revolving around meals, swims, card games with Lotte, efforts by Krista to be nicer; the rise and fall of the burning sun.

On Monday, though, he was there, waiting for her at his gate, when she came walking along the unsheltered road, on her way to the bus stop. It was a few seconds before she noticed him. He watched her move, that careless saunter, and, even as he yearned to call out, remained silent, re-absorbing her face, her peace as she looked down at the sea, relishing the anticipation of her company too much, suddenly, to want to hasten it.

He recognized her dress. He knew her well enough, already, to do that. It was the same striped one she'd worn the night he'd given her that chocolate, with buttons on its short sleeves, and a stitch on the skirt where she'd torn it.

Snagged on a table last summer, she'd said, sitting beneath the tree, tucking the fabric between her knees, then letting them drop against his.

Her hair was in a ponytail again. She had her sunglasses on, her bag slung on her shoulder, and, when she turned her head, glancing his way, her expression transformed, she burst out laughing, running to close the distance between them.

She ran. To him.

And, knowing that the road was empty, the rest of his family safely down by the water, and that he'd been driving himself mad, waiting to do it since Friday, he caught her to him, not kissing her, because she moved first, kissing him – like he was coming to learn she did most things – with every part of her being.

'You're at your gate,' she said. 'You're never at your gate.'

'I decided it was time that changed.'

'Excellent decision.'

'I thought I'd come into town with you on the bus too.'

'*Really?*'

'Really.'

He'd resolved that he would. Resolved too, over the interminable weekend, that he wouldn't give Henri any more excuses for his absence, tired already of the deceit; skulking around as though he were an adolescent boy, in need of his father's permission.

'Good for you,' Krista had said, the pair of them in the kitchen the morning before, grinding beans for coffee. 'I must say I'd like to be present when you tell him.' She'd poured the granules into the stove's copper *briki*, tanned face tense with concentration, braced against her own unpredictable tremors. 'I love it when it's you he's angry at instead of me.'

But Henri hadn't been angry.

He'd said very little at all when, later, whilst Krista, Marianne and Lotte had been gone on a walk, Otto had sought him out on the terrace, telling him that he'd continue to play as many games of cards as was necessary with Lotte, but needed to be able to come and go from the villa as he pleased. Not only to study.

'I've only got a year left before national service,' he'd reminded his father. 'I'll have no control over anything then. Please stop trying to control me now. I won't let you, but I'd prefer not to have to keep arguing about it.'

Henri had studied him from behind his spectacles. All around him had been the client files he'd brought from Berlin; on his lap, what looked like government documents. Although he'd left his firm in the hands of his partners for the summer, he'd told Otto that he still needed to work whilst they were away. *I have to pay for it all somehow. And I have too many people relying on me.* Next to him, Brigit had been napping in her deckchair. Otto had been tempted to entreat Henri to do the same thing. He would have, had he thought for a moment that Henri would have listened to him.

He'd looked so deeply tired.

'Can I enquire where it is that you want to go?' Henri had asked.

'Where I please,' he'd replied, as civilly as one could say such a thing.

He hadn't mentioned Eleni, because he'd seen no reason to, and because Henri would only have set to panicking about Lotte finding out, which Otto had been keen to avoid, for several reasons, not least that he didn't want to be responsible for the way Lotte felt, about anything, and Henri already had more than enough that he was panicking about.

'Will you ever tell him?' asked Eleni, once he'd filled her in on it all, the two of them walking up the dusty, sun-drenched road.

'Maybe,' he said, taking her hand, feeling her fingers lace into his. 'Or, he'll work it out. Krista thinks he will.' She and Marianne alone knew how much time he'd been spending with Eleni; they'd both been at the café, of course, the first time they'd spoken. 'We're living pretty close by . . . '

'And hold hands in broad daylight.'

He grinned.

So did she, her dark cheeks dimpling, the sun bouncing from her hair. 'Well, I don't really mind keeping things the way they are . . . '

'You're sure?'

'I think so. *Papou* might insist on a chaperone, once he finds out.'

'We can't have that.'

'No. So you'd better not sit next to me on the bus.'

'There'll be someone you know?'

'Probably not. But just to be safe, across the aisle will be better.'

'All right.'

'And don't do that thing.'

'What thing?'

'Where you make me laugh too much.'

'That's not a *thing*.'

'It's a thing.'

'It's not. How can anyone laugh too much?'

'It's a thing,' she repeated.

It really wasn't.

And he kept doing it to her.

They kept doing it to each other. That morning, sitting separately on the bus's sprung, frayed seats – arms folded, touching only with their eyes – and on and on from there: bumpy, sweaty, petrol-scented drives into Chania's leafy square that lasted a half-hour, yet passed in the space of seconds. No one worked anything out, not for the entire of that July – not Henri, nor Yorgos, nor Lotte – and, Sundays aside, which Otto grew to dread, he was at his gate every morning, waiting to ride with her on that rickety bus, growing more addicted, with every day that vanished, to the promise of when they'd be together next.

They never ran out of conversation on those timeless journeys, only silences to fill. She'd move in her chair, leaning closer to him, fanning her face against the hot wind blowing through the open windows, talking, her voice raised above the engine, the noise of the other passengers, creating such pictures with her words, it became as though he felt like he knew each one of her relatives for himself; had sat with them all in Sofia's mountain garden, drunk the Vassilis' wine ('You probably have, actually,' she said); watched Little Vassili show off his new army uniform.

She had so many questions too, never seeming to tire of hearing about his own family, her eyes sparking amusement when he relayed Henri's torturous deliberations over Christina's pay, the wodge of drachma Krista, at the end of her patience, had taken from his wallet to settle the matter, then Christina's delight, and Henri's explosion when he discovered just how much Krista had given her. *For Christ's sake, Krista, now I'm going to have to do the same every week.* 'Krista didn't give a damn. Or she pretended she didn't.'

'And what did your mother say?' Eleni asked, bracing herself as the driver coaxed the protesting bus up a hill.

'What she always says. Poor Papa.'

'She must wish she could make it all go away for him.'

'Yes,' he said, seeing Brigit in his mind's eye, not as she was now, but as she'd used to be, running around their house, gathering her scores, kissing them all goodbye before heading off to her students at the university, back when she could still hold a bow. 'I think she wishes for a lot.'

'Like you,' Eleni said.

'Like me,' he agreed, loving how she understood.

He hated leaving her in Chania.

Staving the moment off, he'd walk her to the harbour – both of them drifting closer in the shaded Venetian alleyways, arms brushing, safe in the anonymity of the town. Often, he remained at the café for a drink in the sunshine, a cigarette with Socrates (also there, a lot; *no problem*), catching her eye as she moved around the tables, smiling when she smiled.

But, eventually, he'd have to force himself to say goodbye.

Not for long, though. Never for long.

The rest of the day, he'd spend at the villa, where he'd sit with his mother on the terrace, or head out on one of the several picnics and boat trips Henri organised, or swim with Marianne and Krista from the rocks – the three of them taking it in turns to coax Lotte in ('Maybe tomorrow,' she'd say, from beneath her wide-brimmed hat. 'I'm worried about jellyfish . . . ') – but, every evening Eleni wasn't with her grandfather, he'd head to the bus stop to wait for her, sitting on the roadside, the sea glimmering below. He'd work to pass the time, drawing to the tune of the breeze wisping on the rocks, but stop as soon as he heard the bus approaching.

God, he loved it when he did; that feeling in his chest as he caught sight of her, on her feet already, waiting by the door, looking for him.

Her hair was always loose on those evenings, messy from her siesta swims; her dark skin, latticed with salt trails.

When they kissed, she always tasted of oranges.

He never forgot to bring her something else to eat – more chocolate; bread; biscuits from the bakery – and they never didn't end up beneath their tree, heads together, her legs draped over his, not moving until darkness fell, Yorgos's return became too imminent to ignore, and they were compelled to part again.

'*Kalinichta*,' she'd say, standing close, looking up at him in the moonlight.

'*Kalinichta*,' he'd echo, feeling her fingers slide from his, until he'd pulled her back for one last kiss, because it was never enough, and he'd have stayed with her all night if he could.

They stole two more afternoons back at that beach. Socrates was happy to help them do that. *No problem.*

'Do you think,' Eleni suggested to Otto, 'that it might be . . . well . . . *possible* . . . that he and Dimitri are . . . well, a bit . . . *more* . . . than friends?'

'I'd say it was a possibility, yes.'

'What's so funny?'

'Has this really only just occurred to you?' he said.

The white sands beneath the cliff-face remained as abandoned as they'd been the first time they'd visited, and blissfully alone, *hidden*, they lost hours in the deep, blue sea, racing one another to the rock with its urchin underbelly, drying themselves in the rays, kissing more, then diving back into the water, reaching for one another beneath the surface, neither letting the other go.

'I could drown with you,' he said, pulling her thighs around his waist, 'quite happily.'

'I'd never let you do that.' She tightened her legs. 'Never.'

It was at the end of the month that the Meltemi winds she'd warned him about, hit, lashing across the water, sending shutters slamming, cooling the sweltering heat. Lotte fussed about her hair, Brigit took to wearing a cardigan when she sat out in her deckchair, Henri kept his files inside, and Krista and Marianne complained that the choppy sea was no longer so inviting.

Otto didn't agree.

He still went out in it, every night, on his late swims, because when he did, she'd be at her window, waiting to wave down at him, and how could he have missed that?

She'd become a kind of madness for him, he knew.

There was no point questioning it though.

There was nothing to be done.

When she was near, he thought about no one else.

When he left her, he only wanted to be with her again.

She could make his whole night, just by standing at a damn window; his whole day, with her laugh. He dreamt about her. Felt her touch on his hand when she was miles away. Heard her, if only in his imagination, every dinner he sat through on the terrace. Thought he glimpsed her sometimes, when he was out around the island, only to be disappointed when it was another fair-haired Greek; a poor imitation.

You make me feel not alone, he'd told her, way back at the beginning of the month.

But it had become so much more than that.

She made him feel anchored, centred. When they were together, he almost grew to believe that his mother mightn't die after all, and Krista would live for decades, and his father could lose that permanent pinch in his forehead; wink at Krista like he once had, or throw his arm around Otto's shoulders.

She made him feel safe.

I'd never let you do that.

Really safe.

And deeply, deeply happy.

'Remembering wartime Greece.' Transcript of research interview undertaken by M. Middleton (M.M.) with subject seventeen (#17), at British Broadcasting House, 5 June 1974

M.M: That summer . . .

#17: Yes?

M.M: I get the sense that it all went very wrong, in the end.

#17: You sense that, do you?

M.M: I do.

#17: Well, it finished, of course.

M.M: Yes, but . . .

#17: Nothing is infinite, I assure you. It can feel it, especially at [waves hand] your age, but nothing is, and that summer was no exception.

M.M: You sound so incredibly sad, whenever you talk about it.

#17: I'm a very sad man.

[Long pause]

M.M: Did it, though?

#17: What?

M.M: End badly?

#17: [Sighs] It wasn't nearly so straightforward as that.

LONDON, 1940

Chapter Nine

64 Baker Street, November 1940

It was an unremarkable building, the SOE HQ on Baker Street. Eleni realized that was the point. The people she'd been summoned there to meet, over the ten days that had passed since she'd left Hector Herbert on Vauxhall Bridge, had all appeared, on first impression at least, quite unremarkable too; none the kind to stand out in a crowd, or prompt anyone to wonder what their business might be, as they slipped through number 64's unremarkable doors.

She hadn't seen Hector again. Not until today.

No, she'd been jumping through his hoops.

First had come his promised interviews with native Greek speakers, three in total, each tasked with finding holes in her accent, her turns of phrase; anything that might cause a sharp-eared local to doubt her. The first had been with a classicist from Corfu, now living in Finchley, who'd talked, mainly, of Elgin's marbles. After him had come another classicist, from Athens, much more concerned with Italy's ongoing invasion of Greece, and how hard the coming winter was going be for the men on the Albanian front. 'My cousin's there, actually,' she'd told him, numb, still from Yorgos's wire letting her know that Little Vassili had been sent, along with the rest of the Cretan 5th Division, to reinforce the defence. (*There's no one to shoot, in*

Crete. She could still hear the cavalier way he'd said it, back in Sofia's garden). Finally, she'd met a retired teacher from Patras, with a cool smile that had become rather thinner, the longer they'd talked about Homer.

He was certain he could catch you out, Hector had written, in one of the several notes he'd had delivered to her at the War Rooms. *You perplexed him. I suspect you'll be delighted to hear that. Report back on Thursday at ten. Mr Wood will meet you in the foyer.*

Mr Wood – a middle-aged man with tea stains on his tie, and smudged notes scrawled on his hand – had, leading her up to a dingy, windowless office, carpeted with teetering piles of boxes.

'Sorry for the mess,' he'd said, taking her coat and hat, throwing both unceremoniously on the nearest stack. 'I almost wish we'd get bombed, then I'll never have to unpack it all.'

Once she'd sat, at his command, in the room's only chair – metal, folding, not very comfortable – he'd paced and smoked and briefed her on the various roles SOE operatives might be tasked with overseas (wireless operation, enemy surveillance, sabotage, propaganda dissemination . . . the list went on), and the training required of any recruit in his section, *regardless* of their eventual mission, before he'd consider so much as *assessing* their readiness for active service.

'I want to ask,' he'd said, pausing to light another cigarette, 'how much experience you've had handling firearms?'

'Not much,' she'd admitted.

'Some, then?'

He'd looked so hopeful.

It had been hard, disappointing him.

'None at all, actually.'

'Right.' He'd taken a long drag of his cigarette, frowned. 'And the same goes for explosives?'

'Yes, I'm afraid so.'

'Right.'

'I'm a quick learner . . . '

'Are you?' He'd stared at her through the veil of his own smoke. 'Let's see, shall we?'

He'd unearthed a manual for her to read, then tested her on its various methods of concealing and detonating devices. He'd talked of different models of guns, best practice for clandestine parachute drops, the use of cyanide pills, asking her to repeat everything he'd said back to him, then to do so again, and again . . .

He was rather taken with you, Hector had written. *He believes you have a deal of potential. Honestly, I'm not sure you should interpret that as a compliment, given his line of business, but feel free to do so. And come again on Monday, nine this time.*

That had been yesterday: another language interview, in German this time – *in case your proficiency does become relevant*, said Hector – followed by an afternoon with Mr Haithwaite: a fatherly, affable sort, whose office *had* had a window, a rug on the linoleum floor too, and tea and buns waiting on the desk. As they'd eaten, Mr Haithwaite had talked to Eleni about his daughters – one, a doctor; the other, training to be a pilot with the RAF – assuring her that, unlike certain retired teachers, he had no issue whatsoever with sending women into the field, but did take very seriously his responsibility in ensuring that whoever went did so with a full grasp of the dangers involved.

'I'm here to scare you, Miss Adams. Open your eyes as to what you might face, as an agent of our organisation.'

'My eyes are open,' she'd replied.

'I must insist on opening them more.'

Which he had, detailing to her, quite clinically, the interrogations she could expect, were she to find herself, *God forbid*, in occupied territory, under the arrest of the Gestapo; the tortures she'd face, and near-certain execution.

Cyanide pills had come up again.

They'd come up more than once.

But she hadn't been scared.

On the contrary, she'd felt oddly detached from all Mr Haithwaite had said; like she'd been listening to a story that had no bearing on herself. The more he'd talked, the harder she'd found it to marry any of it with a future that might involve her.

She supposed that was the way, with terrible things: most of the time you got by, believing they'd happen to someone else.

Certainly, she'd had no hesitation in telling Mr Haithwaite that no, she was having no second thoughts about proceeding with her recruitment. Not even in light of all she now knew.

'You'd have nothing to be ashamed of,' he'd persisted. 'You could carry on at the War Rooms, no harm done.'

'I don't want to carry on at the War Rooms.'

'You're sure?'

'Quite sure.'

'Really?'

'Absolutely.'

She could only assume he'd believed her, because now here she was again, sitting in yet another unremarkable office, summoned via yet another note on her desk, delivered first thing that morning.

Just one last hoop, Eleni. I'll be holding it. I hope you haven't forgotten what I said I'll be expecting, when we next meet . . .

She hadn't forgotten.

Hector's words to her on the bridge had played on a loop in her mind, ever since he'd spoken them.

I suggest you be ready with the truth about why you haven't returned to Crete since 1936.

They really weren't something she was likely to forget.

She was ready with the truth, that day.

She gave it to him.

She'd come to accept that, given she had no idea how much he already knew about Otto, and given his trust really wasn't something she could afford to gamble with – and given this final hoop might simply be: was she reliable enough to be candid? – it was pretty much the only path open to her.

Plus, she hadn't actually done anything wrong.

She hadn't.

She'd realized now that she simply felt as though she had because she'd kept it all buried for so long. But the country was littered with people who'd known Germans before the war. They came two-a-penny in the War Rooms. The *king* had family over there.

Why should it matter that she'd had her heart broken by one, years before?

It shouldn't.

It didn't.

'It won't,' she told Hector. 'You have my word, it's in the past. *Well* in the past.'

He studied her from behind his desk, his appraising eyes even more penetrating than she'd recalled. The afternoon was a foggy one. Dim green light, and the muffled noise of Baker Street's traffic, seeped in from outside. He wore no trilby and overcoat today, rather, a tailored charcoal three-piece. His office was directly across the way from Mr Haithwaite's. It occurred to her, as the silence lengthened, that he'd probably been sitting here, so close, the entire time she was with Mr Haithwaite, listening to his tales of the things a skilled interrogator might do to her fingernails.

It was an oddly discombobulating thought.

Distracting herself from it, and the fact that Hector still hadn't said anything, she asked him, '*Did* you know, already, about Otto?'

'No.'

'Oh.'

Damn.

'I realized something must have happened in Crete in thirty-six,' he said. 'Your entire manner changed when I asked you about it. I needed to be sure that, whatever it was, it wouldn't limit your value there now. And I guessed you had some link to Germany . . . '

'Esther?'

'Yes, Esther. Plus, you learnt to speak the language.' He raised a brow. 'With an English accent, I might add, so don't ever consider doing it in front of a Nazi.'

Her heart quickened. 'So, we're still going to push ahead?'

'I'm glad you've been honest with me,' he said, not answering her question. 'And you've certainly impressed everyone here. No one doubts you'd be an asset. Wood's mustard to see how you'll perform in training, thinks you could be handy on the mainland . . . '

'I don't want to be handy on the mainland.'

'No, I know.' He stood, moving to the window, staring into the murkiness below. 'You want to be handy in Crete.'

'It's home.'

'Yet you stayed away so long.'

'I've told you why . . . '

His face, in profile, frowned.

He was still puzzling over something, she could tell.

Before she could ask what, he said, 'Esther arrived in September last year, yes?'

'Yes.'

'Who asked you to sponsor her?'

'The Reich Representation of Jews.'

'It was a very generous thing you did, taking her on.'

'I hardly did it alone. And I'd have done it a thousand times over.'

'Yet you did it for *her*.' He turned to face her once more. 'Why?'

'Because she's an innocent child, and she needed me to.'

'She's four, I believe.'

'That's right.'

'Won't it upset you, having to leave her, if we proceed with this?'

'Of course it will.' Of course it would. She'd been too overwhelmed, when Hector had first approached her, to think clearly enough about that, but she'd agonised over it since, always coming back to the fact that, regardless of her own movements, Esther was leaving London anyway: off with Helen, that coming weekend, to live with Helen's brother in Chester.

'She'll love it there,' she told Hector, and didn't doubt it. Helen's brother had a farm, a new litter of sheep dogs, three children of his own for Esther to play with. *No bombs.* 'It will be better, much better, than here. And Helen's promised her a puppy . . . '

'She likes Helen?'

'Adores her. She really is the one who's spent the most time with her, since she arrived. I'm more like the aunt who spoils her when she shouldn't.' *Let me share this,* Helen had entreated Eleni, before she'd fetched Esther from Harwich. *You're too young, too busy with work, to manage such a little one alone. And I've missed being with children since I retired. I can teach Esther English, care for her. Nothing would give me more joy.* 'She'll be happy with Helen, I'm certain. I really wouldn't be considering going anywhere, otherwise.'

'And do you have any idea what became of Esther's mother?'

'No,' said Eleni, tightly.

Not a day went by that she didn't wonder about that. Or the parents of all the other children who'd been there that early-autumn morning she'd collected Esther. There'd been so many of them, clutching their teddy bears and suitcases, bleary eyes wide and disorientated, exhausted after their long journey from Germany. Theirs had been one of the final *Kindertransports* to leave. It crippled her, picturing the goodbyes that must have taken place, back in Berlin; all the last, desperate kisses pressed against those precious cheeks . . .

'Have you tried to find out?' Hector asked, drawing her back to the moment.

'No,' she said again, more firmly this time, realizing what he was really asking. 'I swear to you, I haven't had contact with anyone in Germany since the war started. I have no more links, no misplaced loyalties . . . '

'Someone must have told the Reich Representation of Jews how to reach you last year.'

'It wasn't Otto.'

'Then who?'

'Lotte.'

'Right,' he said, audibly taken aback, for which she could hardly blame him.

More than a year on, and it still surprised her.

'Esther's mother asked her for her help,' she said.

'And she came to you.'

'I can't imagine she had a deal of choice.'

'How did she come by your address?'

'I assume Otto gave it to her.'

'Right,' he said, again.

What else was there, really, to say?

He returned to his chair, the leather creaking as he sat. She watched him, studying her, his face tense with the movement of his thoughts. He was making his mind up, deciding . . .

'You can trust me,' she said, leaning forward in her own chair, desperate to make him do just that. 'I promise you, I've nothing more to do with anyone in Germany. Nothing. The last letter I wrote to Otto, I told him I never wanted to hear from him again. If he appeared in this room, I'd walk out of it . . . '

'It's all right, Eleni.'

She sat back in her chair. 'It is?'

'I believe you.'

'You do?'

'I do.'

'Good.' Silently, she exhaled. 'That's good . . . '

'And I'm sorry,' said Hector, his business-like manner softening, just perceptibly. 'If someone had done that to me—' he reached across his desk for some papers '—I'd never want to see them again either.'

He authorized her progression into training that same afternoon. It's what the papers were for. He signed them whilst she watched, dizzy with elation, relief that this hoop she'd been dreading was finally behind her.

She realized how hot she'd become; her skin was damp, prickly with sweat beneath her blouse and cardigan. Oblivious to her discomfort, Hector talked, telling her that she needn't return to the War Rooms; further instruction on where she should report to, and when, would arrive in Clapham imminently. Her fellow typists at the War Rooms – who knew only that she'd been interviewing with a different department these past ten days – would be told that she'd been recruited into the navy.

'It should fit,' he said, 'given who your father is.'

He advised her not to speak to any of them further, which she wasn't delighted about – several of them had become friends – but nonetheless accepted. It was going to be trying enough keeping up the deceit about what she was up to at home; she didn't want to have to lie to more people than was necessary.

'A terrible way to live, really,' said Hector, getting up to place her papers in a tray by the door, 'but one becomes accustomed to it.'

Returning to his chair, he detailed what she could expect from her training, which was to take place in a *most secret location*, and would entail a lot more time spent with Mr Wood's handguns and explosives, then crash-courses in interrogation, radio-operation, Morse code . . .

'I'm fine with Morse,' she said, 'Dad taught me, years ago.'

'Did he?' said Hector, smiling, briefly, for the first time that afternoon, reminding her that he did, actually, have quite a nice smile.

It made him seem younger, warmer.

She wished he'd do it more often.

Reaching for a pad, he offered to put in a leave request so that she could spend Christmas in Cheshire. 'I gather Hannukah begins on Christmas Eve this year, too.'

'You gather right,' she said, liking him more, for knowing that. 'And, yes, please, I would like to spend it with Esther, if I can.'

'I'm sure it can be arranged.' He made a note. 'The leave will have to be short, though. I want you on the other side of training, and ready for a final assessment for service ASAP.'

'Fine,' she said, heart pummelling in excitement. 'Whatever you need.'

'Not everyone passes,' he warned her, shutting his pad. 'Far from it.'

'I'm not going to fail.'

'No?'

'No.'

She hadn't just perspired her way through the humiliation of the past hour, reliving one of the most painful episodes of her life – to Hector, *Hector*, so calm and collected and *suave* in his expensive suit, with his crested signet ring, and spearing stare – only to let herself slip up at an SOE training ground. On the contrary, she was absolutely determined now to get through whatever they might throw at her. Crete was within touching distance. She could feel it. Smell it . . .

She did that all the way home, through the damp, wintry, four o'clock darkness, nestled in the taxicab Hector had insisted on hailing for her. ('I don't want another head cold on my conscience.') Unlike on Vauxhall Bridge, he'd talked no more about the people who might or might not betray her in Crete, before they'd said goodbye. She supposed there was time enough for them to debate that further *after* her training. He had however confirmed that – assuming she didn't fail the course, and assuming there were no significant developments in Greece between then and now – Crete, not the mainland, was indeed where she would be sent. 'Possibly as soon as March.'

March.

It would be here before she knew it.

Time really could pass so fast.

She hadn't always thought so, of course.

Infinite, she'd hubristically called that summer she and Otto had met.

What a little fool.

She rested her head against the taxicab's cold windowpane, sinking into her memories of those last days she and Otto had shared – too raw from dredging them all up for Hector to attempt to push them away. They flowed through her tired mind, faded, but unstoppable; like a worn, over-used film reel.

Did you know, already, about Otto?

No.

She was glad, actually, that she'd told Hector, unnecessary and unpleasant as her confession had been. She felt better for it, lighter . . .

Secrets really did carry such a tremendous weight.

She'd felt that, that summer too: the toll things unspoken

took. Complicit as she'd been in keeping her involvement with Otto hidden, she'd grown so guilty about it in the end, especially around her *papou*, who she'd never before concealed anything from. Countless times, she'd toyed with coming clean to him – during their dinners, over their breakfasts, on their weekend drives – yet, she'd struggled to make herself do it. She'd simply cherished her time alone with Otto too much to risk jeopardising it with the rules Yorgos might have imposed.

But eventually – inevitably, she supposed – her and Otto's bubble of two *had* been punctured.

It was on the first Sunday of August that it happened. On a trip to Knossos, of all things.

Spiros's fault.

He had, unbeknownst to Eleni and Otto, met Otto's parents, back at the start of the summer, when Henri had taken Brigit to the surgery for her twisted wrist. At Spiros's suggestion, they'd returned to see him several times over the course of July so that he could keep an ear on Brigit's poor lungs. Neither he, nor Yorgos, had mentioned their visits to Eleni, because they took their Hippocratic Oaths seriously, and also – why would they have supposed it relevant to her? Henri and Brigit had said nothing about them to Otto either, because in their family, no one had talked about anything.

But, somewhere along the way, Spiros and Henri had discovered a shared passion for the ancient world, and Spiros – whose brother had then been part of the team excavating the ancient palace at Knossos – had arranged for them all to visit the ruins, and take lunch with the resident curator.

Wrapping her arms around herself, Eleni stared through the taxi's grimy window, the swirls of fog, feeling again the intense heat and tension of that day.

The first she'd known of it happening had been when Yorgos had come to collect her from her shift at the café the afternoon before. Spiros and Maria had been with him, Spiros intent on booking a caique to take them to Heraklion at dawn.

'Why are we going to Heraklion at dawn?' Eleni had asked, not enthusiastically. For the first time since she'd arrived, she and Yorgos hadn't been expected anywhere that Sunday. She'd been looking forward to a long lie-in; hours doing nothing down at the cove; possibly seeing Otto, if only from a distance . . .

'An adventure, Eleni-mou,' Spiros had declared, heading back along the bustling quayside. 'To the past.'

'King Minos's,' Maria had clarified, with a smile, tucking her arm into Eleni's. She'd been in her usual silk blouse, a pencil skirt, her hair swooped back effortlessly in a bun; always so elegant. 'I'm sorry, I did try to campaign for us to stay here. But you'll have some girls your age at least. Your neighbours are coming . . . '

'What?' she'd choked.

'The Linders,' Yorgos had helpfully supplied.

'Ah, wonderful,' Dimitri, also there, had said. He'd shot a quick wink at Eleni. 'If only I could come too.'

Eleni hadn't been able to see Otto before they went. She and Yorgos had had dinner with Maria and Spiros in Halepa that night, out in the lamplit fragrance of their garden, where everyone had debated the plausibility of a Minoan labyrinth, and seemingly, thankfully, not noticed how distracted she'd been.

It had been after midnight by the time she and Yorgos had returned home. Too late, even, for her to see Otto swimming.

She had, naturally, struggled to sleep, and been exhausted, jangling with apprehension, when Yorgos had woken her before sunrise to leave for the harbour.

There'd been ten of them in total, assembled on the quayside, waiting in the sleepy dawn warmth to climb aboard the fishing boat Spiros had hired: herself and Yorgos; Spiros and Maria; Otto, Krista, Brigit, Henri, Marianne and Lotte.

Lotte had been done up like a Hollywood film star, with a silk scarf round her hair, high heels on her feet, and a tailored cream dress nipped in at her waist.

Eleni, not in her shorts ('Not for lunch with the curator of Knossos,' Yorgos had insisted), but a faded blue dress and sandals, hadn't trusted herself to look at her.

She hadn't trusted herself to look at Otto either.

She didn't think he'd looked at her.

Certainly, they'd kept their distance all the way to Heraklion, sitting on opposite sides of the caique, scudding across the dark blue Aegean, the salty wind in their faces, the breaking sun burning their skin.

Lotte had stuck beside Otto the entire journey through.

Eleni had sat with Krista and Marianne, trying not to wonder what they were both saying.

'You have nothing to worry about,' Krista had whispered to her. 'Really, nothing.'

'Absolutely nothing,' Marianne had echoed, with that contagious smile of hers. 'Hearts will be breaking, all over Munich, when the news gets back . . . '

Oh, Marianne.

She'd liked them both, instantly.

But, even in their company, even discovering their shared love of the pictures, and swing music, and *bougatsa* ('*Mein Gott*,' said Marianne, 'I don't know how I am going to be living without it when we leave'), it had been a very long journey.

Such a long, long day.

The way he'd stood, just behind her, as they'd finally disembarked the boat at Heraklion.

Her knees touching his, in the taxicab from the port.

His fingers, skimming her waist, as – dripping with sweat, flagging with the pounding heat – they'd explored the palace.

Come with me.

She closed her eyes, hearing his voice again.

Back there, again.

With him.

BEFORE THE WAR

Chapter Ten

Crete, August 1936

There was hardly anyone else, besides their motley group, at the palace that Sunday.

The curator, a scholarly British man who'd greeted them when they'd arrived, had, at Maria's quiet request, escorted her and Brigit to his home across the road, the Villa Ariadne, there to wait in the enviable shade, with enviable cool drinks (Eleni imagined), for the rest of them to join them for lunch.

There were a few other tourists dotted around the site, but no workers. Spiros's cousin, Theo, had said the excavation was in a quiet patch, and of those that were digging, all took Sundays off.

Eleni didn't blame them. The ruins were like a furnace. The Meltemi had been and gone, for now, and this far inland there was no sea breeze to wisp across the arid landscape. The sun was ferocious; the screech of cicadas, deafening. Her dress hung limp on her body. She could taste her sweat on her lips; feel the moisture down her back, on her legs.

How had the Minoans survived?

What torture, truly, to have been trapped in their labyrinth, if one really *had* existed.

She couldn't have endured it.

And she didn't want to be here, amid these crumbling rocks

she was struggling to imagine ever having been a palace, taking it in turns with Yorgos and Spiros to translate Theo's impassioned discourse – on baths, and stairs, and flushing toilets – into English, so that Henri and the others would understand.

She didn't.

For the first time since she'd met Otto, she wanted to be where he wasn't.

It had been too uncomfortable, meeting Brigit on the quayside, recognizing Otto's eyes in her wan, beautiful face, feeling the warmth of her smile, only for her to turn it on Lotte, laugh at some joke they shared, and adjust her hat maternally.

It *was* too uncomfortable, walking around the site with Henri, acting like she knew nothing about him, wondering if it was right or wrong that she thought he seemed like quite a nice man, picturing the arguments Otto had told her the two of them had had.

Too hard, noticing the near-constant attention Henri paid to Lotte – helping her when she stumbled in her heels, chatting with her in German, since she alone didn't speak English – swallowing the inescapable truth that it was she, not Eleni, who was part of their family.

And too painful – no matter Marianne and Krista's reassurances – to witness Lotte's unabashed devotion to Otto: how closely she shadowed him, hanging on his every word as he translated Eleni's English into German for her, laughing, at what Eleni truly couldn't think, because she wasn't aware she said anything amusing.

'I must keep missing the joke too,' Krista had muttered, wiping her neck. 'Nothing about this is funny to me.'

She'd stayed with Lotte just now, when Lotte had paused to rest, perching prettily on what had possibly once been a pillar, beneath the scant shadow of a cypress tree. Marianne had remained with them as well, dropping exhaustedly onto the hard-baked ground, winding her plait around her head, her tanned face as flushed as Eleni's felt. Lotte had spoken to Otto, that wheedling tone to her voice that Eleni remembered from the sea. *Otto. Otto Linder.* It had been obvious she'd been angling for him to stay too.

Not wanting to see him do that, Eleni had left, following her *papou*, Henri and Spiros, who'd already set off with Theo, further down the hillside.

She'd hoped Otto would follow her, of course.

She'd wanted to trust that he'd do that.

It had still been a relief though when she'd heard his footsteps behind her; his voice.

Come with me.

They'd slipped inside a crumbling set of walls, barely higher than his head. Not very private, but private enough. She had her back to the stone, her hand to his beating chest, and, as she tried to speak, to say what she didn't know, she realized she was on the edge of tears.

He moved closer, saying nothing either, his green eyes intent, his sculpted features cut by the wall's shadows, the sun's quivering light. Tightening her fingers around his collar, she pulled him to her, kissing him, wrapping herself around him as he kissed her back. In the heat, the cacophony of the cicadas, they kissed harder, with an urgency new to her; all the pent-up strain of the past hours released at once. She felt his lips on her neck, his hands scooping under her thighs, lifting her up, making her forget where they were . . .

'Otto. *Otto, wo bist du?*'

They both went still at her approaching voice.

But neither of them let the other go.

They kissed again, and he dropped his forehead against hers, stroking her thighs with his thumbs.

She kissed him back, closing her eyes, the happiest she'd been all day, yet closer to tears than ever.

It was hearing Lotte. Finally meeting his family, being confronted by what an outsider she was. It had hit her.

Really hit her.

The two of them came from separate homes, separate worlds. It was 2 August, and in less than two weeks, he'd fly back to his world.

Back to Germany.

There was no magic to be done. No alchemy.

This summer of theirs, like every summer before it, really was going to end, and she couldn't bear it.

Lotte didn't discover them.

No one did.

But for the rest of that day, their secrecy, which had become hard enough to carry, ceased feeling like a choice to Eleni, and instead became a burden that hurt.

It hurt as they left their hiding place, and wordlessly went their separate ways.

It hurt over lunch at the Villa Ariadne, where there *were* cool drinks, and there *was* plenty of shade, and place cards on the veranda table, too, with their names side-by-side.

'I've been trying to recall where I've seen you before,' Yorgos, opposite, said to Otto, in English, as they took their seats. 'It was at the café, I think. I saw you there with Eleni, weeks ago . . .'

'Hardly with me, *Papou*,' said Eleni quickly, mind moving to that June evening; Dimitri's music. *My heart beats so that I can barely speak.* 'We did meet though.' She forced herself to turn, look at Otto. 'Remember?'

'Yes,' he said, looking right back at her. 'I remember.'

It hurt on the boat journey back to Chania, through the abiding late-afternoon heat, when he sat beside her again, on the caique's salt-crusted floor, because Krista suggested cards, they needed to form a circle, and Lotte didn't want to ruin her dress, getting off the bench.

It hurt at the harbour, as they all said their farewells, and he turned from her, following his family, following Lotte, away.

'*Kalinichta*,' he called, over his shoulder, with a glance that briefly closed the distance between them, and hurt even more.

She didn't trust herself to say, *kalinichta*, back.

If she hadn't been with her *papou*, Spiros and Maria, she'd have run to the café, found Dimitri or Socrates, and sobbed into either one of their shoulders. She wouldn't have been too proud, and they'd have listened to her, poured her a coffee, given her a hug; told her to pull herself together. She could have done with that . . .

It was lonely, being this sad.

But, since she was with her *papou*, Spiros and Maria, and since they were all keen to head home themselves, she kissed Maria and Spiros goodbye, thanked Spiros for the day, and, taking Yorgos's proffered arm, walked with him, back to where they'd left the motor.

'You're quiet,' he said, patting her hand. 'Tired?'

'Exhausted,' she replied, and, in her upset, felt more tempted than ever to go on, finally tell him everything.

The silence between them continued, and she could hardly think for the noise of her unuttered truths, crowding her mind.

It would be such a relief to let them go, she knew.

All she had to do was open her mouth, start talking . . .

She said nothing.

It wasn't even his rules that she feared anymore. Not now she'd pretended to him as she had, all day long. Lied to his face at lunch.

No, it was something much worse.

It was the idea of his disappointment.

*

Even in spite of her worry, she was so relieved when she saw Otto the next morning, waiting at his gate to walk her to the bus. She'd half-feared, after the strain of the day before – her failure to bid him goodnight – that he wouldn't be. Or that if he was, it would be different between them. But the instant they locked eyes, in her happiness she smiled, instinctively, and so did he.

'There was only one good thing about yesterday,' he said, coming towards her.

'There was a good thing?' she said.

'There was.'

'And where was I at the time?'

'With me,' he said. 'Doing this.' He kissed her. 'It was a good thing.'

'Yes,' she said, kissing him back, wishing, very much suddenly, that she didn't have to go to work, 'I suppose it was.'

'Can you get away this afternoon?'

'I can't.' Yorgos, who'd commented again on her quietness at breakfast, had declared he'd collect her from the café for the siesta, drive her to back to the surgery for a proper lunch, a proper rest. She could kick herself now for not having been more buoyant. 'Hopefully tomorrow.'

But that wasn't possible either. The café was busier than ever in the high summer sunshine, and Socrates couldn't take her shift because, now that it was August, he was busy too, at his new school, meeting his new headmaster, just come from Neapolis, getting ready for September and all his new pupils.

Ioannis Metaxas was also rather busy that day, in Athens, arresting all his opposition, establishing his dictatorship with the support of the much-exiled royal family (assuredly counting on him to protect them from being exiled again), sending the island into uproar, and an incandescent Yorgos to the café again, wanting to make sure Eleni had heard the news.

She could hardly have failed to.

All along the harbour, radios crackled from shopfronts; the hum of anger was everywhere. No one was surprised by Metaxas's move – Greece, fractured, like so much of Europe, by decades of poverty and inequality, had been driven to extremes on left and right, and Metaxas, full of promises for reform, had been building his strength on the right ever since the King had returned from his most recent exile the year before, making him first Minister of Army affairs, then Premier – but it was nonetheless shocking.

Eleni *felt* it.

She watched Yorgos slap his hand on the café's bar, making Dimitri's ashtray jump, and empathised with his rage.

She listened to him rant about what a criminal Metaxas was, Uncle Vassili nothing but a fool for supporting him, and *cared*.

But it didn't take over for her. Not like it did for him, and Dimitri, and so many others (save Uncle Vassili) on the deeply anti-royalist island. She knew it should have, but she also knew that it was Tuesday, 4 August, and she and Otto had just eleven days left.

To both of their despair, they didn't get an afternoon to themselves for the rest of that week. Either Socrates was busy again, or he wasn't, but Eleni was, with Yorgos, who on Wednesday did the unthinkable and reorganised his appointments so that the two of them could drive into the mountains, and he could rail at Uncle Vassili to his face.

'Much difference it will make,' said Sofia, when they got there. 'He says this is a new beginning, that the country will be saved . . . '

'Saved?' said Yorgos, striding inside. '*Saved?*'

'Saved,' said Sofia, and rolled her eyes at Eleni. 'Come, little doll—' she took her by the arm '—we can agree to eat at least. I've made *yemista*.'

The next two days, it was Otto's turn to be caught up; they

were Lotte's last on the island – she was leaving that Saturday, back to Berlin's Olympics – and Henri had organised for the six of them to go on another excursion, stay overnight at a *pension* in Elounda. They didn't return to the villa until late Friday, for Lotte's farewell meal.

Eleni had to ride to the café by herself, both of those mornings.

Walk home from the bus stop alone.

It was horribly quiet.

It came to her, as she passed Nikos's deserted gate on Friday night, that she was getting a taste of what it was going to be like once they'd all left.

It wasn't a nice realization.

Worse, was picturing Otto inside the villa, with Lotte, smiling at her, talking to her; *being nice*.

She tried to stop doing it, but it was impossible.

When, the next morning, Yorgos drove her to the café for her short Saturday shift, she managed to keep up her side of the conversation – agreeing that snapper would indeed be nice for their dinner; thanking him for his offer to return to the café later and collect her – but in her head was imagining Otto at the air strip, bidding Lotte goodbye, because it was entirely impossible not to do that either.

She saw what could only be Lotte's plane leave, at just after one.

She was clearing a table of congealed coffee cups when she heard the roar of its engines and stood straighter, raising her hand to her brow, damp in the day's pounding heat, following its arc upwards. She squinted, watching it become smaller and smaller, and, as it did, felt such an easing within her: of a pressure she'd hardly acknowledged was there.

Lotte was gone.

No longer here.

It took her aback, how relieved she was.

She hadn't absorbed, until that moment, just how much her presence on the island had begun to prey on her.

How miserable she'd become, ever since Knossos, knowing that whenever Otto had left at her side, it had been because he'd had to be at hers.

At Henri's insistence, they'd all gone to the airstrip to bid Lotte goodbye, bar Marianne, who'd stayed behind at the villa, safe from the notice of the SS henchman Lotte's father had despatched to collect her.

'It's fine,' Marianne had insisted, as they'd left her in the driveway.

It hadn't been.

They'd all felt it, even Lotte, who – dressed immaculately for her journey home, in a suit, gloves and hat, a scarf with a diamond Swastika pinned to it – had apologised to her, before getting into Nikos's motor.

She'd shared a room with her and Krista, back in the hot, tiny *pension* Henri had just subjected them to in Elounda. ('Poor Papa,' Brigit had said, 'he doesn't have much luck with hotel arrangements.') Otto's had been adjacent. He'd heard the girls through the wall, talking. He hadn't paused to consider what they might be saying; he hadn't really cared, and besides, he'd been too immersed in making the last adjustments to his house. But it had occurred to him, as he'd measured Eleni's swimming pool (*I won't have it any way but with you*), that he could have been back in Grunewald, listening to the three of them chat there. They'd sounded like the friends they'd used to be.

There'd been no sign of that ease though, in Lotte's stilted farewell to Marianne. Her awkward embrace.

'I'll never tell anyone you were here,' she'd said, doubtless meaning well, certainly making Marianne feel worse.

Otto had seen the effort behind Marianne's smile.

'The day will improve,' he'd told her, ruffling her hair, just as he'd been doing for the past eighteen years, 'I promise.'

'It's fine,' she'd repeated. 'I'm going to sit out on the veranda, play my cello.'

'Well, don't do that,' he'd said, recalling how it had ended the last time she'd played so upset. 'Seriously . . . '

She'd laughed at that, at least.

She'd still looked shamefully abandoned though, standing alone in the sunshine as they'd all driven away, her plait on her shoulder, hand raised in a wave.

'I really am sorry,' Lotte had repeated, in the motor.

'It's not your fault,' Brigit had told her.

'It is a little bit,' Krista had whispered to Otto.

He'd been inclined to agree.

There'd unquestionably have been less need for their furtiveness had Lotte only been stronger; the kind to *insist* to her father that she'd wanted Marianne there with them.

The kind to stand up for her friend.

But that was all old news. Much as Otto *had* blamed Lotte for their ridiculous situation, he'd blamed himself more for going along with it.

And, as they'd drawn closer to the airstrip, he'd found himself feeling almost sorry for Lotte too. She'd been so silent throughout the drive, staring through the window, her pale cheeks tense, one hand to her throat, covering – whether by accident or design – her diamond pin.

'I don't think she wants to go,' Krista had said to Otto, in another whisper, as they'd piled out onto the runway.

'You don't think?' he'd said.

The plane had been waiting, its propellors stilled.

Lotte's father's envoy, smoking beside it, had clicked his heels, *heil*-d, then carried Lotte's several pieces of luggage into the hold.

With a tight smile, Lotte had hugged Henri and Brigit good-bye. 'Thank you,' she'd said, 'thank you so very much.' She'd hugged Krista as well. 'I've had the best summer of my life.'

She'd come to Otto, stalled.

Realizing what she'd wanted, pitying her more, he'd nonetheless only held out his hand.

'Thank you for all our card games,' he'd said.

She'd taken his hand, delicately, but said nothing.

The stormtrooper had called for her to come, and she'd darted him a wary look, like a cornered animal, and scuttled off in her heels to climb aboard the plane.

Uncomfortable as it had been, watching her go, the second the plane had lifted off, it had felt as though the warm, thyme-rich air had filled with oxygen.

Otto had expelled a very long breath.

Krista, beside him, had smiled.

'The best summer of her life,' Henri had said, as they'd driven home. 'She had the best summer of her life.'

Even Brigit had seemed more relaxed, humming, holding Henri's hand.

Otto and Krista had left them now at the villa, sitting on the terrace in the sunshine. Pausing only to collect Marianne, they'd got straight back into the motor, and driven, quickly, to town, the busy harbour.

The day will improve.

Already, it had.

The girls were sitting outside in the thick of the café's packed tables. Otto had introduced them to Socrates – *not* at school, but making the most of his Saturday freedom to be here, with Dimitri, ready to wait tables until nightfall for no wage at all (*Do you think that it might be . . . well . . . possible . . . that he and Dimitri are . . . well, a bit . . . more . . . than friends?*) – and, leaving them to give their orders to Dimitri, had come into the small bar, where Dimitri had told him, in his broken English, Eleni was making orange juice.

Her least favourite job.

He paused in the doorway. She had her back to him, her hair gathered up in a roll, with a pencil stuck through it. She wore her blue dress; the same one she'd been in at Knossos. All the way up her back were tiny, pearl buttons. Above the faded material, her skin was dark; he saw the perfect curve of her neck, a single escaped curl clinging damply to her skin.

The gramophone was playing.

'Cheek to Cheek' again.

It was loud. She hadn't realized he was there. He smiled, seeing the absent way she raised a segment of orange to her mouth, sucking on it.

He hadn't been with her since Wednesday morning.

Just three days, and it felt too much.

Casting a cursory glance at the oblivious crowds outside, he went to her, wrapping his arms around her waist, feeling her start, then relax, and lean back against him as he kissed the side of her neck.

'You're here,' she said.

'I am,' he said, moving his lips to her ear, smiling more at the catch in her breath.

She ran her hands over his, tightening them around her, and said nothing about where he'd been.

Nor did he.

With her, so close, he'd already forgotten about it.

'We've only got a week left,' she said.

'Don't,' he said, kissing her again. 'Please don't.'

'We can't waste any more time.' She turned, raising herself up, pressing her lips to his. The taste of orange. 'We mustn't.'

'So, we won't.' He pulled her closer, feeling himself tense at the sensation of her finger travelling down his spine. 'Not a minute.' He hardly thought about what he was saying, only of her touch, and what torture it would be to go on much longer as they were, snatching kisses, brief minutes alone.

At the start of their summer, it had felt almost enough. She'd told him there'd been no other, and he'd been taken aback, but realized that they could be in no rush.

Now, though . . .

'I want to vanish with you,' she said, her lips brushing his. 'I've missed you so much.'

'Everything will be different now,' he said. 'You watch.' He kissed her more. Then, to himself as well as her, 'It's all going to be so different.'

Chapter Eleven

It was different.

With him back again, by her side, Eleni forgot her upset, she almost forgot her guilt.

For that single, too-quick week, in Lotte's absence, she caught a glimpse of what the summer might have looked like, had she never come, and it was magical.

She and Otto saw one another so much more.

They saw one another constantly.

That Saturday was just the start of it. He stayed at the café until the siesta, helping Eleni juice the damned oranges, carrying the shells to the bins for her, then sitting outside with the others whilst she got on with waiting tables, distracting her, just as he had on so many mornings before, with his smile, his face; the brush of his hand against hers, every time she passed his chair.

They were as busy as they always were on an August Saturday, but with Socrates there to lend a hand, Dimitri found plenty of time to keep on changing the music, rotating his small collection of recordings – Benny Goodman, Ella Fitzgerald – dancing with first Krista, then Marianne, then Krista again. To his obvious delight, they both laughed and loved it. It was bliss, they said, to be able to do it out in the open, unlike in Germany where they could only ever dance in secret, behind locked doors, because swing and jazz had been banned.

'Why banned?' asked Eleni, on her way inside with an order of coffees.

'Because of who performs it,' said Krista, breathlessly, squeezing her right hand with the left. *Pins and needles,* Eleni guessed, and noticed how not only Otto, but Marianne as well, were watching her. 'The Nazis call it *Negermusik.*'

'What?' Eleni frowned. 'So they . . . ?'

'Don't look for reason,' advised Otto, cutting her off, stubbing out his cigarette, taking her tray, then her by the hand, 'you'll only fail.'

'I can't dance now,' she protested, 'I'm too busy.'

'One dance.'

'I can't . . . '

'I thought we weren't wasting time.'

'Go on,' called Dimitri.

'Yes, come on,' Otto said.

So she did.

He was an excellent dancer.

One dance was, quite naturally, not enough.

And although she had to drag herself away from him, from all of them, when the café closed for the siesta, running off to meet her *papou* at his parking spot, she saw him again within hours, from the kitchen window, out swimming in the moonlit water.

She touched her hand to the glass, willing him to notice her.

She didn't move until he had, turning, and raising his arm in a wave.

Smiling, she waved back.

Then, picking up Tips, she headed out onto the dark, balmy terrace, blew him a kiss.

And got a real one in return, the very next morning.

With the entire day free, at last – no lunches in the mountains planned, nor surprise trips to Knossos to contend with – she headed to the cove after breakfast, with a towel, her book, just as she'd told him she would when she'd left him at the café the afternoon before.

She'd thought he'd probably come.

She still felt a thrill of surprise though, when she spotted him, swimming again, around from his own bay.

'*Papou* will shoot you if he finds you like this,' she said, once he'd come ashore and, lowering himself over her, given her a long, lingering kiss. 'Plus, you're very wet.'

'That's the sea for you.' He tipped his head, looking up at the steep rockface, water dripping from his hair, down his neck. 'Is he coming . . . ?'

'He might.' She kissed his throat. 'Any minute.'

'So run up and stop him. Tell him you're coming to ours.'

'What?'

'I'm here to collect you.'

'What?'

He laughed. 'Stop saying what. The girls are waiting. Say they've invited you if you like. Marianne's got you a *bougatsa*.'

'I already ate.'

'As though you mind about that.'

It was a fair point.

'Come on,' he said, kissing her again, jumping to his feet. 'No wasting time.'

She didn't waste another second.

Ecstatic, she ran up to tell Yorgos that the Germans they'd met at the palace had invited her over for more breakfast (it wasn't a lie – at last), and Yorgos – never one to stand between her and food, distracted in any case by the newspaper – said, 'Yes, yes, fine. Have fun,' which was exactly what she proceeded to do.

From the moment she rejoined Otto at the cove, she didn't stop.

Together, they swam around to Nikos's rocky patch of shore, where Marianne did indeed have *bougatsa*, Krista had coffee, and the four of them sat, on the very spot Lotte had called to Otto from (*Otto, Otto Linder*), feet dangling in the water, eating, drinking, sun-baking, swimming and sun-baking again, talking and laughing, *never too much*, about so many countless things, even the hideousness of the hours they'd spent melting at Knossos the Sunday before.

'It was when you translated the bit about the flushing toilets,' said Krista to Eleni, snorting, face down on the rocks. 'And Theo just kept giving you more to say . . . '

'The cisterns,' said Marianne. 'Remember how he kept saying about the cisterns . . . '

'Can we not,' said Eleni.

'No, it was great,' said Otto, in the water, fish darting beneath him. 'I could listen to you talk about flushing toilets all day.' His smile grew. 'And the foundations. They were excellent . . . '

'Not as excellent as Krista's card game on the way back,' said Marianne. 'I thought that was really special. Really. And not at all . . . how do you say?' She considered, freckled nose scrunching. '*Awkward*.'

Krista snorted again.

'Yes,' said Eleni, 'I'd forgotten I needed to thank you for that.'

At two, Henri came to call the three of them up for lunch. He said Eleni was welcome to join them too, and she was sorely tempted, but knew her *papou* would be expecting her.

'Eat fast,' Otto said, lingering on the rock while the others went ahead, kissing her goodbye. 'Really fast.'

'Very best efforts,' she promised, kissing him back.

'You're going to give yourself indigestion,' Yorgos warned, as she inhaled her pasta.

She did a bit.

But, heartburn or no, as soon as the table was cleared, she swam back to the rocks, where she stayed until sundown, and although she and Otto couldn't vanish, because there was nowhere for them to vanish to, they were no longer hiding anymore either, and that was almost as good.

She grew to like Krista and Marianne ever more as the hours passed, for their warmth, their ease, their funny stories of their friends and life back in Berlin, and their interest in her own in England – not least her uncertainty about what she was going to do with herself now she'd finished school, which they sympathised with, having very little certainty of their own.

'I might have gone to university,' said Krista, 'in a less fascist world.'

'You were never going to go to university,' said Otto. 'You need to actually work to do that.'

'I'd have liked to go to university,' said Marianne.

'I know,' he said, less flippantly, turning to look her in the eye. 'I still think that we'll come and see you one day, playing in the *Konzerthaus* . . . '

'Or the Royal Albert Hall,' said Krista.

'Or the Carnegie,' said Eleni, glad she had when Marianne nudged her and smiled.

They stayed behind whilst Otto and Krista went up to the villa to fetch more drinks, talking mainly about Marianne's music, how she loved playing with her papa, and had used to adore doing it with Brigit – 'She was incredible,' said Marianne, 'I wish you could have heard her' – but also about Brigit's illness, which Marianne admitted to Eleni she knew all about, and Krista's diagnosis too. Krista had told her months ago.

It didn't surprise Eleni; she'd suspected as much when she'd seen Marianne at the café, watching Krista squeeze away her pins and needles.

'Please don't tell Otto I know,' Marianne said, squinting. 'Krista made me promise I wouldn't say . . . '

'Does Lotte . . . ?'

'No. *Gott*, no.'

'Is it really so dangerous for them?' Eleni asked. It was stupid of her, but even in spite of all Otto had told her, she still hoped that Marianne would say it wasn't.

But . . .

'It's really so dangerous,' said Marianne, and it was as though the very darkest of shadows had snuffed out the brilliance of the day. 'You hear rumours, all the time, of clinics where they want to stop people having babies. Worse . . . '

'Will it change, though? Get safer?' *Please say yes.* 'Otto said Henri and Brigit believe it will . . . '

'They have to,' said Marianne. 'We all have to believe that. But—' she nudged Eleni again '—I do believe it. I do. Seriously—' she smiled, dispersing the shadow '—how can it not?'

There was no more sadness, after that.

Otto and Krista reappeared, distracting them, Krista carrying glasses, Otto *krassi*, which they drank until it grew too warm ('Like *glühwein*,' said Krista, 'except not very nice'), at which point they fed the dregs to the fish, and idly played at skimming stones, Eleni resting her head on Otto's broad, warm shoulder, the two of them talking, talking . . .

As the blazing afternoon gave way to a barely cooler evening, they slipped back into the water and floated lazily on their backs, the sinking sun on their skin, hands entwined, looking at one another (it never got old), weightless in the translucent swell.

'A good day?' asked Yorgos, when, in the purpling light, she reluctantly returned to the villa, and found him in the kitchen, chopping salad for their dinner.

'Very good.'

'I could hear you laughing from here.'

She smiled.

'Did I see the young man swimming back with you just now?'

She nodded, stealing a piece of cucumber. 'He wanted to make sure I got back all right.'

I'm not leaving you until I have to.

'A gentleman,' said Yorgos, looking up from the fish.

'Hmm,' she said.

There's no one here. No one's looking.

'What a shame they're going so soon.'

'It is.'

'Will you see them again before they do?'

'They said they'll come by the café tomorrow. We might go swimming again at the siesta.'

'All of you?'

'As long as that's all right with you.'

Did he hesitate?

Give her an odd look?

Or was she imagining it?

'Of course,' he said. (She must have imagined it.) 'Lovely.'

'Yes,' she said.

And it was lovely.

She placed the cucumber in her mouth, the cool flesh brushing her lips, where he'd just kissed her at the cove, *There's no one here. No one's looking,* and, with another smile, turned to head up for her bath.

It really was very lovely indeed.

The Meltemi returned overnight, blowing like a rage, bending the island's dry, crackling trees, stirring dust up in gusts from its narrow, winding roads, but Otto didn't much care.

The winds stayed for almost the entire rest of the week, and he didn't particularly mind about that either.

Every morning, he rode with Eleni into Chania, teaching her more German, failing to learn more Greek (she was a perfectionist when it came to pronunciation; it was funny, how impatient she became. 'You're a cruel teacher,' he told her, 'much crueller than you look'), then walked with her to the harbour through the town's by-now familiar warren of streets, where, protected from the wind, overlooked by the brooding mountains, the air once again became hot, became still. In the reprieve, she'd run her finger around her collar, blow air over her face, and – ignoring the scampering children, the laundering women, and elderly men who sat on stools playing backgammon – they'd taunt each other with how it might be if, of all the ramshackle wooden doorways they passed, there was just one they could disappear into.

'Maybe you should buy us one,' she teased. 'I'm sure there must be somewhere for sale.'

He'd have done it if he could.

Too soon, they'd arrive at the waterfront, where the gale resumed, the caiques rocked, masts clinking, and the sun's glare seemed brighter than ever, after the shade of the streets; the sea startlingly blue. He'd walk her to the café, like he always had, but no longer left her there, because while he still had the chance, where would he be but by her side?

He still didn't tell his parents who he was spending his time with. He presumed that Henri, with his lawyer's mind, had put two and two together, but given neither he nor Brigit asked Otto about it, why should he say? When he left them each morning – sitting out on the terrace in their deckchairs, Henri working, Brigit more often than not dozing, her book flipping in the wind on her lap – he said simply that he was going out to work, which wasn't untrue. He still had several assignments, beyond his house, to finish before he returned to Munich, and could think of no better place to be doing that than at the table nearest the café's doorway, his loose papers pinned down with coffee cups.

Whenever there was a lull in customers, Eleni sat with him, winding her hair back up with her pencil, looking over whatever he was doing, eyes moving back and forth over his calculations.

'Do they make any sense to you?' he asked.

'No,' she said, and laughed, *her laugh*.

At his request, she wrote her address in Gosport at the back of his notepad.

'I'll write,' he told her.

'You promise?' she said.

'You really need to ask me that?'

Socrates wasn't able to come to the café any earlier than seven for most of that week. He'd warned them on Saturday that that was going to be the case. The headmaster at his school was a demanding one, as new to his post as Socrates was to his, and, now that he'd arrived from Neapolis, determined to make his mark. He'd planned improvements for the classrooms, training for the faculty, and, with all of his own family and friends still back in Eastern Crete, saw no issue with insisting his staff give up what was left of their holiday to play their part. Without Socrates' help, it was impossible for Eleni to leave the café for anything other than the siesta. The tables there were never less than heaving; Otto didn't need her to tell him how unfair it would have been to ask Dimitri to manage alone. And although he did consider asking Krista and Marianne to help in Eleni's stead, neither of them spoke any Greek, so in that respect really were no use at all.

In another, though, they were very useful indeed.

Every day, they caught their own bus into town, and, just by giving Otto and Eleni the insulation of their company, made it respectable for them to at least spend the siesta together, down on the blustery, sun-drenched sands of the town's beach, as Yorgos had given them his blessing now to do. *All of them.*

'Feel better about that?' Otto asked Eleni.

'In a way I can't begin to explain,' she said.

He would, obviously, have felt better *not* having his sister, nor indeed Marianne, chaperoning them, but he accepted there was little to be done about it. The siesta simply wasn't long enough for him and Eleni to get to anywhere less visible than that exposed bay. By the time the café's tables had been cleared, its shutters closed, they barely had an hour.

So, to the bay at Paralia Koum Kapi the four of them went.

'It's idyllic, really,' Eleni said, the first time they arrived, to a crashing shore break, and whipping sand that stung their skin.

'I think I prefer our rocks,' said Krista.

'Who's for tennis?' said Marianne, pulling out the set she'd brought.

'Me,' said Eleni, dropping her bag.

They'd always play a game or two, wading into the waves. Krista didn't join them, as her right hand was still giving her trouble. ('It will pass,' she'd assured Otto, 'it always does. Please don't say anything to Mama and Papa, I can't stand the fuss . . . ') But when Marianne tired and came back to flop on her towel, Otto would take her bat, head out to rally with Eleni himself. 'Dive, Eleni,' he'd yell, just to hear her laugh again, '*Dive*.' They never played for long, not when what they both really wanted was to swim out to where no one could see their faces. She moved as fast as she always did, glancing at him, the further they went, her smile complicit, her dark-blue eyes alight, challenging him to stop her, until, unable to resist, he would, running his arms around her waist, pulling her legs around his own.

'Don't sink,' she'd tell him.

'I'm not going to sink.'

'Or drown.' *I'd never let you do that.*

'I won't drown,' he'd say.

And she'd smile more, tighten her legs, move her hypnotic face closer to his, then, buoyed by the deep, salty Aegean, they'd lose themselves, finally, in a kiss; each one more impossible to pull away from than the last.

They'd have to pull away though. Even so far from the shore, they both realized how close to the sun they were flying.

And, she had to be back at the café by five.

Marianne and Krista would go with them, there to pester Dimitri to play Fred Astaire again, drink the coffee they'd certainly crave within a day of being back in Germany (and Christ, Otto couldn't let himself think about that), until, as seven approached, Socrates would appear, hurrying along the quayside, pulling at his collar, full of what a *malaka* his new headmaster was, about which they'd all sympathise, and Dimitri would pat his shoulder, hand him a cigarette, then a tray, whilst Eleni took off her apron, ready to leave.

Otto went home with her every night. Their luck, so conspicuously absent when it came to Socrates' time, was far more present with regard to Yorgos's. Or, perhaps it was Aphrodite who got involved.

'Definitely Aphrodite,' said Eleni, who'd pointed out her planet, Venus, to Otto countless times by now.

Regardless, Yorgos made no further amendments to his appointment book. He had no especially early finishes at the surgery, either. Nothing got in Otto and Eleni's way of stealing that last hour of the day to themselves, leaving Krista and Marianne at Nikos's gate, then carrying on to hers.

They no longer sat under their tree, though.

'I want to show you something,' Eleni had said, the Monday after their Sunday on the rocks, tugging Otto by the hand, leading him around the villa, down into the garden he'd never before seen.

He'd taken a moment to absorb it: this place that was hers. The sea view, beyond the end of the steep lawn, was subtly different to the one he'd become accustomed to, the fishing boat lying to his right, rather than his left. The garden itself was wilder than Nikos's too, more charming for its lack of obvious effort, with groves of scented orange and lemon trees, overflowing beds of oleander, and a large vegetable patch. Hidden in pillows of bougainvillea stood a small wooden house that Otto guessed Eleni, and her mama before her, must have played in as a child.

'Here,' she'd said, coming to a halt at the base of the lawn, near to where stone steps dropped down to the shore, and pointing at a patch of earth. 'You remember my peach, that first Friday we went, well . . . ' she'd paused, turning her face to his, the setting sun painting her skin gold, 'swimming with urchins?'

'I do, funnily enough.' How could he have forgotten?

She'd smiled, and crouched down to lay her hand on Tips, who'd joined them. 'You said its pit wouldn't grow into a tree.'

'I know.' He'd remembered that too.

'I've planted it here.' She'd patted the earth, then stroked Tips again, making him preen. 'Maria says I should have given it to her to plant this autumn. Apparently, I've done it all wrong.' She'd shrugged, laughed. 'I still think it's going to be a tree one day.'

'Yes?' He'd crouched too, taking her hand from Tips, which had unquestionably irked him, and felt her fingers tighten around his.

'Yes.'

'I don't, just so we're clear, but I love your faith . . . '

'You love my faith.'

'I love your faith.'

Her smile had become arch. 'Is there anything else you love?'

'I don't know, let me think.'

'I hope you don't need to think too hard.'

'It's quite difficult, actually.'

'Oh, is it?'

'I love how smart you are,' he'd said, dodging her other hand, as she'd made to hit him. 'How you always have something I'm not expecting you to say. I love how you swim . . . '

'I love how you swim too.'

'And tell your customers off when they don't say please.'

She'd laughed.

'And never let Dimitri down, even though I sometimes wish you would.' He'd laced his fingers through hers. 'I love the way you're looking at me, now.' He'd dropped his head against hers. 'I love you, in fact.'

'You do, do you?'

'I do.'

'Ah.' Her smile had grown.

For a moment, she'd said nothing else, making him wait.

Then, with her face still close to his, so that her eyes and the bruised sky behind her had been all he could see, she'd said, 'I love you too, in fact.'

'Ah,' he'd echoed. 'That's an excellent fact.'

'Isn't it, though?'

Tips had mewed plaintively, trying to get between them.

Ignoring him, they'd kissed, and, with no one else there to see, hadn't pulled away, but had sunk into one another, urging each other on, not breaking apart until they'd heard the roar of Yorgos's motor in the driveway, and Otto had had no choice but to run down the stone stairs and swim, fully clothed, home.

'What happened to you?' Marianne, tuning her cello on the terrace, had asked, when he'd got there. 'Actually, don't tell me. I don't think I want to know.'

He hadn't told her.

But to that garden he and Eleni went again on Tuesday evening, then Wednesday, and Thursday too, walking hand-in-hand to the stone stairs, then several steps down, vanishing at last (why had they not done it sooner?), even from Tips, making the most of every second they could in the fading light, the gusting wind, before the tell-tale roar of Yorgos's approaching motor told them they must stop.

Each night, they pushed each other further, and Otto, kissing her throat, her collarbone, feeling her hands beneath his shirt, would, at some barely comprehensible level, remember where they were, how little time they had, and that he really didn't want this to happen for her, rushed, on a set of broken stairs, and, by an effort of will, force himself to pull away.

'Eleni,' he'd say, raggedly.

'I know,' she'd reply, 'I know.'

'Your grandfather . . . '

'I know.'

They both knew all too well.

And somehow, quite suddenly, it was Friday, and he was waking to a morning more silent than he'd known in days. There was no wind to frisk around the villa's walls, nor make its shutters creak. The Meltemi had gone as suddenly as it had arrived, and all was sultry stillness.

He didn't pay it a moment's heed.

He pressed his hands to his face, running them through his hair, and thought only about where all of them would be gone to by this time tomorrow, on a plane that was departing not at one, like Lotte's, but much earlier, far too early, at eight.

He didn't know how it was happening, already.

'It's fairly confusing to me too,' Eleni said, as they sat later, across the bus's aisle from one another, on their final journey into town.

She didn't laugh.

She certainly didn't smile.

She just looked at him, her dark eyes wide and round, and very, very sad.

Hating it, getting – quite abruptly – to the end of his patience with being so damned well-behaved, he moved, reaching for her hand, taking it in his.

She didn't try to stop him, or pull her hand away.

She held on to him, tightly.

Perhaps she'd reached the end of her patience too.

They were having dinner together that night at the villa. Henri had invited them all – Eleni and her grandfather, Maria and Spiros – for a farewell, and thank you to Spiros, for the care he'd taken of Brigit, and that ordeal of a trip to Knossos they'd all enjoyed so much. Eleni said Yorgos wasn't much looking forward to eating in his nemesis's home, and Otto frankly wasn't that thrilled about spending his closing hours with her in full view of their families, but on the positive side, at least they'd be spending them together.

First though, they had the afternoon.

Socrates was, finally, to finish work early enough that Eleni could leave the café when it closed for the siesta and not return. Socrates' headmaster, who visited his family in Neapolis at the weekends, liked to set off at lunchtime, which meant the rest of his unfortunate faculty could too.

Marianne and Krista still came to the café themselves that day. They'd taken a shine to Socrates and Dimitri, and said they wanted to enjoy one last afternoon out in the sunshine, listening to Dimitri's gramophone, drinking so much coffee that they wouldn't be able to sleep that night, and so miss a minute of what was left of the holiday.

Otto and Eleni didn't see them.

Otto only knew for certain that they'd been, because they told him that they had when he returned to the villa, much, much later, to change for dinner.

By the time they arrived at the café, he and Eleni were gone.

He left it to her to suggest where they should go to.

He had his own idea, obviously. But this was her home, her island. She'd be the one who was left on it, when he went, and he cared for her too much to abide the idea of trying to persuade her, in any way.

So yes, he had an idea.

Knew full-well, *in fact*, what he wanted.

But it really had to come from her.

Chapter Twelve

She knew what she wanted too.

She'd known ever since that day in the ruins at Knossos.

The summer might have become one of firsts for her, but she wasn't naive. She'd talked to her friends at school; listened to their stories, gleaned from older sisters, passed on in whispers. Known just what those sailors who'd come to the hotel in Portsmouth – Mr Green, Mr Brown, Mr Smith – had been about. Maria had spoken of it all to her too, over the years, answering the questions Eleni might have asked of her mama, had she still been alive.

'Don't get caught,' had always been at the crux of her advice.

Even now Eleni couldn't decide whether she'd meant literally, or in the sense of having a baby.

Both, possibly.

She certainly intended on doing neither that afternoon. On the baby front, she was confident, from Maria's enlightenment on rhythms, her time spent scouring the villa's medical journals, that she should be safe.

As for *actually* being caught, she felt safe there as well.

When Otto asked her, 'Where do you want to go?' she had her answer ready.

She was sad not to be returning to their beach, with its white sands and sea urchins, but it wasn't the right place for them to be. Not that afternoon. Otto would have had to go home to collect Nikos's motor, and who knew what new obstacle might get in their way there? Not Eleni, and she wasn't willing to take the risk – nor chance the possibility, however remote, that they might run into someone at that beach.

She *was* at the end of her patience.

If the villa had been any closer to town, she'd have taken Otto back to it every siesta that week. She was sure it made her a terrible person, but she'd by now told so many fibs and half-truths to her *papou* that she honestly couldn't see what difference another would make – or, how her going behind his back inside the villa would be any worse than her doing it outside. (Frankly, she didn't much want to be thinking about her *papou* at all.) And while she couldn't be *entirely* certain that the house would remain empty, it was a bet she was willing to take. Yorgos was, after all, performing a tonsillectomy on a child in Souda that afternoon.

'We'll be fine,' she told Otto.

'I'm not going to ask you twice,' he said.

'Just be ready to run, really fast, if you have to.'

They caught the last bus leaving Chania before the siesta.

For once, they said very little to one another on the ride.

Eleni had brought a glass bottle of juice from the café that she sipped intermittently, willing her heart rate down (palpitations!), staring distractedly into the warm air wafting through the bus's window. Every now and then, she turned, looking over at Otto, catching his eye, and every time she did, he smiled, gave a quiet laugh, as though amused, which made her slightly less apprehensive, but not so much that she felt remotely calm.

Now that the moment was almost upon her, she couldn't think what was actually going to happen. How it was all going to *be*.

The villa really was empty though, when they reached it. Peaceful. Even Tips was asleep, snoozing on his bed of blankets, just visible beyond the open kitchen door. Eleni had left the shutters ajar when she'd left that morning, and, through their cracks, thin beams of light seeped, casting patterns on the hallway's shaded walls.

'Do you want a drink?' Eleni asked Otto, easing the front door shut.

'No, I'm fine,' he said, holding her by the waist as she leant back, against the wooden door.

'I'm not thirsty either.'

'Well, you had all that juice on the bus.'

'You noticed that?'

'I did.'

'Are you hungry?'

'No.' He smiled. 'Are you?'

'No, I'm not.' *For the first time in my life*. 'But if you like . . . '

'Eleni,' he said, hand moving not south, but deliciously north of her waist, 'are you worrying?'

'No.'

'Are you sure?' His lips touched her ear. Her legs began to dissolve beneath her. 'Really sure?'

'I'm really sure.'

'I don't want this to be something that will leave you sad.' His lips moved down, to her neck, her collarbone.

'I don't think it could be . . . '

'Good. I won't leave you with anything.'

Was he talking about a baby too?

She thought he was probably talking about a baby too.

She didn't ask.

She felt his hands at her back, undoing the buttons of her dress, one-by-one, until it fell in a puddle at the floor, and she ceased thinking at all.

She hadn't known how it was going to be. She really hadn't known.

But she'd assumed, whenever she'd tried to picture it, that she and Otto would be in a bed.

She'd imagined that they'd at the very least go upstairs.

They didn't leave the hallway though, that first time.

Truthfully, they didn't move from the front door.

Tips didn't wake.

They noticed that, afterwards: how oblivious he remained, snoozing on his blankets.

'Probably for the best,' said Eleni, slumped against Otto on the floor, her slip pulled back on, her head tipped back so that she felt the rise and fall of his chest. He still wore his shirt. They hadn't paused to take it off. 'He'd have been shocked, I think.'

'He'd definitely hate me more,' said Otto.

'He doesn't hate you.'

'I think he does.'

'Maybe a bit then,' she said, and smiled at the vibration of his laugh.

It was a while before they moved. The floor was hard, the door unyielding, but neither of them urged the other to go, not until the kitchen clock chimed the hour (five, already; if only Eleni could keep it from chiming again), and Otto asked Eleni if he could see her room.

Easing herself to standing, she took him by the hand, and led him up to it.

It was shuttered too, but the windows were open, letting in the sound of the sea, *flisvos*, and the lightest of light breezes.

'So this is where you've been all these nights,' he said.

'This is where I've been.'

'So now I know.'

'Hmm,' she said, facing him. 'If only you'd known before.'

He smiled, dipping his head, hair falling forwards. 'If only.'

They kissed, lingeringly, their impatience spent. She undid

his shirt, opening each button in turn, just as he had her dress, and he dropped to his knees, gathering her slip in his hands, pushing it up over her thighs, her waist. She closed her eyes, dizzy with the sensation, the lazy heat, then they were at her bed, sinking down onto the mattress, where, on the cool, crisp sheets, he pulled her slip from her, she removed his shirt, and they did all sorts of shocking things, all over again.

She hardly heard the kitchen clock strike six.

As they collapsed against one another, she ignored how the light, beyond the shutters, had begun to shift, from fierce to subdued. She lay beside him, in the now tangled sheets, staring into his eyes. Outside, the cicadas sang; their chorus, in the sultry peace, was soporific, but they didn't sleep. They talked, and fell silent, then talked some more, and as they did, he ran his fingertips up her arm, down the side of her body, so that she caught silent breath, after breath, after breath.

'I don't know how I'm going to leave,' he said, when, with cold indifference, the clock struck seven. 'I don't know how to go back to Germany, live there again. Not now . . . '

'Don't think about it.'

'I can't stop.'

'Then think about this too,' she said, the idea coming to her. 'One day we'll be here again . . . '

'Yes?'

'Absolutely.'

'Together?'

'Ideally.'

He smiled.

'You'll come from Germany,' she said, shifting closer to him, the pillow's feathers crackling. 'I'll come from England. It will be summer again.'

'And?'

'And . . . ' She smiled. 'Your turn. You tell me the rest.'

'All right.' His hand came to a rest in the dip of her waist 'We'll arrange to meet. Maybe at the square . . . '

'The square?'

'Why not? And we'll see each other, but still have to look twice . . . '

'Like this?' She pulled a face.

'Exactly like that. Actually, do it again.' He laughed. 'Excellent.'

'You do it too.'

'No.' His eyes shone. 'But I will then, because I won't be able to believe it can be true that you're there . . . '

'And then?'

'Then we'll be happy,' he said. 'Really, really happy.'

'I like this story.'

'It's a good one, isn't it?'

'Very good.'

'Do you believe it, Eleni?'

'Yes,' she said, touching her hand to his face, 'I believe everything you tell me.'

He swam home that night, like he'd been swimming home all week, because dinner was almost upon them, Yorgos would be too, very soon, and it felt safer than him going by the road.

Eleni saw him off at the cove. Wrapped in her robe, she ignored the disappearing sun, ignored Venus, already shining in the pale sky, and focused only on him.

They kissed again, then again. *I love you, in fact.* She knew that one of them needed to pull away, but she couldn't make it be her, so in the end it was him – she felt the tension enter his muscles as he moved – and then he was gone.

'I'll see you soon,' he said, from the water's edge.

It felt kinder than goodbye.

In many, many ways, she was glad that they still had their evening together ahead of them. She wasn't sure how she could have borne not being with him, whilst she still could. Nothing was over, she told herself, it wasn't . . .

Yet, as she returned to the terrace and watched him swim from her, disappearing around the bay, she felt such an awful pressure in her throat. She closed her eyes, breathing deep, trying to push the feeling away. Dimly, she registered the thrum of her *papou*'s motor coming into the drive, a trickle of relief that they really had got away with it, but mainly she thought about the hours that had passed, then the night ahead, and how it would, actually, have been better after all not to have had to spend it with his family.

They'd parted now.

Looked one another in the eye and turned away.

It was *done*. She knew just how painful it was.

It hurt, horribly, thinking of having to go through it again.

The dinner Henri and Brigit laid on for them all was, nonetheless, lovely. They'd gone to a great deal of effort, illuminating Nikos's terrace with lanterns, dressing the table with bowls of bougainvillea and flickering candelabras. The meal itself, of melting, slow-baked lamb, was delicious; Christina was clearly worth every last drachma Krista had obliged Henri to pay her, week after week.

'*How* much?' said Maria to Krista, when she related the story.

'*That* much, I'm afraid,' said Henri, walking around the table, topping up everyone's wine.

'But Nikos will have paid her,' said Maria, smiling bemusedly. 'You do know Christina was meant to have been his mother-in-law.'

'Really?' said Henri.

'Nikos was engaged?' said Brigit. 'To whom?'

'A girl not much older than my Petra,' said Yorgos, shortly.

'What happened?' asked Brigit.

'She disappeared to Athens,' said Maria. 'A long time ago now.'

'And Nikos still looks after her mother?'

'I think it's really Christina that looks after him.'

'She feels guilty?'

'I've always thought so.' Maria eased her knife through her lamb. 'She's a very private woman, though. I don't know anyone who knows her well enough to ask.'

'How interesting,' said Brigit.

It was interesting.

On any other night, Eleni might have joined in the conversation, asked Maria to tell her more.

But Otto was across the table from her, in an evening suit.

Every time Eleni looked at him, bathed in the candles' glow, she felt that choking pressure in her throat grow. He'd hold her gaze in his, like he knew what she was feeling, and would fix it for her if he could, but that didn't make it better, because he couldn't fix it; no one could.

After dessert was cleared, at Brigit's request, Marianne fetched her cello to play. She sat on the stool Henri brought out for her, her back to the villa's open doors, facing the night; the black, inky sea.

'Elgar,' she told them, before she raised her bow and began.

She played as exquisitely as before. Eleni, sitting on the terrace wall, watched her, spellbound by the music, her face; how she seemed to have disappeared.

Otto sat beside her, his arm touching hers.

At some point, they must have started holding hands, because Eleni realized they were doing it.

No one noticed.

No one was looking at them.

Everyone's eyes were on Marianne.

Brigit had tears flowing down her cheeks by the time she finished.

Eleni felt closer than ever to weeping herself.

'Are you all right?' Otto asked her, quietly, so that only she could hear.

'No.' She looked at him sideways. 'Are you?'

'No,' he said, with a crooked smile.

She smiled as well.

They were surrounded by people.

What else could they do?

She wanted to leave. She'd become desperate by now to get it over with, since there was no other way but through it. Her desperation grew through the coffees Henri offered everyone, then the brandies.

It still broke her heart though, going.

Determinedly, she held herself together, thanking Brigit and Henri for having her, and wishing them a safe journey home. She kissed Marianne, told her that she really couldn't wait to see her perform in the Carnegie, and kissed Krista as well.

'Chin up,' Krista whispered, squeezing her, 'he's not that special.'

'He is though,' said Eleni.

He was.

She turned to him, and, with everyone else saying their own farewells, offered him her hand, and – feeling the steady warmth of his grasp, knowing that it really was now for the last time – reached up, brushing his cheek with a kiss too.

He held onto her, placing his other hand in the small of her back, not letting her go.

The moment lasted no more than a second.

It was the sweetest, and saddest, second of her summer.

He still didn't say goodbye.

Neither of them said a word.

But, realizing that it was her turn to be the one to pull away, she tightened her fingers on his, then stepped back, towards the others, and didn't look at him again.

She simply couldn't.

She didn't cry either. Not that night.

Not even when she was up in her room, smelling his soap on her sheets.

He's still near. She repeated it over and over. *Just down the road.*

She pictured him there, in a room like her own, picturing her here, in hers.

So this is where you've been all these nights.

Soothed by the thought, she closed her heavy eyes and, utterly spent from the emotion of the day, the week, slept.

She slept so deeply.

When she woke the next morning, to a familiar cramp in her stomach (her curse; it was something), it was already after nine. She rolled onto her side, saw how bright the sunlight coming under her closed door was, and knew he wasn't near anymore.

His plane, which had departed at eight, had long since left.

She'd slept through the moment, and now he was on his way back to Berlin.

Back to his world.

Back to Lotte.

Without her.

She cried about that.

She cried about that for quite a long time.

Chapter Thirteen

She didn't return home herself until the third week in September, a few days before her nineteenth birthday. She'd been excited, back in May, when she'd sat with Timothy, confirming her boat and rail reservations; euphoric that, free of school at last, she was to gain nearly an entire month at the end of her summer.

She regretted that now.

Who had she even been, back then?

She couldn't think.

But those final weeks without him on the island – quiet, hollow, full of lonely bus rides, even lonelier swims, and pretence to everyone but Dimitri that she was fine, *fine* – weren't ones she'd want to repeat.

But nor were they infinite, either.

They did end, in so many last meals – at the villa, in Halepa, up in the mountains – and hugs, and cheek pinches, and a trip to Little Vassili's training ground, where Eleni summoned her very best of best efforts at a smile, told him to not have any accidents with his shiny new gun, and hugged him too.

Then, it was the morning of her departure to Athens, and there were just her final bits of packing to finish; her shorts and swimming costume, which she'd bought with such heady anticipation, to fold away. Tips stood on her bedroom floor, watching her, eyes like saucers in his stripy face, seeming to sense something not entirely ideal was afoot. Picking him up, Eleni kissed his furry head, then took him downstairs to the kitchen, where she made Yorgos promise again that he'd look after him, which he did. He then presented her with the inevitable box of fruits and vegetables she was to take home with her to Portsmouth.

'You are to eat them all,' he said, wagging his finger, white brow knitted, cross, as ever, that she was going. 'If they bruise, you make soup. If they get too ripe . . . '

'I make jam,' she finished. 'I know, *Papou*.' She hefted the box into her arms. 'You don't have to worry about me.'

His frown deepened, worrying regardless, and not only about her diet, she knew. For all she'd tried to keep up her charade these past weeks, she'd caught him looking at her, often, with the same perplexed concern he was wearing now. *No swim today?* he'd kept asking. Or, *Why so quiet?*

She hated that she'd made him anxious.

She wanted to say that to him, but simply didn't know where to start.

They'd run out of time, anyway.

Within the hour, they were in the motor, haring back along the coast towards her ship. She'd changed into the travelling clothes she hadn't worn since June. They felt scratchy and thick; her shoes were already giving her blisters. She thought bleakly of the long, rainy winter waiting for her in England, her prevailing uncertainty about what she was even going to do with herself through it, and, too late, realized what an idiot she'd been, wishing away these last weeks on the island.

'I'll miss you, *Papou*,' she said, on the quayside, her trunk at her feet, the box of food propped atop of it. The ferry was ready to go, chugging in the dark, crystal sea, swallowing the islanders and visiting Athenians streaming onto it, choking the morning sunshine with its smoke. 'Very, very much.'

He huffed a sigh, tipped his head gruffly in assent, and opened his arms.

She wrapped her own around him: the longest and tightest hug of all.

'I'm sorry,' she found herself saying.

'No, no,' he said, 'you have nothing to be sorry for.'

And maybe he'd guessed some of it after all, or maybe he hadn't, but the ship's bell rang, so she couldn't ask, but had to go, struggling up the cargo bay's gangplank with her luggage until Yorgos barked furiously at one of the porters, who came down to help her.

It was a very long journey to Athens.

The ship steamed past other islands, their arid bulks speckled with tiny white towns, and, in the stultifying silence, Eleni almost wished Helen Finch was with her after all. It would have been nice to have had some company to take her mind off everything.

As it was, she sat out on deck, the searing sun moving higher, then lower, and thought of Yorgos returning to the silent villa without her; feeding Tips; preparing his own dinner. Then, of the summer, everything that had happened, and, always, always, of Otto.

You make me feel not alone.

It took every ounce of self-control she possessed not to weep.

She wasn't sure how she was going to last the entire way back to England. All those trains on her own. Facing up to the blackshirts at the Italian border . . .

But then, at Piraeus: a surprise.

The ship's gangplank dropped, scraping onto the busy dockside, and, cutting through the shouts of the quay hands, the ship's churning engines, she heard a familiar, clipped voice.

'Eleni. *Eleni.* Down here.'

Her eyes moved, then widened, settling on her father, pristine in his naval uniform, waiting, ramrod straight, at the front of the jostling melee on the quay.

It was such a shock to see him, she almost thought she might be hallucinating.

'I was worried about you here on your own,' he yelled, by way of greeting. 'All this business with Metaxas.'

'I thought you were meant to be touring the Libyan Sea,' she yelled back.

'It's quite close by, Eleni.'

'Yes, I know that . . . '

'I called in a favour, took leave.' Ignoring the port clerk attempting to block his way, he mounted the gangplank and – ignoring the flood of disembarking passengers pouring past him too – strode towards her. 'What's this? More vegetables?' He took her box. 'Christ, it's heavy.' He frowned down at her, brow denting beneath the white brim of his cap. 'You look well.'

'You do too. Nice and tanned.'

'I haven't been on holiday, Eleni.'

'No, of course not.' She really couldn't believe he was there. 'Are you coming home with me now?'

'What else would I be doing?'

It was too much.

He was coming with her.

She wasn't going to have to get through the journey alone after all.

'Thank you,' she said, and still struggling to absorb that he'd done this for her, she threw her arms around him.

'Now what's all this?' His voice softened. 'Come now.' A quick pat. 'Oh my God, Eleni, are you crying?'

It didn't all come pouring out of her, on their journey home. She didn't sob and take the kerchief Timothy handed her and say how she almost wished she'd never met Otto, because then she wouldn't be so sad now.

They really didn't have that kind of relationship.

Quickly, she pulled herself together, and before their train had even made it out of Greece, began to wish she was on her own again, because it was honestly a lot more comfortable sitting in silence by herself, than with her father beside her, staring stiffly through the window at the parched Greek countryside.

Was he thinking about her mama, she wondered.

Remembering the journey the two of them had made?

Again, she didn't ask.

But her gratitude to him returned at the Italian border, where he was really quite excellent with the blackshirt who took their papers, fixing him with a stare that was pure British Naval authority, and dared him to do anything but quickly stamp them through.

'I wish I had your uniform,' said Eleni.

'You'd look ridiculous in it,' Timothy replied.

And, against the odds, she laughed.

It was raining when, grubby and tired, they reached Portsmouth two days later, and caught a taxicab home to Gosport. Their house, left empty all summer, was cold, echoey from lack of habitation, and scented with damp.

None of this Eleni minded though, because on the doormat was a huge mound of post.

She crouched, gathering it to her whilst Timothy went upstairs to wash and change, and, nodding absently at his request that she put the kettle on, carried on into the chilly kitchen, where she flicked the light, forgot the kettle, and stood at the Formica bench, eagerly sorting through the scores of envelopes that had come.

Most of them were for Timothy, but there were five for her.

The first contained her high-school certificate scores; she did, obviously, look at them, and was happy, but not nearly as elated as she was when she uncovered the four (*four*) letters that had arrived from Germany.

Three were from him.

Smiling, breathless, fingers trembling with impatience, she sat at the table, ripping them open in turn, racing through his words, *Dear Eleni,* then going over them again, more slowly, savouring his every sentence, hearing his low voice in her mind. He told her how much he'd hated leaving her in Crete, how sorely he wished he was still there. *It's a kind of torture, knowing you are, thinking of what you're doing, What we could be doing. I want to be back in your room with you. Or swimming with urchins. Or even carrying your oranges out to that bin.* 'Yes,' she said, under her breath, 'I want that too.' His second letter, he'd written on the train to Munich (she was pleased to read that; it was a relief, it really was, knowing he'd now left the city Lotte was in), and, in his third, said that his tutor had liked her reading nook, but his friends were annoyed; none of them had met any sirens in Switzerland, nor mermaids in Italy, nor Greek girls in Austria, who spoke English like they were on the BBC, and could finish a peach in three bites.

Are you home yet? he asked. *Write soon, please, talk to me like you're with me, then I can fool myself that you are.*

She did it there and then, not even stopping to remove her coat, just grabbing a pad from the dresser, sitting back at the table, filling him in on everything that had passed since they'd parted, down to her delight, just now, finding his letters.

It was like you knew exactly what I needed, she wrote, before signing off.

'Eleni,' said Timothy, startling her by reappearing, waving at the frigid kettle. 'Are you not thirsty?'

She actually was.

Once the tea was made, and Timothy was distracted, rifling through his own post, she opened her fourth letter from Germany, which turned out to be from Marianne, who'd got her address from Otto – *I hope you don't mind, I wanted to say how nice it was to have met you* – and was full of her news from Berlin, where she'd moved into her aunt's flat, which she said wasn't too bad, although they definitely needed to get rid of some of their furniture. *I'm sleeping in the living room, which is strange, but I'm getting used to it. And, much better, my aunt had her baby whilst we were all away. A little girl called Esther, who is quite perfect.* She'd sent a picture of the two of them, perched in an armchair in front of a packed bookshelf. Marianne was smiling into the lens, holding Esther, wrapped in a swaddle.

She certainly is scrumptious, Eleni wrote back. *Look at all her little creases.*

She loves it when Papa and I play her music, said Marianne. *I miss Dimitri's. I wish I could find a copy of 'Cheek to Cheek'.*

Here, Eleni replied, sending her one, *from me to you.*

They stayed in touch from then on.

Eleni stayed in touch with Otto too. They wrote constantly, all through that autumn, winter and spring, sending each letter by return, until she amassed a box full of them, and they became like their conversations on the bus; not as good, naturally, but all they had. She came to know his friends' names, could picture their digs, just off Munich's central square, Marienplatz; the café and bars they all went to, but didn't drink or eat much at, because the shortages were getting worse. *We're not meant to talk about that. It's unpatriotic. Let's hope no one reads my letter.*

Would that happen? she asked, appalled.

You never know what might happen here, he said.

He talked of the heavy snow they had in December, she told him of the heavy rain in England, her quiet Christmas with

Timothy, then Boxing Day at her grandparents in Sutton (*Dad came for once, so we at least left early*), and he said that he'd been home too for the holiday. He didn't mention having seen Lotte, so Eleni elected to believe he hadn't, and was much more concerned anyway with his news of Brigit, who'd come down with another bout of pneumonia that their doctor (Nikos's acquaintance, whom they had no choice but to trust) feared might be her last.

But, thankfully, it wasn't.

I spoke to her on the telephone today, Otto wrote, in spring. *Her voice was stronger. She wasn't wheezing as much. Papa says she's managing to eat more again.*

And how's Krista? Eleni asked.

Fine, he said. *No worse.*

Still taking stupid risks, said Marianne. *It's like she wants to get into trouble. How's your secretarial course coming along?*

Very dull, Eleni told her. *But I need to qualify in something if I ever want to leave Gosport.*

It will be worth it when you get to London, Otto wrote. *Has your father come to terms with you moving yet?*

He finally has, she said. *He's bought me a pot plant for my new room. And I passed my German course too.*

Wunderbar, he said.

It was in June of 1937, after she'd moved, with her plant, to Helen's house in Clapham, and had started as a trainee at Lemos & Pateras Ltd, that he wrote asking her to meet him, not in Chania, but, much closer, Paris. His national service was to commence that August; he wanted, *needed*, to see her before that happened.

She really needed to see him too.

That was the real reason she didn't travel to Crete that summer.

She'd already been resigning herself to not going, even before he wrote, sure that she'd never get so much time off work, not when she'd only been there such a short while. She'd been putting off raising the request with her manager, worried that his inevitable *no* would be awkward for them both, and now decided there was no point in putting them through it. Instead, she asked him for just five days of leave and – wretched at the thought of Yorgos's disappointment, genuinely bereft not to be going to Crete for the first summer in her life – she wrote to Yorgos, apologising, explaining how busy the typing pool was. (*I understand, Eleni-mou,* he replied, making her feel even worse, *there's always next year.*) Then, using the money she'd saved, knowing she could hardly ask Timothy to sub her for such a venture, she caught a ferry across the channel, the train to the Gare du Nord, and from there a taxi to the Hôtel d'Angleterre, where Otto had reserved a room under the name of Fitzhattily.

She ate oysters and drank a glass of champagne in the hotel garden whilst she waited for him to arrive. One of the girls at Lemos's had told her that was what one should do in Paris, and she needed something to distract her from her nerves. She was so very nervous. Her hand jittered every time she brought her glass to her lips. It had been such a long time . . .

But then he was there, appearing at the garden doors, coming to crouch before her on the patio, smiling (his smile. *His smile*), and the months they'd been apart, they disappeared, just like that. Her nerves did too. She smiled as well, cried a bit (the champagne), and touched her hand to his face, running her thumb over his cheekbone. He raised his own hand, turning hers, pressing his lips to her palm.

'It's nice to see you, Mrs Fitzhattily.'

'It's very nice to see you too,' she said, and then she was laughing, pulling him to her, kissing him, like she'd been longing to kiss him every day, every single day, since she last had.

Her grandma in Sutton found out about it.

A church friend of hers, *Meredith,* whom Eleni had apparently met *several times* (she had no recollection of it), was staying at the hotel too, with her husband, *Geoff*, on their golden wedding anniversary, and was on her way out to the garden for a nice cup of tea when she quite lost her thirst, spotting Eleni and Otto *in flagrante* on the patio: one of those ridiculous coincidences that you'd never think possible, until it happened to you.

Strumpet, Eleni's grandma called her, in the letter she sent, which was waiting for Eleni on her return to Clapham. *Absolute strumpet. I'm so embarrassed. Meredith was appalled, naturally. Geoff didn't know where to look. I can't think what to say, I honestly cannot. You're lucky I don't tell Timothy. What would it do to him if he knew? I warned him, I did warn him . . .*

What do you mean, you warned him? Eleni replied.

She heard nothing back.

That was the last contact the two of them had.

And it wasn't fair. She wasn't a strumpet in Paris.

She *wanted* to be one. She really wanted that.

'I wanted you to be one too,' said Otto, holding her hair back as she vomited into their elegant Parisian latrine, just a couple of hours after they'd been reunited, and she'd eaten what had transpired to be some very bad oysters. 'Do you want water?'

'No, I think I'm going to be sick again . . . '

She was really poorly.

For half the week.

She recovered just in time to get her damnable curse.

It started to rain as well, became chilly and grey.

'A disaster, basically,' he said.

But it wasn't. They still had a wonderful time. Even while she was sick, they lay on the bed together, talking and talking. As soon as she felt able to leave the room, they went out, ignoring the rain, walking for miles, losing themselves in the warrens of streets, strolling along the Champs-Élysées, around the Louvre, on to the Îl de la Cité, where they stared up at Notre-Dame, and kissed beneath his umbrella. By night, they went to smoky jazz bars, and danced and drank more champagne. By day, they sipped coffee in the Place de la Concorde, ate oozing, buttery omelettes in the hills of Montmartre, and, when the sun finally reappeared, whiled away hours in the Luxembourg Gardens, collapsed on the grass, her head in his lap, talking more, until it felt unthinkable that they should ever stop, and all she wanted to do was take him back with her to England, keep him close, and as far from Germany, with its new concentration camp in Buchenwald, and the National Service he was so dreading, as she possibly could.

The next morning, at the Gare du Nord, it went against her every instinct to say goodbye.

She was sure it was the same for him.

'Of course it's the same for me,' he said, kissing her on the platform, steam billowing around them, clouding beneath the station's great roof. 'I hate you for eating those oysters . . .'

'I hate me as well,' she said, and realized she was crying. 'I don't want to go.'

And yet, she went.

So did he.

For another year, they kept writing.

His letters, from his camp in West Germany, became shorter, containing no fewer questions about her life, her work, her father, but less and less of himself. When she asked him to tell her about the camp, what he did each day, whether he at least had some of his friends from Munich there, he ignored that she had, and talked instead of his hopes to get back to Berlin on leave.

He went in March, and – with the newsboys shouting of the Nazi annexation of Austria – spent a weekend with his family, which he was also less than forthcoming about, telling Eleni only that Brigit was *not so good*, nor Henri either. He'd run into trouble at work with one of the partners: a badge-wearing member of the party who'd discovered Henri had been helping Jewish families with their visa applications. *It's what he was doing in Crete*, Otto said. *I wish I'd known. He told me he had to work for the money, but his partner's furious because he's largely been doing it for free. So now this man, Friedrich, is questioning his loyalty to the Reich.*

Has Friedrich done anything about it? Eleni asked. *Told anyone?*

Otto didn't reply.

She heard only from Marianne, who'd seen him briefly and said that he'd looked older, had been quieter, badly worried, she'd guessed, for Brigit and Henri, and doubtless miserable at his camp. *He wasn't in his uniform. I think he's ashamed of it. His hair was short.* Eleni couldn't picture that. She didn't want to. *Lotte knows everything now*, Marianne went on, sending her cold. *Her father's asked Henri to join the party. I'm leaving Germany, Eleni. My parents want me to, and I can't stand to go, but I want to, too. I've stopped believing it's going to get better. There was a government exhibition in Munich last November, about how awful we Jewish are. People travelled from all over to go to it. Imagine that. An entire exhibition just to make people despise who we are. Last week, my aunt's windows were smashed, and no one did anything to help. The police didn't care. My father has an old colleague from the university who moved to New York, back at the very start. He hasn't much money, but Henri and Brigit have helped to pay for my passage, and he's managed to get the papers for my visa through. Papa and Brigit say I'll like him, that I'm not to be scared, but I am, Eleni. I feel very alone. Lotte's happy I'm going at least. She came secretly to say goodbye yesterday. I hadn't seen her in such a long time. She looked like she was going to cry when she saw Mama. I think she's ashamed too . . .*

So she should be, Eleni wrote, then scribbled out, because who was she, really, to comment, and anyway, how would it help Marianne?

Instead, she sent her a wire, which she hoped would catch her before she left, telling her to forward on her address in America, write as soon as she got there, *you are not alone STOP,* then, out of desperation, wired Otto too, asking him to please, please just get in touch.

He did.

He apologised for taking so long to do it, *I've tried to write, many times, but it's hard to find the right words here,* and told her he was fine, which he patently wasn't.

Can you get away? she asked him. *Meet me in Paris again, even if it's just for a weekend?*

I want to, he said, *I can't tell you how I want to. But I don't know if I could bring myself to leave you . . .*

Then don't, she said. *Come back with me here.*

It's not possible, he said.

Of course it's possible, she countered.

Are you really being serious? he asked.

Yes, she replied, *Yes, yes, yes.*

All right, he said, *all right,* and her dread, for the two of them at least, evaporated.

It was all going to be fine. *Fine.*

They arranged to meet at the end of June. She told her *papou* that she'd do her very best to get to him in August – fantasising that Otto might now go with her, once they were married, as they were surely going to be – and took a long weekend from the typing pool at Lloyds, which she'd moved to in March, and, once again draining her savings, travelled over the channel to France.

It was a beautiful Friday morning.

She stood out on the blustery deck for the short crossing,

her dress whipping around her, holding her hat to her head, fizzing with anticipation as she watched the French coastline come into view.

He'd told her he'd meet her train at the Gare du Nord.

She waited for him for almost four hours at the end of her platform, but then it started to get dark, and she decided they must have missed each other, so caught a taxicab to the hotel to find him there.

She smiled as she went into the lobby.

She was so excited.

But there was a wire waiting for her at reception.

```
I am sorry STOP I cannot leave STOP Not even
for you STOP
```

The receptionist watched her read it.

She felt the blunt intrusion of his interest as, still somehow smiling, her eyes moved over those words, and a pain, impossible to comprehend, took hold in her chest.

He wasn't coming.

He wasn't coming . . .

Not even for you.

'*Mademoiselle*,' the receptionist said. Distantly, she became aware of his voice. 'Is all well?'

'No,' she said.

Or did she?

She could never afterwards be sure that she answered him at all.

Or whether she managed to contain her tears until she was safely back on the street, in the privacy of the night.

All she was certain of was that, unable to spend another second in that hotel, she returned to the Gare du Nord, where she spent an endlessly cold and lonely night, huddled on a bench, clutching his wire, fighting to make sense of what was happening, failing, utterly.

She wired him of course, as soon as she got back to England.

How could you have done this STOP

He didn't wire back.

For two desolate days, and two more sleepless nights, she waited for him to, and then a letter came: brief, detached, offering no explanations, only saying that he hoped she could forgive him, and was signed simply, *Otto*.

It felt so cold. So final.

She wept, naturally.

She reread every letter he'd ever sent her, and wept a great deal.

Then, growing angrier – discovering that anger was a deal less painful than grief – she dashed off a final letter of her own.

I cannot understand you letting me travel to Paris, knowing you had no intention of coming. I cannot understand any of this. I thought I knew you, and now I feel as though I never knew you at all. You've treated me like I'm worthless. You've made everything we had worthless. Did it really mean so little to you? She cried more, convinced, in her exhaustion and fury, that it must have. *Did I, Otto?* Jerkily, she wiped away her tears. *Never write to me again,* she finished, rashly. *Never.*

He didn't.

And she didn't go to Crete that August, because she was too scared of how much it would hurt to be there, surrounded by things that would remind her of him.

It was a mistake. She regretted it sorely.

She was miserable in Clapham, and cold to boot.

When, in September, Chamberlain returned from his meetings in Munich, waving his and Hitler's treaty, proclaiming 'peace for our time', she consoled herself; *there's always next year.*

Except . . .

'Chamberlain's a fool,' said Timothy, at the twenty-first birthday lunch she returned to Portsmouth for. He bought her a new pen. *From Dad*. 'You watch, it's going to get a lot worse.'

It did, of course.

That November, the newspaper headlines blazed with the horrors of *Kristallnacht*, the Night of Broken Glass. All over Germany, Jewish businesses had been ransacked, synagogues burned, and tens of thousands arrested.

Marianne's father was among them.

I can't stand it, Marianne wrote from her new home in Brooklyn, *I can't, Eleni. He's my papa. He wouldn't hurt a fly. And I haven't heard anything from Krista in months. Has she by any chance been in touch with you?*

She hadn't.

Eleni heard nothing at all from Germany.

Not until May 1939, when, after the German invasion of Czechoslovakia, Lotte wrote to her, in German, which Eleni could only guess Otto had told her she now spoke, at her address in Clapham, which Eleni could only assume Otto had given to her.

Marianne's uncle has been taken, I truly don't know where, but her mama and aunt are very afraid. They won't leave Germany, not without him and Ernst, and I don't think they could go now anyway – there are just too many people trying to get visas, the immigration requirements have become so tight. But, since Kristallnacht, your government has waived them for Jewish children. Have you heard of the Kindertransport? I have spoken to the Reich Representation of Jews and can secure Esther a place, but I need you to take her when she arrives in England. Her mama's terrified she'll end up in an institution. Please, will you help?

Eleni replied to Lotte by return of mail – not asking about Otto, nor permitting herself to dwell on the choice she could only assume he'd made – simply telling Lotte that, of course, she'd do whatever was needed for Esther.

Please tell her mama that she will be loved and kept very safe.

Thank you, Lotte replied. *The Reich Representation of Jews will be in touch. If you're still in contact with Marianne, please can you tell her that I did this?*

Eleni did.

And broke the news to Marianne, as gently as one could do such a thing, that her uncle had been arrested.

When will this end? asked Marianne in reply.

I wish I knew, said Eleni.

In September, Esther arrived, little Esther, carrying her teddy bear, dragging her battered suitcase, which Eleni scooped up for her, scooped her up too ('*Schön, dich kennenzulernen*'; 'it's nice to get to know you'), taking her back to Clapham, where Helen took over, feeding her cocoa and sandwiches, helping her unpack, knowing – after all her decades teaching, caring for her copious nieces and nephews – just how to reassure a small, scared child. She taught her English remarkably quickly. Eleni played games with her at her window, spinning stories about the lives of passers-by, and brought her treats home from work.

In October 1939, Timothy shipped out to the Atlantic (*I miss you, dear. In my way.*); that November, Eleni left Lloyds and started at the War Office. Throughout the next year, she went on a number of dates with a series of disappointing men, then, in November 1940, got a cold, ate lunch on a frigid park bench, and was interrupted by Hector Herbert, who asked her for change for a shilling.

In December she wrote to Marianne, explaining that she had to disappear for a while, but that she'd be thinking of her, always, and of Esther, who was very much loved, and very much safe, *I hope you understand my going* (*This war needs to be won,* Marianne replied, *of course I understand*), then was sent to a *most secret location* (a stately home, in Surrey) where she continued to keep her pot plant alive, learnt to fix a radio transmitter, proved she could type on a Greek typewriter, crawled over a great deal of mud on her stomach, discovered she was quite a good shot, at a close enough range, and, at the beginning of February, days after Metaxas died suddenly in Athens ('Cancer,' said Hector, 'I'm afraid not very sudden at all'), did indeed pass her training.

She wrote to Timothy then too, letting him know she was shipping out, although not where, *I'll be in touch again as soon as I can, please take care of yourself,* and Hector briefed her more thoroughly on the situation in Greece, telling her of the existence of *most secret sources* (radio intercepts), decoded at another *most secret location* (Bletchley), which had made it clear that Germany, massing a vast invasion force in Romania, was planning to attack the mainland imminently. The Greek Army had, he said, mounted a truly heroic defence against the Italians, in the most horrendous winter conditions (*oh, Little Vassili*), but were now exhausted, lower on men and materials than they'd been at the start of the campaign, and stood no chance, however brave, against the might of a ground attack by Germany's panzer divisions. Britain was sending troops over from Africa to help, but couldn't spare many, not now that things had kicked off against Germany there as well.

'I fear the mainland will fall,' said Hector, 'but Crete's an island; the panzers can't roll across the sea, and there truly is no appetite to let it go. Now—' He gave her a sharp look that she'd come to learn meant business, and went on, speaking of the Cretan veterans, the *kapitans*, who'd fought so success-fully for the island's independence from the Turks, and whose cooperation would, it had been decided, be invaluable now, defending it from another occupation. Then, of a man called

John Pendlebury – up until 1935, the curator of Knossos (her heart kicked on the word), now an SOE operative based in Heraklion, ostensibly as the British vice-consul, but really to recruit these *kapitans*. Eleni was to base herself in Heraklion with him – no, no arguments; it was cleaner, less problematic than Chania, and Pendlebury was expecting her at the consulate.

'To do what, precisely?'

'Typing.'

'Wonderful.'

Hector laughed.

She didn't.

'Don't sulk,' he instructed, 'you'll like Pendlebury. And you won't only be typing.'

'No?'

'No. Pendlebury will tell you the rest. No more questions, off you go. They'll be ready for you in Camouflage on Monday.'

Camouflage were ready, with strict instructions that she was to keep as low a profile as possible when she arrived in Crete, no big reunions, no reunions at all ('Wonderful,' she said, again), just a seamless slip into the island's fabric. Her value lay in her ability to present herself as a local, so anyone she met, she was to tell them that she'd come to Heraklion from Chania to work. *The simpler the story, the less questions people will ask.* She was given new clothes ('I'm not wearing these,' she said), manuals on blending in (*brush your teeth only as often as your neighbours*), then a forged set of identity documents under the name of Eleni Florakis, and a bottle of ink-black hair dye, which was apparently part of the blending in, and would also serve to protect her if the worst happened, and she found herself trapped behind enemy lines.

'This is ridiculous,' she told Hector, 'there are other blonde Cretans.'

'I doubt ones that look like you,' he said. 'No standing out. And no finding yourself trapped behind enemy lines either.'

'No one knows me in Heraklion.'

'I don't care.'

He wasn't remotely interested in a debate about that in the end, simply adamant that, should the situation unravel, she'd evacuate Crete for Africa at his first order, at which point they could decide where she'd be most useful next.

'This is important, Eleni. I need your word that you'll cooperate.'

'Fine.'

'Look me in the eye and say it.'

She did that too.

Then she shook his hand, bade him goodbye, took his luck, her forged papers, bottle of hair dye (that she had no intention of using; any fool would spot it as fake a mile off), and her cyanide pills (she had no intention of using those either), went back to Clapham to pack, then spent the weekend in Cheshire with Esther and Helen, where Helen made her apple crumble, placed her plant by the kitchen window, and promised to keep it well watered. On Sunday, Eleni used Helen's camera to snap a photograph of Esther and her new puppy for them to send to Marianne, then, on Monday, kissed Esther goodbye, kissed her puppy, kissed Helen too, and caught a train to Euston, where a car was waiting to take her to an RAF airstrip, and the first of her plane hops over to Crete.

It was 24 March.

A fortnight later, the Nazis moved their massed air and land divisions out of Romania, attacking Yugoslavia and Greece, bombing the harbour of Piraeus.

Less than three weeks after that, the mainland fell, as Hector had prophesied it would, and the Allied troops who'd fought to defend it evacuated to Crete, placed under the command of Major-General Freyberg, the New Zealander leader of Creforce who'd been tasked with holding the island.

The intercepts Hector had mentioned continued to be

decrypted, making it clear that the attack on Crete would be coming very quickly indeed, commencing with raids, culminating in a mid-May invasion, mounted by troops landing by parachute and on glider planes.

Eleni wasn't briefed on that though.

By the time those intercepts were being received, she'd become just what she was meant to be: a young Greek woman, working as a secretary for the British vice-consul, truly doing quite a lot of typing, but also helping Pendlebury – a charismatic caricature of a man, with a glass eye and a swordstick, whom she did like, very much – drawing up lists of local allies, and a few potential enemies, from among the civilian population.

That involved a fair amount of typing in itself, but also shadowing Pendlebury on meetings, *listening*, *watching*, whilst he talked in fluent, if accented, Greek, confirming the loyalty of copious politicians, policemen, journalists. Frustratingly, she spoke to very few such people herself, and met even fewer of the *kapitans*. She wanted to. She ached to feel like she was actually doing something that mattered. Something that would justify her presence on the island; all that crawling over mud on her stomach. But mostly, when Pendlebury went to see the *kapitans* in their villages, he left her behind, typing, and his glass eye on his desk to let them all know in the office that he'd be back soon.

Once though, in the third week of April, he did take her into the mountain's foothills, to a tiny hamlet, where he was greeted with an enthusiastic reception, they were both fed goat and *krassi,* and Eleni, at his request, got to do quite a bit of talking, with the village women, all of whom, she discovered, were as intent on fighting the Germans as the men were.

'Magnificent,' said Pendlebury. 'Excellent work.'

'Was it?' she said dubiously. 'I don't see that I did very much.'

'You got them to open up.'

'So?'

He smiled. 'So?'

'What difference does it make? They're ready to fight, regardless . . . '

'But now you can help them,' he said.

And she did secure that village some additional guns from British supplies. Not half as many as Pendlebury authorized her to request – that was par for the course in Crete, where cooperation between the SOE and the Army still lay somewhere south of optimal – but more than they'd had before.

It felt like the proverbial drop in the ocean though, against the scale of how much was yet needed to prepare. So many on the island remained weaponless, thanks to the confiscation of arms back in 1938, after the revolt against Metaxas. Almost all of Crete's trained soldiers were still trapped on the mainland, Little Vassili included. (What had become of him? Eleni, who, true to orders, had contacted no one in the family, torturously had no way of finding out.) And, even though British forces had been based in Crete since November, they'd done astonishingly little to ready a defence: the island's roads were as narrow as they'd always been, impassable to military vehicles; the scant communication infrastructure was still very weak. It troubled Eleni. For all Hector's assurances that no one wanted to see Crete fall, the British army really was doing an excellent impression of not much minding either way. So, whilst she *wanted* to think that the fact of her having passed on that crate of weapons would have some bearing on the island's safe future, frankly, in the grand scheme of things, it felt terrifyingly insignificant.

Pendlebury, she knew, was also chomping at the bit to do more. He'd vented to her too often of his frustration at their limited resource for her to doubt it. Spoken too vehemently of his anger at the recalcitrance of the British Army to free up their arms to Cretans, or give them an official uniform, and so the protection of the Geneva Convention, should they fall into enemy hands.

It surprised her not at all when, at the end of that April, as the devastating news came that the mainland was lost, and the first evacuating Allied troops arrived on the island – exhausted, hollow-eyed, blackened with blood and dirt – swiftly followed by the Luftwaffe, come to bomb and strafe them all, he abandoned his guise of vice-consul, donned his own cavalry uniform, and declared he'd henceforth be acting in the self-created role of liaison officer between British and Greek military authorities, responsible for unleashing the full potential of the local fighting force in the island's defence.

More privately, in his office, he told Eleni, with his single eye afire, that he had no intention whatsoever of evacuating Crete, should the worst happen, but planned to hide himself in the mountains and run a resistance movement with the *kapitans* from there.

That didn't surprise her either.

'And what will you do?' he asked.

It was an easy question to answer.

Outside the consulate's windows, Heraklion's hot, smoky streets were in chaos, brimming with soldiers, the civilian refugees who'd managed to escape, and airmen who'd been separated from their squadrons, and no longer had planes. With no billets to go to either, many of them slept in heaps on their kitbags, their boots still on. Any minute, the Luftwaffe would return to rain death from the sky, and, in the mayhem, her orders, issued in the calm of a Baker Street office, could not have felt more arbitrary.

Pendlebury wasn't following his anymore.

She saw no reason why she should either.

He didn't argue.

They shook hands, he gave her a gun from his desk drawer as a parting gift, and they wished one another luck.

'Eleni, wait,' he called after her, as she left, 'I've got something else for you.'

He disappeared, and then was back, another gift in hand.

She laughed when she saw it.

He laughed too.

He was that kind of man.

'Better?' he said.

'I don't think it's necessary . . . '

'To be safe though.'

'All right,' she said, taking it. 'To be safe.'

'See you on the other side.'

'See you then,' she said.

And with that, she left, hiding his gifts – one heavy, the other light – in her handbag, running out to take her chances in the treacherous streets, dodging the troops, the jams of chugging army trucks, tense with foreboding, yet also freer than she'd felt in weeks.

M.M: You weren't there, then, for the fall of the mainland.

#17: No, I avoided that privilege.

M.M: I have it on good authority that Joint Planning Staff at Headquarters Middle East were resigned to it happening from the start. I'm told they were drawing up evacuation plans for the troops, even before they shipped them off to fight from Africa . . .

#17: That doesn't surprise me. [Short pause] Have you interviewed many of the men?

M.M: Quite a number.

#17: I've always thought they must have felt . . . resentful . . . to have been selected for such a hopeless task.

M.M: They don't come across as resentful.

#17: No?

M.M: No. They've expressed a deal of sorrow,

actually, about leaving the Greeks on the mainland as they did. Guilt.

#17: There's a lot of that around.

M.M: There is.

#17: [Sighs] I don't think they should feel guilty. It wasn't their fault. They stood no chance. The Greeks understood that. Actually [frowns] didn't the Athenians cheer them off as they went?

M.M: They did. All the way to the ships. [Consults notes] "Come back with good fortune" was the chant. "Return with victory."

#17: And then there was Crete.

M.M: You didn't avoid that privilege.

#17: No, I did not.

M.M: Was that the first time you'd returned, since thirty-six?

#17: It was.

M.M: You and Eleni were alike in that respect, then.

#17: I suppose we were.

M.M: Will you tell me now what it was that happened?

[Long silence]

M.M: What it was you did to her?

[Longer silence]

M.M: When you first answered my advertisement, you said you wanted to [consults notes]

free your conscience, of a wrong you've
carried with you, all these years.

#17: I'm aware.

M.M: Do you still want to do that?

#17: Yes. Yes . . .

M.M: It's only, you seem to be finding it very
hard.

#17: I do, do I?

M.M: Well, this is our third meeting now. You've
told me repeatedly that you're running out
of time, yet we've talked for hours, and
it's been fascinating, it really has, but
every time we come to the point of your
involvement with Eleni during the war, you
digress, take me back to nineteen thirty-
six, or Baker Street, or Paris . . .

#17: [Deep sigh]

M.M: Would you rather we just left it here? Go
home, hold your secret close . . . ?

#17: No. Really, no.

M.M: So, shall we get to it?

[Extremely long silence]

#17: I suppose we must.

M.M: Good.

#17: It is not good. Not at all. [Picks up water
glass] I've enjoyed our conversations,
I must say. I've come to like you . . .

M.M: The feeling is mutual.

#17: It won't be for much longer, I fear. In
fact, I strongly suspect this is where our
short friendship is going to end.

M.M: Why not let me be the judge of that?

#17: Fine. [Drinks] Fine . . .

M.M: Thank you. Now, where shall we start?

#17: With her, I suppose.

M.M: Eleni.

#17: Yes, Eleni.

M.M: She returned to Chania, yes?

#17: A damned fool decision.

M.M: You blame her for it?

#17: No. [Shakes head] No, I've tried to, but I can't. Everyone she loved was there. In her shoes, I'd have gone too. I still wish she hadn't.

M.M: Because that's where you found her.

#17: Exactly. Because that is where I found her.

CRETE, 1941

Chapter Fourteen

Chania, Monday, 19 May 1941

She'd been back in her *papou*'s villa for three weeks already. Three weeks in which thousands more evacuees had arrived from the mainland, staggering from those ships and caiques that had survived the torpedoes, many docking in the harbour at Souda, sitting ducks for the Stuka bombers who dived, trying to sink them there. The Messerschmitts kept coming too, their wings casting ominous shadows on Crete's mountains, bellies making the olive groves shiver as their pilots sprayed bullets at whomever they could trap in their sights. And whilst the British high command had, at last, kicked into gear in terms of readying a defence on the ground – digging trenches, setting up roadblocks, drilling, drilling, drilling – with scant air support from the stretched RAF, it was the Luftwaffe who ruled the skies. Eleni had become almost conditioned to their presence, their menace; the heart-stopping wail of the Stukas' sirens.

Chania, the new British headquarters for Greece, had become a different town to the one she'd grown up with, now overrun with troops and Athenian refugees. With space at a premium, everyone had taken in lodgers: Maria and Spiros had two New Zealander captains staying with them; she and Yorgos had a young British major for their guest – Benedict Latimer ('Ben, please,' he insisted, with his easy smile) – whilst she'd heard tell that the Greek royal family were holed up back in Heraklion, at the Villa Ariadne of all places, exiles once more.

Not everyone was fortunate enough to have a roof over their heads. Far from it. The bulk of the men – many, like Maria and Spiros's captains, from New Zealand, and Australia – resided in tents, hastily erected in those olive groves the Messerschmitts targeted. There were encampments too for the Italian POWs who'd been brought from the mainland: friendly men, for the most part, who seemed only relieved to have the winter battles behind them, and called out to Eleni whenever she passed them by, holding out photographs of their families, waving their letters home, entreating her to take them for posting. *Per favore, signorina.* She didn't – they *were* the enemy, however amiable, and anyway, they'd never get further than the post office – but she did eat the bread they baked. Every islander did. They had to, the Cretan bakers being wholly taken up feeding the Allied soldiers, who, it had been decided, couldn't eat Italian-made bread, lest these POWs, with their dog-eared pictures, tried to poison them.

No one got poisoned.

Day-by-day, meal-by-meal, the troops, so broken when they arrived, started to look less defeated, and – despite the raids, the constant proximity of death, and assuredly imminent invasion coming their way – sprung back to life, swaggering along the streets, whenever they weren't on duty, and larking around on the beaches in their khaki shorts: happy, visibly living for the moment.

Emboldened by their sheer weight of numbers, the unrecognizable faces, everywhere, Eleni had ventured into town often since she'd returned, running errands, disappearing, easily, into the teeming streets. So effortlessly, in fact, that she'd by now dismissed Hector's concerns back in London entirely. When locals spoke to her, they did it immediately in Greek. The troops who invited her to have a drink were the same, pulling out their phrasebooks, calling to her from the bursting *kafeterias* in their blunt, antipodean vowels.

She never accepted their invitations, however comically worded, mindful of all the things she couldn't let herself say. But, in another set of circumstances, she might well have gone to sit with any number of those soldiers, looked at *their* photographs, asked them about the lives they'd left behind. As she observed them all, draining carafes of *krassi*, smoking, their voices raised above wireless sets crackling the world service – or, at Dimitri's, the gramophone playing the Glenn Miller Band – she became increasingly moved by their presence; that they were all of them here, volunteers for the most part – Australia and New Zealand had no conscription – a world away from their homes, come to risk everything to help defend Crete's.

And Crete was going to need them.

Yes, the *kapitans* and their followers would fight when the invasion came; every Cretan Eleni spoke to said they would. But they were still missing their own army. For all the countless strangers who'd flocked to the island, including several divisions of Greek troops, none of the Cretan 5th had managed to escape the mainland before it was cut off. No one seemed to know what had become of them. All over the island, there were missing sons, brothers, husbands, *cousins*. Eleni remained agonisingly ignorant of whether Little Vassili had survived. She couldn't get to the mountains to see Sofia and the others – not with the roads gridlocked with British supply trucks, work parties laying defences – and Yorgos had told her anyway that none of them had heard anything of Little Vassili in months.

Yorgos.

He'd shocked her, when she'd first arrived at the villa from Heraklion, back at the end of April.

She'd shocked him as well.

It had been after dark, by the time she'd reached the house. She'd managed to get a lift in a consulate motor as far as Chania, but had had to catch the bus from there.

Sitting on the bus's sprung seats, that first time, had been every bit as painful as she'd feared it might.

Don't do that thing.

What thing?

Where you make me laugh too much.

That's not a thing.

Hard too, getting off the bus at the stop he'd used to wait for her at, and finding nothing but emptiness, and the lapping sea below.

But her sadness hadn't overwhelmed her. She'd been too full of the adrenalin of the day, and her anticipation at seeing Yorgos, for that to have been possible.

Chin up.

She'd physically raised it, and hefted her suitcase down the moonlit road, passing Nikos's gate – which she'd tried not to look at, looked anyway, and so noticed his diligently blacked-out windows. (He had, she'd since discovered, been in Crete since the start of the Italian offensive, and now had two British captains of his own billeted with him, whom his not-quite-mother-in-law, Christina, still cooked for.) Walking on, she'd reached the tree at the end of her own driveway, with its leaf-strewn patch of ground beneath.

It's very comfortable.

Really?

Not at all.

She'd stared at that too, for a few seconds, then – drawing deep on the night air, making herself feel better with the smells she'd dreamed of – headed down the drive, feeling her aching heart expand as the villa came into view, with its walls and shutters and chipped paintwork that never changed.

Pushing open the always-unlocked front door (oh, that door), she'd let herself into the darkened hallway, set her heavy luggage down, and – quietly, worried that Yorgos might be sleeping – had gone in search of him.

She'd found him on the terrace, not sleeping, but sitting beneath the stars with a very fat Tips on his lap, a brandy at his side, and his eyes fixed in the direction of the smouldering glow over Souda Bay.

'Hello, *Papou*,' she'd said.

And he'd nearly jumped out of his skin.

Tips had yowled, haring off.

'Eleni-mou?' he'd said, like she might have been a ghost.

'It's me,' she'd replied, voice weak to her own ears, seeing the change in him.

He'd aged, so much more than she'd prepared herself for. His hair had grown whiter, thinner; his skin, papery and lined.

I've left it too long, she'd thought. *Hurt him too much.*

Overcome by love, her guilt, she'd rushed to him, throwing her arms around him, feeling him hug her back, enveloping her in his warmth, the scent of his cologne and cigar smoke.

'What are you doing here?' he'd inevitably asked. 'Why have you come?'

She hadn't been honest with him. She'd realized she couldn't do that, and not only because of the Official Secrets Act. It would have been too unfair of her to have burdened him with her secret, dangerous for him, as well as for her. What he didn't know, he could, after all, never be made to pass on.

So, instead, she'd spun him yet another lie (*a terrible way to live, really*), telling him that Timothy had arranged for her to come to Crete, worried about how dangerous London was now, with all the bombs.

'The bombs in London?' Yorgos had demanded, pushing her to arm's-length. 'Has your father had a lobotomy I haven't been informed of?'

'No.'

'Where is he?'

'Somewhere in the Atlantic.'

'Can he get letters?'

He could of course.

Eleni hadn't been about to admit that to Yorgos though.

She'd told him there was no need for him to write to anyone, and entreated him to please calm down.

He had.

Eventually.

In the time since, he'd slowly given up asking her to leave Crete, grudgingly accepting that she really wasn't going to do that, and they'd fallen into their old pattern: breakfasts in the kitchen, dinners on the terrace – sometimes with Ben joining them, if he wasn't at his desk in Creforce HQ, making Eleni laugh with his stories of the personalities there – and Yorgos doctoring in-between, not always at the surgery; a new military hospital had been established nearby, in tents and a disused warehouse, and increasingly he, and Spiros, spent their time there, helping with the casualties from the raids. If they were especially busy, Eleni went along too, not to doctor (obviously), but to help behind the scenes: sterilising instruments, rolling bandages, cleaning.

When she wasn't there, and wasn't running her errands, and there were no Stukas or Messerschmitts in range, she still swam from the cove, relishing the exertion, the invigoration of the clear, cool water every bit as much as she'd used to; finding it more impossible, actually, each time she went out, to believe she could have gone so long without it in her life.

The fishing boat Otto had used to wave to her from had disappeared, she guessed in search of a more protected mooring, but the rocks beneath Nikos's villa were, naturally, still there, and although she didn't especially enjoy the sight of them, or indeed of Nikos's villa – that stone terrace wall she and Otto had sat on, listening to Marianne play – there were, obviously, many, many people contending with a great deal worse.

The weekends, she and Yorgos spent at the villa, or in Halepa with Maria and Spiros (Spiros really had aged so much too; of the three, only Maria looked the same, with her silk blouses and tailored skirts), but, other than them, Eleni saw very few people. Not even Dimitri. She'd passed by his café, unable to resist the temptation, but had kept her distance, making sure he didn't notice her. She hadn't been to see Socrates at the school either.

It felt the most sensible course.

Back in Heraklion, when Pendlebury had confided to her that he didn't intend to leave Crete, should it fall, she'd admitted to him what had long been in her mind too: that, in that eventuality, she had no plans to go anywhere either. Not when she'd only been back five minutes, had achieved so little, but had been trained up to the eyeballs in all sorts of things that really *could* come in useful, and which she'd infinitely prefer to put into practice here, in this place that she loved, than anywhere else in Greece.

'If it holds, I'll go wherever Hector says I should to help, but if it doesn't, I can't abandon everyone here and run away. I simply won't.'

Her resolve on the matter had only hardened when she'd seen how old her *papou* had become.

It had grown stronger yet with each new bomb that had been dropped by a Stuka into Souda; each burst of a Messerschmitt's guns.

This was her home, *their* home, and the Nazis were trying to steal it from them.

If they managed it, she wasn't going to turn tail and run.

No, she was going to help take it back.

She had a plan for what she should do, in that unthinkable future. She'd discussed it briefly with Pendlebury, and he'd approved. She was still hoping, like everyone on the island was hoping, that that future would never transpire, but until it became certain one way or the other, she was keeping a low profile, just in case. The less people she saw now, the less complicated it would be to put her plan into action later.

She didn't wire Hector in London to bring him up to speed with her intentions.

She didn't enlighten him on her move to Chania either.

He'd go apoplectic.

But nor was she was being idle. She'd been running her errands in town, laying the ground, enlisting the support of two people who'd featured high on Pendlebury's list of Cretan allies, the first of whom had been most cooperative, the second, a deal less so – rather, almost as concerned as Hector had been about the dangers of her staying.

'It won't be so dangerous,' Eleni had insisted, 'or certainly no worse than it will be anywhere else I might get sent. Not if you help me. You can do that here . . . '

'I can, can I?'

'Yes, but you won't be able to on the mainland, or any other island. I won't know anyone who can. Do you really want that on your conscience?'

It had been a low swipe, but it had worked.

Reluctantly, they'd come around, given Eleni their word she'd have their support.

For the present, at least, there was nothing more she could do.

There was nothing any of them could do but wait, for the invasion itself.

For the past week, there'd been more German reconnaissance planes circling the island, more intense raids, and fresh whispers, every day, that the assault was coming tomorrow, *tomorrow*.

Yet here tomorrow was, yet again, 19 May, and still there was nothing.

The suspense was agony. Beyond agony.

Needing to do something to distract herself from it, Eleni had done the laundry. As activities went, it felt fairly ridiculous (what use clean bedding, in the middle of a war zone?) but nonetheless, she'd come out into the garden with her damp basket of sheets, and was hanging them on the line. She wasn't alone. Fat, faithful Tips was by her side, stripy head turning with Eleni's every movement, following her with his eyes. Not far away, by Eleni's old wooden playhut, grew a new peach tree. Eleni had no idea if it was from the pit that she'd planted – Maria had taken it upon herself to plant one of her own, in the autumn of 1936, just as she'd said Eleni should have done, so that Eleni wouldn't be disappointed next time she came – but Eleni was electing to believe it was.

She reached for another sheet, feeling the relief of its cool touch on her hot skin. It wasn't yet ten, but the morning was stifling. The sun above seemed somehow larger, its rays beating down with unwavering focus, as though it too was waiting, watching them all for the main act to unfold.

She turned, attention caught by a movement at the corner of her eye: a Hurricane fighter, climbing bravely into the shimmering sky. She was surprised to see it; RAF fighters really never had been a common sight over Crete, and those that had flown had done so against heartbreaking odds, but Ben had told her, only the day before, that the last of them were being withdrawn to safety before the invasion commenced.

She raised her hand to her brow, watching this Hurricane, pulse quickening, her mouth dry with dread. She couldn't hear it. It was too far away. But she didn't lift her eyes from it, as it soared soundlessly upwards.

Please let it be fine, she prayed, like she always did, to whom she didn't know (Ares; Zeus; God), *please let this one be fine.*

But, within seconds, the Messerschmitts it had obviously been scrambled to fight came hurtling towards it, like wasps to honey, and, silently, inevitably, it wasn't fine, but dropped, with whomever was in it, nose first, to join too many others in the deep blue Aegean Sea.

Otto hadn't come to Greece by plane this time.

He'd come by sea, and lorry, on a journey that had taken close to a fortnight, from his bleak training ground in Germany, down through Romania, on to the Attic peninsula, where his parachute regiment had joined the thousands of others waiting, poised to go into attack. Otto hadn't been told, not through any of that epic expedition into Southern Europe, where the attack was to be directed. None of the commanding officers had. As their convoy of lorries had put mile after mile behind it, some of them had started to suspect, Otto had *feared*, but he hadn't known.

It hadn't been a scenic trip, across the Greek mainland. The retreating British Army had left a trail of devastation in its wake, destroying anything that they, the Germans, might put to use, and the smouldering, battle-scarred country had been unrecognizable from the one Otto had held in his memory, all these years. The air he'd breathed had held no nostalgia, no fragrant hit of pollen, nor herbs, only the acrid tang of burning fuel dumps. Alongside the mounds of hastily dug graves, everywhere, had lain wrecks of tanks, roofless stone huts, churches with shattered walls. Locals had stood on the roadside, staring into their transport trucks as they'd trundled by. Otto had been shamed, but not surprised, by the disgust in their eyes; how they'd all held themselves rigid, tense with the effort of their silence, the barely supressed instinct to fight back. He had, after all, been in Czechoslovakia, then France; helped push the British back all the way to Dunkirk; driven past homes demolished and taken; watched Swastika flag after Swastika flag be mounted over countless town halls. He'd looked such hatred in the face, many, many times before.

He was a captain now. A Nazi captain. He'd been promoted, then transferred over to the air force only a few months before, ordered into a newly formed paratrooper division at the request of his old commanding officer from France, a man called Brahn. The two of them had been together from the first day of the French invasion. Quickly, Otto had learnt to trust Brahn: the kind to arrest, not shoot, prisoners, and stop to give a dying man water, regardless of their uniform. Over nights spent at rest in barns, and huddled around fires in estaminets, they'd exchanged their stories. Cradling tin mugs of weak coffee, smoking damp cigarettes, Brahn had talked wistfully of his wife back in Dresden, their home that he missed, and their two small children who he saw in the faces of every French child they passed. Holding his cigarette in his lips, he'd drawn out his pocketbook, shown Otto pictures of his little girls, just as Otto had shown him the drawings he still carried everywhere: of the house he'd designed for Eleni, back in that summer of 1936. In the firelight, his exhaustion, he'd found himself doing what he never did, and spoken about her to Brahn: their time in Crete, then Paris – even the effort he'd gone to, after Paris, to teach himself Greek properly, just as she'd learnt to speak German, naively believing there was a point.

'Was she any good at German?' Brahn had asked, one night.

'Incredible.'

'And what about your Greek?'

'Passable, eventually.'

He wished he hadn't given Brahn that detail now.

Had he not, Brahn might not have brought him here, turned him into an enemy of this place he loved, and made him responsible for the lives of a group of men who were really children.

Most of them in his section – indeed, in all sections – were new recruits, fresh from the Hitler Youth, bloated with pride from the stories they'd been fed back in Germany of how they, the paratroopers, were the elite of the Luftwaffe elite. All the way over, the boys in Otto's lorry had joked and sang, their gung-ho voices raised. Their bravado had been too forced though, too unrelenting; Otto had seen through it; noticed the way some of the youngest had kept looking at the older ones for approval, then him for reassurance. Some of them weren't even eighteen. Most of them had, doubtless, been missing their mothers.

Otto was twenty-six now, and he didn't have a mother anymore. Just a grieving father, and a sister who hated everyone for what Brigit had done.

He'd kept his own grief determinedly buried when they'd pulled up at their campsite in Attica, four days before.

Brahn, who'd come ahead, had been waiting for them.

'I am sorry to do this to you,' he'd told Otto, his lean face earnest. 'I've been selfish. I wanted officers I respect. And your Greek—'

'Is really not that good.'

'Better than mine, however.' He'd grimaced. 'Am I forgiven?'

'Not even close,' Otto had said.

To which Brahn had laughed, like he'd joked, slapped him on the back, and, summoning the other senior officers, led them all on a tour of the parched encampment, with its rows of tents and low wooden huts, then, by motor, on to the airfield, where they'd all stood, deaf to the screeching cicadas, absorbing the sheer number of Junker Ju 52s that had been assembled there, glinting in the sunshine, their empty bellies waiting to swallow them.

'This is just a fraction,' Brahn had said. 'We have six more airfields nearby, and five hundred or so Junkers, then glider planes on top, to transport the ground troops. It's an armada.'

He'd taken his glasses off to polish them, squinting across at the planes. 'There was a hold-up on fuel, but it's on its way now. It won't be much longer before we go.'

Even then, they'd had no official confirmation of where it was that they were being sent.

That had come that afternoon, at an officer briefing in Athens, held at the palatial Hotel Grande Bretagne. General Student, who'd led the victorious airborne attack at The Hague, had chaired proceedings, standing, legs akimbo, his chest strewn with medals, at the front of the sweltering room, pointing at the map that had been pinned to the wall, walking them all through their individual landing zones, targets and consolidation points. He'd spoken of beaches too narrow to bear an invasion, but crucial to opening supply lines, and, in the electric light, the press of sweaty bodies, Otto had stared at the shape of the island he'd never forgotten, reading the names of its towns – *Chania. Rethymno. Heraklion* – feeling his pumping blood run cold at this confirmation, unequivocal, that Crete really was the target.

It's an armada.

In his mind's eyes, he'd seen again those Junkers, then Chania harbour, the café; her villa.

Christ, he'd thought. *Christ . . .*

Student had handed over to an intelligence officer, who'd brought out a series of aerial photographs, which, he'd claimed, made clear that they need expect little in the way of a defence when they landed. The British forces who'd fled the mainland had, he'd assured them, mostly left Crete too, running, like cowards, for Egypt, leaving just a token force behind, most of whom their Luftwaffe would have taken care of by the time they got there. Given that, given the Cretan Army weren't on the island either, taking it, he'd said, should be as easy as a walk in the park.

Otto had narrowed his eyes, unable to believe it could be so straightforward.

And, as Student had stepped back in, claiming that the local Cretans were feeling so betrayed by the British that many of them would welcome them, the Germans, with open arms, he hadn't believed that either.

Rather, with each new word that had left Student's lips, he'd felt like he'd stepped into some warped land of make-believe.

When, at length, the briefing had ended, and he'd headed out through the hotel's plush foyer, into the searing light of the day, he'd tried to get a hold of himself, accept that none of what was unfolding was fiction, but very real. Amid the bustle of the street, the ringing tramcars, and Athenians who'd tried to pretend he wasn't there, he'd lit a cigarette, raised his stare to the Acropolis, with its Swastika flag, and told himself,

This is happening.

The words in his mind had felt every bit as hollow as that promise of a walk in the park had felt, back in the briefing room.

They still felt hollow.

Rationally, he realized they weren't. In the four days since that briefing, preparations across the region had intensified. Every morning, he'd watched fresh waves of bombers and fighters arc overhead, on their way to Crete. He'd been issued with his own map of the island and seen his battalion's target, on the plains near Souda, stark in black and white. Brahn had drilled him, and all of the other officers in their section, endlessly, combing over their objectives, strategies for combatting whatever forces, token or no, they might come up against, emphasising and reemphasising the importance of their weapon cannisters, which, like them, would be dropped on parachutes from the sky.

'Until you locate one, all you'll have is your Schmeisser.' He'd waved his own gun. 'It won't be enough. You must get to the cannisters before the enemy does.'

Otto had tried to visualize himself doing that very thing, just as he'd tried, over and again, to picture himself back in Crete, in this uniform that had become his second skin – dropping from a Junker, like he'd dropped from so many in training, into the island's citrus groves, searching that place that was hers for weapons to take it – but it was too much of a nightmare. He just couldn't make it feel real. The only faces he'd so far managed to conjure had been the ones he knew – Dimitri's, *no problem*; Yorgos's; Socrates'; Spiros's – staring at him as he marched past them in his jackboots, their eyes full of the raw hatred he knew too well, and which he feared might just end him, coming from them.

Never once did he consider that Eleni herself might be in Crete. She'd be in England – somewhere safe, he hoped (every single day). But he'd kept picturing her too, often in the delirium of the past days: in the sea; holding her hair back from her face on the bus; dancing in her shorts at the café; staring down at urchins, up at Venus; lying in her bed . . .

She'd used to make him feel so safe.

This is happening.

He repeated it to himself now, as he strode across the camp's dry, crackling grass, away from Brahn's makeshift office, and his final words of wisdom and luck, on to where he'd left his reports repacking their parachutes for the umpteenth time that day. It was sundown, the eve of 20 May, and the mercury on Brahn's thermometer had been tipping ninety, but, despite the heat, they'd all have to climb into their thick jumpsuits before very much longer, pull on their life jackets; get ready to go. For security reasons, the lower ranks had been kept in ignorance as to where they were headed until only a few hours before. Many of them in Otto's battalion had punched the air when he'd confirmed that they were for Crete, that night – whether in true excitement, or more bravado, Otto hadn't been able to decide, but he'd loathed them for it, no one more than a junior officer called Fischer, who, with his contempt for almost everyone around him, and complete inability to think before he spoke, was a constant thorn in Otto's side. All the way over from Germany, Otto had had to keep disciplining him for getting into fights with the others, then pointing his gun at the locals, making out he was going to shoot them. Not long before they'd arrived, he'd aimed at a child.

'You do that again,' Otto had yelled into his smirking face, holding him up against the wall of the truck, humiliating him, quite deliberately, in front of the others, 'and I will do it to you, only I won't just point, believe me.'

Fischer must have, because, despite his smirk, he hadn't tried it again.

There'd been an unmistakable challenge in his stare though, when, punching the air earlier, he'd sought Otto's attention.

Otto hadn't given it to him.

He'd focused instead on the few who *hadn't* punched the air, but had fallen quiet, their nerves kicking in. Observing their dipped faces, he'd reminded himself that he was all they had, no matter the mess of his own head, and that if he didn't do his job properly for them now, they, and the rest of the battalion, could well end up unnecessarily dead within hours. Pulling a deep, bracing breath, he'd called them all to order, issued them with their own maps, and talked them through their drop zones and day one objectives. He'd been honest about the rosy picture that had been painted by intelligence, but also his own concern that they'd been too optimistic ('I hope they have,' said Fischer, miming pot shots with his hands. 'Shut up, Fischer,' Otto said), then had them polish their guns, check their parachutes again, pack the rest of the weapons into their all-important cannisters, and, when it could be put off no longer, their personal effects into boxes that would be sent on to them if they survived, and home to their families in Germany if they didn't.

Even Fischer had been subdued, doing that.

He'd still jeered at a boy called Meyer though, the youngest of them all, for fumbling over his box's latch.

'Check your parachute again,' Otto had ordered.

'Are you serious?' Fischer had demanded.

'I feel pretty serious,' Otto had replied. 'Do I look serious, Fischer? No, don't answer that. Just check your damned parachute.'

Turning his back on him, Otto had knelt, reopening Meyer's lid, pushing the contents down, spotting a small, knitted comforter beneath some books: the kind given to babies to help them sleep.

'My mama wanted me to bring it for luck,' Meyer had explained, fuchsia with embarrassment. 'She holds on to a lot of things. It seemed important to her . . . '

'She made it?' Otto had asked, mind moving, before he could stop it, to his own mama.

'When I was a child.'

You still are, Otto had thought.

'It's stupid,' Meyer had gone on.

'No,' Otto had said, pulling the knitted square out, the scent of laundry powder with it, and – before Fischer could see – handing it to Meyer. 'It's luck. Take it with you. Don't let it be sent back to your mama, for Christ's sake.'

'Any more beer, *sir*?' said Fischer now, managing, as usual, to make the term sound like an insult.

They'd been given rations the night before: a parting gift.

Otto was glad Fischer asked about it.

It meant he could tell him, 'No.'

'No?'

'You need a clear mind.'

'I could do with a beer.'

'How unfortunate for you.'

The others laughed.

Fischer didn't.

Not laughing either, Otto tipped his head back, looking upwards.

The sky above was clear, a boundless arena of faded blue and pink and grey.

The flush colours, the purity of them, took him back, in a way nothing else he'd so far seen in Greece had: to that white-sanded beach, the first time he'd kissed her . . .

'When do we go, sir?' asked Meyer, dragging his attention back to earth.

'Transport to the airfield will arrive after midnight,' Otto said, and even as the words left him, he felt no trepidation. No fear.

It still seemed so entirely unreal.

'We fly at break of dawn.'

Chapter Fifteen

His strange disconnect lingered with him almost the entire night through, both disorientating, and welcome, in that it at least helped him to remain calm as the sun disappeared, plunging them all into darkness.

The same could not be said for everyone.

With the light gone, a jittery tension descended on the camp-site, all eyes on its gates, waiting for the trucks that would take them to the airfield. No one slept, certainly not in Otto's battalion, even though that would have been the most sensible course. Occasionally, someone sang of the Fatherland, but mostly, all was subdued, and the cicadas dominated, carrying above the hushed voices talking of homes, people loved, and missed.

As midnight finally started to draw nearer, a rumour began to circulate that intelligence had revised its report, and the British *hadn't* fled Crete at all, but were very much still there, waiting to defend it. Otto heard it from Meyer, who'd picked it up on one of his frequent trips to the latrine.

'They say there are thousands of them,' said Meyer, pale-faced in the moonlight.

'There are quite a few thousand of us,' Otto pointed out, then, to distract him, distract them all, ordered everyone to attention, splitting them into their jumping squads, testing them on the objectives they'd gone through ad nauseam that day.

'What's your first priority when you reach the ground?' he asked.

'Getting to a weapon cannister,' they chorused.

'And what colour parachute will they be attached to?'

'Green,' they replied.

'Correctly this time?'

'Red,' they said, and laughed.

For a few seconds.

'Right,' he said, hearing the approach of engines, 'time to get suited up.'

They did, and immediately began to sweat beneath the layers of their uniforms and jumping gear.

'*Mein Gott,*' said Meyer, his zip sticking. '*Mein Gott.*'

The heat only seemed to intensify when, cramming into the transport trucks, they, and the hundreds of others at their encampment, arrived at the blacked-out airfield, where the last of the planes were being fuelled, the Junkers' pilots revving the engines, taxing into place, flooding the frenetic darkness with noise and fumes.

'Linder,' Brahn yelled at Otto, from the back of his own truck, then said something else, which, in the cacophony, Otto couldn't hear.

Almost immediately, he lost sight of Brahn.

There were too many others pouring out of their trucks, torch beams trembling, racing to their respective emplaning points, tripping over their own feet to keep up with one another.

Frowning, not liking how fraught the always calm Brahn had looked – feeling, rather, the first prickling of unease penetrate the detachment he'd been wearing like a shield – Otto commanded his men back into their squads, despatched those not flying with him to their own planes, then ordered the eleven he'd assigned to himself, Meyer included, Fischer too (keep your friends close . . .), to follow him.

He kept searching for Brahn as they proceeded to their allocated Junker, using his own torch to illuminate the dripping, straining faces of strangers, but to no avail. He had a hard enough time just keeping track of his own eleven men, and a grip on Fischer, who kept disappearing to tell others where they should be.

Brahn, however, eventually found him, just as the night's blackness was beginning to fade, and the first hint of the new day was breaking on the horizon. Otto was at his plane, counting the men into its belly, checking their life jackets, their harnesses and straps.

He paused, catching sight of Brahn jogging towards him, weighed down by his heavy kit, his glasses fogged, his face puce with the heat. He looked, if such a thing was possible, even more harassed than he had before.

Otto guessed what it must be about.

It was still a blow though when Brahn confirmed it, telling him what he'd managed to pass on to only a handful of Otto's fellow officers: that the rumour back at the camp had been correct, and intelligence *had* revised its report.

'Right,' said Otto, shoving Meyer, the last to emplane, unceremoniously up into the fuselage, then turning to face Brahn properly. 'How many are waiting for us?'

'Latest estimate is somewhere in the region of fifty thousand.'

Otto stared.

He hadn't expected that.

Cynical as he'd been about their predicted walk in the park, he hadn't expected anything close to that number.

Their own armada paled by comparison.

Fifty thousand.

The assembled paratroopers attacking in the first wave that morning made up barely a tenth of that amount. Even counting the troops currently boarding their glider planes, ready to land with them, their force was fractional.

'Is it certain?' he asked Brahn.

Tell me no.

'Apparently so.'

Otto cursed.

'How did we miss this? How . . . ?'

'I don't know. Some excuse about the vegetation.'

Otto cursed again.

It was too hot. Too damned hot.

He reached up, removing his helmet, running his hand over his shorn, sweaty hair. His heart hammered with adrenalin. *Fifty thousand.* The number did something to him. Shattered what was left of his shield. Made it all feel, quite suddenly, very, very real.

This is happening.

At last, he believed it.

It was happening now.

'I've got to get back to my plane,' said Brahn.

'My other men,' said Otto, ready to run, find them and warn them.

Fifty thousand.

'There's no time,' said Brahn, stopping him. 'Concentrate on the ones in there.' He nodded up at the Junker. 'The others will find out soon enough.'

Otto decided to put off enlightening the eleven in his own squad until they were almost upon Crete, not seeing the point in making them any more apprehensive than they already were. He'd trained them well, he told himself; he'd trained all of them well. The others would be shocked, yes, but they were ready. They were all ready.

It gave him little comfort.

Theirs was one of the last planes to leave. The Junker became like a furnace, and the wait inside it – looking into the soaked, pensive faces of his men, knowing what he knew, listening to the roar of the other planes accelerating, then taking off – was a torture unlike any Otto had ever known.

No one spoke.

Otto didn't test anyone on anything.

When he caught Meyer's eye, he knew he should summon him a smile – that a better officer than him would have done that, that Brahn would have – but he didn't.

He couldn't.

As they taxied, taking their place at the head of the grass runway, the planes taking off immediately in front of them coated them in dry earth, delaying them further since the pilots could no longer see through the cockpit glass, and the screen had to be cleaned.

'We're getting left behind,' said Fischer, surprising Otto by sounding almost as anxious as Meyer looked. 'It's taking too long . . . '

'It's fine,' Otto said, even though nothing was, 'we'll make up the time once we're off.'

Which, eventually, they were, building speed, the walls and floor of the plane juddering, shaking, until Otto felt as though his skull might splinter, the fuselage fall apart, then rising into sudden smoothness, lumbering heavily upwards, up and up, banking right, arcing over the mainland.

Otto turned, looking from the window, watching the sun's first rays blaze across the sky, bathing the basin of Athens in its glow. He studied the city below and thought about the people now waking up to the sight of them overhead. He tried to imagine how they must be feeling, watching this flotilla of theirs leave, off to try and conquer yet another part of their country – the weight of their helplessness, their rage – then averted his eyes, rested his head back against the steel wall, because it was too much. It was all too much.

It did at least become cooler, up in the sky, but the ride across the Aegean wasn't a smooth one. In the turbulence, Meyer and a couple of others vomited.

'Into the bags,' Otto yelled, not in time, and the regurgitated scent of the coffee they'd drank before leaving the camp filled the fuselage.

'Oh, fantastic,' said Fischer, 'seriously, thank you.'

'Shut up, Fischer,' another man shouted, saving Otto the bother.

He wasn't sick, he just felt like he might be, staring back through his window, observing the hundreds of other planes flying in formation with them, and the shadow of their own wings on the sparkling blue sea, recalling how he'd done the same before, flying to Crete the last time, with his mother in front of him, and Lotte by his side.

He didn't dwell on the thought of Lotte. He'd come to feel very differently towards her, since that summer, but she had no place here, in this plane.

Besides, it wasn't much longer before the island came into view, its snow-capped mountains wavering in the sun's glare. Knowing he had only minutes left, Otto did what he must, and turned back to his men, watching the colour drain from their faces as he broke to them just how many tens of thousands of British troops they were, imminently, to face.

'That's more than us, isn't it?' shouted Meyer, eyes darting from him, to the others, back to him. 'That's much more than us.'

No one answered him.

They jerked left, flying into the first puff of anti-aircraft smoke, then again as more came. One of the pilots called from the cockpit that they were to standby, and then their dispatcher was up, opening their door, filling the fuselage with even more noise, the roar of hot air, and the detonation of explosions on the arid land below.

'Fix lines,' Otto yelled, and they were all on their feet, repeating the process that had been hammered into them back in Germany, attaching their clasps to the fuselage's cable, holding themselves steady. He was at the back, with Meyer in front of him. 'What colour cannisters are we looking for?' he asked him, one final time.

'Red,' Meyer said.

'If you can't find one, find a safe place until one of us gets to you.'

'What if no one gets to me?'

'We'll get to you,' Otto told him. 'Got your luck?'

'Yes.'

'Good,' and, with that, Otto gave the signal to the dispatcher for the first man to jump.

He didn't think about Lotte then, either.

But, as one by one, he watched the men disappear through the plane's door, he did, briefly, think about Eleni.

He wondered what she'd think, when she heard, if she ever did hear, that he'd been part of this attack.

Could he stand her knowing?

He didn't think he could.

And he didn't want this attack to succeed. He wanted, with almost every fibre of his adrenalin-charged being, for these fifty thousand Allied troops to win, push them, the wrong side, back to where they'd come from; keep this one, small place, safe.

Yet, he didn't want his men to die. Not even the ones who'd punched the air the day before. He didn't want Meyer to die. He didn't want the officers he'd trained with, to die.

He didn't want Brahn to die, and for a telegram to devastate his wife and children waiting for him in Dresden.

He didn't want to die.

He hated what he'd become, what he did, but he wanted his life; the chance at a future that held none of this in it, where he built houses rather than threw grenades at them.

Christ, he thought, as Meyer leapt through the door, throwing his arms wide, narrowly missing the nose of another plane, flying below them, *I don't want to die.*

I don't.

Then, with nothing else for it, he leapt too.

Eleni had heard the planes before she'd seen them.

She'd been out on the terrace, pouring Tips a saucer of milk, when the milk had started to quiver, the saucer to rattle, and she'd felt herself go still at the distant, grumbling noise, growing louder by the second, like thunder rolling towards her in the cloudless sky.

Tips had hissed, his stripy fur standing on end, and darted inside, but she'd remained where she was, unease rippling through her, her eyes fixed on the horizon.

She'd been up since six, shaken to consciousness by the eruptions of an earlier-than-normal raid. Yorgos had already set off for the hospital, telling her he'd call for her at Maria and Spiros's, where she'd arranged to spend the day with Maria, if she was needed. Only Ben, back from his own night on duty, was home.

He joined her on the terrace – half-dressed, his shirt unbuttoned, braces loose around his waist, towelling shaving foam from his jaw – staring, like her, in the direction of the ominous, guttural, roar, his strong face, intent.

He didn't question what it could be.

Nor did she.

She'd known, instinctively, from the second she'd heard the sound, what it meant, and that tomorrow had, at last, arrived.

The roar grew louder, throbbing in the sky. Everything on the terrace started to shake: the terracotta pots, the grill, the spoon Eleni had left in her bowl from her breakfast; her bones beneath her skin.

Then . . .

'My God,' Ben breathed, as, before their eyes, the horizon shuddered, turning from blue to darkest grey: a wave of metal pushing terrifyingly on towards them, swooping closer, into the storm of ack-ack fire, slowly becoming decipherable shapes: scores of gliders, with their oversized wings, then, behind them, only just visible, hundreds of Ju 52s. 'It's Armageddon.'

He spoke in English, like he always did with Eleni. He knew where she'd grown up – just like Maria and Spiros's New Zealanders knew – but it didn't worry her. She liked Ben, very much. She hadn't known him long, but he'd become a friend; instinctively, she trusted him, trusted them all, but even had she not, she wouldn't have been concerned.

She had her plan.

Never had she prayed harder that she wouldn't need to put it into action than now, watching, redundant, as this foreign, fascist force descended on her home. Her *home*.

The glider planes shifted, splitting in formations, heading to their left and right, far enough away for her not to sprint for shelter, but still very close, up and down the coast.

'They're heading inland,' said Ben, seeming to break from his trance, throwing his towel down, backing away. 'Half the troops are at the bloody beaches.' He said something else, about getting back to work, but Eleni stopped listening, distracted, horrifyingly, by a glider exploding mid-air, caught in the anti-aircraft flak.

The battery from the guns intensified, as though galvanised by the hit, and Stukas screamed downwards, targeting the positions, but still they kept on, firing. Eleni visualized the soldiers operating them – those men she'd seen drinking *krassi* in Chania – sweating, determined, heedless of the exploding bombs, and, in the unfolding carnage, felt more choked, more humbled than ever, by their courage, their presence.

'Eleni,' shouted Ben, his voice straining above the Junkers, which had now reached the island too, and were swarming over it, following the same path the gliders had. 'Eleni . . . '

She turned to face him. He was already at the kitchen door. He'd been up all night, but his eyes were alert, snapping with energy.

'Come too,' he said. 'I can take you to Maria's . . . '

She nodded. It was a good idea. His office, at Creforce HQ, was only a few streets away from her and Spiros's house, and early as it was, she knew Maria would be frantic, wanting to know she was all right. Yorgos would be too. She could telephone him at the hospital though from Maria's. Unlike the villa, they were connected . . .

'Thank you.'

'Give me five minutes,' he said, and disappeared inside.

She intended to follow, try and locate Tips, pack her things for if she needed to stay with Maria.

Yet, she couldn't immediately make herself move.

Ears by now splitting, she returned her attention to the apocalyptic sky, swallowing dryly as, along the coast, more gliders started to go down, losing control, rocketing to the ground. Eleni visualized the men inside them too, torn by hatred and pity.

Then, something else: flurries of canopies, in white, red, green and yellow, spilling from the Junkers' droning bellies.

Parachutes, she thought.

She knew from her training that the coloured chutes must be carrying supplies. The white ones had what looked like black sticks attached to them, sticks that could only be men. She followed them as they drifted down through the smoke, the blinding light, strangely transfixed.

She didn't think of Otto, as she watched them fall.

She hadn't thought of him either, seeing those gliders combust, or the Stukas dive.

None of this violence could live in her mind, with him.

But, as the white canopies neared the ground, the sticks of

men who were hanging from them, helpless to her own eyes, jerked, and then went limp.

She realized what was happening to them.

They were being shot.

Those men she'd seen in Chania, drinking *krassi*, laughing on the beaches, were shooting them as they fell.

They were shooting them in their hundreds, picking them off like toys at a funfair, and it was too explicit, too . . . *human* . . . to see.

Yet, she still couldn't tear her eyes away.

Part of her was aghast at what she was witnessing: the same part that had known pity just now, seeing those gliders burn.

But another part, a part she could feel expanding within her, with every pulse of her racing heart, willed the shooting gunmen on.

You can't let compassion in, Mr Wood had once counselled her, back in training. *Detachment is your friend. Without it, you'll find a trigger a great deal harder to compress.*

She didn't doubt that the soldiers on the ground were living by that lesson now.

She was getting there herself.

These sticks couldn't be allowed to land, she knew that. They'd only be the ones to start killing otherwise. They, and their brothers, had bombed and shot and panzered their way across Europe, and they *had* to be stopped.

Shame on them, truly, for having come.

Shame on all of them.

Yet, even as she thought it, she couldn't find it in her to triumph in their deaths.

Rather, as more canopies fell, and lurched, and sunk, she remained rooted to the spot, her eyes settling on one stick in particular. She wasn't sure what it was about it that drew her focus. But as it dipped lower and lower, nearing the ground, in the heat of the morning, she kept following it with her eyes, and felt no bloodlust, no hatred, nor vindictiveness.

She felt nothing but dread.

And an overwhelming sense of grief.

Point at their feet.

Otto heard the frantically barked command over and over, rising up from the Cretan ground. He was further inland than he was meant to be, at least a couple of miles from the coast, pushed off course by the air's currents, the planes' slipstreams, and sudden gusts triggered by explosions.

Aim for their toes, you'll get their heads.

Constrained by his harness, he snatched looks left, right, down into the haze of heat and gunfire, breath racing at the sight of the jolting canopies beneath him, filling his throat, threatening to choke him. He didn't know which men were being shot – whether they were part of his own battalion, or someone else's; if they'd been among the few that had been warned of the Allie's strength, or the majority that could only have been horror-struck by it – only that what was happening to them was grotesque. They couldn't aim with their guns, not until they were free of their chutes; their only hope was in the air itself, and where it carried them: to open ground, where those beneath them would have a clean line of sight, or somewhere sheltered, somewhere they might have a chance to defend themselves.

He kept thinking of Meyer, his blanket.

That's more than us, isn't it?

He thought of all his reports, cursing, turning, craning his neck, watching more canopies jolt, his entire body taut with impotence as he hung, drifting, waiting to find out what had become of them, or if there was someone on the ground staring at him through their eye-piece, trigger-finger tensed, taking aim . . .

Point at their feet.

He was still waiting for the shot when, as always happened on a jump, his descent ceased feeling so slow, and became suddenly fast, the earth abruptly close enough to rush up to meet him, winding him as he landed, feet first in the thick of a grove of olive trees, on the hard, solid soil.

He didn't stop to gather himself. Even as he strained to fill his shocked lungs, he moved, wrenching off his harness, pulling out his Schmeisser, his eyes – raw from the smoke he'd drifted through – raking his surroundings, combing the shade of the pale, parched trees. After the vast auditorium of the sky, it all felt very closed in, exceedingly small. Quiet too.

Chance had been on his side.

There was no one else there.

But, as he set off, crouched low, head still spinning from lack of oxygen, he heard other feet close by, tripping in the undergrowth.

He stopped, gun raised, ready to fire.

'Don't,' came a familiar voice. Fischer's voice. He broke from the olive trees, cradling his arm, blood seeping through his fingers. 'They already shot me once. I've been *shot* . . . ' He'd been crying as well. Otto could tell from the smears in the dirt on his face.

He lowered his gun.

'They're killing us,' Fischer said, another tear escaping him. He'd be hating himself for it. Hating Otto, for seeing it. 'They're killing us all.'

As though to reinforce the inescapable truth, there was a burst of machine-gun fire from not very far away. Seconds later, the ground beneath them shook in the force of an explosion. Otto could only guess it was another glider going down.

Fischer sunk to his knees.

For a brief moment, Otto considered walking away and leaving him there. Of all his men that he'd thought about on the way down from the plane, Fischer had featured the least. He saw him now, bleeding before him, and saw him again, pointing his gun in the face of that petrified child on the mainland; taking pot shots with his hand at the camp before they'd left.

Let him bleed, a voice inside him said. *Let him.*

The machine-gun started up again.

Fischer cowered.

Exhaling an expletive, knowing he could never live with himself otherwise, Otto bent down, ripped silk from his parachute, and went to him, hauling him to his feet, using the silk to tourniquet his wound. Tightening it, ignoring Fischer's yelp of pain, Otto asked him if he'd seen any weapon cannisters.

Fischer hadn't.

'Then let's go,' said Otto.

'To do what?' said Fischer.

'Survive,' said Otto, and thought, out of nowhere, of Marianne, little Esther. 'We survive.'

'And win?' said Fischer. 'We'll win, yes? Get our own back.'

Otto pushed on through the grove, not answering, not straight away.

He still hoped they wouldn't win.

Even after the massacre he'd seen just now, he hoped they'd have no choice but to retreat, pull out.

Get our own back.

He wanted no part in that.

But . . .

'Yes,' he said, flat to his own ears, 'we'll probably win.'

'How do you know?'

'I don't.' He readied his gun, seeing the bright light of a clearing ahead, and gestured at Fischer to get down, move left. 'But we always tend to in the end, don't we?'

Chapter Sixteen

They did win.

They shouldn't have.

It was said often, after the battle, after the Allied Force's second evacuation from Greece in as many months, that Crete should never have been lost. In the stunned silence that descended on the island, little more than a week after that first, bloody day of the invasion – a silence broken only by the marching of jackboots, crackling megaphones ordering Crete to welcome its liberators, and the chilling staccato of gunfire, echoing from the mountains' walls, as Nazi execution squads moved to work, *getting their own back* – a horrified disbelief descended.

How had it happened?

Eleni heard the question everywhere.

How?

At first, it truly hadn't felt possible that it *could* happen.

Too many Germans were killed, that first day. Too many planes went down, all over the island. Eleni wasn't able to see any more of the battle for herself, once she'd moved to Halepa, but the mood that night in those packed, buzzing streets, thronging with diplomats and officers, was pure optimism. The aircraft had been tallied, calculations had been done; word quickly spread that Jerry had landed nothing like their number of troops on the island. Nazi officials hadn't even announced the invasion back in Germany yet, too afraid to do so after such a catastrophic start.

But that was all that first day was: the start.

Too quickly, the story began to change.

Eleni could never fully grasp how it happened herself, nor even when the precise point was that the Allied forces flipped from being on the winning side, to the losing one.

Ben helped give her some idea though.

She saw him often, before the moment came for her to disappear.

Not back at the villa. She didn't return there; for the first time in her life, it didn't feel safe, not when it was so isolated, so close to Souda, around which the fighting only intensified. She remained in Halepa with Maria, and a sincerely spooked Tips – whom Ben had helped her to manhandle into his motor before they'd left the house (and, oh, but the image of him, square-shouldered and uniformed, fighting to contain pudgy Tips in a headlock, wasn't one she'd soon forget) – setting up residence in the garden-facing room she'd used to take her childhood naps in. The New Zealanders who'd been boarding at the house had left, off to fight with their unit (Maria worried about them, constantly. 'Such good boys,' she kept saying. 'They always made their beds so neatly.'); Yorgos and Spiros were gone too, working around the clock at the hospital, defying their age to help with the inundation of casualties flowing through its warehouse doors. Eleni spent every day there as well, Maria with her – rolling more bandages, washing endless vats of linen – but each evening, once they'd walked home, weaving through the troops and supply trucks jamming the dark roads, Ben would call by, sometimes to snatch a wash, or change his clothes, always keeping Eleni and Maria appraised of the unfolding nightmare.

It was the airfields that were at the root of it. Even as early as the first night of the invasion, he was concerned about them falling. Once the Germans had gained a runway, he said, they'd be able to land their troop carriers with ease – not to mention keep their Messerschmitts and Stukas up in the air for longer, since they'd no longer have to fly them back to Athens to refuel and rearm them. The Allies needed to hold the bases at all costs, but they still had too many of their own troops standing idle at the coast, on standby for the seaborne invasion General Freyberg was adamant must also be on its way.

'Is it?' Eleni asked.

'I don't know,' Ben said, 'but we're in the middle of an air-borne one, so it feels fairly counterintuitive not to be prioritising that.'

Eleni was inclined to agree.

No invasion fleet did arrive across the water, but, the next day, more paratroopers arrived, countless transport planes too, swooping overhead, sending men swarming for Maleme airbase, where the Allied troops fought determinedly to hold them off ('For hours,' said Ben), but couldn't keep going forever, not when the Germans kept coming, managing, eventually, to overwhelm them.

'They took a lot of prisoners,' said Ben, who stopped at Maria's that night only long enough to break the news. He refused Maria's offer of a meal. He didn't even remove his cap. His sun-darkened face was grim, sober. 'We're told they forced them to clear the runway so they could keep it operational to land reinforcements. Shot anyone who refused.'

'But, the Geneva Convention,' said Maria.

'I suspect they were feeling even less inclined than normal to respect it, after yesterday.'

'And now they've got Maleme,' said Eleni.

'They have.' He turned for the door. 'We need to take it back. We need to have done it hours ago. It's madness that no one's given the order. Freyberg's obsessed with keeping men at the coast . . . '

The order to launch a counteroffensive was eventually issued the next day.

'Too damned late,' said Ben.

The forces allocated to it were too few as well. They stood no chance against the might of German troops who'd by then landed on their repaired runway, consolidating their defence. And, although Cretans did come out in support of the Allied Army – 'Women as well as men,' said Ben, 'we're seeing it everywhere.' (Eleni pictured them in their headscarves, rifles raised to their shoulders) – the attack failed.

Almost immediately, the inauspicious rumour spread that the royal family had fled Crete.

It was Yorgos, not Ben, who brought that particular piece of news to Eleni's attention, the following afternoon, seeking her out in the hospital scullery, where she was boiling more bandages.

'They're gone,' he said, craggy brow furrowed.

'The Germans?' she said, without any hope.

'No. Our king and his family.'

'I suppose that's not much of a loss either.'

He told her how they'd left: of the armed escort that had taken them over the white mountains to the port at Sphakia, then the naval one that had carried them to Alexandria.

'Perhaps your papa was involved.'

'He's in the Atlantic.'

'He wouldn't want you here anymore.'

'Probably not,' she conceded.

'If it makes sense for the king to leave—' he wagged his finger with each syllable '—it makes sense for my granddaughter.'

'I don't have blue blood,' she pointed out.

'Neither do they.'

'Nonetheless, they're the ones who've been whisked away.' She heaved the bandages from the vat, into the basket for the mangle, barely noticing as another distant explosion puckered the air. They were all long past that. 'How do you suppose *I* could get to Sphakia, *Papou*? Shall I walk there on my own? And what boat am I meant to get on?'

He didn't have an answer for that.

'No, you see,' she said. 'It's not time for me yet.' She turned her attention to the mangle, unwilling to face him for any more of her deceit. (*A terrible way to live, really.*) 'When everyone else evacuates, that's when I'll go. But let's not give up just yet, please.'

She didn't want to.

No one wanted to.

The rumours kept coming though, two-a-penny, of more ground lost and retaken and lost again, ricocheting them all from their hope, to despair. As the third day of the invasion gave way to the fourth, Ben said they were struggling even at HQ to keep track of what was going on; the rudimentary wireless system kept going down, cutting communication between the far-flung towns and battle grounds, and they were having to resort too often to guesswork about what ground was in which hands. As more troops were shunted from crisis to crisis, Crete's roads – which should have been widened, but never had been – became more blocked than ever, the vast jams making easy pickings for the circling Luftwaffe.

The noise of the planes, the bombs, and the rat-a-tat-tat of machine guns, simply never stopped, not even in the dead of night. Ammunition dumps and fuel supplies went up in flames, filling the already stagnant air with even more smoke, so that by the morning of the twenty-fourth, when Eleni walked with Maria to the hospital, the stench of burning had obscured almost everything else: the sea, the flowers, the thyme ('Will we ever breathe such things again?' said Maria); only one scent penetrated the acrid haze – a ripe, sickening scent that Eleni had never smelt before, and never wanted to again: of the dead, drifting on the breeze from the battlefields.

At the hospital itself, they'd long since run out of room in the old warehouse for the endless waves of wounded, and stretchers had had to be placed on the surrounding pavements, with nothing to shield the men from the sun. Eleni heard them groaning, even from down in the scullery, and hated how little she could do to help them, other than fetch them pans of drinking water, and wash their dressings.

She was desperately worried for Yorgos and Spiros as well. They were by now on their fifth day of constant service at the hospital, and for each one they'd spent there, setting breaks, irrigating wounds, assisting the surgeons in theatre, they looked to have aged twice as many years. They refused to stop though, or even discuss returning to Halepa for a night's sleep.

'So you'll sleep when you're dead,' Maria had snapped, at both of them. 'It won't be long if you keep this up. You are seventy years old.'

They simply wouldn't be told though, not when there weren't enough doctors to go around, and always more lives to be clutched back from the edge.

It wasn't only men from their own side that they did it for.

They cared for Germans too.

There weren't many of them at the hospital, not in comparison to the rest. They were kept in an area of their own, at the very back of the converted wards, sectioned off by surgical screens. Sometimes, when Eleni had found herself close by, cleaning the floors, she'd heard them rambling, delirious, talking of their homes, their friends, and especially their mothers, weeping because they wanted them so much.

It had been beyond her, when she'd listened to them do that, not to let that pity she'd felt back on her terrace – watching those gliders burn, those stickmen fall limp – rise in her again, regardless of what they'd all been brought here to do.

She'd never felt any urge to go to them though.

She didn't think she could bring herself to offer them comfort.

Until, on that morning of the twenty-fourth, her *papou* asked her to do just that.

He found her this time outside, in the shaded rear courtyard, where she was filling buckets at the pump. He'd come from theatre. His white jacket was stained with blood. There were deep shadows beneath his sagging eyes.

'*Papou*,' Eleni began, ready to *insist* that he get some sleep.

'Eleni-mou,' he interrupted, waving her wearily down, telling her of the young man who'd been brought in the night before with bullet wounds in his stomach and shoulder. They'd removed the bullets, he said, but the boy had been lying out in the open for too long, and sepsis had already set in; in all likelihood, he didn't have long.

'He's just a baby,' he said, sitting heavily on the courtyard's crumbling wall. 'He doesn't understand anything we're saying to him.' He pressed the heel of his hand to his forehead, as though to push the hideousness of it away. 'Sit with him, will you? Pretend he's your German boy.'

Otto was still so distant from her mind, it took her a second to realize who he meant.

'*My* German boy, *Papou*?'

He exhaled a short, sad laugh. 'You think I was born yesterday?'

'You knew?'

She felt no panic as she asked it, no worry. Not like she would have, that summer.

War, if nothing else, afforded tremendous perspective.

'I got there in the end,' he said. 'I raised your mama, before I got to you, don't forget.'

'She didn't tell you about Dad?'

'She didn't tell me about a lot of things,' he said, which wasn't quite answering her question, but it was hardly the time to press him on it. 'I know she'd be kind to this child now though, so please, can you?'

She didn't want to.

Even whilst they'd been talking, more German troop planes had flown overhead.

Less than an hour before, she'd bent to give water to a man on a stretcher, only to find he was already dead.

The last thing she wanted to do was go and be kind to a Nazi.

But, at the same time, there really wasn't much that she wouldn't have done for her *papou*, had he asked.

'I'll try,' she told him.

'Thank you,' he said, and ushered her inside, on to the stifling, chemical stillness of the ward.

The boy hadn't been put with the rest of the Germans, but in a small, screened cubicle of his own.

'Like I said,' Yorgos sighed, 'he probably doesn't have long. Kindness, Eleni-mou, yes?'

'All right, fine,' she said, and, far from confident of being able to manage it, nonetheless slipped behind the screens.

She did manage to be kind that morning though.

In the end, it came very easily.

For the short time she spent with that boy, she forgot her hate, forget her detachment, and felt nothing but the compassion Mr Wood had warned her against.

A baby.

She saw immediately that Yorgos had been right. This boy, lean and slight beneath his thin sheet, with his tufts of hair, and smooth cheeks, couldn't, she guessed, have been much more than sixteen. He was whimpering, when she first went to his side, but stopped when he saw her, and stared up at her, his gaze wide, terrified. He was trembling with his fever. His skin was waxy, yellow with loss of blood. She could smell his sepsis, smell his fear.

'You're safe,' she found herself whispering to him. 'You're safe.'

His eyes filled with tears. 'You speak German.'

'Shhh.'

'I'm so scared, *fräulein* . . . '

'I know.'

'I don't want to be here.'

Did he mean in the hospital? Or in Crete?

She didn't ask.

'It's all right,' she told him. Then again, 'You're safe.'

'I am?'

'Yes, of course.' She perched on the bed beside him, and, without thinking, pulled his hand into hers. She felt his fingers flicker, flailing to grip onto hers, hot, and so very weak, and held them tighter. 'I'll sit with you.'

'You won't go away?'

'Not for a while.'

'Please don't.'

'I won't.'

His fingers flailed again. 'Thank you.'

He didn't ask for his mother.

He continued to stare up at her and said nothing more at all.

Within no time, his eyes started to droop. It was as though now he felt secure, he could let them go.

His hand in hers went limp, entirely trusting, and he fell asleep, becoming more of a baby than ever.

He was still fast asleep, when, eventually, she stood to go.

She stopped just once at the screens, glancing back at him before she left, such a heaviness in her chest. She watched his lips move, how his eyelids flickered in a dream. Perhaps of the battle that had brought him here.

Pretend he's your German boy.

She hadn't done that.

She hadn't needed to.

She'd forgotten, she really had forgotten, whilst she'd been holding his hand, what he was doing in Crete.

She wanted him to be all right.

It startled her, how much she wanted that.

She didn't ask after him though, once she'd left him.

She spared him not another single thought.

Within just a few short hours, the compassion she'd known had left her entirely.

Because that afternoon the Luftwaffe did the unimaginable, and carpet-bombed Chania, demolishing the Venetian town, setting it – with its palaces, its streets of wooden balconies, and wooden roofs, ablaze – burning homes, burning families, burning everything, breaking all of their hearts, and shattering, for Eleni at least, the last lingering shred of hope she'd been clinging to that the invasion was going to end any other way but the one she'd been most dreading.

She wasn't immediately able to absorb her own conclusion, not whilst the raid was going on, nor for the hideous hours that followed.

She was too busy.

The hospital was, at least, far enough from the town not to be touched. She remained there for the raid's entirety, so saw none of it, but she heard it: the throbbing planes, the bombs, as bad as any of the worst nights of the blitz. She *felt* it. With each new explosion, the metal beds crammed into the wards shook; dust scattered from the ceiling, and the warehouse's loose glass windowpanes trembled. As she helped drag the patients away from under them, and ran, at the orderlies' commands, to ready the triage room, she pictured the inferno in Chania, and wanted to weep.

Not here, she silently begged the droning planes, *please don't do that to here.*

But they did.

They kept on and on and on doing it.

Then, the casualties came, cramming into triage, jostling to be seen by the too-few doctors: toddlers wailing and staring in horror from their blackened faces, carrying burns that would be with them for the rest of their lives; a pregnant woman, having her baby too soon, clutching at Spiros from her stretcher as he tried in vain to assure her that they'd do their best; countless others with broken ribs, more burns, concussions, sobbing in shock, calling for their families. Then, a little girl, about the same age as Esther, who was silent, and couldn't be helped, but whose mother had brought her in anyway, because she just couldn't bear the truth of it; she simply couldn't bear it.

'Why not sit with her?' Eleni heard Maria tell the mother as she passed them by, on her way to fetch more gauze. 'Just sit here now, together, for as long as you like.'

Seeing the mother do just that, amid all the noise, the smoke and fear, Eleni stopped, stilled by the unimaginable pain she must be feeling. She thought too, like she so often found herself thinking, of Esther's mother, back in Berlin, and had to bite her cheeks to contain her grief.

She couldn't let herself break down. She realized it would be appalling of her to do that, on many levels.

She didn't.

She took a breath, then another, and, leaving Maria to care for that poor woman, and her poor little girl, went to get the gauze.

She carried on like that all through the rest of the night.

Everyone did.

It was close to dawn before she and Maria returned home.

Relieved as they were to find it, like the rest of the suburb's streets, intact, they did both cry when they got there, slumped beside one another on the garden steps, breathing in the town's charcoal fumes, not looking at the brightening sky, because the smoke had obscured it, just leaning against one another for support.

'I keep seeing that little girl,' said Eleni, pressing her fingers to her eyes.

'I know,' said Maria. 'I know.'

'I hate them. I hate them for doing this.'

'We all do.'

'They didn't need to . . . '

'All of this has been unnecessary.'

'God, that little girl . . . '

Eleni kept thinking about Dimitri too, with his asthma. *Come, Eleni-mou, let's be in heaven.* One of the ambulance drivers had told her that the bombers had left the harbour undamaged – their commanders mindful, no doubt, of the use it would imminently be to them. But how could she know Dimitri had even stayed there? His family's home was right in the very centre of town. Knowing him, he'd have run straight for them.

'I'm sure he's fine,' said Maria.

She couldn't be sure, though.

None of them could be.

Eleni ached to find out for certain that he was. And Socrates.

She was desperate to know what had become of everyone she loved, and not only in Chania, but up in the mountains too.

What was happening to her great-aunt Sofia, and the rest of them?

Did they even know the world was ending, down here?

And what of Pendlebury? Where was he? Still in Heraklion? She couldn't think how to find out.

It wasn't the time, anyway.

For now, deeply as she cared, she had other, more pressing, concerns.

It was then that it really hit her.

Chania was burning. God only knew what was going on in Heraklion and Rethymno. Troops were scattered all over the island, fighting their isolated battles, unable to communicate with each other. The roads were blocked, airfields had fallen, and the Luftwaffe had near free-reign in the sky.

The fascists were going to win.

They were going to do it soon.

The realization swept through her coldly. She felt no more grief, no more anger.

She was too exhausted, too blunted by the day, to feel anything beyond grim resignation.

She was ready.

She'd long been ready.

She had her plan.

She was going to need it after all.

The events of the following day did nothing to disabuse her of the notion.

When, after a brief sleep, she and Maria returned to the hospital, it was to learn that the lieutenant-colonel in charge had ordered preparations for its evacuation to commence, since they'd need to move at a moment's notice. The doors had been shut to any further casualties, and Eleni was tasked with shadowing one of the MOs around the wards, noting those patients he assessed well enough to be transported, then, those he reluctantly pronounced too critical to move. They, he told her, would – like the German patients, and those from the raid – be left in the care of her *papou*, Spiros, and the handful of other Greek medics remaining, until the Germans arrived, at which point they could all but hope that their doctors would continue to look after them as diligently as they'd tended to their men – and show more respect for the Geneva Convention than their compatriots had at Maleme.

'We're not leaving you behind however,' he said, tiredly. 'I've put you down on the list of staff.'

'That's fine,' said Eleni.

It worked well for her.

Maria, Spiros and Yorgos were all more than happy to hear about it too, when she told them.

'Thank God,' said Spiros.

'Now I can sleep tonight,' said Maria, clasping her face, kissing her on both cheeks.

'I might myself,' said Yorgos, pulling her into his arms.

'Please do,' she said, hugging him, tightly, acutely conscious of how few such opportunities she might have left.

'This is a weight from me,' he said, holding her closer. 'Such a weight.'

She'd known that it would be.

She felt no guilt about telling this lie.

It had always been her intention that everyone she knew in Crete should believe she'd left, if it was to fall. It was why she'd been so careful about whom she'd seen since she'd returned. It was simple mathematics: the less people she'd made aware of her presence, the less people she'd have to worry about convincing she was really going, if, *when*, the time came. The lie was for their good, not her own. She felt no more concern that they'd betray her now than she'd had back on Vauxhall Bridge. On the contrary, she was sure that they'd die before they'd do that. But she didn't want them to have to die for her (obviously); she'd realized how little she wanted them to have to lie for her at all. It *was* a terrible way to live. She couldn't inflict it on them. Plus, bluntly, not everyone was particularly adept at it. Spiros in particular, she feared would flounder, if put on the spot. And whilst he, or Maria, or Yorgos, might one day mention to Dimitri or Socrates, or Sofia, or indeed anyone, that she'd been on the island, they'd tell them in the same breath that she'd

268

departed, in full, authentic, *convincing*, trust that what they were saying was true.

Still,

'I can't stand leaving you here,' she said to Yorgos. 'I can't—'

'I survived the Turks,' he said. 'I can survive this.' He kissed her on the head. 'I couldn't survive anything happening to you though, Eleni-mou. You are to be careful when you go. Extremely careful.'

She would be that.

She assured Ben of it too, that night.

He called one last time, just before nine, catching her alone, since Maria, who was almost seventy herself, had gone to bed, off to sleep the sleep she'd declared herself so certain of.

Eleni had been looking for Tips when she heard Ben's familiar knock. She hadn't seen his fat stripy form since the raid and was getting worried. He'd stuck to the house since they'd moved from the villa, never straying further than the courtyard garden, and, whilst Eleni could only suppose he'd been scared enough to make a run for it when the bombs had started falling, she couldn't think why he hadn't come back. She'd wanted to take him with her when she went. She'd *really* wanted to do that. She was going to have no one else, and whilst she realized that he was a cat, *just a cat*, he was *her* cat, who'd come into her life with him, Otto, *your German boy,* and, actually, she couldn't abide to think that he might be hurt.

Ben's news was hardly the cheering kind, either.

He told her, once she'd beckoned him into the dim hallway, that the staff at Creforce HQ had moved out of Halepa, to Souda, although he didn't expect they'd be there long. Student, the German general who'd masterminded the invasion, had now arrived on the island to oversee its completion. Back in Germany, the Nazis had finally announced it was happening on their radio stations too, confident enough of their victory to make it public.

'There's still a deal of fighting going on,' he said, 'successfully, we believe, in some sections. No one wants to give up. But too much of the island has fallen. Freyberg's about to signal Cairo and let Joint Planning Staff at HQ Middle East know that Crete can't be held.'

Eleni didn't know why it came as such a blow.

She'd already accepted the battle was over.

It was crushingly final though, hearing that Freyberg had too.

'We won't be able to evacuate from Souda,' Ben went on, his jaw tense with what she could tell was regret, and suspected, to her distress, was also shame. 'Jerry's too close. We're seeking permission to do it over the white mountains, leave from Sphakia . . .'

'Like the king,' Eleni said numbly.

'Yes,' he said.

She tried to smile, but couldn't, because what was there to smile about?

'I won't be able to get back here again now,' he said. Outside, beyond the front door, more ambulance bells clanged. Distant gunfire snapped. 'I'm sorry to say this is goodbye.'

'I'm sorry about that too.'

She really was.

It came to her, now that he was leaving, how much she'd grown to enjoy his company, to depend on the promise of his visits. Every night, no matter how busy he'd been, how frantic, he'd come to her. Always, he'd told her everything he could.

'Good luck,' she told him, and, in the stuffy, narrow hall, placed her hand on his shoulder, and raised herself up to kiss his cheek. It was coarse with stubble; his skin was hot. Beneath her palm, his broad shoulder was steady. For a brief moment, overwhelmed as she was by tiredness, and worry – about so much – she wanted only to sink against him, let herself rest.

He'd be a perfect kind of person to rest on, she thought.

Solid. Capable.

Good.

'Are you going to be all right, Eleni?' he asked her quietly, seeming to sense some of what was going through her mind.

'I'll be fine,' she said, knowing that she had to be, and pulled back. 'Absolutely fine.'

His eyes, in the darkness, were glassy with fatigue, but warm.

'I'm so sorry,' he said. 'I am so sorry that this has happened to your home.'

'It's not your fault,' she said, which it of course wasn't.

'What are you going to do?' he asked.

'Leave,' she said, needing him to believe it too. *Just to be safe.* 'Over the mountains.'

'Perhaps I'll see you in Alexandria.'

'Perhaps you will,' she said, even though he most certainly wouldn't.

'Until then,' he said, raising his hand in a salute.

'Until then,' she echoed, saluting him back.

He went to the door, opened it, then paused, turning back to her.

'I really do hope we meet again,' he said.

'So do I,' she replied. Then, struck by sudden certainty, 'I have a feeling we will.'

It was two days later, on 27 May, that the signal arrived from Cairo, authorizing the evacuation of all Allied forces on Crete to Africa, via the port at Sphakia. The hospital had already cleared out the night before, unable, with the Germans closing in, to wait any longer to forge their path to the mountains.

Eleni, who still hadn't found Tips, had gone with them.

In the close, smoky darkness of the warehouse forecourt – amid the stretchers and ambulances and walking wounded streaming away – she'd said her impossibly painful goodbyes, to Maria, to Spiros, and to Yorgos, her eyes burning with the effort of not upsetting them more with her tears.

'Please look after yourself,' she told Yorgos, clinging to him, 'please.'

Then, taking the package of oranges, bread and cheese Maria had cobbled together ('Eat it slowly,' both Yorgos and Spiros instructed, 'so the energy lasts'), she forced herself to leave them, running before she could weaken and turn back, joining the rest of the staff heading inland, towards the mountains. In the masses of others congregating on the chugging road – the retreating soldiers; the diplomats, and their families; the refugees from Athens; the Greek girls dressed up in uniform so as to try and escape with their soldier boyfriends; the troop trucks racing against their tide, heading for the fighting, horns blaring in their urgency to hold the advancing Germans back for as long as they could – it really was too easy to slip away, lose herself in the melee.

And disappear.

'Remembering wartime Greece.' Transcript of research interview undertaken by M. Middleton (M.M.) with subject seventeen (#17), at British Broadcasting House, 6 June 1974

M.M: Did she ever find the cat?

#17: Excuse me?

M.M: The cat. Did Eleni find it?

#17: I must say I'm a little surprised that you're asking about that, given everything else I've just spoken about. It was just a cat. With a very foolish name . . .

M.M: Did she though?

#17: What?

M.M: Find him?

#17: No.

M.M: Oh.

#17: [Sighs] The cat found Yorgos. He got all the way back to the villa. Does that make you feel better?

M.M: Eleni knew?

#17: Yes, she found out.

M.M: Good. That does make me feel better.

#17: I'm so glad.

M.M: Where did she go though?

#17: Eleni? Not far at all. [Shifts in seat] She told me that she did consider returning to Heraklion. She knew that in many ways it would have been the most straightforward path. She'd become familiar with the town, had made useful contacts there, with Pendlebury's help. But . . .

M.M: She wanted to keep an eye on her family?

#17: It wasn't only that. Not even primarily that, I don't believe. She'd decided, well before the invasion commenced, that, given the British had chosen Chania for their headquarters, it was more than likely any occupier would too. She wanted to position herself at the centre of things, where she could be of the most use. She really was very single-minded about being useful.

M.M: Never more so, I imagine, than after having lived through the invasion. Then the reprisals . . .

#17: Yes.

M.M: They must have angered her, tremendously.

#17: They angered a great number of people. Shattered a lot of hearts.

M.M: More than a thousand Cretans murdered, in just the first three months. Most of them without trial. Entire villages razed to the ground . . .

#17: They were a travesty. A crime of . . . wicked proportions. [Long silence] I remember, just before the surrender, there was a plane that flew over the

island, dropping pieces of paper warning
Crete what was coming. I picked one up. It
made me feel . . . [Sighs] [Shakes head].
For years, decades, the words were . . .
tattooed on my memory. [Brief silence] I'm
struggling to recall them now . . .

M.M: I have them. [Consults notes] [Quotes] It
is certain that the civilian populations
including women and boys have taken part
in the fighting, committed sabotage,
mutilated and killed wounded soldiers. It
is therefore high time . . .

#17: To undertake reprisals with exemplary
terror. [Bows head] Yes. Yes. I do
remember.

M.M: Then [reads] there are the listed threats.
Shooting. Fines. Burning of villages.
Extermination of male populations.

#17: Like I say. Wicked. Evil.

M.M: Did you see any of it?

#17: Enough. [Draws deep breath] [Closes eyes]
I saw enough.

M.M: Where were you?

#17: [Shakes head] [Places face in hands]

M.M: Let's take a short break.

#17: [Nods]

[Recording stopped]
[Recording resumed]

M.M: Are you ready?

#17: Yes I'm ready.

M.M: The reprisals then . . .

#17: Not all Germans agreed with them. The
parachute division's chief of staff refused
to give his support. Plenty wouldn't take
part in the executions. But of course there
were those who raised their hand. There
were enough of those. [Silence] Women had
their shoulders examined for bruises from
rifle butts. If they had them, they were
executed too . . . [Presses fingers to
eyes] There was a lot of resentment, from
General Student downwards, at how fierce
the resistance had been to the invasion.
No one had expected so many men to die. It
enraged Student that Cretans had helped to
defend their home. He despised guerrillas.
Feared them too. There was a great deal
of fear, from the very start of the
occupation, of the Cretan resistance.
Especially of the *kapitans*. You've visited
Chania, yes?

M.M: I have.

#17: Then you'll have seen the way the mountains
loom over it. You can't ignore them,
when you're in the town. Everywhere you
look, there they are. I feel absolutely
certain in saying that there wasn't
a single occupying soldier who didn't, very
often, glance at those mountains and feel
absolutely chilled at the thought of those
who were up there, hidden in their caves,
looking down at them, waiting to do what
they couldn't imagine next. General Student
and his successors, General Andrae, General

Bräuer, General Müller [draws breath],
they were determined to keep the population
subjugated. So they carried out their
reprisals, all through the occupation,
General Bräuer more moderately than Müller.
Müller really was a man of unutterable
cruelty. But even Bräuer continued with
them. Those first three months of the
occupation were just the start. For every
German soldier found dead, every act of
sabotage, a patrol would be sent out, men
seized, women and children taken away while
their villages were burned, but [coughs]
with quite the opposite effect to the
one intended, only causing more [coughs]
hatred, more determination to resist.

M.M: For Eleni too?

#17: Yes, for Eleni too. [Coughs] Could I have
some water please? I have been talking
a great deal.

M.M: Yes, of course. Here, let me. [Fetches jug]
[Pours glass]

#17: [Drinks] Where were we?

M.M: With Eleni. Did she know anyone who was
killed in the reprisals?

#17: No. Not in the reprisals. But they still
devastated her, naturally. Like the bombing
of Chania had. She was never able to
forgive that either. Although [drinks more]
she did comment that it had made it a deal
easier for her to slip back into town
undetected, before the surrender. So many
people had had to find new homes. If anyone

277

ever did ask her where she'd come from, she simply told them that her family's house on the other side of Chania had been hit, and that she'd lost them all. People shy from tragedy. No one pushed her . . .

M.M: What had she been planning to tell them if Chania hadn't been bombed?

#17: I don't know. [Frowns] [Further drink] She'd have come up with something though. She was an incredibly unruffled liar.

M.M: Where did she live in town?

#17: A small apartment, in the basement of an old Venetian building. Quite beautiful actually. The gods were on her side, at that point, and it had survived the fires. She'd leased it before the start of the invasion, filled it with essentials, and went straight to it as soon as she'd left the others evacuating from her hospital. The whole town was still smoking, largely abandoned, save for the rats. No one saw her go in.

M.M: She must have felt very alone.

#17: I suspect she did. You'd never have got her to admit to something like that though. She made herself busy anyway, disguising herself . . . compellingly. I didn't immediately recognize her myself, the first time I saw her again. She wore these [gestures with hands] shapeless clothes that the SOE desk back in London had issued her with. She hated them . . .

M.M: I can't imagine they suited her style.

#17: [Frowns] Her style?

M.M: You mentioned about her shorts.

#17: Oh yes, the shorts. [Smiles briefly] [Shakes head.] No, these were nothing like those. She had a headscarf too, that Pendlebury had given her before he was killed. [Brief silence] She always spoke of him fondly.

M.M: Everyone I've met who encountered him, does.

#17: She'd joked with him about not wanting to dye her hair, that was why he gave her the scarf. But she dyed her hair anyway. Just to be safe, she said. It was her motto. Just to be safe. [Picks up water] [Stares] [Sets glass down]

M.M: What colour did she dye it?

#17: Not black, like they'd wanted her to in London. She claimed it would have looked too obvious, and was probably right. She'd got hold of some brown dye. She was incredibly beautiful, I have to tell you. Those blue eyes. A not dissimilar shade to yours, but even more . . . vivid . . . once her hair was darker . . .

M.M: An assassin dressed up as a goddess, you said before.

#17: Indeed. A Greek goddess though. She looked entirely Greek. No one seeing her would have had cause to question it. It made it all the more startling when she broke into English, as she still did with me. She had to be so careful though. As soon as the

dust settled, she started work as a typist
in the town hall . . .

M.M: The town hall?

#17: Yes. She'd decided, quite rightly, that
it would be an excellent place for her
to pick up intelligence. Chania's mayor,
Skoulas, helped her do it. She didn't
suppose any German working there would
have reason to suspect she understood the
language . . .

M.M: Clever.

#17: Very much so.

M.M: And brave. To work in the thick of . . .

#17: Nazis? Yes. Incredibly brave. She was
in excellent company in that respect.
Every act of resistance back then, small
or large, took unfathomable courage,
and [raises hands] there were so many
at it. There were thousands of men left
behind on Crete after the evacuation.
There was simply no time for the ships
to get everyone off. Many were interned,
of course, but the prison camps were
poorly guarded, and there were plenty
of escapes. I doubt there was a single
Cretan community that didn't have some
combination of Kiwi corporals, Australian
diggers and British Tommies concealed
within it. They had so little food, and
yet they kept them fed. Safe until they
could move . . .

M.M: Even with the anvil of reprisals hanging
over their heads.

#17: Indeed. But to me, their awareness of the dangers only made their bravery more admirable.

M.M: You admired them?

#17: I did. I admired Eleni. One of the things she did, very quickly, was build a network of women, working in administrative posts like her, who helped get warnings out to the villages of planned patrols, so people had time to move, and hide. She was under no delusions about what she'd face if she was discovered. She kept her cyanide pill with her always. She was by no stretch naive. Alive, in actual matter, to the threat of traitors. She always had her eye out, just not directed, in the end, at the right place . . .

M.M: You mean at you?

#17: I do.

M.M: Can you go on?

#17: I can. But [Coughs] I . . . [Reaches for handkerchief] [Wipes head] I'm becoming rather tired. Could we please have another break?

M.M: Of course.

#17: Thank you.

M.M: Another brief question first though, if I may?

#17: You may.

M.M: How long into the occupation was it before you saw her again?

#17: Oh, it was months. It had been going on for almost a year.

M.M: Where did it happen?

#17: Where did I see her?

M.M: Yes.

[Long silence]

#17: Chania.

M.M: At the town hall?

#17: No. No. [Long sigh] I saw her in the main
square.

CRETE, 1942

Chapter Seventeen

Chania, April 1942

It was Friday, close to seven. The days, lengthening now after the chilling, endless winter that had been, were still much shorter than the summer ones Eleni had once only known, and already there was the tint of approaching dusk to the old town's pixelating tones of blue, pink and grey. She'd come to the square from work; another week at her typewriter behind her. Would her grandma in Sutton be proud of this secretarial post she'd taken? Eleni, wanting very much not to care (*strumpet, absolute strumpet*), nonetheless found herself hoping that she would. Although she suspected that not even she would want her fishing for a husband from the pool of men she was now surrounded with: the Nazi officers who spent their days processing requisition orders for the islanders' livestock, issuing fines for non-compliance, keeping a tally of the provisions they hoarded for themselves behind Chania's locked market gates. Not that any German was permitted to fraternise with a Greek woman. It was an arrestable offence. They had their military-run brothels. Let that be enough for them.

Hardly any of them at the town hall spoke Greek. Mainly they got by with English, and the help of bilingual Cretan translators: women who, unlike Eleni, could admit to having learnt English at school. It was useful that, whenever they spoke confidentially to one another – on all manner of matters: patrols; rumoured landings of British spies; the ongoing war in that unreachable world beyond Crete's shores, silenced now to the rest of them, thanks to the prohibition of outside news – they did it in German.

It worked really quite well for Eleni that they did that. (And had a tendency to hover near her desk.)

She'd overheard nothing of particular interest that day though. If she had, she'd have taken it directly to Socrates: her only real link now to her past.

The two of them had, to their mutual happiness and amazement, been reunited the June before, introduced, covertly, as fellow resistance fighters by Eleni's employer, the mayor, Mr Skoulas – himself much amused at their already knowing one another (and even more by Socrates' shock at Eleni's appearance). Back then, Socrates' main business had been in assisting POWs on their escape to Africa, *no problem,* using his runners – old students of his – to identify hideouts in the mountains, then navigating the soldiers to them. These days, with so many of the POWs safely gone from town, he and his runners focused on speeding any information Eleni, or another of her colleagues, fed them, to whichever village, or hidden British radio operative, or *kapitan*, it was most pertinent to: a veritable network of whispers that travelled the entire island.

The Cretan Wireless, it was becoming known as.

Its existence absolutely maddened the Germans. They were always trying to recruit informers to help them get to the bottom of who was part of it, and the wider resistance movement, seldom successfully. Whilst they had managed to bring some locals into their fold, there were very few prepared to help them, which only maddened them more. Eleni had heard tell of occasions when they'd disguised themselves as straggling British soldiers, trying to infiltrate the villages and sniff out partisans that way, but as soon as they began their enquiries into who, locally, had a means of contacting agents to help them with their escape, the villagers turned on them, feigning outrage at the suggestion that any of them might consider such a heinous crime, dragging them to the nearest Nazi guard post for arrest as a traitor to the Reich.

Eleni enjoyed those stories.

They really were quite far from her mind, however, in the square that evening.

She was at its edge, lingering by the entrance to the alleyway that would take her home, inspecting a handful of *horta* at a stall. The harbour wasn't far away. Over the earthy scent of the *horta*, she could smell the sea. *Will we ever breathe such things again?* They did now. Those of them that were left. The square itself was busy, filled with scores of off-duty soldiers taking their leisure in its *kafeterias*, drinking, smoking, writing letters, playing cards. A pair of guards sat, bored, on the wall of the central fountain, leaning on their rifles, staring out at the Cretans passing them by: the office workers, children with their mothers, and farmers leading donkeys, who resolutely ignored their attention. In the bustle, Eleni had, for herself, just been speaking with a man in peasant clothes – the type of breeches, cummerbund and waistcoat that the Vassilis favoured – passing on, at Mr Skoulas's, request, an address outside of town. Nothing more than that. But, as she'd done it, she'd noticed a young soldier at the nearest *kafeteria* eyeing her.

'Go,' she'd told the man, 'slowly,' and, as he had, she'd decided to stop and buy the *horta* she was now holding, not wanting to tempt any more of this soldier's interest by being on her way too hastily, knowing it would only make her brief conversation appear too much like the assignation it had been.

Handing the bunch of *horta* to the stallholder, she asked her how much, then, if she had any eggs, or cheese, or meat, realizing she wouldn't – the Germans had, from the start of the occupation, pilfered almost all the island had – but eliciting a cackle.

'What a shame,' said Eleni, laughing too, glancing around to check if the soldier was still there. He was. 'And there I'd been hoping to make *kleftiko*.'

'Ah, *kleftiko*,' the woman said, emitting a nostalgic sigh. 'I'll dream of it tonight.'

'I'm sorry.'

'No, I'll enjoy it. Here, give me your basket.'

Handing it over, then her drachma, Eleni risked another look at the soldier, feeling her pulse quicken as his eyes caught hers. *Damn. Stupid.* Smiling at a non-existent person to his left, she adjusted her shawl, then, *casually*, thanked the woman for her change, remarking on how glad she was that the week was at an end. The first one of April.

This time the year before, she'd only just arrived in Heraklion, met Pendlebury. Each morning when she put on his headscarf (*to be safe*) she thought of him, still unable to believe, even after all this time, that he, with his glass eye, and expansive, generous laugh, was gone. Killed, in the last days of the battle, just outside of Heraklion.

Mr Skoulas – so high on his list of allies, and such an ally to Eleni, from the day she'd first approached him, before the invasion, with her request that he give her a post at the town hall, should Crete fall – had been the one to tell her.

We carry on for him as well now, yes?

'I've snails,' the woman at the stall said, with a nod at her feet. 'Want any?'

'Not really,' Eleni replied, having failed repeatedly through the hungry winter to condition herself into liking them, 'but I'll take some anyway.'

More cackling.

The pair of them were really hitting it off.

'Just a few,' Eleni cautioned, as the woman ducked to add the unfortunate molluscs to her pile of greens. Whilst she did, Eleni risked one more look back at the soldier in the *kafeteria*, frowning when she saw he'd disappeared.

Was that a good, or bad thing?

Ordinarily, she wouldn't have let something so minor needle her. She'd long stopped reacting to every glance, or request for her papers, or barked command, or even shy smile, that a German threw her way. She'd had to. She'd never have survived for so long, in the thick of so many of them, otherwise; her edginess would assuredly have given her away, jeopardising everyone else whose secrets she shared, by association.

But this evening . . .

This evening she *was* uneasy.

It wasn't only the thought of the address she'd just given that man, of a nearby safehouse that Mr Skoulas, and several others – SOE agents and *kapitans* among them – were to meet that coming Sunday. The imperativeness of it remaining secret. There was a strange energy to the cool evening. A low-level tension that was making her senses prickle.

'Thank you,' she said to the woman, taking her full basket. 'Enjoy your dreams.'

A final cackle.

Eleni smiled, and set off.

Where the hell had that young soldier gone?

It wasn't a long walk home. Just a few minutes. The darkening alleyways were quieter than the square had been, but not empty. Not like they had been when Eleni had first returned to Chania. Then, the smouldering town had been so silent that, at night, she'd been able to hear every scurrying rodent, each drip of water that had been used to douse the Luftwaffe's flames.

She had been lonely. Grieving too, for all that had happened, and was happening. The Swastikas that were hoisted above Chania's roofs. The bursts of gunfire from the reprisals.

That little girl in her mother's arms.

She was still grieving. Still lonely. She had, early on, briefly taken in a couple of British soldiers, before Socrates had arranged for their transport back to Egypt, but they'd been with her less than a week, and gone nearly a year. Now, other than her landlord, and Socrates – who was in any case often out of town – she had no friends nearby. Weekends were the hardest. She always missed her *papou*, and everyone, most through them. She never ventured near Halepa, nor the surgery, nor any place they might be. Over the winter, she'd got into the habit of walking, for miles, to keep herself from giving into the temptation to seek them out. Sometimes though, she'd weakened, taken herself up to the hillside above the villa, there to conceal herself at the vantage point she'd discovered, where she'd remain for hours, in all weathers, waiting for glimpses of Yorgos. She even saw Tips.

She'd been so happy, the first time she'd spotted him.

And things *had* got easier. These days, there were at least people like that woman in the square for her to talk to. And the other secretaries at the town hall (they'd formed quite a collective). Nonetheless, she still felt isolated enough to be grateful for the companionship, however silent, of the other islanders she passed by in the alleyway, if not the odd, inevitable German, heading in the direction of the square.

Nor, indeed, the one who was following her.

She saw him, about thirty yards behind her, when, unable to shake her earlier disquiet, she paused, setting her basket down and picking it up again – as though *horta* and a few snails was any kind of burden to carry – casting a furtive glance back. He slowed too, in tandem, seemingly still making his mind up about coming forward.

Mouth dry, she set off again, holding herself back from checking if he'd done the same, hoping that, if he had, he'd lose interest when he realized how unconcerned she was. Every instinct compelled her to hurry. The muscles in her legs burned with the urge.

She took a turning, into a narrower alley, chequered with the gaps of blitzed houses. It was quieter than the one before, she was the only one in it, but only a minute or so now from her own front door. All remained silent. No boots behind her. She held her breath, uttering a silent prayer that none would come.

But just as she reached her next turning, there they were.

They were getting closer too, their tread irregular, shuffling, deepening her impression that the young soldier wearing them hadn't yet made his mind up to stop her.

Her breath quickened, making her dizzy.

She turned again, keenly aware that she was taking herself into ever-gloomier, deserted alleys, but also that, short of turning on her heel and facing up to this soldier-boy behind her, she had precious little choice in the matter.

What did he want with her?

Could he have guessed what she'd been saying to that man before?

Or had someone else got wind of why she'd been sent to meet him, and asked this soldier to bring her in?

She didn't think it was that. He would surely have arrested her already.

Perhaps this boy had his mind on something else entirely.

Damn, she thought.

Damn, damn, damn.

She darted left, finally permitting herself to speed up as she took a last turning, reaching the crooked stone steps up to her own row of Venetian terraces, with their chipped bricks, faded paintwork, and balconies that were iron, rather than wood, so had survived Chania's inferno. Most of the houses stood vacant. Two had had Jewish families in them: one couple with a sweet little baby, the other with a trio of teenage sons. Eleni had met them only briefly before they'd disappeared, just like that, one night at the beginning of the occupation, no one knew where to. She'd tried to find out, but not even Mr Skoulas had been able to help her. *I wish I could.* Other than them, the terraces had emptied when work had dried up in the town, their tenants returning to families in the villages. Although a couple were still occupied, their residents, like Eleni, kept themselves to themselves, and certainly didn't peer from their windows now as she broke into a run, intent on slipping down into the alcove of her front door before her soldier-shadow had a chance to reach the alley himself.

The view of the mountains was clearer than ever, above the rooftops; she fixed her eyes on their peaks, still capped with snow – the white bathed in the sun's final beams, all the brighter for the darkness that was thickening by the second around her – thinking, fleetingly, of everyone up there who'd be willing her on.

Then,

'*Fräulein*,' came the boy's voice. '*Fräulein. Halt.*'

She cursed, stopped.

He was still a little way behind her. At the head of the stairs, she guessed.

There was something familiar about his voice. She couldn't place it.

She didn't turn towards him either.

Needing to calm herself, she forced a long, deep breath.

'*Fräulein*,' he said again, then broke off as another set of boots, much surer than his, came up the stairs.

She heard a murmured conversation.

'*Jawohl*,' the boy said.

And the new boots carried on, towards her.

Not quickly.

Not hastening, like she'd hastened.

Not hesitant either. Just taking their time, even as the boy sounded to turn, and retreat.

Eleni almost wanted him to come back.

He, young and uncertain, had sounded far easier to manage than whomever was wearing these boots.

She was ready for the hand that seized her.

It still shocked her, when it came.

The gentleness of the grip that closed around her arm, shocked her.

Then, a voice.

A voice she didn't doubt she'd heard before.

His voice.

'Come with me,' he said.

'Remembering wartime Greece.' Transcript of research interview undertaken by M. Middleton (M.M.) with subject seventeen (#17), at British Broadcasting House, 6 June 1974

#17: It had been so long since I'd seen her. She'd changed.

M.M: You've said about her disguise . . .

#17: It wasn't just that. She'd changed in herself. It shouldn't have been a surprise. Everyone was changed by the war. But she . . . She'd become . . . [searches for word] harder.

M.M: Harder?

#17: Tougher.

M.M: I suppose she had to be.

#17: I suppose she did. Even so, it was a . . . jolt. I would never have believed, back in thirty-six, that she could have killed someone. Then [shakes head], then, I didn't doubt it.

Chapter Eighteen

'Come with me.'

He spoke in English, for no other reason that it was what they'd always done with one another. He did it quietly though. For her ears only.

She said nothing in reply. Not at first.

She didn't move.

For a few seconds, she did nothing but stare.

He stared back at her, into those eyes he'd never forgotten, but which he'd given up on ever seeing, so close, again. He'd given up on a lot of things, over the course of the year that he'd served here in the *Festung Kreta . . . Fortress Crete*. He no longer hoped he'd one day leave it.

He'd lost any belief he deserved to.

He watched her eyes move, in just the same way as they had the first time they'd met, down on the harbour, with Fred Astaire playing. Then, she'd been smiling. Now, as she took in his cap, his uniform, the insignia on his chest, his sleeve, her lips turned in disgust. And God, it hurt. He'd known it would, but not like this. Not as bad as this . . .

'Where are we going?' she asked, finally speaking, also in English, as quietly as he had, but not so quiet that he didn't catch the edge to her tone. An edge that let him know that, even in her hatred, she was remembering other things too. Like the hours they'd lost, sitting beneath their tree; how they'd kissed in the rain at Notre-Dame (and no, he hadn't gone near it, when he'd marched through Paris); the way they'd used to wrap themselves up in one another, drifting in the sea.

He didn't know why the thought of her memories hurt even more.

'Are you arresting me?'

'If we stay here much longer, and Weber decides to join us, I might not have much choice.'

'Weber?' she said. 'That's his name?'

'Let me worry about him.'

'I'd rather not, if it's all the same to you. Tell me who he is.'

'Fine.' Still holding her arm, he pulled her on, in the opposite direction to the one he'd ordered Weber to return. 'First we need to move. He might still be watching. I won't keep you long.'

He didn't intend to.

And he hadn't thought for them to go far. He didn't want to risk the pair of them running into anyone else. He knew these streets. They need only get to the next one, and would have their pick of abandoned bombsites to hide in.

Wordlessly, they walked.

As soon as they rounded the corner, he dropped her arm.

'Here then,' she said, slipping into the doorless, roofless shell of a home.

Inside, it was all blackness, broken stones, and smashed furniture.

'Make you proud?' she said.

He ignored the question.

She set her basket down on the remnants of a dresser, and tipped her head back, looking up at the first stars pricking the April sky. It was getting colder. He saw how she held her shawl wrapped around herself, the chill sheening her skin. He followed her gaze upwards, seeing Venus. He'd searched for it every night he'd been back on the island, even the first one he'd come, when he hadn't dared chance sleep, but had slumped against a tree, his gun in his lap, the few who'd been left of his men around him, and Fischer whimpering about his arm. Always, when he'd found the star, he'd thought of her.

He didn't tell her that now though.

Make you proud?

She wouldn't want to hear it.

He could understand why Weber hadn't been sure she was who he'd suspected she was, just now. In her thick stockings and old-fashioned dress, that cloth scarf covering her darkened hair, she could almost have fooled Otto.

He was often in Chania, only able to take so much of existing between his billet, and the division's parade ground at Souda. Whilst it was invariably hideous, being in town, facing up to the disgust directed at him from almost every corner, the thought of her kept pulling him back. Everywhere he looked, he saw the ghost of her, with the ghost of him – happy, careless, laughing, *never too much* – and, when he did, felt human again, like he still had a soul.

He got that most in the square.

He'd never forgotten that promise they'd made to one another in her bed, that they'd meet again there.

We'll see each other, he'd said, *but still have to look twice . . .*

He supposed, part of him at least, had been waiting for this moment.

He'd been alone at a table, writing to Krista (*I don't know how much longer I can go on*) when he'd looked up, and, seeing her talking to that Greek man, felt his entire body go still. He hadn't taken his eyes from her, so had noticed the glances she'd kept throwing in Weber's direction, quickly suspecting that all was not right.

Then Weber had moved from his table, circumnavigating

her, clearly trying to get a better look, and he'd *known* all was not right.

Otto actually quite liked Weber. He hadn't led him during the invasion. It was only after the surrender that Weber, having lost his own CO, had been put under his command. He reminded Otto, in many ways, of how seventeen-year-old Meyer, with his mother's blanket, had used to be. Before Fischer had done what he had to him. He was even younger though, only recently turned seventeen. Traumatised, still, from the battle. He'd been badly wounded, taken prisoner. Nearly died . . .

'Did you nurse?' Otto asked Eleni now, drawing her attention down from the sky, back to him. 'During the invasion?'

She frowned, bemused. 'I wasn't a nurse . . . '

'But you helped in a hospital?'

'Yes . . . '

'Were any of your patients German?'

'Any . . . ?' she began, then stopped, her expression clearing in understanding. 'That was *him*?' Her eyes widened in alarm. 'I spoke to him in German . . . '

'It's fine. He wasn't certain it was you.'

'*Papou* said he didn't have long . . . '

'Well, he's still here. I've told him I'll take you in for questioning.'

'You followed us?'

'Yes.' Once he'd found them again. It had taken him a minute. 'I reminded Weber of the trouble he could get into for chasing a Greek woman home at night.'

'*I swear, sir*,' Weber had stuttered, '*I wasn't planning to do anything. I just want to see if it's her . . .* '

'*Do you speak Greek?*' Otto had asked.

'*No.*'

'*Then you'll scare her, if she's not who you think. Go back, leave this with me.*'

298

'You're not worried about getting into trouble?' Eleni asked him, coldly.

'No,' he said, wearily. 'Come on—' he moved back towards her '—it's probably safe for you to go home now.'

He didn't want her to. God knew he didn't want her to.

But he didn't want this either.

'How long have you been here?' she asked, remaining where she was, looking up at him, her entire body tense with restraint. Like those Greeks on the mainland who'd stared into his truck. All the French. 'How long . . . ?'

'From the start,' he said, wishing he had a different answer. 'I landed at the start.'

'On a glider?'

'In a parachute.'

She stared.

'You were one of them?'

'Yes, I was. Come—' he turned '—let's go.'

'Did you take part in the reprisals?' she asked.

Slowly, he turned back to her.

Her eyes, glinting in the darkness, burned into his. She clenched her hands in fists.

'You're seriously asking me that, Eleni?'

'I am seriously asking you that, Otto.'

It was his turn to stare.

Go to hell, he so nearly told her.

'I got demoted,' he said instead, stepping closer, 'for refusing to.'

'Yes?'

'Yes.'

She flicked another look at his insignia. 'What were you before? A general?'

'A captain. I got promoted again.' He had Major Count Von Uxkall, the parachute division's chief-of-staff, to thank for that.

'I have not shot a single Cretan. Not even the ones who killed my men . . . '

'Should I thank you?'

'No.'

'How can you be here?' Her eyes were by now liquid. She was trying not to cry.

It took him back to when they'd stood in another set of ruins, in the heat, not the cold; at Knossos. He'd hated it for her then. He hated it now.

'Eleni, please . . . '

'Shame on you.' She struck him on the chest. Then again, and again. '*Shame* on you, Otto.'

'Shame on me, yes. Shame on me. I am drowning, Eleni.' He caught her wrists. 'I am drowning in my shame.'

'God, Otto,' she said, and wasn't hitting him anymore.

She was pushing him away, scrambling over the rubble to go.

Never write to me again, she'd said, in her letter.

'Don't you dare follow me,' she told him now. 'Don't you dare come near me.'

Don't you dare follow me.

She didn't want him to.

She got herself from that building without a backwards glance, her hands smarting from where she'd struck him, and only hated him.

She hated him.

How long have you been here?

From the start . . .

She didn't care that he could so easily have been one of those sticks she'd watched fall limp, on that first day of the invasion.

She didn't.

She couldn't have given less of a damn about the flash of fury in his eyes when she'd asked about the reprisals.

No, the sobs rising in her, filling her chest, her throat, as she blindly retraced the steps they'd just taken, making for the lonely sanctuary of her basement, had nothing to do with her pain at his obvious pain, nor any compulsion she'd felt to go to him. She'd known she couldn't go to him. Not like she'd gone to that boy, *Weber*. (*Don't let compassion in*. What an idiot she'd been.) She'd felt no compulsion. She hadn't been disturbed by any treacherous happiness either, when she'd heard his voice. *Come with me*. He was her enemy. All of their enemy. *That* was why she was having to fight back her tears.

Shame on him.

She ran down the steep, shadowy stairwell to her front door, jaw set against the memory of his words.

Shame on me, yes.

I am drowning, Eleni, in my shame.

She reached her door, and, needing her key, slammed her hand against the wood, realizing she had, in her haste, left it, along with her basket, behind in the ruined house.

It tipped her over the edge. Giving into her tears, she sank her head against the door, and wept.

I could drown with you, he'd once said to her, swimming, in the water beside that rock with its urchins.

I'd never let you, she'd told him. *Never*.

She hated the thought that he was drowning now. She did. At least as much as she hated him.

Why did he have to be here?

Why?

Finding no answer to her own impossible question, but needing her key, she pushed herself from the door and, wiping her eyes, returned through the chill night to the rubble.

He was still there, sitting on a pile of stones, his cap off, his head in his hands, fingers pressed into his short, short hair.

She wasn't surprised to see him.

It came to her that she'd known she would.

Had she left her basket on purpose, then?

Wanted, on some subconscious level, to grant herself this excuse to return?

He raised his head, as though hearing her silent question, and, as his green eyes met hers, she felt her heart, her treacherous heart, catch.

Silently, she went to the dresser.

He watched her move. She felt the pressure of his stare on her skin.

She reached her basket. It had tipped when she'd put it down, and there were only three snails left inside, gorging on the leaves. Two had made a break for freedom and were inching painstakingly across the shattered wood, silver trails reflecting the moonlight; their version of a sprint.

She left them to it.

Good for them, really, to have got away.

Impulsively, she set their friends free too, and picked her basket up.

Don't look at him, she told herself, *just go.*

Even as she thought it, she turned, facing him. His eyes, fierce with feeling, once again held hers, transporting her to a thousand different moments when they'd looked at her, so differently.

She'd loved him. She'd loved him so much.

Goodbye, she needed to say.

'How is your mother?' she heard herself asking instead.

'She died,' he said, and the words, his pain, struck her, wrong-footing her all the more. 'Just before I was meant to meet you in Paris.'

'Oh, Otto.' She closed her swollen eyes. *Never write to me again.* 'Why didn't you tell me?'

'It was too . . . hard. Complicated.'

'I am so sorry,' she said, and was, in spite of everything. Deeply,

deeply sorry. She pictured Brigit as she'd briefly known her; frail and wan and kind. The way she'd smiled whenever she'd looked at Otto or Krista that day at Knossos, then over their last dinner at Nikos's villa; her tears on her cheeks, watching Marianne play. 'I'm so very, very sorry.'

'Thank you.'

She thought of how devastated Marianne was going to be. Then, Marianne's worry, all this time, over Krista's silence, never writing to her, not even before the war . . .

'Krista isn't . . . ?'

'No.'

Thank God.

'Why didn't she write to Marianne?'

'She said she didn't know how to, without telling her about Mama . . . '

'But why wouldn't she? Why didn't you . . . ?'

'For what purpose?'

'Marianne adores her.'

'She's lost everything, Eleni. Why add to it?'

'Because,' Eleni began, then stopped, unsure what to even say. He sighed, deeply. 'You stayed in touch with Marianne?'

'Yes. Until I came here.'

'How is she?'

'Well, the last I heard, the man she lives with, Hans, your mother's old colleague, he was helping her to apply for a scholarship at his music school.'

'Music school?'

'Yes.'

'That's good. God—' he filled his lungs, as though the goodness was oxygen – which to him, perhaps it was. 'I'm happy for her.'

'Yes,' said Eleni, hit now by more disorientating memories: of how he'd used to tug Marianne's plaits, and fling her in the water, teasing her, like he'd teased Krista . . .

'And Esther?' he said.

'Esther's fine,' she said. Then, needing, finally, to be certain, 'You gave Lotte my address?'

'Yes.'

'Did you marry her?' The question was out before she knew it was coming.

'What?' His brow creased. 'No, Eleni. *No.*'

'No?'

'No.'

No.

Relief washed through her.

She shouldn't be relieved.

She shouldn't . . .

'How could you have thought that?' he asked.

'I assumed,' she said, 'when she wrote to me . . . '

'I told her she should. That you'd want to help.'

'I did,' she said, numbly.

'And Esther's really fine . . . ?'

'She is.' Hector kept her assured of that. He, still incandescent at her *going rogue,* as he put it, nonetheless always included news of Esther in the communications he sent. Eleni could only guess at the story he'd spun Helen about her own protracted absence. 'I didn't imagine I'd be gone this long. But she's living on a farm, with Helen Finch, my old—'

'Landlady. I haven't forgotten.'

'No,' said Eleni, still reeling. 'She has a puppy, friends to play with. I left her happy.'

'Happy,' he echoed, and, briefly, smiled.

That smile.

Oh God, she thought. *Oh God . . .*

Leave, she told herself.

Turn around and leave.

It would be such a betrayal, to so many people – the women

at her work, Mr Skoulas, Pendlebury, the *kapitans*. Socrates, Dimitri, Little Vassili; the list was endless – if she didn't.

'Otto,' she began.

'I know,' he said. 'It's all right, Eleni. Go.'

'I don't want to.' Again, the words were out before she could stop them. 'I don't . . . '

He said nothing.

He wasn't going to ask her to stay.

He, drowning in his shame, would never do that.

Go.

Cheeks working, seeing little else for it, but unable any more to leave him hated, not like she had before, she set her basket down, then crossed the rubble to him, intent, however much it hurt, on giving him a final kiss farewell.

She stood before him.

He looked up at her.

His face, in the darkness, was achingly familiar: those cheekbones; that dent in his nose from when he'd been a child, sledging with his sister, who'd lost her mother too.

Instinctively, she touched her fingertip to it, then moved her hand to his head, tracing her palm over his short hair, around the base of his neck.

Still, he kept his eyes locked on hers.

Tears by now overflowing, she leant down, touching her lips to his forehead.

She made herself say it. 'Goodbye, Otto.'

But the words rang hollow to her own ears.

It wasn't goodbye.

It was already too late for that.

It had been too late, she realized, from the moment he'd touched her arm.

Perhaps he knew it too.

Or maybe he was asking her to stay after all.

Either way, he placed his hands to her waist, pulling her to him, and then they were kissing, properly kissing, as hungrily as they had in those ruins in Knossos, clinging to one another in the bombed-out ruin his Luftwaffe had made of someone's home, he in his Nazi uniform, her in her Cretan dress, the moon beaming down on them, and Venus shining coldly above.

Chapter Nineteen

'Why are you here?' he asked her, much later that night. 'Why are you still here?'

'Because I need to be,' she said.

'You want to die, Eleni? Is that it?'

'No,' she said. 'Do you?'

'Not here,' he said. 'Not with you.'

'Don't ever want it,' she told him. 'You mustn't.'

They talked about a lot of things that night.

Not at first. Not hidden in the rubble, where a kiss would never have been enough. Giving herself over to the inevitability of it, no longer fighting, because she didn't want to, she pulled him to his feet, and he, not fighting either, gathered her up, backing her further into the building's shell, the deep darkness of its stairwell, where, with his lips on her throat, her hands at his belt, he pushed her against the wall, and neither of them said a word – not of stopping, nor of the risk they were running, nor of anything – but were only silent, and desperate, and reckless, and stupid, and not alone.

Not alone at all.

'I think you'd go to prison for that,' Eleni said, when it was over, and he leant against her, his head sunk in the nook of her neck.

'I think I would,' he said, speaking for the first time in Greek, making her, for the first time, laugh.

It felt wrong.

Even after what they'd done, laughter felt too much.

She swallowed it.

'No,' he said, in English again, moving his head so that he was looking at her, 'please don't.'

'I have to,' she said.

Only she didn't.

It shocked her how quickly she stopped that night.

He couldn't stay with her for all of it. He was billeted, along with three other officers, at a house close to his barracks in Souda. ('What's happened to its owners?' said Eleni. 'I don't know,' he said. 'You don't want to know,' she corrected. 'You're wrong,' he said. 'You're very wrong about that . . . '); he needed to return to Souda at a reasonable hour otherwise the others in his billet, and a man called Fischer particularly, would start asking questions.

'You don't like Fischer?' she guessed.

'I despise him,' he said, a hardness edging his tone that she'd never heard before. 'He's been looking, all year, for an opportunity to get me demoted again. I'm not going to hand it to him. Or risk him finding out about you . . . '

They had just shy of three hours together.

They spent them in her flat.

They didn't return to it together. That would have been too foolish, even on a street as empty and disinterested as hers. She, key in hand, went the front way, and gave him directions around the back, through the entrance to the yard.

'You need to look for a crooked gate, with blue paint . . . '

'It's fine,' he said, 'I'll find it.'

He did, slipping through that blue gate just as she was, very quietly, easing open her back door.

'Must we always be hiding on this island?' he said, as she tugged him inside.

'I think we must,' she said.

He looked around, eyes raking the darkness, taking in her simple living room, with its high, shuttered windows, woven rugs, and old-fashioned furniture, all provided by her landlord: the second of Pendlebury's allies, after Mr Skoulas, whom she'd approached on her return to Chania, asking for his support.

'*It won't be so dangerous*,' she'd insisted, when he'd protested at her plan to stay, '*or certainly no worse than it will be anywhere else I might get sent. Not if you help me. You can do that here . . .* '

He more than had, and not only by giving her this flat. Over the winter, sometimes he'd come by with boxes of black-market food, as heavy as any her *papou* had packaged up.

'This is quite a hideaway,' Otto said.

'It serves the purpose,' she agreed.

He turned his attention back to her. 'I have . . . *endless* questions.'

'So do I.'

Yet still, they didn't ask them. They were together, somehow they were together, in the midst of so much that was hideous, and it felt too raw, too tenuous for Eleni to do anything other than step towards him, even as he reached for her, the two of them kissing again, with no less intensity than they had in the rubble, just more time. She pulled him with her, into her bedroom, with its wrought-iron bed, tugging at the stiff buttons of his uniform, needing him to not be wearing it. He helped her undo them, his hands brushing hers as he wrenched his jacket free, needing, she no longer doubted, not to be wearing it either.

Then he moved away from her, just slightly, running his hands around her face, to the nape of her neck, loosening the knot of her headscarf so that it fluttered to the floor, and her hair, which had grown much longer than it had used to be, spilt down her back.

He watched it fall.

'Look at you,' he said.

'Can you tell it's dyed?' she asked.

'Yes—' he kissed her neck, unfastening her zip '—obviously . . .'

'No, I meant if you hadn't known me before.'

He paused. 'You're asking whether your disguise would fool a Nazi?'

'I suppose I am.'

'Fine,' he said, running his fingers up her exposed spine, turning her legs liquid beneath her, pulling her dress from her shoulders, 'I think it probably would. And these—' his eyes found her stockings '—definitely would.'

She laughed again at that.

Took a little longer to stop herself.

And closed her eyes as, lifting her onto the bed, he pulled those thick stockings, inch by inch, from her skin.

There was no more talking then, either.

That came after, as Eleni lit her bedside oil lamp, and, in the flickering glow, they lay wrapped in her eiderdown, facing one another on the pillows.

There really was such a lot for them to talk about.

Too much, for the couple of hours they had left, but they did their best, their words, held back for too long, flowing between them as freely as they ever had – under their tree, on the bus, in her garden – slowly filling in the years that had passed.

They spoke, before anything else, of his mother.

'How did it happen?' Eleni asked. 'You said it was complicated . . .'

'It was.' He moved, looking at the ceiling, the pillow's feathers creaking. 'Very.'

'Tell me about it,' she said. 'Please.'

So, he did.

He didn't hold back, like he had in the letters he'd sent from his training camp, but confirmed what she'd already pieced together: that he'd loathed his time there. He'd had no one he knew with him – all of them in Munich had been sent to different camps – only scores of Hitler Youth graduates, and commanders who'd drilled them relentlessly, until he – falling in, marching to their rhythm, *heiling* their *heils,* colluding in his failure to do anything else – had made himself numb, because he hadn't known how else to manage it.

'Your letters were . . . everything,' he said. 'When I was reading them, it all went away.' He looked at her. 'You have this . . . knack . . . for making life feel possible.'

She touched her hand to his face, feeling that old swelling in her chest, her throat.

She'd almost forgotten how he did that to her.

She really had almost made herself forget.

He reached for her hand, took it in his, and went on, reliving how everything had crumbled that spring of 1938, after Germany had annexed Austria, after that partner at his father's firm, Friedrich, had found out about Henri helping Jewish families with their visas.

'He and my father were never that friendly. Papa was senior to him. He'd always won more cases, brought in more clients . . .'

'Friedrich was jealous?'

'Bitter. He had friends in the Gestapo. He gave them Papa's name. Lotte's father told her he'd done it, and she asked him to help us, so he said Papa should join the party, that it would prove his loyalty.'

'Did it?'

'It must have. He wasn't arrested. I went back to camp thinking it was behind us. Then you wrote about Paris, and I should never have said I'd come, but I wanted to. I requested leave, booked my ticket . . . ' He broke off. 'I don't think I've ever wanted to do anything more. You need to believe that.'

'I do,' she said. 'I think I always have.' It was part of what had made his not coming so impossible to accept. 'I found the way you told me . . . harder . . . '

'I know.' His brow pinched. 'I wasn't thinking straight . . . '

'Because of your mother.'

'Because of a lot of things.'

He told her that he'd received a wire from his father, two days before his train for Paris. 'He asked me to come home, said that he couldn't tell me why. I knew that something bad must have happened. I assumed it was to do with him. I didn't think . . . I *couldn't* . . . ' He stopped, jaw set against his grief.

Saying nothing, knowing there was nothing she could say, she held his hand, and waited for him to be ready to go on.

The lamp crackled beside them, and, in the lengthening silence, her dread about what was coming next grew. *She died. Just before I was meant to meet you in Paris.* It had been no peaceful passing, she felt sure of it now.

'When I arrived back in Berlin,' he said, 'the house was so silent. Papa was just sitting on the stairs, staring at the door, like he'd been waiting for me for hours.'

She swallowed, seeing it, all too easily. Henri, exhausted, full of anguish . . .

'Friedrich had been . . . upset, that nothing had happened to Papa, and decided to go after Mama.'

'He knew she had multiple sclerosis?'

'He knew she'd been ill. And there'd been dinners that he and his wife had been at with my parents. His wife, Andrea, had noticed Mama's hands. Papa said she'd called around, a couple of days before, told Mama she wanted to apologise for Friedrich going to the Gestapo the way he had, said that she was mortified. Really, she'd just been having another look at her.'

'That's evil . . .'

'Mama was very weak by then. Much worse than when you saw her here. Her tremors were . . . bad. Andrea told Friedrich, and he reported Mama for investigation that same afternoon. Lotte's father came home with the news . . .'

'He couldn't do anything?'

'He promised Lotte he'd try. I don't know if he did. She didn't trust him anyway. She got a message to Krista, told her that the house was being watched, and that none of them should try to contact Mama's doctor . . .'

'Nikos's friend.'

'Yes. Lotte went to him herself, that night, warned him what was happening. He destroyed Mama and Krista's records. There were others he was helping too. He got rid of everything, saved their lives, then left Berlin.'

'I can't believe Lotte did that.' She tried to picture her, running furtively around a dark city, putting herself in danger . . .

'No,' said Otto, 'I never would have believed she had it in her either. She was shaken up, after. Really shaken up. And it didn't help Mama. A letter came the next morning, instructing her to report to a government clinic for tests. Papa said she wasn't scared for herself, only for me and Krista, and what it would mean for us if they found out what she had. Krista had been fine, she still is. No one's ever suspected there's anything wrong with her. Mama thought they'd insist on testing us both, though, as soon as they got her results.'

'Would they?'

'Probably. Papa wanted to try and get her away, to France, or Switzerland, but she thought the Gestapo would arrest her if she moved . . . I don't know.' He expelled a sigh. 'Maybe they would have.'

Eleni tightened her fingers around his. She saw now what had happened. She saw . . .

'She took an overdose,' he said, confirming it, and she felt her stinging eyes fill, because it was so incredibly, unutterably sad. 'She didn't tell Papa she'd decided to. They went to bed, and when he woke, she was gone.'

'I am so sorry.' Words had never felt more useless. 'I can't tell you . . . '

'Yes,' he said, face tense with pain, 'I'm pretty sorry too.'

'Why didn't you say?' she asked him, just as she had in the ruins.

'I didn't know how to. Lotte's father had me brought into Prinz-Albrecht-Strasse . . . '

'What?' It sent her cold. 'You were taken into the Gestapo?'

He smiled, not happily, not at all happily.

She felt sick. 'You must have been . . . '

'I wasn't anything,' he said, before she could say *terrified*. 'I couldn't feel anything. I'd only just got home. Lotte's father must have had someone waiting for me outside. I thought maybe he wanted to talk to me about my mother. But he wanted to talk about you.'

'Me?' She felt even sicker. 'How did he know about me?'

'The Gestapo are pretty efficient at that kind of thing. He knew about our letters, that we'd been to Paris, and were planning on meeting there again . . . He really enjoyed telling me all about it.' Anger hardened his voice. 'He knew plenty about Krista too. Her pamphlets. Her swing friends. He said it was only because of him that she was still safe, that our father was. It seemed really important to him that I understood how much he'd done for our family.'

'Because of all your parents did for Lotte?'

'Probably. I'm pretty sure he's always hated them for it. Hated that they were so much better than him. I think he's felt . . . ashamed of how hard he's made Lotte's life, knows what a bastard he's been to her, and wanted to . . . I don't know, *punish*

314

me, for not fixing that for him.' He gave a short, humourless laugh. 'He asked me what was wrong with me, that I'd chosen an English girl over his daughter. He told me I'd humiliated her, and him by extension, but that no one would ask any more questions about Mama's death, or Krista, or Papa, so long as I stayed in Germany like the loyal Nazi he knew I was, and toed the damn line.'

Eleni struggled to absorb it; that it had all been going on, whilst she'd been in London, excited, happy.

'Did he tell Lotte he'd done it?' she asked.

'Yes. Like he was giving her a gift,' she said. 'She came to my house to apologise. She was upset. Embarrassed . . . '

'So, she knew about us?'

'She did then,' he said, the anger in him softening. 'We could have told her that summer, you know. We all trod on eggshells with her, but it wasn't fair. She'd never have let something like that get in the way of trying to help Mama. She loved her. Really loved her. She was heartbroken at what she'd done. She cried, cried and cried . . . '

Eleni found she could picture that.

'I'm sorry,' she said, again.

'She wanted me to get the train to Paris anyway. She said she'd take care of her father, make sure he didn't do anything to hurt Krista, or Papa . . . '

'Then?'

'She'd never have been able to stop him. She'd have tried, and then he'd have shouted her down, and she'd have given in, because she always has with him, and I couldn't let that happen.' His eyes bore into hers, entreating her to understand. 'They're my family, Eleni. All I've got left.' His voice strained on the painful truth. 'If I'd left them, deserted the army, I don't know what might have happened to them. How could I have done it?'

'You couldn't.' She really did understand that. And how

impossible it must have felt to put any of it in a letter, knowing that that letter would have been intercepted. 'It's all right.'

'No,' he said, heavily. 'It's not.'

'It is,' she insisted. Then, before he could protest again, 'Where's Lotte now?'

'Still in Berlin. Krista sees her. She's the only person she's got now, other than Papa, who she can be honest with . . . '

'And what about Friedrich?'

'He was killed in Poland.'

'Good.'

'Yes,' he said. 'I thought so.'

'I hope a bomb finds his wife.' She said it quite coldly, quite detachedly, in much the same way as she passed the names of traitors on.

Did it shock him?

He didn't look shocked.

He only studied her in the mellow lamplight, as though she were one of his sketches, and it had dawned on him that there was a room he'd yet to fill in.

'I hope it does too,' he said.

'I'm glad you told me.'

'I'm glad you know. It means . . . a lot.'

'Have you told anyone else?' she said. 'Had anyone *you* can be honest with?'

She knew what she was really asking.

So did he.

'I haven't wanted anyone,' he said.

'Not in all this time?'

'Not in all this time. And you?' He continued to appraise her. 'Have you?'

'No one like you,' she said, kissing him. 'No one.'

'No?'

'No.'

'All right,' he said, kissing her back. 'Selfishly, I'm happy . . . '

'You're allowed to be.'

For a little while after that, they said no more, just lay there, their foreheads touching, his hand moving up and down her back.

'So,' he said, at length, 'my questions . . . '

'Oh, your questions . . . '

'Yes.'

'I probably won't answer very many of them,' she warned.

And he smiled, lifting the sadness that had descended over them, making her do it too, she wasn't sure what at, only that it was good, so incredibly good, after all they'd spoken of, and been through, to be smiling again, with him.

She was true to her word though.

She didn't answer many of his questions at all. Whilst she did tell him that her father was fine, no longer in the Atlantic, but sailing other seas (another thing she knew thanks to Hector), and was happy to pass on more news of Marianne and Esther – like of Marianne's Brooklyn home, and part-time job in a local store; Hans's kindness; Esther's English, and funny little ways – she refused to confirm his suspicions about what she was doing on the island, or why she was hiding herself away as she was.

'I'm not stupid, Eleni,' he said. 'I don't need you to. It's fairly obvious.'

'I'm not saying anything,' she said.

Nor would she about when she'd come, or how she'd found her job, or this flat. And, when he asked her who, if anyone, she still saw from their past, she was silent about that too, not because she didn't trust him – she did, she'd never have brought him home with her otherwise; she'd probably never have left her basket behind in the rubble – but because it wasn't her right to share anyone else's secrets but her own.

'You're being very . . . perplexing,' he said. 'I'm perplexed.'

'I can see that.'

'Tell me at least that you know your cousin is alive?'

'I do know that,' she said, and it was her turn to be perplexed, that *he* did.

All through the winter, members of the Cretan 5th Division had trickled home from the mainland, brought at night on caiques that had evaded German naval patrols. Little Vassili had come in November, and been working as a runner ever since, carrying messages across the mountains – all the warnings, and news of incoming British parachute drops, and plans to hijack patrols. She hadn't seen him, much as she longed to. He, like almost everyone else, had no idea she was here. *Just to be safe.* The British SOE operative she'd come to know had made his acquaintance though, along with Sofia's, and Katerina's, and the others Vassilis. Their wine cellar, he'd told her, when she'd asked if he'd ever passed through their village, was a favoured hiding place. *Your aunt's an excellent cook.*

Given their hospitality, given Little Vassili's work, she couldn't help her growing alarm that Otto knew he was here, regardless of how much she trusted him, because it was suddenly feeling all too plausible that he'd heard his name mentioned in Nazi circles.

'Stop panicking,' he said.

'I'm not panicking.'

'Well, you are, and you don't need to. I've known he's been back five months and told no one.'

'But who told you?'

'Your grandfather.'

'What?' *What?* 'You've seen *Papou*?'

'Yes.'

'What?' she said again, stupidly. 'How have you waited this long to tell me that?'

He laughed. 'I'm sorry. I don't know . . . '

'When did you see him?'

'For the first time, months ago. My billet's only a couple of miles from the surgery.'

'Go back,' she said, 'start from the beginning.'

Which he did, saying how, when he'd first been posted to Souda, the summer before, he'd resolved to call in on Yorgos and Spiros at work, before they'd have a chance to run into him. 'I felt it was a small respect I could pay, to not hide.'

'That was very brave of you.'

'That's a generous way of putting it.'

'What did they say?' she asked, at once dreading, but somehow not dreading, the answer.

Kindness, Eleni-mou, Yorgos had told her, in the hospital.

She didn't think that he, or Spiros, would have had it in them to have been cruel to Otto. Especially not when he'd gone to the effort of seeking them out. Not like she'd been cruel to him, earlier.

Sure enough . . .

'They made it easier than I expected them to,' he said, shifting his weight, trailing his hand around her waist. 'They thanked me, actually, for coming. Said it meant something.'

'I expect it did.'

'I've been taking them medical supplies. Antiseptics, sulphonamides, morphia . . . '

'You steal them?'

'Yes,' he said, carelessly, like it was nothing. 'It helps, I think.' He frowned. 'I don't know. Maybe it does.'

'It must,' she said, moved, deeply moved, that he'd been doing that.

The smallest acts, Mr Skoulas had said to her, only a few hours before, when he'd given her that safehouse address to pass on, *can change the course of lives*. She'd been unhappy about being excluded from the planned meeting. Only male attendees, naturally. *Be proud of the risks you take, Eleni. I am.*

She hadn't been especially proud. She wasn't now.

She still wanted to be doing a lot, lot more.

She didn't tell Otto that he should be proud either. She realized it would be pointless.

'You'll have made people better,' she simply said, 'taken away their pain.'

'You sound like your grandfather. And Spiros.'

'Good,' she said. Then, acclimatising, slowly, to the shock of him having been with them, asked, 'How are they?' She'd never got close enough to Yorgos to be able to tell. 'Please say they're well.'

To her relief, Otto did. 'Older than I remember . . . '

'I know . . . '

'But they seem fine.'

'I hope they're sleeping. They weren't sleeping at all when I was last with them.'

'Don't worry about that. They have plenty of energy.'

It was the dry way he said it.

It made her laugh.

He did too, properly laughed, low and warm, and, remembering how much she'd always loved that sound, loving that she was hearing it again, she kissed him, loving too how he pulled her onto him, kissing her back.

'Have you seen Maria?' she asked, when they broke away.

'No.'

'That's disappointing.'

'I apologise.'

'Did you tell *Papou* and Spiros about your mother?'

'Yes.'

'They must have been very sad.'

'They were,' he said, and spoke of the letter his father had sent for him to pass on to Spiros, thanking him for the care he'd given to Brigit, saying he hoped there'd come a day when they could meet as friends again.

'That's a very big hope,' said Eleni.

'That's exactly what I told him,' Otto replied.

They didn't have much longer, after that.

They talked for a few minutes more, no longer of the present, but reliving their past: that first night they'd seen one another in the water; the chances they'd taken, staying out so late; how he'd swam home from her villa to avoid her *papou* ('We didn't fool him,' she said. 'I know,' he said, in the same dry tone as he'd spoken of his energy, making her laugh more, 'he's made that clear'), then of the café, and Dimitri's music, but very little of Dimitri, because they'd run out of time.

'You'll come back though,' she said, as he climbed from the bed and it dawned on her how much lonelier, how much more silent, her weekend would now feel, without him in it.

'I'll come back,' he said. 'You'll be here tomorrow night?'

'I'm always here at night.'

He pulled on his trousers, sat on the edge of her bed to shrug his shirt back on. She got up too, fetching her robe.

It was as she was tying it, that he mentioned Nikos Kalantis. 'Did you know they use him as a translator at HQ?'

She paused, still holding her tie, taken aback at hearing that name, from him. 'You've seen him?'

'I have.'

'You work at HQ?'

'I'm there enough. Briefings, reports on my men. Sometimes, I translate too.' He gave her a long look, reading her face. 'You knew about him then?'

'Yes,' she said, realizing it made sense that he did too. She just hadn't expected it. 'His name comes up a fair bit.' He wasn't widely trusted. The women she worked with especially talked about his fluent German – such an exception, on the island – and how he made the most of it to earn a Nazi wage, making up for all the money he'd lost since trade for his clothing business had dried up. 'He's come to a couple of meetings at the Town Hall as well.'

'Christ, Eleni . . . '

'It's fine. He's never looked at me.' He hadn't. 'It wouldn't matter if he did . . . '

'What do you mean, wouldn't matter?'

'Stop panicking,' she said, just as he had to her, about Little Vassili.

He didn't pretend he wasn't panicking though, like she had.

'This is insane,' he said.

'No, it's not,' she said, moving back to him, placing herself between his legs, taking his face in her hands, intent on reassuring him. 'He'd never know me . . . '

'I knew you.'

'You've seen a lot more of me than he has.' She smiled. 'A lot more . . . '

'He was watching you, Eleni, remember? That Sunday we met, at Dimitri's.'

'You think he was watching me.'

'I *know* he was watching you.'

'And what if he was? I was an eighteen-year-old girl in white shorts, with blonde hair. Look at me now . . . '

'I am,' he said, the lamp throwing golden shapes on his face. 'I'm looking.' He placed his hands to her hips. 'I'm terrified for you.' It was then that he said it. 'Why are you here? Why are you still here?'

'Because I need to be.'

'You want to die, Eleni? Is that it?'

'No,' she said. Then, thinking of his words, *I am drowning in my shame*, 'Do you?'

'Not here,' he said. 'Not with you.'

'Don't ever want it,' she said. 'You mustn't.'

'You shouldn't be here.' He sounded like Hector. 'If you're

caught, they will torture you, and then they will kill you. They will kill you,' he snapped his fingers, 'like that.'

'No one's going to kill me,' she said. 'I have cyanide.'

'Don't joke.'

'I wasn't . . . '

'Please, promise me you'll think about going.'

'No,' she said, abruptly tired, so tired, of lying. *A terrible way to live, really.* 'I'm not going anywhere, and we're going to fall out if you keep telling me I should.'

'Then we'll fall out . . . '

'I'd rather we didn't. I'd rather we focused on surviving this. We need to survive.' She leant down, kissing him, feeling him resist, for a moment, then relent. 'We need to get to the other side.'

'You think there'll be one?'

'I do,' she said. 'I have to. And I want you there, with me, because it won't be as nice if you're not.'

'Don't . . . '

'Don't what?'

'Make me believe it could happen.'

'Believe it,' she said. 'Please . . . '

He made no promise.

But he kissed her again, making her tumble forwards as he pulled her with him, back onto the bed, and she decided that that was promise enough.

Chapter Twenty

He did return the following night, bringing food – tomatoes, bread, jam – which he refused to share with her, saying she must keep it for herself. 'I hate thinking of you hungry.'

It was certainly a theme among the men in her life.

She waited for him, perched on the steps by her back door, reading a novel by torchlight, her ear tuned for the click of her crooked blue gate.

She hadn't been there long, when he came.

The day, gusty and rainy, had been a busy one.

In the morning, she'd called by on Socrates.

Not at his old flat, that he and Dimitri had decorated with such care; no, that had been cruelly flattened in the raid, and he'd moved to an apartment much closer by, not far from his school. He was the headmaster there now, the previous head – who'd been so determined to make his mark that summer of 1936 – having returned to his family in Heliopolis after the mainland had fallen. (A fortuitous move, it transpired. Heliopolis, along with the rest of the east, had been placed under Italian jurisdiction, their bakers POWs no more; it was kept entirely separate, an island now in itself, but, if the rumours were to be believed, existed under an occupation that was managed a deal more leniently than theirs in the German zone.) Socrates was, much like his old head, gone from Chania almost every weekend. Eleni had known he probably wouldn't be home.

She'd needed to try him though, desperate to talk to him about Otto, and her guilt at what they'd done – which had returned as soon as he'd left her, gnawing at her all night – trusting, instinctively, that Socrates would understand. He, after all, had spent years loving someone the law, and his family, and any number of others, would condemn him for.

'*It's painful,*' he'd confided, the better they'd grown to know one another over the winter just gone, '*but I made a choice, long ago, not to let the idea of anyone's judgement taint what, for me, is good and true. I hide to be safe, not because I'm doing anything wrong.*'

She realized her and Otto's situation was different, but she supposed, as she rapped on Socrates' door, that what she really wanted was for him to tell her she wasn't doing anything wrong either. He'd known Otto. Drank coffee with him. Taken her shifts so that the two of them could run off together.

Surely, he wouldn't think she was doing anything wrong?

She wasn't able to find out.

On Eleni's second rap, the woman from upstairs stuck her head from her window, calling down that he'd left the night before. Up to the mountains, Eleni guessed.

Deflated, she trailed home through the drizzle, only to find a note pushed under her door, which on any other day would certainly have lifted her spirits, but the wind was picking up, the sky darkening, and the hut this note had requested her to present herself at would take her a good couple of hours to reach – or, as the runners tended to talk about distances, twelve cigarettes. They never used traditional measurements; they said it was pointless when a mile on a road took a quarter of the time as a mile scrambling through a ravine, and a tenth of one climbing a steep rockface – which was what they most often found themselves doing.

Eleni at least had no rockfaces to climb that afternoon. She didn't smoke any cigarettes either. Pulling on her worn-through boots (there was no leather left on the island; she'd had to repair them with old car tyres), she reached for her basket, hid Pendlebury's gun beneath a blanket, and set off, west out of town. At each checkpoint, she showed her papers to the damp, disinterested guards, appearing, she had every confidence, as though she was on nothing more sinister than a snail-hunt.

She did collect some snails as she walked, for show, swallowing her bile as they suckered from the ground. She wouldn't cook them, she decided. She'd liberate them, just as she had their sisters the night before, once she was back in her yard. Turn them from country-snails to town-snails.

'Lucky snails,' said Stephen, the same SOE operative who'd praised Sofia's cooking, pulling her into the windowless hut she'd first met him in, back in October. Then, he'd sent a runner to fetch her, and had been all seriousness. Now, he wore a lopsided grin. 'Hello, Hector's rogue.'

'Hello to you,' she said, pulling a face at the musty smell. 'When did you last wash?'

'Not for days. I've been on the move. Only got here this morning. Had several near-misses with patrols on the way.'

'How near?'

'Not as near as they'd have liked,' he said, grin spreading.

'Good,' she said. 'It's nice to see you.'

It always was. She could count on one hand the amount of contact she'd had with him since she'd arrived, but when she was with him, it was like the most delicate, wavering thread spun out, across the mountains, across the Libyan Sea, connecting her to the bureaucracy and security of British HQ in Cairo, from which he'd been sent, and with whom he, unlike her, was in regular wireless contact. It was incredibly comforting. She'd never thought to be homesick for Britain, like she'd been homesick for Greece. But she was. Often, she was. And she missed her dad. She hadn't seen him now for almost three years, and she missed him in *her way*, which was a lot . . .

'I'm sorry to drag you out like this,' said Stephen, grimacing. 'I need to be on the move again tomorrow though, straight from this meeting . . . '

'You got the address?'

'Yes, yes.' He waved his hand. 'But I need to talk to you.'

They spoke in a mixture of English and Greek, like they always did with one another, breathing ice. It was somehow even colder in the hut than it had been outside. Stephen never lit fires, lest the smoke drew the interest of a passing German. They weren't alone. There were two others there, both playing cards, obviously Cretans . . .

'Narkover,' Stephen said, following Eleni's stare, letting her know the men were for the SOE training school that had been set up in Palestine – nicknamed after the fictional British boarding school of *Boys Will Be Boys* fame, but more officially known as ME 102. It was one of the things he did on the island: selecting Cretans to attend, despatching them by sub from Sphakia for a crash course in 'Resistance Warfare', which Eleni could only assume covered much the same syllabus as she'd been put through in Surrey (camouflage; codes; explosives; crawling on their tummies over sand, rather than mud). Little Vassili was, he'd told her, chomping at the bit to go, but was proving too useful here for the moment.

Stephen was very Greek in appearance too, with his thick moustache, and dark hair. He, like her, had a Greek mother, from the Peloponnese rather than Crete, and had lived in London since infancy. He'd fought with the British Army on the mainland, then again here, in Rethymno, and although he'd managed to evacuate before the surrender, he'd also been one of the first agents to come back, the autumn before.

'Felt the least I could do,' he'd said to her.

His main objective was in organising the resistance, working with local leaders to create a pan-island movement that would cut through politics, call a halt to the *kapitans'* sporadic attacks on Germans – which always brought more reprisals down on everyone's heads – and aim instead for orchestrated acts of sabotage that could be passed off as being of British, rather than Cretan, origin, so avoiding more bloodshed. It was an ambitious endeavour, and what the meeting the next day in that safehouse was to be about. The one that Eleni hadn't been invited to attend, because she was a woman. (*Boys Will Be Boys.*)

She didn't for a moment suppose it was what Stephen had summoned her to discuss. No, she assumed he had a message from Hector to pass on. It was why he usually wanted to talk to her. It was why he'd sent a runner to fetch her the first time she'd come.

She'd written to Hector after the surrender, using the code she'd been trained in, and sent her letter care of one of the British soldiers she'd helped hide in her basement. She'd done her best to explain herself, refusing to apologise, *not for this*, but – mindful of how little she wanted to be arrested, when, if, she made it back to England – entreating Hector to authorize her staying on the island as an agent.

You don't disappoint, he'd written, by way of reply. *I'll authorize it though, since you've given me no choice. Those poor Germans. Also, I've let your father know where you are. I expect he's as displeased as I am.*

She expected he was too.

'Any more word of my father?' she asked Stephen now.

'Nothing new,' he said. 'But nothing bad either.'

It was something. 'And Esther?'

'Bonny.'

'Excellent. So, what else has Hector said?'

'That if you're dead, it's no less than you deserve, and if you're alive, well done.'

She had to laugh.

'Also,' said Stephen, 'excellent work on the plane count.'

'He was pleased with that?'

'We all were.'

She had, since January, been working with Socrates and his network to gather up-to-date numbers on the Luftwaffe's strength in the region, logging the movement of their planes in and out of Crete. Their bombers used the island as a launching post for raids on North Africa – one of the very reasons everyone from Churchill down had been so reluctant to see it fall – and keeping tally of their comings and goings, without arousing suspicion, had been a huge task. But they'd done it, and fed the information into the *Cretan Wireless*, with very little idea of what use was going to be made of it.

'Can you tell me now what's being planned?' she asked Stephen.

''Fraid not,' he said.

'How irritating of you.'

Another grin.

'Is that it?' she asked, stepping back as another man entered the hut, looking in dismay at the intensifying downpour outside, impatient, really impatient, to get back.

Will you be here tomorrow night?

'No, that's not it,' Stephen said, 'I wouldn't have dragged you out here just for that. I got a signal last night. Sorry to say you won't be seeing me for a while after this.'

'Oh?'

'I know, such a bore. The desk back in Cairo has split us agents up though. I'm going East, so Robbie here—' he slapped the back of the dripping man who'd come in '—will be bringing your messages from now on. I wanted to give you the chance to make proper acquaintance.'

'Hello,' said Robbie, in Greek, pushing his wet hair from his face.

'Hello,' she said, holding out her hand, 'nice to meet you.'

'Right,' he said, shaking water from his hand, then taking hers, 'yes, I was just getting some fresh air . . . '

'I don't blame you.'

He laughed. 'I must say—' he released her hand, rubbed his again through his hair '—well done on getting the better of Hector. You've become rather famous.'

'Oh no.' She grimaced. 'That can't be good.'

'It is, it is . . . '

She turned back to Stephen. He was smiling, she had no idea what at, but it was a familiar conundrum with him, and she wasn't going to give him the satisfaction of asking.

'I need to go,' she told him. 'I want to get home before this weather gets worse.'

'It's just a shower . . . '

'A rather heavy shower.'

He rolled his eyes. 'Come on, stay. I've got biscuits.'

'Really?'

'No. But stay anyway. Robbie knows Arthur Dillon . . . '

'Arthur?' That made her look at Robbie twice. Arthur was the solider with whom she'd despatched her letter to Hector. She hadn't got to know him well, but he, and his friend, had been very nice, unfailingly courteous, for the short time they'd stayed with her. 'How is he?' she asked Robbie. 'Well, I hope.'

'It was the last I saw of him.'

'In Africa?'

'Yes. Fighting in the desert now.'

'You're friends?'

'Good enough. He spoke very warmly of you, when I mentioned I was coming here. Said how impressive you are . . . '

'Oh no, can we not?' interjected Stephen. 'Really. I'm enough British not to be able to bear gushing . . . '

'So am I,' said Eleni.

Robbie laughed.

'Are we going to sit?' said Stephen.

'Fine,' said Eleni, and did, but only for a bit. Just long enough for Stephen to introduce her to the Greek pair as well, her to wish them luck in Palestine, and become, as Stephen had intended, properly acquainted with Robbie, learning that he'd been stranded on the island for several months after the evacuation, escaping in January, only to have come back again the week before, keen to do his bit, and put his rusty Greek to use. She told him a bit of her own story too (the parts Stephen and Arthur hadn't already filled him in on), then Stephen set to reminiscing about Pendlebury, who he'd been at Cambridge with, the pair of them apparently having got up to all sorts of high jinks. *Boys Will Be Boys*.

It was all very companionable. Under normal circumstances, Eleni really would have been happy to stay on, talking more. But the rain drumming on the hut's roof was getting no lighter, and time was ticking on.

'You'll be all right getting back?' Robbie asked, as she stood to go.

'I'll be fine,' she said. 'But that's very nice of you.' She smiled. 'I expect *you* would have invited me to this meeting tomorrow.'

'No, he wouldn't,' said Stephen. 'You play your part, Eleni, and let us play ours.'

'Fine.' She wasn't going to stop and argue it now. '*Bon chance*, Stephen. Watch out for your pronunciation of your o's when you're out and about, won't you? You have a tendency to slip into RP.'

'Sod off, Eleni. And *bon chance* to you too. Don't do anything I wouldn't do.'

'Of course I will,' she said, and didn't add that she was, for example, racing back to spend the night in the arms of a German officer.

That would probably be too rogue, even for him.

She still felt guilty about it, chasing the darkness home. She jogged, the wet grass soaking her legs, replaying each moment of the night before, anticipation building at the one ahead, growing ever guiltier, the more excited she became.

Her guilt got worse as she neared the town, presenting her papers, again, then again, and hastened to her flat, letting herself in, running around to light the lamps, out to the yard to release the snails ('Off you go,'), then back into her bathroom, where she threw off her drenched clothes and breathlessly hurried to bathe before he arrived.

It kept building as she dressed, pulling on the stockings she wanted him to take off, and settled down to wait, her stomach fluid with expectation, at the base of her back stairs.

It remained with her even as her heart lifted, hearing the yard gate's catch, then his footsteps, coming closer.

But as soon as she saw him at the top of her staircase, looking down, relief flashing across his face that she was there, her guilt evaporated, replaced by her own relief, that he'd come.

And, just like that, she no longer needed to hear Socrates tell her that what she was doing was all right.

It *was* all right.

Everywhere, *everywhere*, there was violence and danger and hatred, yet the two of them had found one another. They'd found one another, and it was *good*, and it was *true*. The only wrong that she could have done that night would have been in trying to deny it. Otto wasn't her enemy. He was *him*. As he came down the steps, her mind flooded with everything that made him that: how he'd stolen medicine for her grandfather, ridden on a hot, sweaty bus with her each morning of his summer, swam at night just to wave at her, sent her letter after letter after letter in England, held her hair in Paris, danced with her in jazz clubs, could well have saved her life the evening before, and had been through hell, lost too much, become so beaten that he was drowning, but deserved better.

He deserved so much better.

'Hello,' she whispered, smiling, setting her torch and book down. 'Did you have a good day?'

'Not particularly,' he whispered back. 'How about you?'

'Too cold and wet,' she said. 'Shall we make it better?'

'Yes,' he said, kissing her as she stood, the two of them moving inside, him kicking the door behind them, 'let's do that.'

Chapter Twenty-One

He showed her his house again that night; the one he'd designed over the course of their summer. It was late when he did. Almost time for him to go again.

He'd long since removed her stockings.

They'd talked more as well, about their past, and the island as it was now. She'd told him, smugly, about their peach tree, although not that it might have grown from a different stone ('I know, Eleni,' he'd replied, laughing, 'I know Maria planted another one. Your grandfather said . . . '); he'd told her that he'd been back to their beach, found the urchins still there – not killed by any bomb, but hanging on, unknowing that the world had unravelled above them – and she, wishing she'd been with him, had said how much she missed swimming, it being another thing – like gathering in groups, enjoying freedom of any kind – that had been prohibited. 'It's going to be even harder, now it's spring.'

'I'm sure there must be some place you can do it safely,' he said.

'I don't know . . . '

'I can bring you a shell.'

'I don't think that's going to cut it.'

He handed the drawings to her when they were still in bed, leaning over the edge to pull them from his bag.

'I want you to have them,' he said. 'They're yours.'

She sat up, unfolding the sheets, smiling as, in the lamplight, she saw the once-familiar lines and notes. *Eleni's nook.* 'I can't believe you've carried these around with you.'

'You never gave me a photograph. These were all I had.'

She shook her head, flicking through the pages, finding the address she'd written; the swimming pool.

I can't imagine you ever being trapped, he'd said. *You'd swim away . . .*

'You used to call me a mermaid.'

'I did.' He looked at the pool too. 'I used to take these out in Czechoslovakia, and France.' He frowned. 'There was one night in France, we'd come across a smashed farmhouse, and found these children hiding in the cellar. The whole building could have fallen down at any second, so I carried them up. They kicked and screamed, like I was going to murder them.' He stared, remembering. It hurt her, physically hurt her, to watch him do it. 'Everywhere I've gone,' he said, 'I've been hated, but whenever I looked at these, I remembered . . . well—' he drew breath '—I remembered you.'

She felt tears form in her eyes. 'You did?'

'I did.'

'So I was with you,' she said, and was glad, beyond glad, that she had been.

That he'd had her to lean on.

You make me feel, not alone.

Slowly, she leant forwards, pressing her lips to his.

'You aren't hated,' she said, 'you are loved, always. But—' she glanced down at the drawings '—I can't take these. You need to keep them.'

'They're yours.'

'You need to build this house one day.'

'No—' he shook his head '—I'll never build this. Please. Take them. It's important to me.'

She thought about protesting.

'Please, Eleni,' he said.

'All right,' she said, folding them, moving, her knees sinking on the mattress, to set them on her table, 'I'll keep them safe then, for when I've convinced you that you should build it.'

He laughed, like it was a nice kind of fantasy; sweet, but fiction nonetheless.

Don't make me believe it could happen, he'd said to her the night before, when she'd talked about a life beyond this war.

Believe, she'd told him then.

'You mustn't give up,' she insisted now. 'You can't . . . '

'I'm trying not to,' he said, moving too, onto his knees, taking her face in his hands. 'You're helping.'

He was with her every night he could be, from that point on. It wasn't always possible. Sometimes he was on duty at his barracks. Occasionally, he had to attend some meeting. She didn't ask for detail. She didn't want to think about him with his fellow officers. What mattered, the only thing she could *allow* to matter was that, whenever he was able, he came to her.

She was always waiting for him on her steps when he did.

She told Socrates about him. He called by at her flat the Sunday of that first weekend; the woman above him had said that his *young lady* had come knocking, and he was worried, wanting to check Eleni was all right.

'I'm fine,' she said, 'I think.'

'You think?'

'You'd better come in,' she told him, and – at her kitchen table, over tea, and a plate of Otto's bread, spread with Otto's jam – out it all came.

Socrates didn't tell her what she was doing was all right.

He was concerned ('Deeply,' he said), not because he blamed her for having involved herself with Otto again – he really did understand why she had – but because of the risk, to both of them, if they were caught.

'I don't just mean prison,' he said, speaking over her attempts to assure him that they *wouldn't* be caught. 'Have you thought what the people around here will do to you, if they see you? How the women at your work will react?' He took her hands in his. 'I don't want to come looking for you, and find you strung up . . . '

'I don't want that either.'

'Then end this. End it now.'

'I can't.'

'You can.'

'I *can't*. Would you be able to, with Dimitri?'

He looked away, across at the range, saying nothing.

'You see?' she said.

He clicked his tongue, not wanting to see anything.

'How was he?' she asked.

'You're changing the subject.'

'I am,' she conceded. 'But I still want to know how he is.'

It was to Dimitri Socrates went whenever he left town at the weekends.

He'd moved out of Chania after the raid. He'd survived, but his parents, tragically, hadn't. Their house had, like Socrates' old flat, been struck by a direct hit, only unlike Socrates, who'd been at school when it had happened, they'd been sheltering inside their home. Dimitri *had* tried to get to them when the raid had started, but in the smoke, his asthma had got the better of him, and he'd ended up in a casualty clearing station. He'd blamed himself for not saving them, but the Germans more, for their bombs. Unable to stomach the prospect of living in the town under their occupation, he had, as soon as he was recovered, shut up his café and moved to live with his father's brother in the mountains, where German soldiers were a lot fewer and, for the most part, terrified to go.

All of this Eleni had learnt when she'd first reencountered Socrates. He'd told her how Dimitri's uncle – a goatherd – was one of those who took in escaping POWs, concealing them in his cheese hut until their passage to Africa could be arranged. Dimitri in turn helped lead them across the mountains to Sphakia – not on foot (his asthma) but by donkey – dodging German patrols, getting them on to British boats. He'd helped with several British parachute drops too, heading up into the plateaus as soon as word was transmitted from Cairo that one was on its way. There, he'd camp out, lighting fires to signal the plane in, grabbing the supplies they sent drifting down and hastening them away for distribution by Stephen and his cohorts, before any nearby Germans could arrive to take them for themselves.

Eleni liked to picture him camping beneath the stars.

She wanted to think that he was by now healing enough to hum Fred Astaire to himself, through the cold mountain nights.

'He's getting there,' said Socrates, reaching for another slice of bread. 'Although I don't know what he'd say about this.'

He wouldn't tell him. Dimitri was another who didn't know she was here. She and Socrates had agreed it was for the best. He had enough secrets of his own to keep.

'Have you told Otto you've seen me?' Socrates asked.

'Of course I haven't.'

'You can,' he said, with a sigh.

'I don't need to.'

'I want you to. Tell him I'm sorry about his mother.'

'You could always stay now, tell him for yourself.' She knew it was a lot to ask, but also how much it would mean to Otto if he did it.

'Agh, Eleni . . . '

'Just for a minute.'

Another deep sigh. 'Fine, fine.'

'Yes?' She placed her hand to her chest. 'Really?'

'Really . . . '

'Thank you.'

'I'm not sure you're welcome.'

'I do feel terrible about it,' she said, and did. Her sense of remorse had returned the instant Otto had left her and been growing again ever since. 'Horribly guilty. I don't want you to think I'm in this lightly . . . '

'I know you better than that.'

'Good.'

'And the guilt will ease.'

'How do you know?'

'Because guilt always tends to in the end.'

Did it?

She wasn't convinced.

She supposed it all rather depended on the scale of the consequences.

Socrates was right though. As the April days passed, her guilt *did* cease to prey on her quite so persistently. Possibly, she simply conditioned herself into living with it, knowing that it was either that or live without Otto, which, now she had him back, truly wasn't an alternative at all.

And oh, his face when he saw Socrates that Sunday in her kitchen.

'My God,' he said, grasping Socrates' proffered hand, shaking it warmly, happy in a way that made Eleni so . . . *happy*. 'It's good to see you.'

'It's surprisingly good to see you,' said Socrates, smiling, for which kindness Eleni could have kissed him.

'So, Eleni does have someone . . . '

'She does,' Socrates said.

He didn't linger with them for long, *understanding*, but left as soon as he'd paid his respects to Otto about Brigit, asked after Krista ('I don't know where to start,' said Otto), and dodged Otto's own enquiries into Dimitri.

'Eleni mentioned he'd moved,' Otto said. 'Do you still see him?'

'Yes, yes,' said Socrates, gathering his jacket. 'Now I must go. Be careful, both of you.'

'Dimitri's working with you, then?' said Otto, once he was gone.

'I'm not saying a word,' she said, wrapping her arms around him.

'You'll tell me about Socrates, but not Dimitri?'

'I didn't tell you anything about Socrates. He lives around the corner, wanted to say hello, that's all . . . '

'Eleni . . . '

'Otto?'

He stared down at her a second longer, then gave a short, frustrated laugh.

'Fine,' he said, 'fine . . . '

'Thank you.'

'Are you hungry?' he asked.

'Always.'

'I thought so.'

He'd brought her food again.

He kept bringing it. He never had much – even with the German's pilfering, there were too many of them on the island, and they, he said, often went short too – but whatever he could come by. As the weather grew warmer, he brought her the season's first oranges, and peaches.

'Better than snails,' he said.

'Anything's better than snails,' she said.

'Your great-aunt Sofia brings your grandfather all sorts.'

'I'm sure she does.' It was well known that, up in the mountains, out in the ungarrisoned villages, Cretans were more able to hold onto their food. Some of the women at the Town Hall had relatives who secreted them packages. Eleni, of course, had received her own, thanks to her landlord, although he'd brought her nothing recently; they'd had cross words . . .

'You should visit Sofia,' said Otto, 'eat some goat, and keep going to Sphakia, one of your submarines . . .'

'Not this again,' she said, 'please.'

He kept on with that too, though. He never stopped trying to persuade her to leave the island.

But they didn't fall out about it.

They didn't fall out about anything.

The brightening nights passed, the balmy air sweetening with fragrant bougainvillea, and, holed up in the cocoon of her basement, the two of them shut the world out, tumbling into her bed, cooking in her kitchen (eventually she convinced him to share the dinners they made), playing cards at the table, protesting when the other won, talking, laughing, *never too much*, so entirely, blissfully, the opposite of alone.

At the end of the month she discovered, to her relief, that there was no baby on its way. They'd thrown caution to the wind, that first night, and although they'd taken better care since (mostly), she'd been anxious.

'No more taking chances,' she told him, at the table, picking an ace from the pack.

'I don't think a baby would be so bad,' he said.

'Don't you?' she said, drily.

'No, you'd have to leave then . . .'

'I'm far too busy for a baby,' she said, rearranging her hand, saying no more, because her work on the island still remained one of the few things they never spoke about.

She certainly made no mention of it when, towards the end of April, her new SOE contact, Robbie, came by the flat, heavily disguised, anxious about the worsening situation for the Allied

Forces in North Africa ('We can't lose there too'), delivering her a coded message from Hector, with strict orders that, should the Nile Delta fall, she really was to evacuate Crete. *I mean it this time*. Robbie also had a request for her: that she and her network keep an especially close ear out for any new Nazi informants. There was something brewing, he said; something that should ruffle a few feathers before long, and no one wanted the plan leaked.

'Does this have anything to do with the plane logs?' she asked.

'Possibly,' he said, which was more information than Stephen would have given her.

'Are you all right?' Otto asked her, the next night.

'I'm just trying to work something out.'

'But I can't ask what it is?'

She heard his frustration.

She sympathised with it.

'There's plenty I'm never told,' she said, 'believe me. It's safest though . . . '

'You think I'd give away your secrets?'

'I think secrets only work if they're never passed on.'

'Eleni,' he said, 'I don't want to know your secrets. Honestly. Tell me or don't tell me what you like. I don't give a damn. All I need to know is that you trust me.'

'I do,' she said, and she did. She *did*. 'It's this war I don't trust.'

'No,' he said, with a sigh. 'No. I don't trust it either.'

His war was the other thing they seldom talked about. Besides that story he'd told her of those children in France, he hardly shared any of his memories. She didn't press him to, not when it was so obvious it would cause him pain. Only once did they discuss his experience of the invasion: how numb he'd felt, when he'd learnt Crete was to be their target; the Luftwaffe's dawn flight over Athens; his grief for the men he'd watched killed, before their feet had touched the ground.

'Plenty of them had families,' he said. They were on her armchair. She sat with her legs over his, her head on his shoulder. 'They loved their children. They weren't all evil . . . '

'I know that,' she said, and – haltingly, feeling more of a traitor than ever, but needing him to believe she understood – found herself admitting to her own sense of grief, back on her *papou*'s veranda, watching so many gliders combust; all those sticks go still. 'There was one I watched, all the way down.' She moved, looking at him. 'I keep wondering now if it was you.'

'Yes?' His eyes shone into hers. 'I hope it was. I like that idea, somehow.'

'Did any of your men survive?'

'Not many,' he said, then, that nearly all of the officers he'd trained with had been killed too. One of the few to have survived had been his CO, Brahn; he still reported into him. 'Now he *is* a good man.' Fischer wasn't. He'd led an execution squad in the initial wave of reprisals. 'I saved his damned life, just for him to do that. He bullied a boy called Meyer into taking a place on the squad with him. He was only seventeen. He carried his mama's blanket with him when we dropped. She won't know her son, I don't think, when he goes back to her. If he does . . . '

'Was he sorry afterwards?'

'Maybe. I don't know.'

'Does Fischer worry you? You said he wanted you to be demoted . . . '

'Don't let him bother you. Seriously. He's an . . . insect. One that needs to be swatted. It will happen. Forget him, please.'

So she did.

And enjoyed it much more when they talked of other things, like his ongoing visits to her *papou* and Spiros, who he gave her more stories of, indulging her insatiable appetite for news of them both: what they'd said; how well they still seemed; the door hinge they'd been trying to fix one afternoon in mid-May, shouting at one another because they, who'd performed countless tonsillectomies and appendectomies, hadn't been able to do it.

'They had it on the wrong way,' said Otto.

'You told them?' Eleni asked.

'I did. Naturally, your grandfather had known all along.'

'Naturally,' said Eleni.

He called on Maria too.

'Just for you, Eleni.'

'How was she?' Eleni asked, thrilled.

'Exactly the same as I remember.'

'Was she in a pencil skirt?'

'I have no idea what that is. But she's definitely convinced that you're not here anymore.'

'How do you know?'

'She was pretty damned triumphant about it.'

She smiled. 'Was she nice to you?'

'Not particularly.'

It made her laugh.

'It amuses you?'

'It does amuse me. Maria's a kitten.'

'She wasn't with me. She was furious that I hadn't been to see her before. Then she cried—' he grimaced, making her laugh more '—said my uniform was ugly, but that I was a good boy for all the medicine, and kissed me, because of my mother.'

'What a whirlwind.'

'It was exactly that.'

They spoke of his family, as well. He grew more open with her, the longer they spent together. ('I remember how you did this before,' he said. 'Did what?' she asked. 'Reminded me how good it is not to think before I talk.') Henri, he said, wrote weekly. The kind of letters he'd stopped believing it possible

344

his father *could* write to him. Warm letters, kind letters. 'He's still at his firm. He spends a lot of time with my grandparents, on my mama's side. I think it helps . . . '

'And what about Krista?'

'Christ, Krista,' he said, and didn't put her off, like he had Socrates, but told her how shattered she'd been, by Brigit's death, blaming everyone, and herself most of all. They'd fallen out before he'd come to Greece; she'd been taking more risks than ever, refusing to listen to his own, and Henri's, and Lotte's, warnings, but going to her illegal dance clubs, helping to print pamphlets, as well as distribute them. 'I told her to think about what Mama had done. How pointless it would have been, if she throws her life away.'

'Have you made up now?' she asked.

'We write.'

'Is she still dancing?'

'Probably. She has a death wish as well.'

'I don't have a death wish.'

And back they went again, to him asking her to leave.

It got to the stage where she had to laugh about it, he was so persistent.

'Are you growing tired of me?' she said, towards the end of May. 'Is that why you're trying to get rid of me . . . ?'

'I don't want to get rid of you,' he said, not laughing. 'I can't stand the idea of you going.'

'Then stop this.'

'I can't. You used to make me feel safe. You really did. But you don't anymore.'

She stopped laughing at that.

'You think I'd do something to you?'

'I'm not worried about *me*. It's you. Every hour I'm not here, I'm scared, petrified, that something might have happened to you . . . '

'It won't.'

'You don't know that.'

'It's been a year, and nothing has.'

'That doesn't mean nothing will.'

'Otto.' She moved her face closer to his, ran her hands down his arms. 'Please, enough. I am not leaving Crete. Not until your army does . . .'

'Eleni . . .'

'You need to accept it.'

'I won't.'

'You have to.'

'I can't. I know, I *know*, that if I do, we'll both end up regretting it.'

'No, we won't,' she said, kissing him, drawing a line beneath it, in her mind at least. 'We're together. How could we possibly end up regretting that?'

Chapter Twenty-Two

How ow *could we possibly end up regretting that?*

Her words stayed with him, as he made his way home that night.

All too easily, he could think of ways that they would.

Fischer was slouched on their billet's front step when he reached it, smoking a cigarette in the blackness, a bottle of raki, the local liqueur, beside him. Otto wasn't surprised to find him waiting. He was most nights, drinking alone. His face had grown flaccid, in the year since they'd arrived; his eyes watery and bloodshot.

'Where have you been?' he asked Otto. (A familiar question.)

'Town,' said Otto. (A familiar answer.)

He didn't know why Fischer bothered with the tired exchange. Vain hope, maybe, that, one of these nights, Otto would throw him a rope to help him catch him out. He'd never forgiven Otto for the tears he'd seen him shed, back when he'd been shot; even less for the pledge Otto had made him, after the reprisals.

I will see you pay for this. I swear to you, one day, I will make you pay.

'What were you doing in town?' he asked Otto now, picking the bottle up, taking a swig, then frowning, confused, into the neck, finding nothing left.

'That's not really your business is it, Fischer?' said Otto,

passing him. 'The last I checked, I was still your superior officer.'
He needn't have had Fischer billeted with him, just like he
needn't have had him in his jumping squad, but he was as intent
as he'd ever been on keeping him close. He'd meant it when
he'd told Eleni that she shouldn't let Fischer bother her – he
didn't want her giving him room in her head; God knew she
had enough filling it as it was – but that didn't mean Fischer
didn't bother him. 'Where's your salute?'

Fischer raised a lazy one.

'Want to know what I've been doing?' he said, as Otto opened
the door.

'Clearly you want to tell me.'

'I've been recruiting.'

'Right.'

'Made a friend in Souda.'

'Congratulations . . . '

'He's going to keep an eye out for me.' He belched. 'Says he's
got connections to agents . . . '

'And how did you convince him to say that?'

'I didn't convince him into anything. I just . . . ' Another belch.
'*Commented*, on how pretty his daughter is . . . '

'You're disgusting . . . '

'Don't worry.' Fischer laughed, tinnily. 'I'd never actually go
near her. I'd never touch a Greek. They're all little teases. Filth . . . '

'No, you're confused,' said Otto, carrying on inside, where
he was greeted by a wall of stale heat, and the sound of their
housemates – a teacher from Frankfurt, and a jeweller from
Bavaria – snoring. 'It's you that's filth, and them who would
never touch you.'

He didn't take Fischer's talk of an informer particularly seriously. Fischer had bragged of making too many such friends
for him to do that. When he'd first started with it, the summer

before, Otto, with little alternative, had passed the names he'd mentioned on to Brahn, who'd dutifully fed them up to the head of counterespionage for investigation. These days, Otto and Brahn had agreed not to bother, on the basis that it was a complete waste of time, and too embarrassing all round when it transpired that Fischer's friends had access to information no more valuable than the name of a disliked neighbour who might or might not have once sheltered an allied soldier.

'How's our secret weapon doing?' someone would inevitably ask Otto, whenever he was at HQ. 'Won the war for us yet?'

'Give him time,' Otto would reply.

And whenever he did, Nikos Kalantis was somehow always nearby, always listening.

Otto had to go to HQ again the next morning, ordered there for a briefing, along with Brahn and several other officers. They went on a bus from the barracks. Before they left, Otto inspected his men, and gave them their orders for the day: drilling, rifle cleaning, supply inventories; anything to keep them occupied, and their malaise and homesickness at bay.

'You may as well go and see your new friend,' he told Fischer, who was sweating with his hangover. 'You can walk into Souda. God knows you could do with the exercise.' He sent him mainly to annoy him, although that wasn't the only reason. 'Apologise to him about his daughter, find another way to keep him on side, if you think he can be useful.'

Fischer stared.

'Fine?' said Otto.

'Fine,' said Fischer. 'Leave it with me, *sir*.'

'Weber,' Otto said, once Fischer was out of earshot, summoning the young soldier who'd followed Eleni: the one whom he'd given his word to that Eleni wasn't who he'd thought. (*She was beside herself when I took her in. I feel bad, I want her left alone.*) 'I've a job for you . . .'

That sorted, he made his way over to the chugging bus, and on to HQ.

Nikos Kalantis was once again there when he arrived, suave in a three-piece suit, and deep in conversation with two staff officers outside the office door of General Andrae, the *Festung's* commander. Otto studied them, wondering what they were talking about.

Catching his stare, Nikos raised a brow.

They'd hardly spoken, over the past year, only ever exchanging the briefest of civilities. Otto hadn't, for example, told him about his mother. He'd never forgotten how he'd lied to him about watching Eleni in the café, nor the curt way he'd told Marianne that her cello music had bothered him (*You disturbed me a great deal*), and simply hadn't felt any inclination to share something so personal as his mother's death with him.

Yorgos approved.

'A good judge of character,' he'd said.

'Ah, Yorgos,' Spiros had sighed, 'is it worth hanging on to such hatred?'

'Yes,' Yorgos had replied, and been very happy to remind Spiros of why, counting off his various grudges against Nikos: the strip of land their grandfathers had fought over; the collaboration of Nikos's father with the Turks; how he'd stolen the disputed land, *stolen it,* from Yorgos's papa, when the Turkish authorities had granted him the deed in his name. ('What bit of land?' Otto had asked, trying to visualize it. 'It's just a strip,' Yorgos had said impatiently; 'it's not the point.') Then, how Nikos had fawned over Melia, whilst she'd been alive ('Eleni's grandmama,' Spiros had explained), and made Petra ('Eleni's mother,' said Spiros; Otto had known that), as distraught as Yorgos had known her, back during the last war, coming to the villa whilst Yorgos was at work, railing at her.

Otto had had to ask. '*Do* you know why?'

'Yes, I know why,' Yorgos, well into his stride by that point, had said. 'Petra was friendly with his fiancée, Christina's daughter. Ida, she was called. It was her, back then, who'd been Nikos's housekeeper, until she ran off with her boy to Athens, but not—' he raised his hand '—before she told Nikos that Petra had known all about the pair of them, and was two months gone with Eleni.'

It had been the way he'd said it.

'She wasn't married to Eleni's father?' Otto had guessed.

'They weren't even engaged,' Yorgos had said.

And Spiros had sighed, as though it was all coming back to him.

Otto had wondered how he could have forgotten such a thing.

'I hadn't forgotten,' Spiros had said, 'just stopped remembering. These things happen as you get older. Well—' he'd cast Yorgos a weary look '—to some of us.'

'Nikos was furious Petra hadn't warned him about Ida,' Yorgos had gone on. 'Took it all out on her. That was when I found out she was having Eleni. I'd suspected something was wrong. She'd become . . . withdrawn . . . but when I got home and found her the way she was, I got it out of her. Nikos had called her . . . No—' his frown had deepened '—it doesn't matter what he called her. But he'd told her how ashamed Melia would have been of her.' He'd stared. 'He, *he,* had had the nerve to tell Petra what my wife, her mama, would have thought of her. She wouldn't have been ashamed . . . '

'No,' Spiros had agreed.

'She'd have been angry,' Yorgos had said, 'at first. I was too. I admit it. But not ashamed. That wasn't who she was . . . '

'She was proud,' Spiros had agreed. 'Doted on Petra.'

'Worshipped her,' said Yorgos.

'Why did you never tell Eleni any of this?' Otto had asked.

'Her papa didn't want her to know. He'd left Crete before Petra had discovered she was pregnant, only came back when Petra wrote, telling him. He was on a ship, her letters took weeks to reach him. By the time he arrived, she'd given up on him ever returning. She was heartbroken, convinced she'd have to raise Eleni unmarried, without him. He's always been ashamed of that . . . '

Otto had debated whether to tell Eleni himself. Not for long though, no matter her father's wishes.

He couldn't conceal such a thing from her.

And she'd seen no shame in it, just as he'd known she wouldn't ('That would be fairly hypocritical of me, don't you think?' she'd said); nor had she been upset: not by it having been kept from her ('I'd have been more shocked if Dad *had* told me'), nor, especially, Nikos's behaviour.

'I suspect he lashed out because he was hurt,' she'd said. 'He probably regrets it.'

'You think?' he'd said, sceptically.

'Well, he can't have been all bad, for Christina to have kept looking after him all these years.'

'I don't understand why you're defending him . . . '

'I'm not.' She'd laughed. 'Really, I'm not. I just don't know him. And this was all years ago. A stupid row. I've got too much that is real to worry about . . . '

'You look so much like your mother, though,' he'd persisted. He hadn't forgotten that photograph of the two of them in her bedroom. Yorgos had others on his desk. 'More, now your hair is darker. I'm certain he's recognized you . . . '

'He'd have said something by now, if he had. *Told* someone . . . '

'Maybe he's just biding his time. Waiting for when the information will be most valuable to him.'

'Or maybe, given he's never looked at me twice, he's got other things on his mind too.'

Part of Otto was tempted to confront Nikos.

How could he though, without giving Eleni away?

He watched him as he broke away from the men he'd been talking to, picking up his hat, carrying on, past Otto.

'Good morning,' he said to Otto, in his perfect German.

'Good morning,' replied Otto, in his imperfect Greek. 'Where are you going?'

'On some business,' Nikos said, moving swiftly on, leaving Otto wondering whether he'd imagined the furtiveness in his hooded eyes.

Did Eleni see him at the town hall that day?

Otto didn't ask her.

To his frustration, he couldn't get to her that night, nor the next two.

The briefing he attended that morning was about a recent spate of murders of 'Bad Greeks', as the locals termed them: Nazi-recruited locals who'd acted as informers (real, rather than of Fischer's imagining), leaking the locations of *British collaborators* to counterespionage. General Andrae was incensed that the resistance had once again got the better of them, and adamant that those who'd committed the murders be punished, lest other Cretans become too scared to help them.

'You, Linder,' he said, pointing at Otto. 'You speak Greek. Have you heard anything that might lead us to someone?'

'No, General,' he said, without hesitation.

'Keep listening. All of you, ears to the ground. I don't know what is wrong with these people. Why they must keep *fighting* us.'

'It's a conundrum,' said Brahn to Otto, as they left.

They were each ordered to take patrols out into the surrounding villages, where, in the blazing May heat, Otto, loathing himself, nonetheless instructed his men to round the inhabitants up, *civilly,* gathering them in whatever large space they could find – cobbled squares, churches, patches of sun-dappled olive grove – supervising those he trusted least while they guarded the villagers ('Anyone who shoots outside of my order will be shot'), leaving the others to search their homes, looking for wireless sets, spies, anything incriminating.

'Does a tin of bully beef count?' Weber asked Otto, quietly.

'No,' said Otto. 'It could have been from last year.'

Besides that tin, they found nothing, beyond more hate-filled stares.

'You're free to go,' Otto told the seventh and final group of Cretans who they rounded up on Sunday morning.

'We're not free,' a teenage boy hissed at him, before his mother dragged him away. 'We haven't been free for a year.'

'Fischer would have shot him for that,' said Meyer, who might or might not still have his mother's blanket, and possibly was sorry for the bullets he'd fired in the reprisals.

'He would,' Otto agreed. It was precisely the reason he hadn't selected him to come.

He finally got to Eleni that night, making his way to her yard in the silver-blue light of dusk. The streets around her house were, as usual, silent, save for the clattering song of the thrushes that thronged in Chania's trees, and nested in its countless shattered roofs. The evening was thick with the lingering heat of the day, the illicitness of those meeting for clandestine Sunday gatherings, behind their closed doors.

She was waiting for him, like she always was waiting, at the base of her stairs.

He stopped short, seeing her there, hating that he'd left her waiting, these past nights. Hating *why* he'd done it.

She stared up at him, her dark-blue eyes wide, unsmiling, hating it too.

She wore no stockings, but had her feet in a bowl of water;

her hair wasn't wrapped in her scarf, but piled up on her head, off her neck.

She was hot, it was obvious.

She'd have been hot, he realized, all day.

She, who'd used to swim with such freedom, in this place that was meant to be her home.

He carried on towards her.

She watched him, tipping her face up to him, the closer he drew.

'I'm sorry,' he said, crouching before her, unclear what part of it all he was apologising for.

'You were on patrols?' she said.

'You know about them?'

'I do.'

'Did you know those murders were going to happen too?'

Her gaze held his. He tried to read it, to unpick the emotion he saw. There was too much there: pain, he thought, anger too; love; sorrow; resolution.

Regret?

'You did?' he said.

'Ask me a question I can answer,' she said.

You don't trust me?

I don't trust this war.

'Fine,' he said, making his mind up as he spoke. 'Do you want to go swimming?'

'What?'

'You heard.'

To his joy, his relief, her face softened; her lips moved in a smile. 'You're joking . . . '

'I'm not.' He'd been thinking about it, ever since she'd told him how much she missed it. *There must be some place you can do it safely.* He'd been looking for one.

He'd been given a motor to carry out the patrols, and still had a hold of it. Normally, he caught a transport truck into town – they were always shuttling back and forth from the barracks – but that night, he'd driven. She could easily hide in the car's back. He was sure it would be safe. No one ever stopped him at checkpoints. All they needed to see was his rank.

'I feel like it's either tonight, or never,' he said.

'It should probably be never,' she replied.

'Probably,' he agreed.

They still went, of course.

Not straight away. They waited until the night – a dark one, thanks to the waning moon – had had a chance to descend into deep blackness.

She went first to the motor, which he'd parked a couple of streets away, slipping out through her gate, her bare feet silent as she crept up the alleyway, blankets in her arms.

It was impossible not to be impressed, watching how assuredly she moved, stealthily opening the motor, disappearing into its back.

Someone, somewhere, had trained her well.

'Comfortable?' he asked her, getting into the driver's seat, and loved her more for her laughter, emanating from the blankets; that she was excited, when almost every other person he knew would have remained at home, rather than chance such a venture, for a swim.

'I'm boiling,' she said. 'Drive, please. God, if Hector could see me . . . '

'Who's Hector?'

'Not *now*, Otto. Drive.'

Laughing too, he did, out of town, on to one of the coves he'd discovered, and which he was sure would be abandoned. He was relieved, but not surprised, by the salutes of the checkpoint guards as they waved him on; he'd never have suggested any of this had he believed he'd be putting her in danger.

'Are you coming?' she whispered to him, once they'd parked at the cove, and she'd resurfaced from beneath the blankets, picking her way down several feet of rockface to a strip of shingle, too shallow for defences.

'I'm going to stay here,' he said.

'You don't want to swim with me?' Did she smile as she said it?

It was too dark for him to see.

It sounded like she'd smiled.

He knew he heard her undo her zip.

'Of course I want to swim with you,' he said. 'But I want to keep you safe more.'

'All right,' she agreed, quickly, letting him know that she was more nervous than she'd been letting on. 'I won't be long.'

'Be as long as you like,' he said. 'I'm here. Enjoy it.'

There was a short silence.

This time he knew she was smiling.

Then, she moved. He watched her silhouette wriggling from her clothes, dropping them on the shingle, then stepping into the water, her fingers trailing through the starry surface. Briefly, she stopped. He imagined her filling her lungs, looking out at the distant horizon, thinking, he was certain, of what was beyond it. Then she raised her arms into the V he'd seen her form so many times before, and dived.

He watched her for a few moments longer, forgetting the hideousness of the past days, thinking only of her, and her enjoyment. Then, keeping her safe, he moved to the other side of the motor, reached for his cigarettes, lit one, and, leaning on the bonnet, kept his eyes fixed, unwavering, on the deserted road. Just. In. Case.

She was gone a while. Long enough that he started to imagine what it would be like if she ever did agree to go, and not come back. He'd hate it, he knew.

He was as resolved as ever to convince her to do it though.

'Good?' he said, once she was with him again, breathless, her hair dripping, her dress, which she'd pulled back on, sticking to her body.

She wrapped herself around him, pressing her lips to his.

She tasted of salt, the orange she'd eaten before they'd left; it transported him in the instant to her kisses at that bus stop, when he'd used to wait for her at the end of her shifts.

'You have, if possible,' she said, 'just made me love you more than I've ever loved you before.'

'Yes?'

'Yes,' she said. '*In fact.*'

And he laughed, remembering that too (*I love you, in fact*), kissing her back, not drowning, not anymore, not when he was with her, only living. *Wanting* to live.

She'd done that for him, again.

Somehow, she'd made life – a good life, a better life – feel possible once more.

'Let's get you home,' he said, 'out of these wet things,' then she was laughing too.

They were both of them laughing, on the pitch roadside, and dangerous and stupid as it was, he wouldn't have been anywhere else.

He couldn't have been anywhere else, but with her.

Chapter Twenty-Three

He was sent away though. For all of June, he was gone with his unit, over the mountains on the south coast – now prohibited to Cretans, in a futile attempt to curtail the landings of British boats – taking a turn guarding a garrison post in Sphakia.

'If you could get word out to your *kapitans* not to shoot me on the way, I'd be grateful,' he said to Eleni, before he left.

'They're not *my kapitans*,' she said, 'so keep your wits about you, and a helmet on.'

It was more than five weeks before he returned. Every night, she sat on her steps reading by torchlight, listening out for the click of her gate, *hoping* that that would be the one he'd reappear.

She missed him, in a consuming, debilitating kind of way.

The month was made no easier by the grim whispers of ongoing Allied retreats in North Africa – whispers the Nazi authorities were only too happy to fuel, feeding everyone's fear that Britain might well be defeated there too, and where would that leave them? Eleni had no clue, and even less inclination to think about it, so she tried, determinedly, not to. But it was hard, when she had so much time to herself to *think*.

Then, towards the end of that June, she finally discovered the truth of why she, Socrates, and so many others, had been tasked with gathering intelligence from across Crete's aerodromes. The *something* that had been brewing turned out to be explosive attacks on two of Crete's most major airfields by British and French special services teams. They focused on Heraklion and Kastelli Pediados, destroying large numbers of aircraft, vast amounts of fuel, and most certainly ruffling German feathers.

Eleni felt little elation at the victory. As soon as she'd learned of it, she heard, via Mr Skoulas, of the reprisals that had been enacted, with *exemplary terror*. Despite the saboteurs having gone to lengths to take responsibility for the devastation, leaving plenty of evidence that it had been them, not locals, involved, fifty Cretans had been executed.

'A warning,' Mr Skoulas said, 'to anyone who helped hide our allies, not to do so again. A warning to us, Eleni. And a reminder of why we must keep doing as we do.'

Several of those executed had been Jewish prisoners, taken from Agia prison, where, it had become clear, they'd been interned since the start of the occupation. It tore at Eleni's heart, thinking of their fear, the brutality of their ending. She kept remembering the couple from her street, with their chubby baby; those teenage boys, all wide eyes and gangly legs.

Had they been shot?

Could an execution squad really have taken aim at them?

She knew the answer.

They all knew the answer to that.

The saboteurs themselves hadn't all got away either. A number of the French group had been taken prisoner when their hiding place had been betrayed to Nazi authorities by a *bad Greek* – Eleni had no idea who, she only wished she did.

'I feel responsible,' she said to Stephen, her old SOE contact, a couple of days after her conversation with Mr Skoulas, shaky still from the shock of it. She'd come to meet Stephen in another derelict building: a house this time, on the outskirts of Chania. He'd surprised her by being in town. ('I thought you'd gone

East,' she'd said. 'Best laid plans,' he'd replied.) 'All those planes we logged . . . '

'They legitimised the attacks,' he said, 'that was all. Believe me, there were many people who played a far larger part in the planning of this, than you. You are not responsible. Eleni. Stop frowning, and look at me.'

She did. He was a wreck, his dark hair greasy, and his skin coated in days-old dirt.

'This was not your doing,' he said.

'I feel like I must have missed something, though. I should have been able to warn someone . . . '

'You can't warn everyone. You found out about those patrols last month. Gave Robbie time to get everyone moved . . . '

'That wasn't me. I was just the messenger.'

'There's no such thing as just the messenger.' *The smallest acts.* 'Honestly, I simply won't have you beating yourself up about this. No one imagined there'd be reprisals. These executions were senseless, no one's fault but the Nazis', and nothing to do with you.'

Slowly, she nodded.

He was right, she knew.

And she didn't want to make him work any harder to convince her of it. Not when he was so obviously on his knees. It wasn't fair to him.

She'd walked to meet him at the house direct from work, it being a Tuesday. He'd sent a runner, letting her know he was there. The evening was a sunny one, but windy; the Meltemi had arrived, early, and was frisking around the building's dilapidated walls, making a loose shutter upstairs bang. Every time it did, Stephen glanced in the direction of the noise.

He was uncharacteristically jittery, but then there really was a great deal going on. He'd been in Chania to hold emergency meetings with several influential supporters of the island-wide resistance movement he was part of trying to build. There was always a degree of anti-British feeling in Crete after any reprisal, and he feared it would inevitably be worse with this one, given it had come about as a direct result of British action; Mr Skoulas's allegiance, he didn't worry about, but he'd been assuring the others he'd met with of the efforts the sabotage teams had gone to, to avoid bloodshed. He'd wanted to meet them himself, he'd told Eleni, because he had the most established relationships. 'Keeping their loyalty is too important a job to be delegated. Plus—' he'd smiled, exhaustedly '—I get to see you.'

He'd just been updating her on the deteriorating situation in North Africa, which was the other reason he was so wrung out. The last he'd heard, Tobruk was perilously close to falling, and staff in Cairo had been put on standby to burn all classified documents, lest that city follow.

'I want to get on the move,' he said, as the upstairs shutter slammed again. 'These damned long summer days. I hate being out of radio contact this long.'

'You get used to it,' said Eleni.

'Do you?' He gave her a dubious look. 'Cairo could be falling now, and none of us would know.'

'Don't jump to a future that hasn't happened.'

'One we don't think has happened.' He ran his hand through his greasy hair, then laughed. 'You're so *cool*, Eleni. It was almost reassuring, just now, seeing you worked up about those planes. Truly, I've wondered whether anything can unsettle you . . . '

'Plenty unsettles me.'

'Does it?'

'Yes. And you can talk. This isn't like you.'

'No, I know. Very boring, sorry.'

'You need to take a breath. It's dangerous, being this edgy.'

He laughed again, then surprised her, taking her by the arms and kissing her on both cheeks.

'You're a tonic,' he said, 'you really are.'

'I do my best,' she said, abashed.

'I've never doubted it.'

She smiled.

So did he.

'Africa won't fall, you know,' she told him.

'No?'

'No,' she said, discovering as she spoke that she believed it. 'One of these days, this war has got to start going our way. I think that day's coming soon.'

'I'll love it if you're right.'

'I am right.'

'If you are, we'll most certainly have to celebrate.'

She was right.

The tide did turn in North Africa. Not before plenty of classified documents *were* burned in Cairo, but the city itself never fell, and, by August, it was the Germans who were on the backfoot.

Stephen didn't come to celebrate with Eleni though.

He was already in Egypt himself by that point, having been ordered back on leave care of a wireless transmission from Cairo. Eleni was pleased for him, when a runner found her with his message telling her that he was off. *I'll bring you back a present.* He really had been at the end of his rope. He needed a rest.

Fortunately, there'd been no chance of him crossing paths with Otto at Sphakia. Otto, to Eleni's overwhelming relief, returned to Chania within a day of Stephen's note arriving – thinner, after his weeks on a garrison, darker too, from his days beneath the high summer sun, but uninjured.

'Thank God,' she said, throwing herself into his arms, the sultry July night he made her heart explode by appearing at the top of her stairs, losing herself in his kiss, the dizzying joy of his face, his hands, his eyes, his smile. 'Thank God, thank God, thank God.'

He was the one she raised a glass to the shifting fortunes on the Nile Delta with. Socrates raised one too, in her basement kitchen. Despite his (deep) prevailing concern at herself and Otto's involvement, he took, at her invitation, to joining them more, over the course of that July and August, sneaking into her flat after dark to share their cobbled together meals: *krassi* and feta; olives and oranges; bread and rabbit stew.

Socrates was the one who brought the stew.

'I nicknamed the rabbit Goebbels before I killed it,' he said, in Greek. It was what they mainly spoke on those evenings, Otto being more proficient in it by now than Socrates was in English.

'Why did you nickname it Goebbels?' Otto asked.

'To help me break its neck. I'd have struggled otherwise. One of my students told me the trick. You should try it with snails, Eleni.'

'I've given up on snails,' she said.

She loved those nights, the three of them reaching over one another for more wine, talking about books, and music; friends near and far ('I caught Dimitri humming "Cheek to Cheek" at the weekend,' Socrates told Eleni. 'This is excellent news,' she said); they were such a wonderful world away from the silent ones she'd known too much of. And whilst there would, indisputably, be hell to pay if they were caught, there would be hell to pay for so much of what they did.

'In for a penny, in for a pound,' said Eleni, switching to English, since the expression didn't bear translation.

'What does this mean?' Socrates asked.

'That if you're going to do something, you might as well *really* do it,' Eleni said.

'So basically, the rule you live by,' said Otto.

'Basically,' she said, smiling across at him, catching the

reflection of her own enjoyment in his eyes. His hair had grown longer again, over the course of his time away; lighter. It made him look more like he'd used to: that boy who it hadn't been treachery for her to love. 'What's the point, otherwise?'

He laughed. 'I don't know. But—' he reached for a cigarette '—I also don't know that it's the *best* approach to breaking Nazi laws.'

'Perhaps not,' said Socrates.

'Maybe,' she agreed, with a sigh.

But they kept breaking them anyway.

Not flippantly. They joked like that because it was easier to pretend that they weren't living in permanent, gnawing dread of being caught. But Eleni never forgot the cruelty of the regime they were living under – the innocent thousands whose lives had been stolen in reprisals; her neighbours; those wide-eyed teenage boys; that little girl, silent, in her mama's arms after the raid – and she knew that neither did they.

They were all of them always, *always* careful.

'Do you know what I miss?' Otto said, once Socrates was gone, and they were alone again, leaving the dishes, backing one another towards her room. 'Walking down a street with you.' He picked her up, drawing her legs around his waist. 'Holding your hand.'

'Dancing,' she said. 'To jazz.'

'Falling asleep. Waking up . . . '

'Swimming,' she said, catching her breath at his kiss on her neck. 'Together.'

That was a risk they never took.

She didn't go swimming again herself. She fantasised about doing it, all through her long, blistering summer days at the Town Hall, ignoring the blatant, idle stares of the sweating German officers there, and through her even longer nights, sleepless in damp, tangled sheets. Over and over, she relived the night he'd taken her to that tiny bay: the sense of peace that had washed through her as she'd stepped into the water, and felt the clear, cool Aegean lapping at her toes; her elation as she'd swam, kicking the shackles of the island free, losing her breath, forgetting – or almost forgetting – the prison that her home had become, thinking only of him, up on the roadside, keeping watch, keeping her safe.

You have, if possible, just made me love you more than I've ever loved you before.

He had done that.

He did it every day.

But she wasn't going to ask him to chance such a dangerous escapade for her twice.

'You can,' he said, because that was who he was.

'I can't,' she insisted.

So he did the next best thing, and brought her sand from their white beach; bottles of seawater, for her to run over her hot, swollen hands, cramped from typing; the urchin shell he'd promised her back in April.

'For until we get to the other side,' he said, handing her the shell at her door, grinning, ruefully, tucking his hair behind his ear.

'God, I hope we get there soon,' she said, pulling him in, to her. 'I really hope it's soon.'

She hoped it with all her being.

And yet, those cooling autumn months that took them on to Christmas, weren't unhappy. No, they – starting with first her birthday in September (twenty-five!), then his, in October, (twenty-eight!), peppered with dinners with Socrates, her solitary weekend walks to spy on her *papou* and Tips at the villa – were, contrarily, some of the happiest she'd known. Because every evening, she took her book, wrapped herself in her shawl, and went to sit on her steps, waiting for *him*.

Occasionally, there were other visitors who came. Those were quiet months for the resistance, but there were still warnings of patrols to be passed on, messages of troop movements, and garrison reinforcements, to be shared. At the start of November, Robbie appeared again, bringing the bizarre gift of Marmite from Stephen, now returned from leave, details of a parachute drop for Eleni to give to Socrates, and a message from Hector that she should continue to sit tight, now the immediate danger in North Africa had passed (*indulge me by permitting me to believe you'd have left had I asked*). Robbie also had an utterly unexpected verbal communication to recite from her father, who was currently on leave himself in Cairo.

'What is it?' she asked eagerly.

'That you are to be most, most careful,' he said, in his own, clipped RP.

'Oh, I can almost hear him,' she said, hugging her shawl around her. 'Robbie, I could kiss you for that.'

'Next time,' he laughed, leaving. 'Meanwhile, enjoy the Marmite.'

'I'm not a fan,' she admitted.

'It's full of vitamin B,' he said. 'Eat it.'

She'd still barely touched it, when, later that month, another communication, far more sobering, reached her ears, of two Cretan resistance workers – Andreas Polentas and Apostolos Evangelou – who'd been betrayed to the Germans, and incarcerated. They were tortured, then, eventually, executed.

It was Mr Skoulas who broke the news to her. She stood in his office, staring mutely at his careworn face as he talked, running cold at the thought of what Polentas and Evangelou must have endured; recalling, vividly, the grim detail Mr Haithwaite had gone into, back in Baker Street, of the interrogation methods Nazis used. She'd felt so detached from all he'd said, then; like it was an irrelevance.

Now, it couldn't have seemed less so.

They will torture you, Otto had warned her, *and then they will kill you.*

It was a man called Komnas who'd double-crossed the pair. Eleni didn't ask Mr Skoulas what would happen to him. She knew. That much didn't shock her: when he was dealt with, like all traitors were dealt with, and executed, silently, in the Chania safehouse he'd been moved to by Nazi authorities.

'How was it managed?' Otto asked Eleni. 'That street is packed with billets. There would have been officers everywhere.'

'I don't know,' she said, truthfully. Then, also truthfully, 'But I'm glad it was.'

'Does it not terrify you, what happened to Polentas and Evangelou? Please, tell me you have sense enough that it's terrified you.'

'I have plenty of sense,' she said. 'And yes, it's terrified me.' Her voice fractured on the admission. She hated saying it out loud; it made it feel too real. 'I'm meant to be terrified though. All of us are. They want us subjugated. That's why we can't give in.'

'Christ,' he said, shaking his head, 'I wish I could make that not make sense.'

He couldn't though.

It was one of the many reasons she loved him so: that, in spite of his desperation for her to leave, he understood, absolutely, why she stayed.

There were still some evenings that he couldn't be with her. On those, she'd wait for him until, leaden with disappointment, shivery with the cold, she'd reluctantly return inside, go to bed, and set her thoughts on the promise of tomorrow.

Mostly though, he didn't leave her waiting.

Mostly, he came.

To her delight, as the days shortened and the darkness lengthened, he did that a little earlier, every night.

'Did you have a good day?' she'd whisper, setting down her book, looking up at him.

'No,' he'd reply, helping her to her feet. 'How about you?'

'Pretty miserable,' she'd say, then smile, because they both knew what was coming. 'Shall we make it better?'

'Yes,' he'd say, smiling too.

And they always, always did.

As Christmas approached, an undeniable sense of hope began to lift the chill island air. For Cretans, that was. Morale for the Germans sunk pleasingly low. To add to their woes in North Africa, their renewed assault on Russia, launched earlier that year, had once again faltered with the onset of winter, against a fierce defence in Stalingrad. And it had been a year now since the Americans had entered the war, lending their strength to the Allied side. For the first time, it really did begin to feel possible that the Nazis might, in the end, lose.

There could be no overt celebrations, naturally. Christmas gatherings that year were as illegal as they had been the year before. Still, Eleni knew many of her fellow secretaries were excited at the prospect of forbidden family parties; meals of goats that had been secretly fattened over the autumn. Yorgos, Otto had told her, had one of his own, care of Sofia, which he was planning to share with Maria and Spiros. Eleni was glad of it. Glad that they'd all be together, even if all she could do was imagine herself with them.

She didn't invite Socrates over for Christmas Day, knowing he was off to spend it up in the mountains with Dimitri, and Dimitri's uncle.

'Does his uncle know about you both?' Eleni asked, before he went.

'What do you think?' Socrates said, with a short laugh. 'Remember the mountains, Eleni? Remember the way people are?'

She did, and was sorry for it. Sorry for them both.

'We'll be all right,' Socrates said, kissing her goodbye, 'happy. *No problem.* You concentrate on being the same.'

She didn't have to concentrate on feeling anything that Christmas.

It all came quite, quite effortlessly.

The day itself was quiet. She ventured out briefly in the morning, heading, in her scarf and shawl, to church, wanting to light a candle for her mama and *yiayia*, who, lately, she'd been feeling especially close to. She went early; the church was empty, but nonetheless aglow with candles others had already left burning for their lost ones, their sweet waxy scent filling the small space with longing; love.

She knelt before the pair she set flickering, dropping her head to her hands.

I hope you're there, she silently told her *yiayia,* who she'd never met, and her mama, who she only wished she could remember, *I hope you can see me.* She closed her eyes, giving, for a few short seconds, free rein to her fear, but also feeling them – whether truly, or by wishful thinking – all around her. *Please keep us safe.*

Then, starting at the steps of another arriving – not a local, but a German, come to pray too – she left.

Once she was home, bathed and in more comfortable clothes, she spent the rest of the day in bed, reading, eating the pistachios Mr Skoulas had given her, watching the diminishing light through her window, growing happier, the darker it got, knowing that he'd arrive, *soon.*

As he did, at not much past five, scooping her into his arms, swinging her around and making her laugh, then setting her down, reaching for his canvas bag and setting it on the kitchen table.

'I have gifts,' he said. 'They're the worst gifts I've ever given anyone for Christmas . . . '

'Oh no.'

'I know. And much less than I want to give you, but—' he grinned, producing first chocolate ('Oh my God,' she said), then a jar of honey, some cinnamon, and bread. 'You can maybe make something a bit like a *bougatsa*,' he said, looking at the jars and bread, brow furrowing, 'I don't know . . . '

'A bit like,' she said, running her arm around his waist, resting her head against his chest. 'I love it all, thank you.'

'You are very welcome.'

'I have something almost as good for you.'

'Something a bit like *kaiserschmarrn*?'

'No.' She detached herself from him, collecting her own soft package from the kitchen counter. 'Something a bit like this.'

'You knitted for me, Eleni?' he said, tearing the paper, pulling out the long, blue strip of scarf, which had taken her weeks to produce, and only had a few snags in it. He shrugged off his jacket, looped the scarf around his neck, looking down at it, then back at her. 'You *knitted*?'

'I did,' she said, proudly. 'I've decided I need to get better at it.'

'Why?'

'Let's eat first,' she said. 'I'm hungry.'

He'd brought eggs already, the night before. She'd scrummaged together some greens, and a tomato. Together, they made omelettes for their Christmas feast, which they ate, by candlelight, along with his bread, honey and cinnamon ('It isn't *not* like *bougatsa*,' she said, closing her eyes at the sweet hit), and some more covered in Stephen's Marmite.

'My God, that's disgusting,' said Otto. 'What is it?'

'Yeast extract.'

'A new weapon of war?'

'No,' she said, kicking him, softly, laughing more. 'It's very good for you.'

'You eat some then.'

'I can't. I hate it.'

'Right,' he said, laughing too, casting his slice aside. 'Right.'

'Maybe if you add some honey to it . . . '

'No,' he said, 'don't waste the honey. Although—' he picked up his slice again '—I think this should be a tradition for us now.'

'Stale bread and Marmite?'

'Yes, exactly.' He leant across the table, taking her hand; the warmth of his fingers, closing around hers. 'No matter where we are in the world, or how much food we have, we'll always have it on the table.'

'And bread with honey and cinnamon?'

'Yes,' he said, nodding, his smile lighting him up, 'that too.'

'All right,' she said, agreeing, very willingly. Loving that he was talking about more Christmases. Loving that he really had started to believe they were possible. 'And, something else . . . '

'Oh?'

'Yes,' she said, nervous, suddenly, that the moment had arrived. She'd been keeping this particular surprise to herself, wanting to be really sure before she told him about it. But it had been more than three months now, and it was getting that she could no longer do the button of her skirt up, so she was pretty sure. She was, *in fact*, really very sure.

Because they hadn't always been as careful as they'd agreed they would be.

Mostly, they had.

But that night he'd returned from his weeks away in Sphakia, for instance, they hadn't been.

Even after that, they'd taken the odd chance.

They'd taken at least one of those too many, and she couldn't regret it, not now it had happened. She was too happy about it. Frightened, yes, deeply, *deeply* frightened (*please keep us safe*), but happy. She was almost certain he would be too.

But it was a big thing to be telling him.

So yes, she was nervous.

'What is it, Eleni?' he said, his expression, in the lamplight, becoming anxious. 'You are all right, aren't you?'

'Oh, I'm fine,' she said. 'Really. Fine. I've been a bit tired, that's all. Not sick though . . . '

'Why would you be sick?'

She drew breath, hesitating a second longer, eyeing him across the table, feeling a tug at the corner of her lips, in her cheeks. 'Otto,' she said, 'we're going to have a baby after all.'

And his face.

His *face*.

*'Remembering wartime Greece.' Transcript of research interview
undertaken by M. Middleton (M.M.) with subject seventeen
(#17), at British Broadcasting House, 6 June 1974*

M.M: She was pregnant?

#17:   She was.

M.M: My goodness . . .

#17:   Yes.

M.M: And you never suspected?

#17:   No. Please [shakes head] don't look so
           disbelieving. I realize it was foolish
           of me, but she'd given me no reason to.
           I honestly had no idea. None. She'd hidden
           it very well.

                    [Long Silence]

#17:   You have no more questions for me?

M.M: Sorry. I'm digesting it.

#17:   I see that.

M.M: So, that's why she decided to leave the
           island . . .

#17:   Yes. She accepted she couldn't stay. She

was an unmarried pregnant woman in Nazi-
occupied Crete. That wouldn't have ended
well for . . . anyone. If it had got out,
there would have been judgement on . . .
[coughs] every side. It would have been
very, very hard. For her especially.

M.M: I assume she didn't want to put the baby at
risk either.

#17: No. [Dips head] No.

M.M: When did she leave Chania?

#17: It was several weeks later.

M.M: She kept working?

#17: Yes. She thought it would have looked
suspicious if she'd suddenly stopped, and,
I suppose, she wanted to carry on. Stay
busy. I must tell you, getting her, anyone,
off Crete, it wasn't a straightforward
thing to do. It's not like today, where one
can simply walk down the road to a travel
agent and book a ticket . . .

M.M: No, I do realize that.

#17: It all had to be managed, arranged. The
Royal Navy had stopped sending submarines
by that point. There was a nasty incident
at Antiparos, and they switched to motor
launches. The lieutenants who captained
them were tremendously courageous, shuttling
back and forth from Africa, bringing more
[reaches for water] agents, supplies,
taking others who needed to return, back.
But the service wasn't like a bus . . .

M.M: No.

#17: No. [Shakes head] The boats could be weeks

apart. Eleni's space on one had to be
arranged via wireless transmission. Then,
before it could sail, the moon needed to be
on the wane, the tides right. Her journey
across the mountains had to be timed too,
so that she wouldn't be left waiting too
long at Sphakia. That would have been
incredibly dangerous. It really was very
heavily guarded. And this was January
forty-three, don't forget . . .

M.M: I don't.

#17: It was a jumpy time, all around. After
the reversal in North Africa, there was
a strong sense across the island that
Britain was going to reinvade, use Crete
as their base to liberate Greece, which of
course the Axis powers couldn't allow.

M.M: Of course . . .

#17: Massive reinforcements were sent to
defend it, Italian as well as German. The
fortifications at Souda were strengthened,
more garrisons were added to Sphakia. It
felt, very much, like an island on the edge
of another battle. Really [drinks water]
one has to wonder whether the path of the
war in Russia might have gone another way,
had Hitler not felt compelled to divert
such a scale of resource to Crete . . .

M.M: Yes, but back to . . .

#17: Many Cretans believe it was their
resistance that decided the fate of
Russia, you know?

M.M: I do. But . . .

#17: I think they can certainly claim some credit. But it was an attack by Britain that was most feared.

M.M: Can we . . . ?

#17: Britain encouraged the fear. It was an excellent diversionary tactic. They even built a dummy invasion fleet at Tobruk for shufti planes to pick up. But then of course it was Sicily that was invaded . . .

M.M: Yes, in July.

#17: That's right. But . . .

M.M: [Interrupts] I assume Eleni had had the baby by then?

[Short silence]

#17: What?

M.M: Eleni. The baby. You've just been deploying another diversionary tactic of your own, taking us off subject . . .

[Longer silence]

#17: I digressed again.

M.M: You did.

#17: I am sorry. [Sighs] We're coming to the end, you see.

M.M: I rather thought we might be.

#17: It's hard.

M.M: I'm sure. Would you like to take another break?

#17: Just a brief one, if we might.

M.M: So Eleni needed to leave the island.

#17: Yes. And it was a huge loss, to many. It really was. She was . . . dismissive, to me at least, of the work she did, talking of it as though it was of minimal importance compared to everyone else's. That British part of her that refused to . . . gush. Certainly, her name has never reached any history books. Not like those of Xan Fielding, Patrick Leigh Fermor . . .

M.M: Stephen Garton.

#17: Indeed. Perhaps because she was a woman.

M.M: That feels like a fairly safe supposition.

17: [Brief smile] She was on Crete anyway for almost two years. I've spent a deal of time thinking about what she achieved during her tenure there. I can't estimate the number of lives she helped to save, with her secretarial collective, sniffing out [coughs] . . . informers . . . getting all those warnings out to . . . villages. It's impossible. But it would have been a great, great many. [Coughs more]

M.M: Here. [Pours water]

#17: Thank you. [Drinks] [Sighs]

M.M: When exactly did Eleni leave Chania?

#17: At the start of February.

M.M: And Crete?

#17: Crete? No. No. [Shakes head] She never left Crete.

Chapter Twenty-Four

Not a night passed, through that dark, wet January, that they weren't together. Otto came to Eleni, every single one.

'No briefings?' she said to him. 'No guard duty?'

'Let me worry about that,' he told her.

It was the end of the month before the date for her departure was agreed, and the uncertainty about how long they had left hung over them, tinging the sweetness of those last evenings with inescapable sadness.

But they weren't ruined.

Nothing ruined them.

Together, they cooked, they ate, they went to bed, held onto one another, made everything better, and, more than ever, talked.

'I can't believe this is real,' he said, so often, his eyes cast down to the growing curve of her tummy, his thumb moving over her skin. 'A child. Our child. From all . . . *this*.'

It was the baby, mainly, unsurprisingly, who they spoke about. Before the new year had even dawned, Otto reclaimed his house designs from Eleni's bedside cabinet, just long enough to add a nursery. ('So, maybe I will build this thing one day after all,' he said. 'Maybe.') They pondered, as generations of parents before them had assuredly pondered, whether the child would be a boy or a girl, agreeing they didn't mind either way. *So long as it's all right.* They discussed endless practicalities too, such as how Eleni was going to manage, alone and unmarried, until the day came when the two of them *could* marry ('Is that a proposal?' she said, wriggling closer to him beneath the eiderdown, slipping her freezing toes between his warm legs. 'Why not?' he replied grinning, then starting at her cold touch. 'Christ, Eleni, your feet . . . '); she told him of her conviction that her father would stand by her, like he had her mama ('I trust it,' she said, 'I trust him'), then, of her half-baked plan to return to England from Egypt, and move in with Helen and Esther in Chester ('Helen won't judge,' she said, 'I trust that too.'); Otto told her of the ring he was determined to get her before she went, so that she could tell anyone who *would* judge that she had a husband, away with the war, waiting to come home to her.

'You must do that,' she said to him, at the end of the first week in January, her dread that he wouldn't be able to, normally kept so determinedly at bay, rushing in before she could stop it, making her want only to cling to him, keep him safe, with her, whilst she still could. 'Promise me you will.'

He wouldn't though.

Not then, nor any night afterwards.

'I can't,' he said. *I don't trust this war.* 'You know I can't.'

'You can . . . '

'No.' He smiled a wry smile, to make light, she knew; block the fear before it became overwhelming. 'But I'll make you another promise.'

'Oh?'

'Yes. That I will think about you, and the baby, every single moment I'm not with you.' He tipped his head forward so that his green eyes were all she saw. 'I *swear* to you, that so long as I'm alive, it will be because I'm trying to get to you.' His eyes moved, across hers, reading them. 'Is that enough?'

'No,' she said, and realized, as he wiped her tear, that she was crying, 'of course it's not. But I know it's going to have to be for now.'

They guarded the secret of her pregnancy close, neither of them so caught up in their happiness as to question the abhorrence their news would be met with by almost everyone else on the island. It simply wasn't something they could risk getting out. Nor could Eleni chance anyone guessing that she was preparing to leave; there'd be too many questions about why she was going, and where to – from the other women in the office, the Nazis who worked there – so, at the Town Hall, she enlightened only Mr Skoulas of her imminent departure, unable to do him, who'd done so much for her, the disrespect of simply disappearing.

'What?' he said, from behind his desk, when she told him that the SOE desk in Cairo had issued an order for her to evacuate. 'Who is this, issuing these orders?' He raised his shoulders, held his weathered hands wide. 'Who?'

She laughed, regretfully, but gave no answer, since it would have been another lie. (*A terrible way to live, really.* She couldn't wait to stop.)

'I'll miss you,' she said.

He nodded, as gruffly as her *papou* would have done, and asked her how long she intended to carry on working.

'For as long as I can.' It was important to her that she did that, and not because it was a distraction. Grateful as she was that she *could* go, and keep this child safe, it didn't sit well with her that she was fleeing when so many had no choice but to stay. Whilst she was still here, she needed to keep playing her part. 'What will you tell everyone, once I have gone?'

'I suppose that you've left to marry some lucky farmer,' he said. 'I've lost plenty such secretaries that way.' He sighed. 'I will never forget you, Eleni Florakis.'

'Adams, actually,' she said, in a whisper, in English.

And he laughed, quite as hard as John Pendlebury had when he'd given her the headscarf she now wore, the last time she'd spoken to him.

'You must look after yourself,' she said, overcome by a surge of affection for him: this good, good man, who cared so deeply, and took such risks of his own. 'Escape if you need to, yes? Leave yourself time . . .'

'Yes, yes,' he said, waving her out. 'You worry about yourself. And make sure someone gets word to me, once you're away from Sphakia. Socrates is arranging it all?'

She nodded.

Socrates was.

He, she and Otto did tell about the baby, and he at least was sweetly happy for them, if even more (deeply) concerned about Eleni, and now the baby's, welfare.

Fuelled by that concern, he wasted not a moment sending a runner off into the mountains to secure her place on the next Royal Naval motor launch that would land. They agreed a story to tell that runner, and anyone else whose help they were going to need along the way – Stephen, Robbie, the SOE desk in Cairo – which was, simply, that she'd received a warning that she was being watched, so had to vanish.

The plan for her to do so, which came together really very quickly, was straightforward, as all the best plans were.

It was on a Sunday, the penultimate of January, that Socrates returned to the flat to run Eleni and Otto through it.

'So,' he said, the three of them sitting around the kitchen table, the oil lamps flickering, rain beating down outside, 'this is how it will be.'

Eleni was to leave town on a Friday, in the afternoon, since that was when Socrates would be free to take her. 'I won't trust this with anyone else.'

'Good,' said Otto. 'Thank you.'

'Yes,' said Eleni, relieved she'd be with him, not a stranger, at least to start with. It made the prospect of this long journey, at more than four months pregnant, slightly less daunting. 'Thank you, Socrates.'

They'd travel by donkey and cart into the mountains, on the same route Socrates had covered countless times before to visit Dimitri, telling any guards they passed that Socrates was, true to Mr Skoulas's story, couriering Eleni to her wedding. Then, on reaching Dimitri's uncle's village, she'd rest a night in his cheese hut.

'I'll see Dimitri?' she said, hopefully.

'You'll see him,' said Socrates. 'He knows about you now.'

'He does?' She smiled. 'What did he say?'

'Nothing,' said Socrates, with a laugh. 'He's not speaking to me. He's furious I haven't trusted him with it before.'

'Oh dear . . . '

'It's hard,' said Otto, with a raised brow, 'being kept in the dark.'

'I've told him it was your decision not mine,' said Socrates, to Eleni.

'Oh *dear*,' she repeated, laughing too.

'He'll forgive you. He's too happy to be seeing you not to.'

She was happy to be seeing him. As silver linings went, it was certainly a shiny one.

As was the news that, the day following her night in the cheese hut, Dimitri himself would take her to the top of the Samaria Gorge. There, Robbie or Stephen or whichever agent they chose to delegate the responsibility to, would meet her, with a runner, who'd take her the rest of the way to Sphakia on foot.

'It's the safest route, with all the fortifications,' said Socrates, 'but Dimitri doesn't know it well enough. You need to be with someone who does.'

Before they entered the gorge, a secure bay at Sphakia would have been selected for them to depart for Africa from, based on the advice of scouts whose responsibility it was to reconnoitre the area, charting the shifting German defences. A Royal Naval launch would also have been despatched across the Libyan Sea, ready to wait offshore for the signal to approach. All that would be left to Eleni was for her to arrive at the designated bay, on the designated night, where she'd find others waiting to travel to Africa with her, and an agent with a torch ready to flash the agreed Morse code out to the launch, at which point it would chug stealthily in, and carry them all away.

'You make it sound too easy,' said Otto.

'There's no such thing as too easy,' said Socrates. 'Only too hard.'

'Will it work though?' he asked.

'It almost always does,' he replied.

'*Wunderbar*.'

'It will be fine,' said Eleni.

And, for her, he smiled. 'I know.'

'When do I go?' she asked Socrates.

'The fifth,' he said.

She looked at Otto.

He looked at her, not smiling, not anymore.

Neither of them were.

It was already 24 January.

They had less than a fortnight left.

And, it went.

In a haze of long days in the office, and too-short nights with him, it went so fast.

Before it was over, Eleni had one last visit from her landlord: the second of Pendlebury's allies whose help she'd so depended on, these almost two years, and who, like Mr Skoulas, she couldn't bring herself to leave Crete without saying goodbye to, even if the two of them had drawn only the most tentative of truces after their cross words the April before.

They had seen one another since, just not as often as they'd used to. The first occasion had come when he, still fuming, had sought her out at the Town Hall, back in May (just a tap to his ear as he'd passed her desk, letting her know he wanted to speak to her outside); he'd needed to warn her of the search patrols he'd heard were being sent out to the surrounding villages – a warning she'd passed on to Socrates, who'd got it to Robbie, ensuring that when Otto and the other German search squads had carried out their raids that week, they'd found nothing more than a tin of bully beef.

After that, he'd called at the flat sporadically, never less than incensed about her involvement with Otto – which itself had been the source of their row in April (Eleni had told him about it, furious that he hadn't told *her* Otto was in Crete in the first place. 'How could you have kept something like that hidden from me?' she'd demanded. '*How?*' 'Because I was worried you'd endanger yourself by running after him,' he'd defended himself, '*quite* correctly.') – but nonetheless forgiving her enough to deliver more parcels of homecooked food.

Eleni was going to miss that food.

Wanting to thank him, again, for bringing it to her – and for all the generosity he'd shown her, however reluctantly, since the day she'd stunned him, back in May of 1941, knocking on his villa door and asking for his support in supplying her with a hideaway ('*I know you have the means to help me . . . You can do that here.*') – she'd enlisted Socrates' aid in getting a message to him, asking him to call on her if he could.

He came the Sunday following Socrates's briefing on her escape: her very last in Chania. She found him waiting for her in the kitchen when she returned from church. She'd been lighting more candles for her *yiayia* and mama. (*Please, keep us safe.*) He'd let himself in, made himself a pot of the black-market coffee his German colleagues at HQ kept him supplied with. It didn't surprise her that he'd made himself at home. Waiting on a doorstep wasn't his style, especially on this street where he owned every house – previously for the use of his employees, but now, since trade had dried up, left mostly empty, save for those other lodgers he'd given keys to, and who kept themselves so determinedly to themselves: resistance workers as well, Eleni guessed, but didn't know (*secrets only work if they're never passed on*), kept safe by this complex, taciturn man's charity.

He raised his hooded eyes to her.

'*Yiassou*, Eleni,' he said, with a long, troubled sigh.

'*Yiassou*, Nikos,' she said.

He'd guessed that she was pregnant.

'You are your mama through and through,' he said, pushing the cinnamon biscuits Christina had made her across the table. 'And now you're leaving too.'

It was him, not Otto, from whom she'd first heard the truth about all of that. He'd admitted, early in their acquaintance, to the guilt he'd long carried at how cruel he'd been to Petra over her pregnancy. 'I was an ogre,' he'd said, 'when all I'd ever wanted was to treat her kindly. I used to leave her gifts you know, at Easter, on her birthday . . . ' Eleni hadn't known that. 'She was scared, terrified, at her . . . predicament . . . and I made it worse. It is me that your *yiayia* would have been ashamed of, not her.'

He'd loved her *yiayia*, Eleni was certain; it was the way his stiff manner had always softened whenever he'd spoken of her. He'd been devastated, he'd said, by her death, from typhus. *An awful, lonely time.* Then, again, by Eleni's mama's. 'She was too young. Far too young. I blamed you for it.' He'd given her a long look, and she'd had to wonder whether part of him still did. 'I thought, if it hadn't been for you, she wouldn't have gone to England, and become so unwell. I wouldn't have said the things I'd said to her. I really never felt any inclination to see you.' He'd frowned. 'I *heard* you, the first summer you came. You screamed.' He'd turned his lips in distaste. 'Occasionally, I've heard you since. I haven't always been away for the start of your visits, and your laugh, it . . . travels.'

She'd almost felt compelled to apologise.

He'd told her that he'd got into the habit of summering in Thessaloniki, long before she'd come along, preferring it for its cooler weather. But that year of 1936, when the Linders had come, he'd delayed his trip long enough to greet them. He'd been out for a walk when Eleni had arrived from the port with her *papou*, and seen her in the driveway. 'In all your British clothes.'

'I didn't see you,' she'd said, bemused.

Which was when he'd told her about that spot above the villa, from which one really could get the most remarkably clear view of the house, and which she'd been using ever since to steal glimpses of her *papou*, and Tips.

He'd said how shocked he'd been by her face.

'You are the image of your mama. Apart from you have different coloured . . . ' he'd pointed at his eyes '—and—' he'd gestured at his hair. 'I had to sit down. Then, I walked, for a long time. When I set off home, there you were again, running down to the water. In the *dark*.' He'd narrowed his eyes. 'What was your *papou* thinking, letting you go swimming?'

'That I was a grown woman . . . '

'I had no idea if you could do it,' he'd said. 'But you were like a fish.' He'd shaken his head. 'I trod on that damn cat while I was watching you. I left him for you to take care of. I knew it would irritate Yorgos . . . '

'I think he likes him.'

'Yes, I've noticed he's got fat.'

'Otto saw you at the café, watching me dance . . . '

'I wasn't watching you. I was angry at you, for being there again. All I'd wanted was a coffee in peace. Then there you were, reminding me of . . . too much.'

'You lied to Otto . . . '

'I didn't want to have to explain myself to your boyfriend.'

'He wasn't my boyfriend then.'

'I've seen many things, Eleni. It was easy to deduce, it was only a matter of time.'

'And what about my parents?'

'What about them?'

'Did you ever see them together?'

'No. No . . . '

She'd fallen silent. It had been impossible not to wonder if Timothy, barely twenty at the time of her conception, *had* really loved her mama as much as Yorgos had always claimed. Or, if he'd resented her, Eleni, at least at first, for having forced his hand in returning to the island . . .

She'd found herself saying as much to Nikos. 'Maybe *that* was why he sent me back here, when I was so tiny . . . '

'Perhaps he sent you because he found you difficult,' Nikos had replied. 'You really did cry a . . . *great* deal. And he was alone, working to provide for you.' He'd given a rare, very sad, smile. 'A young man, I think, trying to do his best for his daughter.'

He always had done that.

It was what made Eleni so certain he wouldn't let her down now that she was leaving Crete in the self-same condition her mama had (just hopefully with a different end); also, why she missed him so.

That whole conversation had taken place well before her and Nikos's row over Otto.

In that first year after the surrender, the two of them had become, if not friends, then amicable. Every few weeks, they'd shared a meal, and some *krassi,* and he'd told her stories of her grandmother, and Sofia, then more about Christina too, who'd been a widow from when Ida was a year old, and become lonelier, even than Nikos, since Ida had run away. He'd asked Eleni about her life in England, and become almost animated as he'd spoken of his own passion for travelling, describing the journeys he'd undertaken around Europe and Asia to build his business, and his love for Germany particularly, where he'd spent much of his early twenties, having a number of clients there. He'd become ill with pleurisy one year, which was how he'd come to know Brigit's doctor: the brother of one of his clients.

He'd been upset when Eleni had told him what had happened to him, and Brigit. Hopeful that his friend, at least, had managed to escape Germany.

Happy too that Marianne had, and was now living safely in New York.

'It grieved me so, that time I heard her play her cello,' he'd said. 'So much sorrow, in such a child.'

Eleni had entreated him, often, to let her tell Otto of all the good work he did. She'd kept it from Otto, not because she enjoyed the deceit (*A terrible way* . . .), but because she knew that giving him the truth *had* to be Nikos's decision.

But Nikos remained adamant that Otto shouldn't know. He said that it was too much of a risk, with both of them so frequently at HQ.

'Please let me do it,' she implored him again now, reaching for the coffee pot. 'A parting gift?'

'Absolutely not.'

'You can trust him.'

'I won't trust anyone I don't have to. You never know what someone might do to save their own life.'

'Otto would never betray anyone.'

'I hope for your sake that you're right.'

'I know I am.'

His heavy eyes contemplated her, unconvinced.

'I have a favour to ask of you,' he said, changing the subject.

'Oh yes?' she said, intrigued.

'I want you to see your *papou*.'

'What?' she said, nonplussed.

'This, you—' he waved at her '—is a secret he would want to carry.'

'You know I can't let him do that.'

'And I can't let you make that decision for him. Heaven knows we have our . . . *past*.'

'Heaven knows you do.'

'But you're going now. What harm can it do? And you have no idea if you'll get a chance to see him again.' He reached for her hand, taking her aback all the more. His grasp was strong, insistent. 'You are all he has left of Melia and Petra. Let me tell him that you're here. Let him see you once more. Please.'

Chapter Twenty-Five

She didn't give in.

Not immediately.

So, Nikos intercepted her on her way home from work the next day, asking her again.

And again the day after that.

Otto was suddenly at it too, that final week she had in Chania, pleading with her to let him visit Yorgos, tell him the truth about everything.

'He'll kill me,' he said, 'but it will be worth it for you to see him before you go. Don't gamble on the future, Eleni. We can't know what's waiting.'

Eventually, on Tuesday evening, she relented, still far from convinced that it was the right thing to do, but, in the end, wanting it too much to be able to resist their combined powers of persuasion.

She told Nikos that he needn't call on Yorgos, Otto would. But Nikos either didn't believe her, or didn't want to – needing, perhaps, to pay this penance to his old enemy for the guilt he'd carried – because, by the time Otto got to Yorgos, on Wednesday morning, he was already well across their state of affairs.

He didn't kill Otto.

'Not quite,' said Otto, grimly, that evening.

But he had been very, very angry.

'Very,' said Otto.

'About the baby?' said Eleni.

'A bit about the baby, yes,' said Otto, in a harassed way that somehow managed to make her smile. 'But mainly about the danger you've been putting yourself in, and me lying to him. And the two years he's missed out on seeing you.'

'It was for his own good.'

'I dare you to say that to him.'

'I will if I have to.'

He eyed her. 'Who told him?'

'I can't say.'

It was his turn to smile, then curse, in German. 'Of course.'

'I would if I could,' she protested. 'I've asked him if I can, but he won't let me.'

'It's all right. I think I've guessed . . . '

'I sincerely doubt it.'

'I don't. I've been suspecting a while. Then your grandfather obviously disliked the man, said he couldn't believe he'd had to hear about everything from him. It's Nikos Kalantis. Ha—' he pointed at her face, slapped his hands together '—it is.'

'Otto . . . '

'You're not that good a liar, Eleni. Not to me.'

'Otto . . . '

He laughed, triumphant, and she had to fight her smile – that he was finding it amusing, where so many would have been put out.

'*Mein Gott*,' he said, 'the stories you have spun me about him. Is it him that owns this flat?' Another laugh. 'It is, isn't it?'

'Otto . . . '

'You don't need to say anything. Just nod if it's yes. Or blink.'

'It's impossible not to blink. I . . . '

She stopped, silenced by the firm knock that sounded at the door.

Yorgos's knock.

'Christ,' Otto said, laughter gone. 'He's here.'

He was indeed most angry.

Eleni saw that from the set of his jaw as Otto opened the door, and he stalked silently past him, removing his hat.

But then his eyes locked on Eleni. His face, rigid with fury, crumbled.

His anger, it went.

'Ah, Eleni-mou,' he said, striding towards her.

Then she was in his arms, inhaling his scent, feeling his strength and love close around her, wondering how she could possibly, possibly have done without him, all this time.

'I'm sorry, *Papou*,' she told him, realizing now how very wrong she'd been, resisting this farewell. 'I am so sorry.'

'You are forgiven,' he said, holding her tighter. 'Of course, you are forgiven.'

'And Otto?' she said, as they broke apart. 'Can you please forgive him too?'

Yorgos shot him a forbidding look. 'I'll find that easier once he's married you.'

'I'd have done that yesterday if I could,' said Otto.

'Seems to me you should have done it several months ago,' Yorgos riposted.

'It's not his fault, *Papou*,' said Eleni.

'It's at least half his fault,' said Yorgos.

'For which I apologise,' said Otto, in a way that let Eleni know it was most definitely not the first time he'd said it. 'I am deeply sorry for everything I have not told you, and for the way things have happened, but not for anything—' he moved his gaze to her '—*anything*, that's happened.'

She held his stare. Smiled.

And Yorgos sighed, shook his head.

'This is a world run mad,' he said, setting his hat on the kitchen table, his doctor's bag beside it. 'That much at least is neither of your faults.' He pushed his fingers to his temples, rubbing them, and, with another sigh, told Eleni he'd brought her food.

'Naturally,' said Eleni.

'I want to take your blood pressure too.'

Which he did, pronouncing it fine, 'Miraculously,' then they all sat, and he held Eleni's hands in both of his, telling her, when she asked, more about his conversation with Nikos, who'd apparently called at the villa at daybreak.

'He didn't stay long,' Yorgos said. 'He apologised for not speaking to me about you sooner.' He paused, as though replaying Nikos's words. 'He apologised for a great deal.'

'And what did you say?' Eleni asked.

'I thanked him.'

'You didn't argue?'

'No,' Yorgos said, so plainly she knew he was speaking the truth. 'He *should* have come to me before, but what matters is that he's done it now.' He squeezed her hands. 'He spoke to me for the first time in decades, to give me you. How could I have argued with that?'

She smiled, leant over to kiss his cheek.

He talked on, saying how sorry he was that he wouldn't be able to stay for long. Petrol was a luxury he hadn't had in months, and he would need to catch the bus home before it got too late. Spiros and Maria were waiting for him, eager for his report. 'They wanted to come, but there'd have been too many of us. We couldn't put you in that danger.'

'Or yourselves,' said Eleni.

'We've lived our lives. It's you, and you—' he gave a grudging nod to Otto '—we care about.'

He quizzed her on her upcoming journey. Otto had already

run him through the details, but he needed to hear from her how safe she trusted she'd be, so she told him, assuring him of the friends she'd be with on the way.

'And you'll make contact with your papa, as soon as you can?' he said.

'As soon as I can,' she promised.

He nodded.

Like her, he didn't doubt that Timothy would help her.

He had other things to say about him, besides – quashing the idea that Timothy could ever have resented her, once and for all.

Nikos, it seemed, had done her one last favour, letting her *papou* know that he should.

'He's never felt anything but grateful to have you,' he said, weary eyes full of regret that she could have thought it any other way. 'He struggled when he was left with you. There's no shame in that. I struggled with your mama. But he never wanted *rid* of you . . . '

'No?'

'*No*. He simply wanted you to be here, in this place your mama loved.'

Eleni looked across at Otto. He'd said something similar to her once, that first afternoon they'd kissed. *Maybe he thought you'd be happier here, in your mama's home.*

He smiled, remembering too.

And Yorgos talked more, giving her long-coveted details of how her parents had met, down at Souda, where Timothy's ship had been docked. 'Your mama had been to the market, and punctured her bicycle on the way home. Your father saw her, offered to carry it for her.'

'He did?' Eleni pictured it: Timothy in his crisp white uniform, her mama beside him, chatting in the English Yorgos had taught her.

'He did.'

'I'm assuming they didn't tell you they'd met?' She hadn't forgotten that either: what Yorgos had said to her of her mama, back in that warehouse hospital. *She didn't tell me about a lot of things.* It had been just before she'd sat with Weber, letting her compassion in. 'Mama kept it secret?'

'Yes,' said Yorgos, 'you are not the first young woman to have worried about a chaperone.' He went on, saying how Timothy had returned to the villa, to fix Petra's bicycle. Then again to make sure it was still working. Then again, and again. 'She told me none of it until she admitted she was carrying you. She was scared, because your papa hadn't replied to her letters. She believed her life was over. Then Nikos said what he said to her, and . . . ' He sighed. 'I wasn't innocent either. I said things I shouldn't have. And I was ready to kill your papa. But then, a few weeks later, there he was, on the doorstep. He'd been disciplined by his commander—'

'He wouldn't have liked that,' said Eleni.

'Maybe not,' said Yorgos. 'But he still came back. You should have seen your mama, when she saw him.' He smiled in recollection. 'So happy. They were both so happy. She brought something out in your papa, I think. Helped him become who he might have, had he not been incarcerated in one of your damned British boarding schools. He never wanted to send you to one.'

'I know . . . '

'I wish you could have seen him, back then. It broke my heart, that summer he brought you here, and tried so hard to remember how to be like that for you.' He squeezed her hand. 'It was very important to him that this felt like home to you. He couldn't give you your mama, Eleni, so he gave you her home.'

She nodded, struggling to talk, for the tears she suddenly felt building. Understanding, really understanding, for the first time, just how shattered her father had been, losing her mama . . .

'Your English grandparents were angry that you were born

so quickly after the wedding,' said Yorgos. 'I don't think they approved of your papa marrying a Greek girl.' He expelled a sound, much less than a laugh. 'Petra said your *yiayia* called her a . . . what was the word . . . I can't think . . . '

'Strumpet?' Eleni choked.

'Yes. *Yes.* How did you know?'

'A guess,' said Eleni, thinking of Paris.

'They had such a short time together,' said Yorgos. 'Such a short, short time.' He raised Eleni's hand, kissed it, then reached over, patting Otto's shoulder; an olive branch. 'I hope you both have longer. I hope with all my heart for that.'

It was utterly awful, saying goodbye to him that night.

'I have never felt prouder,' he said, hugging her in the darkness at her back door. 'When I see you next, I will tell you off for these secrets. But for now—' he pressed his lips to her head '—know how proud I am of you, Eleni-mou. Know how proud we all are.'

Tightening her arms, she told him she was proud of him too, and entreated him to take care of himself. 'Don't work too hard.'

'You said this when you were meant to leave before.' He pushed her sternly to arms' length. 'I hope you are going this time?'

'I am.'

'She is,' said Otto.

And, as Yorgos held her again, she recalled that farewell at the hospital; how she'd had to make herself run from him, Maria and Spiros, wrenching herself away before it became too impossible to go.

He pulled back from her with the same jerky resolution.

'Be sure to eat plenty on the journey,' he said, putting his hat on, 'and rest as much as you can.'

Then, with a final touch of his hand to her face, he opened the door and disappeared through it.

Gone.

'I almost wish he hadn't come,' she said, into Otto's chest, as he enfolded her in his own strong embrace. 'This is too hard.'

'I'm so sorry,' he said. 'I wish there was something I could do.'

But there wasn't.

There was nothing either of them could do.

And really, what was one more goodbye, in this war of millions?

She still wept though, not only in sadness at this parting from her *papou*, but for her mama, who'd had so little time, and her dad, who'd loved her as he had, and who still couldn't bear to so much as look at a photograph of her, but had tried that once to return to this island, for Eleni's sake; she wept for how much she wanted to thank him for doing that, and for sending her back here, year after year. *A young man, I think, trying to do his best for his daughter.* Then, tears unleashed, she wept for the war, and everyone who had died and was dying, and even for those New Zealanders who'd boarded with Maria and Spiros, and Ben Latimer, who'd boarded with herself and Yorgos, because she had no idea what had happened to any of them. Otto held her closer, she felt his heart beneath her cheek, the surety of his love, and she wept for every one of those millions of goodbyes, but most of all for the one that was coming for the two of them; a goodbye that, now she'd said this one to her *papou*, felt far too real, and much too close.

'Don't think about it,' he told her, as she'd once told him, back in 1936, when it had been him about to depart Crete. 'Don't.'

'I don't want to,' she said, pushing the heels of her hands to her eyes in a doomed attempt to stop her tears, then her face back against his chest, 'I'm sorry. I hate doing this . . . '

'You don't do it much,' he said, kissing her. 'You know it's all right.'

But it wasn't all right.

And nor was their goodbye, which *was* too real, and came, before either of them were ready for it, the very next night.

She was waiting for him on her stairs when he arrived that Thursday evening, for the last time.

Her bag was packed, filled with a change of clothes, her soap and toothbrush, the urchin shell he'd brought her, and his house designs. She wouldn't return to the Town Hall again. She'd let Mr Skoulas know as she'd left that that would now be it. (*Good luck, Eleni Adams,* he'd said.) Socrates had arranged to start his weekend early, and they'd be leaving Chania the next afternoon, whilst it was still light.

It didn't feel real to her.

She heard the click of her gate, tried to tell herself that she'd never hear that sound, or his footsteps crossing her yard, again, and that didn't feel real either.

'I don't like this,' she said, looking up, seeing how he'd paused at the top of her stairs, looking down at her, as though painting her image in his memory. 'I don't like it at all.'

'No,' he said, coming down, helping her to her feet, *one last time.* 'Nor do I.'

'Shall we make it better?'

'I think we should try.'

They couldn't though.

Nothing could make it better anymore.

The baby did its best to help, moving that night, for the first time. They were in bed when it happened, holding one another in the lamplight, not talking, just *being.* The kick that startled Eleni was a proper one, none of the flutterings she'd felt before, but an unmistakable pelt to her tummy; a little elbow, or fist, or foot, pushing its way against her.

'Feel it,' she said to Otto, taking his hand, pressing his palm to the place the kick had come. Almost immediately, another followed, as though the baby had sensed its papa's touch. 'Yes?'

'Yes,' he said, raising himself up on his elbow, staring at the spot, his face, that she loved, entranced; his bright, slanted eyes, in awe. 'Yes.'

It kicked again.

He laughed.

She laughed too, and the baby kicked more.

'For you,' she said.

'For me,' he said, and lay back down, leaving his hand on their wriggling child, resting his head beside hers.

The baby was still again when later, much later, as midnight approached, she sat on the rumpled bed, fighting her tears as she watched him dress, and he came and crouched before her, offering her the ring he'd sworn he'd bring her.

His mother's ring.

His father had sent it to him from Berlin.

'I couldn't risk telling him exactly why I needed it in my letter,' Otto said, slipping the delicate gold band onto her finger, the grief that had been straining his face softening, momentarily, when it fitted, perfectly. 'He's pieced it together though. He said that he feels filled with hope. And that I'm to ask a certain proficient linguist to take good care of herself.'

She smiled, eyes swimming.

'He wants me to write to him of her assuredly delightful and clever child, as soon as I can.'

'Does he?'

'He does.'

She nodded, drawing a ragged breath, determined not to let her tears go again – not while he was still with her – staring at the gold on her finger.

'I love that I have this,' she said. 'I love that it was your mother's.'

'I feel like you'll be safe now,' he said. 'Is that madness?' He looked at it, brow creasing. 'Maybe it's madness.'

'No,' she said, thinking of the candles she'd lit, 'not madness. I wish I had something to give you. Something to keep you safe. And happy.' She couldn't forget how he'd been when they'd found one another again; the loneliness she was leaving him to return to. 'I don't want you to drown.'

'I won't.'

'You mustn't. You must come home to me. To us.' She dropped down onto the floor so that they were facing one another. 'As soon as the baby's born, I'll get a message to Socrates . . . '

'I know.' They'd gone over this before. 'God—' he closed his eyes, tipping his head against hers, running his hands around her waist '—I wish I could be with you. I wish I could meet our baby . . . '

'You will, Otto.'

'Promise me that whatever happens, you'll take him or her to see Papa and Krista.'

'*You* will take the baby to them . . . '

'Promise me, Eleni. Please. I need to hear it. I need to know they'll know my child.'

'Otto . . . '

'*Please.*'

'I promise, then,' she said, kissing him, feeling his warmth, his *life*. 'I promise.'

A tear did break free from her then.

More came, as she walked with him to her door, and clung to him there.

'It's all right,' he said, and kissed her liked he'd kissed her in Knossos, that ruined house, and so many unforgettable times since. 'This is not the end. It's not.'

'No?'

'No,' he said, and did then, in that, their last moment, finally give her the vow she'd craved. 'I will see you again, Eleni. I swear it, I will see you again.'

Did he truly believe it?

Or did he say it to her as a kindness, because he wanted her to believe that he did?

She didn't ask.

She didn't want to know.

'You will,' she told him, 'you will.'

He smiled, holding her face in his hands.

She smiled too.

I love you, in fact.

Then, with one last kiss, she did what she must – what they'd already taken it in turns to do for each other too often – and pushed him softly from her, letting him go.

Chapter Twenty-Six

Her journey out of Chania did at least go smoothly.

She felt no fear, as she and Socrates left the town behind the next afternoon, presenting their papers at the gates, then clopping on in their cart, up into the mountains. She was too numb with sadness to have room in her heart for very much else at all.

It was a long and cold ride to Dimitri's uncle's village. As darkness descended, and the stars appeared, the steep mountain roads grew icy. Wrapped in a sheepskin Socrates gave her, Eleni huddled against him, staring down at the black ravines, the babbling streams twinkling in the waning moonlight, and, as Socrates talked, trying to distract her with stories from his classroom, she thought of Otto, what he would be doing, baffled by the reality that, whatever it was, he wouldn't be catching a ride from Souda to see her.

But since that *was* the reality, however brutal, and since she couldn't be with him, she was glad that it was Socrates, and Dimitri, who she was with. They were both of them wonderful, as was Dimitri's uncle – an older, swarthier version of his nephew, who'd roasted a goat for dinner in her honour. He didn't know she was pregnant; Dimitri did – Socrates had told him ('This will be a beautiful baby, I think,' he said, when they at last reached his village, and he lifted her down from the cart) – but his uncle was a traditional man. One whom, if Socrates's hunch was to be believed, had high hopes that she, Doctor Florakis's grand-daughter, would one day make babies for Dimitri. *No problem.*

'Erm,' Eleni said.

'Yes,' said Dimitri, thick eyebrows raised. '*Erm.*'

It was, against the odds, a good night. Not happy – Eleni couldn't manage that – but, in spite of the plummeting February temperature, warm. Packed together in Dimitri's uncle's small, smoky home, they ate, they talked – of Dimitri's parents, all of their families, and the many soldiers they'd each sheltered and helped – then, before Eleni and Socrates retired to the cheese hut, Dimitri wound up his gramophone, letting Fred Astaire play.

'And you wanted to throw it away,' said Socrates, as the notes filled the room, making the stone walls hum.

'I never would have,' said Dimitri, smiling at him (how did his uncle not see how they loved one another? 'People see what they want to see,' said Socrates, later). Then, to Eleni, 'Come.' He reached for her hand, pulling her to standing. 'Let's be in heaven. For old times' sake.'

'All right,' she said, placing her hand to his shoulder, her head to his chest, closing her eyes as he turned her around the tiny space.

It was so very nice being with him again, after their years apart.

So deeply comforting to sleep not alone that night, but a few feet from Socrates, who must have risen at some point to put more blankets over her, because when she woke the next morning to a frigid dawn, she was covered in them.

Mostly, though, it was hard, parting with them both, when the time came.

She at least got to put her goodbye off to Socrates for several hours, since he decided to go with her and Dimitri as far as the Samaria Gorge.

'I'm putting it off myself,' he said, helping her on to Dimitri's donkey.

'Like Mary,' she said.

'Less virtuous,' said Dimitri.

It was a fair observation.

Their trek that day was spectacular. Eleni, who hadn't been into the mountains in daylight since her visit with Pendlebury in 1941, and never in winter, couldn't fail to be stunned, in spite of her sadness, by the view: the sun, bouncing from the frosted cypress trees; the icicles, dropping from the cliffs; the vastness of it, all around her. With Socrates and Dimitri both there, keeping her company, pontificating on what might be coming next in the war, suggesting Greek name after Greek name for her to give the baby, she would have happily gone on as they were for many miles more.

But all too soon they arrived at a stone hut, nestled in the cliff-face near the top of the gorge, and their inevitable farewell, which needed to be said before the near-moonless night closed in, was upon them.

They had an audience for it, in the form of an SOE agent called Dusty whom Eleni had never met. He was young – 'Twenty-two,' he told Eleni, when she quizzed him – fresh from Narkover training, and heavily camouflaged in traditional Cretan breeches, layers of sheepskin, and hair that had been dyed SOE-grade black.

'It looks ridiculous,' Dimitri told him. 'Don't go anywhere you might see a German until it's faded.'

'I don't understand a word he's saying,' said Dusty to Eleni, in English.

'Don't you speak Greek?' she said, appalled.

'Ancient,' he said.

'What use is that?'

'Not much,' he said, 'clearly.'

It was probably good that he was there for the goodbye. It meant it couldn't be too drawn out, which in itself made it feel kinder than it otherwise might have been.

'Thank you,' she said to Socrates, holding him tight, 'thank you from the bottom of my heart, for everything you have done.'

'Thank *you*, Eleni,' he told her. 'You have been a true friend.'

'We will see you soon,' said Dimitri, stepping into Socrates' place, lifting her from her feet as he hugged her. 'Very, very soon.'

'Oh, I hope so,' she said.

She watched them go, leading the donkey off together down the craggy, narrow pass, until their broad backs vanished around a turn. Dusty watched them with her, silent at her side, saying nothing until they'd gone, at which point he said he hoped Eleni wasn't too anxious at the prospect of spending the night on an isolated mountain with an Ancient-Greek-speaking stranger, and offered her a cup of tea.

He told her, as they headed inside, that couriering her to Sphakia was to be his virgin assignment ('Right,' she said, anxiously), and that Stephen had said it would be a good one for him to cut his teeth on, given Eleni was such an old-hand.

'I gather you've got into a bit of hot water in Chania,' he said.

'Quite hot, yes.'

'You'll be sipping mint tea in Cairo before you know it.'

'Well, now, that sounds nice.'

He set to making theirs – 'Breakfast, not mint' – stoking the meagre fire he had burning, setting a kettle to boil atop it, telling her, in response to her question about where their runner was, that he was still waiting for him, Christos, to return. He'd gone off to get confirmation about which part of Sphakia they were to head to the next day. 'We've had a few wireless sets go on the blink,' he said, scratching his dyed head, leading Eleni to a discomforting suspicion of fleas. 'Christos has been trying to find one that's operational. He should be back already. I'm sure he can't be far though.'

'You're not worried?'

'Not at all. We'll be on our way before you know it.'

For the rest of the evening, he was at chivalrous pains to put her at her ease, heating them a dinner of baked beans, laying blankets on opposite sides of the hut for them to sleep, and making a courteous clatter tidying his cooking utensils when she headed out, shivering into the starry night, to hitch up her skirt and empty her bladder.

'I think you must be getting bigger,' she whispered to the baby, moving more, now it had started. 'I'm not sure I'm going to be able to hide you for much longer.'

'Tired?' asked Dusty, when she returned inside.

'Exhausted,' she said.

'Best get some sleep then. We've a long walk tomorrow.'

Except, they didn't.

Dawn broke, and Christos wasn't back.

Lunchtime arrived, and there was no sign of him.

The hours passed, the wintry sun setting behind the mountains' peaks, and still he hadn't appeared.

'Now, are you worried?' Eleni asked Dusty.

'No,' he said. 'He's probably just had to go further than planned for a set. He'll be with us tomorrow.'

He wasn't.

'I'm getting a bit worried now,' said Dusty.

To pass the time, they swapped their war stories, drank more tea, and cleaned their guns.

'Oh, I like yours,' he said, as she brought out Pendlebury's. 'It doesn't look like it needs cleaning at all. Have you ever used it?'

'No,' she said, honestly. 'But I know how to.'

'Definitely?'

'Definitely.'

'Show me,' he said, a challenge in his smile.

So she did, shattering a glass bottle he placed on a rock, several yards out from the hut.

'Right.' He nodded his head. 'Yes. That was pretty good.'

They ran out of baked beans that night, so the next morning, Eleni – feeling as grubby as she was used to Stephen being, and aching from the discomfort of sleeping on the hut's stone floor, not to mention constantly trying to conceal her bump – went foraging for snails (*Hitler, Goebbels, Goering, Andrae, Student . . .*) that she again never ate (*lucky snails*), because, at midday, with clouds building, looking to threaten snow, their runner, Christos, finally appeared, clambering up the mountainside. To Eleni's intense relief, he had Robbie, who didn't need to cut his teeth on anything, with him.

Robbie was full of apologies that they were having such a complete damned nightmare with their wireless sets, assurances that it was all sorted now, but also (less relievedly) the tidings that, with all the delays, there was going to be a wait before they could move to Sphakia. A three-week wait, to be precise.

'Stephen's call,' said Robbie, 'and he's right. We've missed the moon now, and can't know how long these clouds will stick around.' He looked to the heavy sky, then back to Eleni with a sorry smile. 'Can you bear it?'

'I can,' she said, since what choice did she have?

She was at least happy to know that Stephen had a handle on everything. Irksome as he could sometimes be, she trusted him, absolutely.

Trusted Robbie too, who (another relief) had no immediate plans to leave her, Dusty, and Christos. Rather, he suggested they all move, *just to be safe*, up into a cave he and other agents made use of, where there was a now-functional transmitter, food supplies, a stream for drinking water, and enough isolation for them to be able to safely light a proper fire.

'It's not the Ritz,' he said, hauling Eleni's bag onto his shoulder, 'but there are mattresses.' He rubbed his face, tired, obviously in a need of a good night's sleep himself. 'It will be better than this.'

It was a bit better.

Freezing, still, in spite of the fires they kept burning – the snow started before they reached it, and didn't stop for two days, the thick flakes creating a gusting film across the low, rocky entrance, so that the world beyond felt even more removed, and the cave a land alone in itself; it was dirty too, littered with old food cans and empty bottles, which rodents crawled over at night, their scuttling taking Eleni back to Chania's streets, after the raid. There *were* mattresses however, and cans of food that hadn't been emptied – bully beef, more beans – plus tea, and rusks.

Eleni could bear it.

Those three weeks she spent in that cave though, concealing her stomach, smashing ice from the nearby stream to collect water for them all to drink and wash, watching the day's light shift through the cave's opening, waiting for another to disappear – wondering, hopelessly, if Otto had any idea she was still on the island – were, without question, the longest and most strained of her life.

For the first of them, it remained just her, Dusty, Christos and Robbie.

With nothing else to do, Robbie read, and sketched, and played solitaire. Sometimes, Eleni played solitaire too, or rummy with the rest of them, or poker for pebbles. She also decided to teach Dusty – who she grew to like more, the more time she spent with him – modern Greek. Christos tried to help her, exclaiming at Dusty's archaic conversation (clearly having warmed to their green, good-natured friend himself), but it was an uphill struggle, so Eleni banned English between them entirely.

'What, *completely* banned?' Dusty said.

'Completely banned,' she confirmed.

'They've turned you in Chania,' he said. 'You've become a Nazi.'

'I am when it comes to Greek. Honestly, the hoops I had to jump through to convince Hector I could speak it, and here you are, no better than Homer.'

'He won't be mixing that much,' chipped in Robbie. 'Not like you.'

'I don't care,' she said. 'If you're going to do something, you might as well do it properly.'

'You were more fun when I'd only heard stories about you,' said Dusty.

Once the snow stopped, they were able to venture out for the occasional walk beyond the stream. Robbie, declaring he'd had enough of beans, clambered up to the closest village, in which he was known and trusted by the locals, fetching goat's milk and cheese. Eleni, starved of exercise, went with him as far as the hamlet's limits, and waited there, getting her icy breath back, staring out at the sweeping valleys of sun-kissed snow, stomping her tyre-soled feet to stay warm.

On their way back to the cave, they crossed paths with a local gendarme, who was on his way to buy cheese himself. He was a friendly man, and didn't demand to see their papers, but simply enquired of Robbie what he was doing, dragging his wife out on such a cold day.

'I'm having a baby,' Eleni said, answering for Robbie, whose accent was better than Dusty's, but not watertight. She slipped her arm though his, smiling up at him, quite as though he was Otto, grateful that it was him she was with, and not Dusty, who mightn't have had the presence of mind to smile back at her, just as adoringly. 'I have such jittery legs. The only thing that helps is walking.'

'Ah,' the gendarme said, with a chuckle, 'my wife was just the same.'

'Did anything help?' Eleni asked.

'Walking,' he said.

They all chuckled at that.

'God, you're good,' said Robbie, once they'd bidden the man goodbye, and carried on their way. 'I could almost have believed you were having a baby myself.'

'Imagine that,' she said.

At the start of their second week, the sun grew a fraction warmer, setting off a thaw so that the snow turned to slush and the stream, liberated, flowed again. Eleni listened to it at night, her hand to her moving stomach, preferring to focus on the purity of its ripples over the rats' claws, and the heavy breathing of the others.

Two more men briefly joined them in the cave, both Greek, and well acquainted with Christos, from the enthusiasm with which he greeted them at the entrance.

'Who are they?' Eleni asked Robbie, eyeing them.

'Christos's cousins,' he said, patting her shoulder, going to greet them himself, 'you have no need to worry.'

They stayed a night, and were gone again at dawn, continuing their long climb upwards to wait for a parachute drop.

'More replacement wireless parts,' said Dusty, proudly, his Greek by now having become modernised enough that he'd managed to garner as much from the pair.

'Well done,' said Eleni, throwing him a rusk.

Two days later, another agent came and went, on his way to sit tight with another traveller waiting for their delayed launch, and the day after that, a runner arrived, despatched by a *kapitan* in search of Robbie, bringing a request for more arms.

'It's like Piccadilly Circus in here,' said Eleni, edgy at all these strangers.

'It's fine,' Robbie said, with a smile, 'you're not in Chania anymore. There are no Germans for miles.'

'None that we know of,' she said.

'None at all,' said Stephen, who appeared as the second week gave way to the third, up from Heraklion where he'd been holding more meetings. 'I've had a proper recce. They're all staying warm in their guard posts.'

He was much more relaxed than the last time Eleni had seen him, when he'd kept flinching at that banging shutter (clearly his leave had done him good), although no less dirty.

'People in glass houses,' he said to her, 'should not throw stones.' He looked her over, taking in her hair, that she'd rinsed, but couldn't properly wash, and which she'd scraped into a ponytail; then, the breeches she'd begged from Dusty, since they were warmer, and roomier, than her dress, and the thick, oversized army-issue jumper she'd also convinced him to donate her, which swamped her sufficiently that she didn't need to worry so much about her now five-month bump. 'How are we faring?'

'All right,' she said.

'Not long now.'

'I know.'

'And, good news.'

'What's that?'

'Hector knows you're on your way, as does your father.'

'Really?' Her heart lifted.

That did feel like good news.

'Really.' Stephen's dark eyes gleamed. 'Hector managed to get a signal to him. I rather suspect he'll be hand-selecting the lieutenant who comes to fetch you.' He laughed, looked at the others. 'Imagine that responsibility.'

'Do you know where Dad is?' Eleni asked.

'I don't, I'm afraid. But you'll find out soon enough.'

'I suppose I will,' she said, properly happy, for the first time in such a long time.

Cairo, and safety, and *home*, were all suddenly feeling a lot closer.

Hector's news wasn't all good though.

To her regret, he'd come to take Dusty and Christos away, on with him to Sphakia, where they were to keep watch on the new bays that had been earmarked for the launch's landing, ready to get confirmed coordinates out to everyone by radio.

'Jerry's got a bit busy with their defences,' he said, 'we need to remain agile. And you—' he cast Dusty a look '—aren't cutting your teeth on anything up here.'

'I'm better at Greek,' he protested, in Greek.

'Solid work, Eleni,' said Stephen.

And, with promises to see her again in Sphakia, in six days' time ('You can give my clothes back then,' said Dusty), off the three of them went.

Eleni and Robbie were only to stay in the cave themselves for another four days. After that, they'd return to the hut Eleni had first met Dusty in, where they'd spend one last night before finally heading down into the gorge.

It was quieter, without Dusty and Christos there. Eleni missed Dusty especially. He'd been such easy company.

She hoped he'd be all right in Sphakia.

'He'll be fine,' said Robbie. 'He's the safest person on the island at the moment. He's with Stephen.'

Robbie was good company too. He was.

But six days was a long time to be with only one person.

Or, at least, one who wasn't Otto.

She never wasn't thinking about him: where he was, what he was doing; how, if he could only be with her, the discomfort and cold and boredom of the cave would become anything but. For all she knew though, he imagined her in Cairo already.

With nothing else for it, she got on with getting through those last days before she could leave.

She and Robbie went for more walks, and sat for hours by the stream, cradling mugs of tea, warming their faces in the sun's glow. They gathered sticks for the fire, cooked their meals, washed their clothes, and talked and talked.

She learnt about his elderly parents, who'd sent him away to school at just seven, where, to Eleni's distress, he'd been bullied, until he'd got big enough to stand up for himself, which, he supposed, meant it had made a man of him in the end. She told him about her dad, and her mama, and her *yiayia*, and Tips, fat Tips, and Maria and Spiros, and all of them.

She even told him about Otto.

It was the morning after the others left that she did that. They were sitting by the stream, and, as her ring caught the light, throwing gold on the rocks opposite, he asked her who'd given it to her.

She didn't want to lie, not about that.

'A man called Otto,' she said, and realized how desperate she'd been to say his name. 'It was his mother's.'

'A German man?' Robbie asked.

'A German man, yes. A good German man. They do exist.'

'I know that. One of my closest friends at university was from Frankfurt. I often wonder what's become of him.'

She smiled, nodded, and turned her ring on her finger.

'Was he with you in England before the war?' he asked.

'No, not in England. We met here. And went to Paris together . . .'

'Paris?'

'Yes.'

'I love Paris.'

'So do I.'

For a while, they spoke more about what they loved; the jazz bars, the food. Then, they fell silent, each in their own memories.

'Is Otto in Crete now?' Robbie asked, at length, interrupting

Eleni's thoughts of Notre-Dame, speaking in a way that let her know he'd guessed he was.

'Yes,' she confirmed. *In for a penny.*

'Did he take part in the reprisals?'

'No.' *You're really asking me that, Eleni?* 'No, he did not.'

'Good,' said Robbie.

'I'd never have anything to do with a man who had.'

He nodded, squinting at the water. 'I saw some of them.'

'The reprisals?'

'Yes.'

'Do you want to talk about it?' she asked, sensing he did.

'No,' he said, but talked anyway: of how, a fortnight after the surrender, when he'd been hiding in a village in the Chania foothills, concealed in the bell tower of its church, the execution squads had arrived, roaring into the square in their trucks. He'd watched, helpless, whilst the soldiers had rounded the inhabitants up, leading the men off into the trees.

'Some of them tried to talk to the guards as they went,' he said, voice straining at the memory. 'They were trying to reason with them.' He looked at her as though to say, *can you picture it?* She could. She could. 'I don't think they believed it would really happen.'

'Did you see it?'

'I heard it,' he said, and, choking on his own words, brushed his forearm over his eyes. 'Everyone left in the village heard it. I should have done something.'

'You are doing something,' she said. 'You came back.'

'It doesn't feel enough. Nothing feels enough.'

'No,' she said, 'I can empathise with that.'

They talked about that too: how insignificant so many things that they did could feel – an address handed over here, a whisper passed on there – but that in the end, it all, hopefully, added up.

'We're like bees in a hive,' Eleni said, quoting Mr Skoulas, throwing a pebble into the water, watching its ripples spread, 'all playing our part.'

'Stinging the bastards,' said Robbie, 'time and again.' He frowned. 'Hopefully avoiding death in the process.'

'Ideally, yes.'

As the days crept by, the baby – kicking more, growing stronger – remained the only thing the two of them didn't discuss.

Eleni thought she probably could have told Robbie about it. He'd understood about Otto, so she was almost certain he'd understand about their child. But she wasn't completely sure. Not enough to be prepared to chance it.

She felt too protective of the tiny wriggling thing, so innocent and unknowing inside her, to want to do that.

Instead, she left Robbie believing the party line: that she'd been betrayed, and was escaping arrest.

The simpler the story, the less questions people will ask.

Robbie had a revelation for her though.

He delivered it on their last morning in the cave, just as they were packing up to set off for the gorge.

'You don't remember me, do you?' he said, squatting on his haunches, quenching the fire.

She paused, midway through folding a blanket. 'What do you mean?'

'Last April,' he said, 'in the square in Chania. It was me you gave that safehouse address to. I was dressed like a villager. You saw a German soldier looking at us and told me to leave . . . '

'That was you?' She looked at him afresh, struggling to see it. In truth, she hadn't thought twice about the exchange since. She'd been distracted by Weber watching them. Such a lot had happened since. 'I can't believe I never realized.' She laughed. 'It was the next day, wasn't it, that I met you?' That much she did remember: her long walk through the rain to see Stephen in his hideaway; her impatience to return to Chania, and Otto. 'You were in different clothes, I'm sure . . . '

'I was. I hate those cummerbunds. Stephen still thought it was most amusing that you didn't know me.'

'I'm sure he did,' she said, more coming back to her: Robbie's stilted response when she'd told him it was nice to meet him (*Right . . . yes*); Stephen's odd smile. 'I'm so sorry. I feel rude . . . '

'Not at all.' Robbie stood, dusting off his hands. 'You were so business-like in the square. So in-command. I was shocked, actually. You weren't at all the way I recalled . . . '

'Recalled?'

He grinned, sheepishly. 'I was here, before the invasion. I called to you from one of the *kafeterias*, asked you to come for a drink. I recognized you.'

'*How?*'

'Agh, no—' he shook his head '—ignore me. I feel like an idiot, telling you all this . . . '

'Well, you can't stop.' He couldn't. She was too intrigued. 'How did you recognize me?'

'I was here before. Back in that summer of thirty-six. I fell a bit in love with you, I'm afraid.'

'Oh . . . '

'Yes—' he grimaced '—sorry.'

'No, I'm sorry.' She was. She felt bad now for having pushed. And quite awkward.

It was disconcerting finding out someone you'd believed a new acquaintance had kept hidden that they were anything but.

She finished folding the blanket, set it down.

'I used to come to the café you worked at,' Robbie said, 'all the time. I remember seeing you in your shorts, dancing with . . . what was his name?'

'Dimitri.'

He nodded. 'Dimitri. Then talking to that German of yours. The way you switched from Greek to English.' He expelled a laugh. 'Pure Vivian Leigh.'

She laughed too, to dispel her awkwardness. 'I wish I was Vivian Leigh.'

'I wished I was your German—'

'Oh no, don't say that.'

'It's all right.' He raised his grimy hands. 'I'm recovered now.'

'Good.'

'You threw an apron on my head, though, when you left with him one day . . . '

'That was you?'

'That was me.' His smile became reflective. 'I thought you were a goddess. I still do, for what it's worth. In an entirely platonic way.'

She didn't know what to say.

Recovered he might be, but the compliment was too much.

'I'm not a goddess. Far from it.'

'You certainly wear a good disguise then.' His eyes moved to her gun, atop her bag. 'It's probably what's made you so effective, all this time. And so dangerous.' He reached down for the gloves she'd left drying by the fire, turned them in a ball and threw them to her. 'People want to trust you. You're an assassin dressed in a goddess's clothes.'

She caught the gloves, held them up. 'These clothes you mean?'

He laughed. 'Metaphorical clothes.'

'I'm not an assassin either, you know. I've never killed anyone.'

'Maybe not with a bullet,' he said. 'But you've still done it.'

She didn't argue.

She knew he was right.

'Don't look like that,' he said. 'You have nothing to feel guilty about.'

'I don't know . . . '

'I do. This is war. None of the normal rules apply.'

'I'm not sure about that,' she said, thinking of Otto, and how he'd stood up against the reprisals. Then, of those names of traitors she'd passed on, with such determined detachment. Betrayers, yes. But deserving of no trial, no second chance? She threw the gloves at her bag. 'Maybe we've all just got too good at forgetting that they should.'

#17: We still hadn't had full confirmation from
Stephen when we left the cave about the
coordinates for the bay. He'd radioed, but
our set had cut out halfway through his
transmission. They were . . . temperamental.
As I've mentioned, there were several others
assigned to travel with Eleni to Africa. More
recruits for Narkover. A couple of operatives
on leave. Another Australian we'd learnt was
being hidden. [Shakes head] You couldn't open
a cellar door without finding one. Anyway
[sighs] I knew I must get to one of them,
be certain of which spot in Sphakia to head
to. I couldn't risk a chance. It would have
been like . . . [considers] . . . heading
into a lions' den blindfolded. But nor
could I let Eleni go to the gorge alone. It
was a precarious walk. She didn't know the
way . . .

M.M: And was five months pregnant.

#17: No, I still didn't know that then. I didn't. [Coughs] You must take my word on that. I had no idea.

M.M: She must have been showing.

#17: It was only just March. She was [coughs] covered in layers.

M.M: [Pours water] [Offers glass]

#17: Thank you [Drinks]

M.M: So, you took her to that hut?

#17: I did. The afternoon was still light, so I left her there and went to another nearby that I'd used for shelter, hoping I'd find one of the others in it. But [drinks] it was empty. So I went to another . . .

M.M: You were anxious?

#17: I was. It was getting dark. That wasn't a problem. I was used to travelling at night. But I was worried for Eleni. I really did care for her . . . very much.

M.M: Not platonically?

#17: Of course not.

[Long silence]

M.M: So, what happened?

#17: Bad luck. Simple bad luck.

M.M: You came across that gendarme you'd met? The one buying cheese . . . ?

#17: No. No. [Shakes head] He really was a nice man. No. I'd got quite far down the mountain by that point, and it was two others I ran into. They asked for my papers, I showed

them, and perhaps I was too silent, or
looked too suspect, but they arrested
me . . .

M.M: You didn't have a gun?

#17: I did, but so did they. Two of them. They
bound my hands, led me to the nearest
Nazi guard post, where I tried to convince
the duty officer I was a farmer. [Frowns]
One of the men who'd arrested me told him
I had a strange accent, so he locked me
in an old sheep pen, and an hour later
a truck arrived to take me to a garrison in
Souda. [Reaches for glass] [Drinks] There
was a truly detestable human being called
Fischer on sentry duty there. He was . . .
thrilled . . . at the diversion of my
appearance, when they pulled me from the
truck. I've never spoken much German, but
I understood what he said. I'll take it from
here. That's what it was. [Dips head] I'll
take it from here. [Silence] I knew what was
coming then.

M.M: He hurt you?

#17: He did, yes. He locked me in another room
and hurt me . . . quite badly. I've had some
beatings in my time, but this was . . .
different. It was . . . [searches for
word] . . . venomous. I gave him nothing.
Not at first. Then he left me for . . .
I don't know . . . half an hour, maybe.
I was bleeding, in a lot of pain. When he
came back, he had a Greek man with him. My
heart it . . . plummeted, when I saw him.

#17: You knew him?

M.M: [Nods] Alexis, he was called. He'd helped me from time to time, bringing news of shipping movements, troop arrivals, that kind of thing. He looked [pauses] terrified. I don't blame him for telling Fischer I was British. I understand why he did it. Fischer gave me a choice then. He took out his gun, held it to my head, and told me that unless I gave him the name of other agents, he'd bludgeon me to death. [Stares at glass] I had no doubt he'd do it. I was scared, I admit it. Very, very scared. Pain can . . . do that to you.

[Long Silence]

M.M: What did you do?

#17: I gave him Eleni's name. You're not surprised, I see that. You were expecting it . . .

M.M: I had an inkling.

#17: I'd been told she'd already been betrayed you see. I thought, what harm would it do, betraying her again? She was on her way off the island. I believed she'd be safe.

M.M: You'd left her in a hut with no idea what bay in Sphakia to head to. How to even get there . . .

#17: She was incredibly capable. I trusted she'd work it out.

M.M: You just said it would have been like walking into a lion's den blindfolded.

#17: Her name wasn't enough for Fischer anyway. He said he'd be laughed at by his superiors, if that was all he gave them. He wanted more from me.

M.M: How much more?

#17: He wanted to know where Eleni was.

M.M: You didn't tell him?

#17: I tried not to. [Dips head] I really did try not to. But he struck me and struck me, and I became desperate, forgot the rules. [Presses fingers to eyes] I gave her away to save my skin. [Shakes head] Then, because I was a beaten, cowardly jealous bastard, I went a step further. I told Fischer that she'd been having an affair with one of his own. I told him she was involved with Captain Otto Linder.

Chapter Twenty-Seven

Otto hadn't been imagining her in Cairo.

He'd been acutely aware, these past weeks, that she hadn't left the island. Yorgos had told him that her boat had been delayed, having been educated as to that unsettling state of affairs by Socrates.

There really was such a thing as too easy.

They'd all known she was hiding, just not exactly where. So many damned secrets, on this island. Socrates had assured Yorgos that she was with other agents, *safe*, but hour in, hour out, Otto had been able to think of nothing else but whether she truly was.

He knew the answer to that now.

There were four of them sent to arrest him at the house.

Fischer wasn't among them. No, he'd gone after Eleni, grabbing a couple of others and racing off in a truck before the responsibility could be delegated to someone else, apparently. Otto couldn't think whose authority he believed he'd been acting on, all night, but the idea of his enthusiasm to get to Eleni – the *thought* of him, breathing the same air as her – sent him cold.

The four who'd come for him weren't all strangers.

Three of them were.

One though, Otto knew. He knew him well. Well enough

not to doubt how much he'd be despising the duty, and to be grateful to him for the kindness of volunteering for it.

'Let's go then, Weber,' he said, to that young man who'd never really believed Eleni hadn't been Eleni, when he'd tried to convince him of it.

'Yes, sir,' said Weber. 'Let's go.'

Eleni didn't sleep that night.

She'd realized, well before the misty dawn now breaking, that something very wrong must have occurred.

I won't be long, Robbie had said, when he'd left her. *Save me some dinner please.*

She'd long since thrown that plate of congealed beans away.

She hadn't considered setting off alone for Sphakia. Not in the darkness. Not with no idea where to go. It would have been suicidal.

The only path open to her had felt to be the one she'd taken: waiting.

So, she'd waited.

And waited.

She was still waiting, standing at the hut's window, staring out at the cold, silent mountains, watching as they were thrown into gradual relief by the rising sun: the trees turning from grey to green; the rocks from black to misty pink.

She rested one hand on her stomach, and with the other held Pendlebury's gun.

She didn't tremble. She refused to be afraid.

No weakness.

But she was alert.

In the mountains' shadows, she sensed the presence of others.

Whether they were friend, or foe, she couldn't guess.

*

They arrived on foot: the three Nazi soldiers. The pass up to the hut wasn't wide enough for a truck to climb, so she heard none, and by the time she saw them approaching, it was too late for her to run.

She stepped out from the hut, arms folded, and filled her lungs with the morning's frost-scented air. She was, much against her will, growing afraid now. Her pulse was racing, and the baby kicked, unsettled.

Calm, she told herself, *calm.*

Then, the three men were upon her, red-faced and panting from the climb.

One was very young. As young, almost, as Weber. He leant over, hands on his hips, catching his racing breath. He raised his stare to meet Eleni's for a moment, then dropped his attention to his boots.

The second who'd come was older, squarer, with glassy blue eyes, and greying stubble on his jaw. He wore a passive expression as he looked Eleni up and down, like it was all just another day at the officc for him.

The third soldier – who Eleni guessed was in charge, from the way he stepped forward – had a wide, slack face, and a leering smile.

'I'm going to speak German,' he said, 'because I know you understand it.'

'Can you speak anything else?' she asked, somehow sounding calm.

You're so cool, Eleni.

God, what she'd do for Stephen to appear now.

'Why would I need to?' he said. 'You have a gun hidden somewhere. I know that too. Tell me where it is.'

'It's here,' she said, drawing it out from within the copious folds of Dusty's jumper, unable to see what other option she had; not with three of them to contend with. She wasn't that good a shot.

'Drop it,' he said.

She did that too, hoping she was far enough away from the men that none of them could see how much she'd started to shake. It landed on the rock at her feet, and the sharp metallic knock echoed through the valleys.

'Are you going to arrest me?' she asked.

'I could,' the ringleader said, 'I could take you back with us and you'd be tortured.' Or—' he shrugged '—I can shoot you here.'

'Fischer,' said the young one. 'We can't shoot her.'

Fischer, she thought, registering, even in the noise of her panic, who he was: the boy Otto despised. The one who'd led a squad in the reprisals.

Somehow, Eleni had pictured him taller, stronger.

Less pathetic-looking.

'Of course we can shoot her,' said Fischer.

'We'll get in trouble.'

'We'll just say she tried to run away. Or fight.'

'But she's not fighting. She's dropped her gun.'

'Shut up, Meyer.'

That name was familiar too.

Mouth dry, her heart beating so hard it was making her head spin, Eleni looked at the boy's smooth, flushed face again, recalling the blanket Otto had told her he'd used to carry.

'I'm pregnant,' she told him, certain it would mean nothing to the other two, but desperate, *desperate*, for it to mean something to him. 'Look.' She smoothed her quivering hands over her stomach. 'See?'

He stared.

What did Fischer do?

She didn't know.

She was too preoccupied with searching Meyer's expression. He felt like her chance.

He really did feel like her and the baby's chance.

But the third man was giving no one any chances.

'Get on your knees,' he ordered Eleni, raising his gun, 'or stay standing, I don't care. This needs to be done, so let's get it done.'

'I said I'm doing it,' said Fischer, raising his gun too.

'I'll do it.'

'*I'll* do it.'

Then the shot sounded.

And it was done.

#17: Otto's commanding officer, a man called
Brahn, came to tell me that she'd been
pregnant when she was shot. I was in
a cell by that point, at Agia prison. Otto
was held there too. Brahn was most . . .
upset, about everything. I wasn't executed,
because I'd given them what I'd given them,
but Brahn kept me imprisoned, thinking
about what I'd done, for the rest of the
time he was on the island. Then, when he
was re-posted, to France, I believe, he
had me shipped to a concentration camp
in Germany so I could think about it
some more. [Dips head] [Stares at table]
I don't believe Stephen, or anyone else,
ever discovered what I did. I'm sure they
all assumed I'd been betrayed too. I've
never had the courage to search them out.
I couldn't . . .

[Silence]

M.M: What happened to Otto?

#17: He was executed. Later that summer. Brahn
told me about that too. Otto held a scarf
Eleni had made him when it happened. Oh no,
no, you're crying . . . Please, don't cry.
Please. This was a long time ago. Please.
I warned you that you'd hate me . . .

M.M: Let's leave it here, shall we?

[Recording stopped]

ENGLAND, 1974

Chapter Twenty-Eight

Oxfordshire, 7 June 1974

The road was a sheltered one, lush with willow and ash trees. The houses, large and graceful, peeked from the foliage, concealing gardens that backed down to The Isis. All was quiet, all serene. After the pollution of White City, then the sweaty, Friday afternoon traffic Martha had just sat in on the M40, it was idyllic.

She hadn't come on the BBC's time. She'd taken a half-day. She had no intention of using anything gleaned on this visit to add to the mountain of material she'd by now amassed for the program, due to be broadcast in October, on the thirtieth anniversary of the liberation of Athens. It was well into production. It already had been by the time her anonymous witness, subject seventeen, had taken it upon himself to reply to her advertisement, placed in the Sunday papers all the way back in February.

Did you serve in Greece during its fall or liberation? Would you be willing to share your experiences? If so, we at the BBC would be most grateful to hear from you . . .

Martha, a lowly researcher, had telephoned him, the first time they'd spoken, wanting to thank him for being in touch, but ready to explain that his offer had nonetheless come a little late to be useful.

It was the way his voice had faltered in disappointment, *Oh, I see*, that had made her think again.

When she'd collected him from the foyer for his first interview, she'd been taken aback by how young he was. Not even sixty. He'd sounded older on the telephone, very frail. He'd been recovering from flu; it was what had made him cough so much when they'd been talking, but not what was killing him. He'd told her, during that first interview, that he'd been diagnosed with early-onset dementia. Soon, the memories that were torturing him would be gone.

I've done two people a grave wrong, he'd said, *and remained silent. I can't let you use my name, I'm too ashamed, but nor can I let my actions go unaccounted for any longer.*

She'd been intrigued, naturally.

Then he'd mentioned that one of the people whom he'd wronged had been Eleni Adams, and she'd become even more so.

His testimony would contribute to only a single section of the hour-long episode that would air on October 12: a snippet to join the other stories of traitors she and her fellow researchers had unearthed. She'd known the quote her producer, Ali, would want to use, the moment he'd uttered it. *None of the normal rules applied. Or at least one could forget they should.* Yet, she'd let him go on for hours. Nine in total.

'*Nine* hours?' Ali had said, when she'd come across the tapes. 'Nine, young lady? He must have had a very interesting story indeed.'

He had that.

Pulling in through the last of the road's gates, Martha continued up the gravel driveway and, coming to a halt at the house, shut off her ignition, climbing from her oven-like car. A duck, up from the river, stared at her, quacked, then waddled away.

The front door opened.

'What a surprise,' came a warm, familiar voice. 'To what do we owe this pleasure?'

'My impulse,' she said, walking into his hug.

She hadn't seen him for several weeks.

He'd given her material for the program too.

Subject one: Benedict Latimer. Serving Major with the British Army on HQ staff for both the fall of the mainland in April 1941, and the fall of Crete in May 1941, for which time he was billeted with Doctor Yorgos Florakis (Subject Five). Transferred, at own request, to active service in Africa after evacuation from Sphakia. Awarded the military cross for bravery in 1942 and promoted to Lieutenant Colonel. Took part in the D-Day landings at Sword Beach in May 1944. Present at the liberation of Athens.

She was very proud of her dad.

The fact of his service had, along with a couple of other ticks in her favour, undoubtedly, helped her secure this, her first research position with the BBC.

'Is Jack coming too?' he asked, of her husband.

'Probably.' She'd telephoned him at work, left a message that she was on her way, and was sure he'd leap at the opportunity to follow. They'd been married less than a year and were midway through renovating their derelict Victorian money-pit of a house on their own stretch of river, in Barnes. They currently had no electricity, nor hot water, and it was miserable.

'We'll be a full house,' her father said, his arm around her shoulders, walking with her through the porch, into the front hall. There was a chicken roasting. She could smell the garlic, the lemon. 'Georgie's back for the weekend from university. Sleeping, naturally, since it's still daylight, but she'll be delighted to see you.'

Martha smiled, pleased to be seeing her younger sister too.

'Briony's promised to call over from Windsor tomorrow,' Ben went on, 'with her parents . . . '

Martha laughed at that. Briony was two months old: the daughter of her twin brother, Josh, and his wife, Lily.

'I'll call Rafe and get them all here as well,' said Ben.

'Rafe's meant to be sorting our hot water . . . '

'It's the middle of summer, you'll be fine.'

'Is that who I think it is?' Another familiar voice.

Martha turned towards it.

And there she was, coming into the sunny living room through the garden doors: the real reason for Martha's long Friday drive from London. She was wrapped in a towel, her fading blonde hair dripping, clearly just back from a swim in the river.

'Martha, darling, hello.'

Subject number two: Eleni Juliet Latimer, nee Adams. Agent with the SOE on Crete, not that she ever says much about it.

'Hello, Mum,' said Martha.

She was stunned when, a little over an hour later, Martha came clean about who she'd been with all week.

The two of them were in the back garden. Eleni had showered, dressed (in shorts; she still wore shorts), and poured them chilled glasses of wine, which they'd taken to drink on the patio. Ben was down by the riverside, sleeves rolled up, doing something to the engine of the chug-boat they'd had for as long as Martha could remember.

Martha didn't watch him work.

She watched her mum, who'd turned completely still, like she'd slipped from their plane of existence into another one entirely.

Then . . .

'We've talked on the telephone this week,' she said to Martha, finally speaking. 'Several times.'

438

'I know.'

'Why didn't you tell me you'd met him?'

'I couldn't talk to you about it on the phone.'

'Did you tell him you were my daughter?'

'No. At first, I was worried he'd clam up, so I pretended I didn't know you.' All that nonsense about not knowing about Tips. She'd slipped, just once: when he'd mentioned Eleni's shapeless SOE clothes. *I can't imagine they suited her style.* 'Then I didn't know if you'd want me to tell him.'

'Why wouldn't I want that?'

'He thinks you're dead, Mum. He thinks he killed you.'

Eleni stared.

'They told him when he was in prison that you'd been shot,' said Martha. 'They said that you'd been shot pregnant.'

Eleni closed her eyes. 'Oh, Martha . . . '

'Was Otto Rafe's father, Mum? I think he must have been.'

'Martha . . . '

'And I suppose Henri's Rafe's grandfather? Krista's his aunt? Not your old college friend at all. What about Marianne? And Esther? Lotte? Where do they all fit in? Because . . . '

'Martha, stop,' said Eleni, fixing her with a firm look. (She was back on their plane again, now.) 'Stop talking.'

'Are you going to start?'

She sighed a long sigh.

Took an even longer sip of wine.

'What do you want me to start with?'

'Whether Rafe is Dad's son.'

'Yes, he's Dad's son.'

'But also Otto's?'

Another sigh. 'Yes. Which he knows about, by the way. He's just never wanted the rest of you to.'

'Why?'

She drew breath to speak, then stopped, a dent of indecision forming between her eyes. 'I shouldn't be talking to you about this . . .'

'No, don't you dare . . .'

'It's not as straightforward as this being only my story to tell, Martha. Rafe has had a lot to deal with. Such a lot.'

'Please, tell me about it.'

She hesitated a moment more.

Then, 'You have to understand, when he was born, we were still in the middle of the war. He started school in forty-eight, with children whose parents . . . *despised* Germany, hated Germans. I took him back to Crete, as soon as the civil war was over, and they hated them even more there. I told him his father was a good man, because he was, but I couldn't tell him that he'd been German, not to start with. Not whilst he was still such a baby. I told very few people that.'

'Did you tell Dad?'

'Of course I told Dad.'

'When did you tell Rafe?'

'After you and Josh were born. Dad and I told him together. He was still only six, but if we'd left it longer, it would have become impossible to do. And he'd grown to love Henri and Krista by then, Miriam and Nicolas . . .'

'Yes,' said Martha, who loved them too. They'd spent enough Christmases together. Countless June half-terms visiting Krista's lakeside home in Berlin; long, hot holidays through which Krista had let them all run wild, staying up too late, playing music too loud. (*Live for the moment,* said she, still very much living with her MS.) Martha had long known she and her husband, Claus, had built their house from designs Krista's lost brother had drawn, she just couldn't believe she'd never clicked that their children, Miriam and Nicolas – who, now she considered it, bore a marked resemblance to Rafe: those cheekbones she'd always envied – were Rafe's cousins.

'How did Rafe react?' she asked.

'He was quiet for a while. Very clingy, with your dad espe-cially.' Eleni glanced down at Ben at the boat. 'He was wonderful with him. He always has been. I think that was probably part of what made Rafe so anxious about you and Josh finding out he wasn't his son. He worshipped you. Got very tearful about it . . . He was so little still. In the end we told him he didn't need to tell you anything he didn't want to. That it could wait. By the time Georgie came along, it wasn't even a conversation anymore.'

'Does Rafe ever talk about it now?

'Sometimes. He's felt guilty about lying, as he's got older. Lies become a habit though.'

'This one certainly has.'

'He is proud to be his father's son. Really, he is. Look at what he does for a living.'

Martha nodded, *looking*. He was an architect, increasingly well known. He'd given her and Jack the drawings for their renovation as part of their wedding gift, and was helping them manage the build too (hence his involvement with their hot water).

'He named Brigit after his grandmother,' said Eleni, 'gave Stella her ring, when he proposed. He flew over to Berlin, actu-ally, after Brigit was born, to apologise to Henri and Krista. I think having her brought home to him just how much Otto—' she paused on his name '—*lost*.'

Such a lot of sadness, packed into one word.

'Did you marry him?' Martha asked, softly.

'No.'

'When did you really marry Dad?'

'Not in Crete in forty-one.'

'No, I'd rather hoped not.'

Smiling, briefly, Eleni told her they'd met again in the summer of 1948, at a dinner party Hector Herbert had invited them each to. 'We got married the following autumn, after Rafe and I came back from that first trip to Crete. Dad proposed to me before we went. I thought about it . . . constantly . . . while Rafe and I were away. I felt like it would be . . . faithless, to Otto's memory, if I said yes. *Papou* gave me a stern talking to . . . '

'I can imagine he did.'

'So when Dad met Rafe and me off our ship, I said yes.' She looked again at Ben, face soft. 'I honestly didn't believe I'd ever want to marry anyone, after Otto. I didn't think it could be possible. But I fell in love with your father. I hope you don't doubt that, Martha.'

Martha didn't.

Never once in her twenty-five years had she doubted how much her mum loved her dad.

But nor did she doubt, after all she'd heard, that she'd loved Otto too.

Do you believe first love can be real love?

She absolutely believed it. How could she not?

She'd married Jack, the boy she'd sat next to on her first day of primary school, after all.

'Was Otto really executed, Mum? Please tell me he wasn't.'

'I can't, darling. I wish I could. But he was. That September.'

'For being with you?'

'No, no. He went to prison for that, but that wasn't why he was shot.'

'Then . . . ?'

'After the Italian surrender, there was a lot of unrest on the island, more reprisals. You know that. Otto had been released from prison by then, but someone decided he should prove his loyalty by taking part in the reprisals. He refused, like he'd refused after the surrender, but this time he was court-martialled.' She stared sightlessly at her wine. 'His CO, Brahn, spoke for him, tried to get his sentence commuted to internment, but . . . ' She filled her lungs, exhaled a shuddering breath. 'For his last night, Brahn let *Papou* into Otto's cell to sit with him.' She looked across at Martha, her blue eyes full. 'He was with him to the end.'

'I am so sorry, Mum.'

'It was war. An awful war.'

'He died standing up for what was right.'

'He did, yes. That was . . . who he was.'

'Rafe's father.'

'Rafe's incredible father.'

They talked about him more, over that noisy, sunny weekend they all came together: Martha and Jack; Georgie; Josh, Lily, and tiny Briony; Rafe, his wife Stella, four-year-old Brigit and two-year-old Seb. For the very first time, they talked about him openly.

Rafe said they could.

Eleni and Ben broke it to him when he arrived on Saturday morning, fresh from seeing to Martha's hot water, that she'd discovered everything.

'Really?' he said.

'Really,' said Eleni.

And he exhaled, took a while to digest it, then, at length, decided to tell the others.

'Oh my *God*,' said Georgie, with nineteen-year-old theatricality. 'No *way*.'

'Doesn't make any difference to me,' said Josh, more profoundly, hugging Rafe. 'None.'

'How does it feel?' Ben asked him, later that evening, as they stood by the smoking barbecue.

'Better,' said Rafe, holding Seb on his shoulders, keeping one eye on Brigit, cartwheeling towards the river. 'Much better to not be lying.'

'It always is,' said Eleni. (*A terrible way to live, really.*)

'I don't know why I haven't stopped sooner,' he said.

'You needed a push,' she said, 'that was all. We all need those sometimes.'

Delivering that push, liberating them all from the lie, was at least one good thing Robbie had done.

In return, Eleni had by now resolved that she needed to liberate him from his.

She understood why Brahn had deceived him as he had. She'd never met him; he'd been killed in France in 1945, and never made it home to his wife and children in Dresden. From all she'd been told, though, he'd been an honourable man, one who'd cared for Otto, and she could only assume he'd wanted to punish Robbie for his treachery.

But he'd been punished now for thirty years.

He'd been imprisoned, sent to a concentration camp.

She'd always hate what he'd so nearly done to her, and Rafe, but he was dying, and it was in her power to give him some peace. He hadn't killed her. It would be wrong, pure and simple, to allow him to go on any longer believing that he had.

'You're sure?' Ben asked dubiously, when, on Sunday evening, after the children had all gone, back to their respective homes and college halls, she told him of her intention to contact him. 'I'd let him stew. I'm sorry, I would.'

'I'd do exactly the same,' said first Dusty, then Stephen, when she telephoned them the next day, telling them everything. Martha had interviewed them both for her program as well (*subject three and subject four*); Stephen was her godfather; Dusty was Rafe's. They'd all of them known for decades that Robbie had turned on them. It was why none of them had ever felt the remotest inclination to look him up.

'Let him go,' Stephen said to Eleni. 'You owe him nothing.'

'Nothing,' said Dusty. 'Don't let compassion in, remember?'

But she'd never had much time for that lesson.

She'd let it in with Weber (*kindness, Eleni-mou*), and look what had happened there.

He'd led Otto back to her, in April 1942.

Helped save her life in March 1943.

It was time for her to give Robbie back his.

She couldn't bring herself to visit him. It would be too much.

She wrote to him instead, going to the study to do it as soon as she'd put the telephone down to Dusty – the windows open, letting in the smell of the river, and cut grass – unpicking everything Robbie had thought he'd known.

Otto knew about Fischer's informer in Souda, she began with. *He'd had one of his men, Weber, follow Fischer to him, many months before. Weber had told the man that he should seek him out if Fischer ever bothered him again, which was precisely what he did, as soon as Fischer had released him from your interrogation. Major Brahn did take a squad to Otto's house to charge him, but, thanks to Weber, Otto had already left by the time they arrived. Together, they went to Socrates, and Socrates led them to me. I had more cavalry coming in the form of Dusty, whom Stephen had despatched to collect us when he'd realized our wireless set had gone down.*

I was very afraid before they reached me, Robbie. When those three soldiers came – Fischer, Meyer, Schmitt – I thought I was going to die. I do understand the fear you must have felt, in that room with Fischer. I don't know if I'll ever understand what you told him, but I do understand your fear. Mine made me drop my gun, too readily. It's confused me since, how quickly I did that. I reached for it again, when it became clear Fischer and Schmitt intended to shoot me, but I didn't need it. Dusty, however abysmal at Greek, had a truly excellent aim. He shot

Schmitt, Otto shot Fischer, and the third man, Meyer, I called out for them to let live. He was a child, just a child.

We were all of us so young, really.

We took Meyer to Sphakia with us. Otto and Weber came too. It was deep night by the time we reached the beach, and too windy for the launch to come ashore, so we had to swim out to it. It was freezing. But, one of those strange coincidences, my cousin, Little Vassili, was there ('Eleni-mou!'), a last-minute passenger, finally off to Narkover. My dad was waiting for me too, on board . . .

She paused writing, reliving the shock she'd felt, seeing Timothy's face, taut with fear above his turtleneck, peering over the deck, eyes searching the beam of his torch as he'd looked for her in the water.

'Dad?' she'd said, gasping with the cold. 'What are you doing shuttling a launch?'

'You think I could have let someone else come?' he'd said, climbing over the launch's rails, reaching down, dragging her sodden form up and to him, five-month-bump and all, wrapping her in a blanket. 'You think I could have done that?'

Weber came aboard. He would, of course, have been arrested had he returned to Souda, so we took him prisoner, back to Egypt, and he survived the war. I believe he trained as a teacher afterwards. My father offered to take Otto too. He saw, very quickly, the lay of the land. But Otto refused. I'd known he would. We'd debated it, at length, on the way. Schmitt and Fischer had been shot. Otto was adamant that he and Meyer needed to move their bodies, then return to Souda to testify that they, and Weber, had fallen from a precipice, into a stream. He didn't trust Meyer to see the story through. He was right, I think. I don't need to tell you that, had the Nazis got wind of the resistance playing any part in the death of German soldiers, more innocent people would have been killed in reprisals.

She'd accepted, in the end, that Otto had had to return to Souda.

It had still devastated her, though.

'Time to swim away, Eleni,' he'd said to her, on the beach. 'We'll do it together, yes? One last swim, you and I.'

As for me, we decided that Otto should tell Brahn I'd already escaped the hut by the time they'd reached it. The simplest stories, and all that. I have no idea if Brahn believed I'd escaped all alone. I suspect he didn't.

You almost took everything from me, Robbie. And perhaps you really did take Otto's life. Perhaps, if he hadn't been arrested because of his involvement with me, he might never have been ordered to take part in those reprisals. But he might have. Or he might have been killed another way. The war still had over two years left in it, then. And, in all you took, I can't forget that you also gave us something. Because of you, we did see one another again.

That much had been a gift, she'd come to realize.

Even now, she felt it: her choking relief when she'd glimpsed Otto, crossing the rocks beyond that hut, towards her.

'I told you it wasn't the end,' he'd said. 'I told you . . . '

We spent one last day together, she wrote. *A day that I have held close for more than thirty years. We talked about endless things. We talked about what we should call the baby.*

'Did your mama have a middle name?' she'd asked Otto.

'Miriam,' he'd said, as they'd slid, loose rocks tumbling beneath their feet, down the side of the gorge.

'And your father?'

'Rolf.'

She'd pulled a face. 'We can't do that to a child.'

He'd laughed.

His laugh.

'Rafe then,' he'd suggested.

'Rafe,' she'd said. 'Yes. I love that.'

He was born on a farm in Chester, in the middle of a very hot night. Helen Finch's sister-in-law delivered him, Hector sent me flowers, my father came to visit me, and my grandmother from Sutton did too.

'I am so sorry, dear,' she'd said. 'I'm a foolish old woman who should have learnt better by now. I hope you'll find it easier to forgive me than your father has.'

Esther loved Rafe immediately, and the two of them have remained close friends. Esther plays with the New York Philharmonic now, just like Marianne used to, and Helen Finch watches her whenever she can – as does Lotte, who travels all over the world, just to be in the front row at her first night performances. Esther's parents didn't survive the camps, and nor, devastatingly, did Marianne's. Lotte's father was killed himself, after the plot to depose Hitler in 1944, which Lotte never discusses. But she has done much work since, trying to support those the regime wronged. Esther has a wonderful husband, and three children. Marianne had five in the end. I'm losing count of her grandchildren. Ben and I have four children. Rafe, you know about. Martha, you've met. Josh is a doctor. Georgie is a terror. I am fiercely proud of them all.

I have had a good life, Robbie. I have had a very, very good life. I continue to do so.

You did not take that from me.

She signed off, and stared at the slant of her own hand, trying to imagine how he'd react when he read it all.

She didn't expect to ever know.

She posted that letter, and didn't think she'd hear from him again.

His reply, though, arrived by return of post.

It was short, and to the point.

Thank you, it said.

Then . . .

Just one more question, if you'll indulge it. Did Otto discover he had a son before he was killed?

He did, she replied, touched, more than she was prepared for, that he'd been compelled to ask. *He knew all about Rafe. My grandfather saw to that.*

CRETE, 1943

Chapter Twenty-Nine

Agia Prison, Crete, September 1943

It had taken weeks for Eleni's message to reach the island, via Hector.

It had got through in the end, though.

Little Vassili, fresh back from training, had carried it direct to Yorgos, who, as soon as he could, brought it to Otto.

He brought it to him on a Wednesday night.

The same Wednesday night that Brahn smuggled him into Otto's cell, so that he could keep Otto company, until his last dawn.

'I have a son?' Otto said, sitting on the edge of his low bed, his hands, shackled, clasped before him. 'We have a son?'

'You have a son,' said Yorgos, coming to sit beside him, laying his old, steady hand over Otto's. 'A healthy boy, called Rafe, who you have not let down.' He tightened his hand on Otto's. 'You have not let him down.'

Otto closed his eyes and tried to picture him.

He tried very hard to do that.

'I can't,' he said to Yorgos. 'I can't do it.'

'So you wait a few hours,' said Yorgos, still holding his hand. 'Then, when you are standing outside, shoulders square, spine straight, because you are not going to let them see you are afraid, you won't be afraid. You'll know that, in just another moment, you'll be looking down on your boy.'

'You really believe that?' Otto asked, desperate to himself.

'With all my heart,' said Yorgos.

It was a long night.

Otto had thought the hours would go quickly, but they passed incredibly slowly.

He didn't sleep.

Yorgos, seventy-two years old, didn't either.

Outside, through the cell's small window, the cicadas nested, and Yorgos talked, giving Otto the only thing that could have calmed him, which was story after story of Eleni: her babyhood; her childhood; her teenage years, 'We won't dwell on them,'; then, how happy he'd watched her become, that summer she and Otto had met.

'She made me happy,' said Otto, seeing her at least, very easily: by the window on the bus; eating a peach; laughing down at him from that sea-urchin rock, *do you need to catch your breath*; sitting on her step; reading her book . . . 'She has made me incredibly happy.'

'She knows that, my boy. She knows.'

Gradually, the light lifted.

Outside, the September dawn broke.

It was Brahn who came to lead Otto out to the courtyard. He hadn't delegated the responsibility, just as he hadn't delegated it when Otto had had to be arrested.

'I don't judge you,' Brahn had said to him, after he'd returned from Sphakia. 'If my wife had been here, I'd have done no differently.'

'It's time,' he told Otto now, his eyes, behind his spectacles, heavy with pain. He pulled out a key, unshackled him, and embraced him. 'I will do it,' he said, into his ear. 'I will do it for you, and you will not know a thing about it. I swear.'

Otto nodded. 'Thank you.'

He turned to Yorgos, who, face rigid (*he always looks crossest when he's upset*), opened his arms, embracing him as well.

He held him very tight.

'Hold your head up,' he said. 'Stand proud. I can find sense in none of this, but you are to stand proud.' He squeezed him harder. 'You have a welcome committee waiting for you. Your mama, she's waiting. And Eleni's mama. Melia will be too. They are all waiting.'

Otto nodded again.

He found he couldn't talk.

'Come,' said Brahn. 'Come.'

And, unable to make sense himself, of his moment being here, Otto went.

He paused at the cell door, turning back to face Yorgos.

Yorgos, standing straight in the centre of the cell, *shoulders square,* stared back at him.

'One last thing,' said Otto, rediscovering his voice, 'before I go.'

'Anything,' said Yorgos.

'Tell Eleni she must never feel guilty about being happy. Tell her how much I need her and Rafe to be happy.'

'I will,' said Yorgos. 'And they will be.'

From deep within him, Otto found the strength to believe it.

He kept believing it, as Brahn led him on, out to the courtyard, where the sun hit his skin, and the scent of thyme filled his senses.

He walked to the post, past the men with their rifles, seeing not them, but Eleni again, and, at the last, their son with her; both of them smiling, both of them laughing.

He reached up, touching his hand to her scarf, and, leaving the island, felt their happiness all through him. He knew nothing but that.

And it was everything.

CRETE, 1974

Epilogue

Crete, August 1974

Eleni hadn't missed a summer in Chania since the one she'd returned with Rafe, back in 1949. That visit had been hard, in many ways, but also good, and full, and *happy*. Nikos – whom Yorgos had slowly, painstakingly, reached an accord with – had called, often, parking himself on the veranda, telling Rafe stories as he held him on his knee; the Vassilis had pinched Rafe's cheeks and taken him around their vineyards, lifting him high to pick grapes; Maria and Yorgos and Spiros and Sofia and Socrates and Dimitri had spoilt him, endlessly; and Eleni, she'd taught him to swim, introduced him to *bougatsa*.

She hadn't felt guilty about the happiness.

Yorgos had given her Otto's last message.

In time, she'd brought Ben back to the island as well. It was a second home now to all of their children. Each one of them relished the deliciousness of cinnamon-dusted pastries for breakfast, and had taken their first strokes, down at the cove.

Beloved faces had disappeared, as time had wound on, but new ones had appeared. Little Vassili had married, and – to Katerina and Middle Vassili's delight – produced his own noisy brood. Dimitri had reopened his café, he and Socrates had adopted a dog. Tips had, without doubt, fathered many stripy kittens.

With the passing years, it had, eventually, become easier for Henri and Krista to think of returning to Crete, and there'd been several summers now that they'd flown in from Berlin, staying not in Nikos's villa – 'Too painful,' said Krista – but in one of the new hotels that had started to spring up. Marianne had frequently joined them from New York, and Lotte had even come, once, as well.

No one was forgotten.

The war wasn't forgotten.

Two cemeteries had been built: one, at Souda, where John Pendlebury, and hundreds of other fallen Allied soldiers rested, and another at Maleme, in which more than four thousand Germans lay. Eleni had visited both, and she'd taken Rafe to Otto's grave. Always, when they went, they brought him a peach, plucked from the tree that still grew in the villa's garden.

'Do you think he knows?' Rafe had asked Eleni, earlier that August morning, setting the fruit beside the urchin shell she'd long since left there, and which no one had moved.

'I think if he does,' she'd said, 'he's probably wanting to tell you that the tree grew from Maria's stone, not mine.'

She'd smiled.

He had too.

When they'd returned to the villa, Yorgos had been on the terrace with Ben and Timothy – who, for Eleni, and for Rafe, had accompanied them on their trip back in 1949, and kept on accompanying them since – helping them to prepare the snapper they'd caught on their morning's fishing trip. Marianne, come again that year, had been with them, resisting Yorgos's entreaties that she get out her cello, pleading jetlag, promising that she'd do it tomorrow.

'You're telling a man who's a hundred and three years old that he should wait until tomorrow?' Yorgos had said.

Eleni could hear Marianne playing now, the chords sending familiar shivers down her spine.

She was down at the cove, sitting on the shore, watching the others in the sea. The sun blazed with typical August intensity. There was no wind. The sea lapped back and forth, over her legs, brushing the shingles. *Flisvos*.

Not everyone had arrived for the holiday yet. Martha and Jack, busy with their jobs, and their house, wouldn't be flying in until the following weekend. But the rest of them were there: Georgie, flummoxed on a lilo, her face to the beating sky, probably not wearing any lotion, and oblivious to Josh, stealthily approaching, about to tip her in; Josh's wife, Lily, not far away, turning little Briony through the water, cooing as her chubby feet skimmed the surface; Rafe and Stella, deeper, playing rather more boisterously with Brigit and Seb.

Eleni let her attention settle on four-year-old Brigit.

Of them all, she resembled Otto, and her great-grandmother, the most. She had their brown hair, their slanted green eyes; skin that turned to bronze the instant the sun touched it.

That grin.

It was all over her delighted little face as Rafe raised her up, high above him, turning her around and around.

'Daddy, do it now,' she squealed, 'throw me now.'

'Not until you say it in Greek,' he said, in Greek.

So she said it in Greek.

And, in the same moment that Josh upended Georgie from her lilo, Rafe launched her through the air.

As she flew, her eyes, full of the thrill, locked on Eleni's.

Do you think he knows?

Eleni thought, perhaps he did.

Brigit splashed joyously down, limbs flailing, into the clear sea, and Eleni believed he must.

Author's Note

It has been an incredibly moving experience, writing *The Officer and The Spy*, which was inspired, in no small part, by the experiences and stories of my own family. My grandmother, Maria, was in Athens throughout the Nazi occupation. She, along, with my great-aunt Noola, and great-uncle Yorgos, survived it, whilst my great-grandparents, and other great-aunts, tragically, did not. My grandmother met my English grandfather at the liberation, and left with him for England before the start of the civil war. She couldn't afford to return to Greece until more than a decade later, when she took my dad and his siblings there by train: a trip my dad still talks about with huge emotion.

I have been lucky enough to grow up spending every summer of my life in Greece, and now take my own family there every year. Throughout my childhood, I was told stories of my relatives' experiences in the war, many sad, some happy: of rabbits named after Nazi generals; of German soldiers that were too young, and very hungry; of my dad's oldest friend, who is only alive today because, when his own father was lined up to be shot in a Nazi reprisal, he somehow found the strength to jump the six-foot wall behind him, and run. One of my own earliest memories is sitting on my uncle Yorgos's lap, by the sea, and him leaning down, resting his cheek against mine, and pointing up at the sky, telling me to look, 'Not a cloud there.' I never met my grandmother, but Yorgos, and my aunty Noola, were like grandparents to me, and a story set in their home, that I think of in so many ways as my own, has long been growing in me. I hope so much that I have done it justice. I hope that they, and my grandmother, would have approved.

The Officer and The Spy, whilst entirely a work of fiction, is nonetheless rooted in real-world events, and there are a number of books that I found invaluable in my research: *Crete, The Battle and the Resistance*, by Antony Beevor, is an excellent study, examining the battle from every side; *The Cretan Runner*, by George Psychoundakis, is a vividly written memoir which brings to life what it meant to be a local member of the Cretan Resistance; *Ill Met by Moonlight*, by W. Stanley Moss, and *Abducting a General: the Kreipe Operation and SOE in Crete* by Patrick Leigh Fermor, are both gripping memoirs of British SOE operatives active on the island; finally, the Second in Evelyn Waugh's Sword of Honour trilogy, *Officers and Gentlemen*, provides an unputdownable account of the battle from Waugh, who experienced it first-hand.

I have tried to provide as faithful an account as possible of the battle for, and defeat of, Crete, in 1941, but there is no one simple answer to why the island fell. Given the Nazi invading force was so much weaker, numerically, to those waiting to fight them, it is perhaps no surprise that there has been such heated debate, ever since, into the reasons behind the island's defeat. Undoubtedly, Freyberg's belief that the Nazis would attack by sea as well as air was crucial, resulting, as it did, in the fall of Maleme airbase, but there were other factors involved: poor communications; narrow, blocked roads; the sensitivity of the *most secret* wireless intercepts, which the Allied Forces couldn't risk the Nazi commanders guessing they'd decoded. What is incontrovertible is that, in May 1941, Crete did fall, and massacres swiftly followed, inflicted on Cretans by way of punishment for their defence of their home. Whilst there were German soldiers, like Otto, who protested against the travesty of these reprisals – the Parachute Division's Chief of Staff was, as mentioned in the novel, one such man – plenty didn't, and, by the occupation's end, thousands of men, women and children had been murdered. Scores of villages had been burned to the ground.

The occupation lasted for four years, with the last Nazi forces not leaving Crete until 1945, several months after the liberation of Athens. The reprisals were, tragically, far from being the only atrocity. Many Jewish Cretans, like Eleni's neighbours, were arrested, and murdered in the executions following the 1942 attacks on Nazi airbases. Even more remained in prison until May 1944, when, after further island-wide arrests, they were forced onto a ship bound, horrifically, for the death camps of Europe – a ship that was mistaken as a military vessel by British naval forces and, devastatingly, sunk, with almost everyone on board drowned. Only a few escaped, to remain hidden with Greek families until the end of the war.

On the island, countless cruelties were inflicted, but so too did a fierce resistance flourish, made up of both Allied and local operatives. It was whilst I was researching their incredible work that I came across a small but unforgettable reference made by Antony Beevor to the bravery of local Cretan women, employed as translators and secretaries by the Germans, who risked their lives to feed the resistance vital information. I knew immediately that I wanted to explore a woman fulfilling such role in this novel – neither Greek, nor British, but a mix, like my own family is a mix, of the two.

The first British SOE agents returned to Crete within months of the surrender, initially to help evacuate the stranded Allied soldiers, but thereafter also to support resistance efforts. Whilst there were, undeniably, Cretans who acted as informers, such collaborators were the exception; by far and away the majority of Cretans took huge risks to resist. As one SOE operative, Ralph Stockbridge, is quoted as saying in Beevor's book, 'Everything depended throughout on their magnificent loyalty. Without their help as guides, informants, suppliers of food and so on, not a single one of us would have lasted twenty-four hours.'

Almost all the characters in this novel are fictional, but there are a handful of references to individuals alive at the time. I have already mentioned the German parachute division's chief of staff, and, in addition, all the generals I refer to are historical figures. On the British side, John Pendlebury was indeed based in Heraklion before the invasion, tasked with building the support of Cretan *kapitans*, and, according to contemporary accounts, intended to remain on the island to continue fighting, if it fell. Tragically, he was killed during the invasion, and is now buried in the Allied cemetery at Souda Bay. Chania's mayor, Nikolas Skoulas, such an ally to Eleni, was highly active in the resistance and worked, throughout the occupation, with members of the SOE to form a pan-island movement. Finally, I mention, briefly, SOE agents Xan Fielding and Patrick Leigh Fermor, and also Cretans, Andreas Polentas and Apostolos Evangelou, all of whom were heavily involved in the resistance too.

At the end of the war, those Nazi generals and senior officers who'd led the occupation were tried, and punished. For years, the German soldiers who'd fallen – so many, on the first day of the invasion, so many of them conscripted – lay scattered across the island. But, with the passage of time, it was decided that they, as well as their Allied counterparts, should be moved to a single resting place. The cemetery at Souda was built for the Allied soldiers, and the cemetery at Maleme for the Germans. It is hard to imagine what must have gone into the task of exhuming and moving the fallen men; when I read that the burial of the Germans was undertaken not only by their surviving comrades, but also Cretans, including members of the resistance, it moved me to tears.

In the summer of 2021, I took my children to Maleme cemetery, where, in the Cretan sunshine – surrounded by many others, of all nationalities – we read the headstones of those who had died. All around us, we heard the same murmured words. *So young*. We've visited, of course, the cemetery at Souda as well, and heard the same refrain repeated again, and again there.

In May of 2021, ceremonies were held around the world to commemorate the eightieth anniversary of the Battle of Crete, attended by the last surviving veterans, all remembering, all honouring. Never has it felt more important than now to remember that war, that awful war, in which so much was lost, and taken, and given, and from which the perpetual echoes are still being felt, generations on.

Acknowledgements

I want to say a huge thank you to everyone that has given their time to read *The Officer and The Spy*. It is my sixth novel, which feels almost impossible to believe, and I never forget what a privilege it is to share my stories with others. Nothing makes my day like hearing from a reader – it really can lift me from the deepest of plot holes – and I'm so very grateful for all the support I've received.

This novel is one I've long been waiting to write, and I couldn't have done it without the belief and encouragement of my brilliant agent, Becky Ritchie, and equally fantastic editor, Manpreet Grewal. I'm a firm believer that a novel is made in the editing, and it's such a joy to work with Manpreet, who always manages to know just where I want to go with my stories, and how to help me get there. Thank you to Deborah Schneider, and to Alexandra McNicoll, Prema Raj, and Tabatha Legett at AM Heath, for all their work in finding my books international homes. And thank you to Melanie Hayes, Lily Capewell, Sarah Lundy, Janet Aspey, Donna Hillyer, and everyone at HQ – I am so lucky to be working with such an inspired, talented team.

I also want to thank all the writers, bloggers and bookstagrammers who are so generous with their time, reading and reviewing, and who keep my TBR pile teetering with their fantastic recommendations. I cannot say thank you enough to wonderful friends, Iona Grey, Sarra Manning, Cesca Major, Claire McGlasson, Kate Riordan, Lucy Foley, and Katherine Webb, nor to Dinah Jefferies, Hazel Gaynor, Gill Paul, Eve Chase, Tracy Rees, Liz Trenow, and Heather Webb – it would be a lot tougher, and a lot less fun, without you all.

Thank you to my husband, Matt, and to our children, Molly, Jonah and Raffy, for always being by my side. Thank you to my mum, for everything, and to my dad, for everything too – and, in this case, most of all for telling me so many wonderful stories of my grandmother. Thank you to all my family in Greece, especially my cousin Nestos, for being on the end of the phone and answering all my questions. Thank you too, to Philippa Viglakis, for her hospitality and sharing so much local Cretan knowledge.

Finally, thank you to my grandmother, Maria, my great-aunt Noola, and my great-uncle Yorgos. I can't say this to them in person, but without the love they each left behind, I would never have written this book.

ONE PLACE. MANY STORIES

Bold, innovative and
empowering publishing.

FOLLOW US ON:

@HQStories